# WHY YOU SHOULD NEVER KISS YOUR EX-HUSBAND

## WHY YOU SHOULD NEVER...

## ERIN NICHOLAS

# THE SERIES


**Why You Should Never...**

Kiss Your Boss (Ben & Jessica)
Kiss Your Blind Date (Sam & Dani)
Kiss A Grump (Mac & Sara)
Kiss Your Fake Boyfriend (Dooley & Morgan)
Kiss Your Ex-Husband (Kevin & Eve)
Kiss Your Brother's Best Friend (Ryan & Amanda)
Kiss Your Ex (Shane & Isabelle)
Kiss Your Enemy (Nate & Emma)
Kiss Your Best Friend (Cody & Olivia)
Kiss Your Roommate (Conner & Gabby)

# ACKNOWLEDGMENTS

And a very special thank you to Angela Gebhardt, Sarah Caldwell, Molly Dougherty and Wendy Kahland for answering all of my questions about child custody issues, guardianships, social work and everything else. Your patience, time and expertise were greatly appreciated!

# ABOUT THE BOOK...

*He may now kiss his bride...again...*

Kevin Campbell just found out that he's been designated the guardian for a half-brother he never knew existed. And that's not even the craziest thing about this night. The annulment he thought he got twelve years ago? Yeah, that never went through.

Eve is shocked to see him again, but not surprised they're still married. After all, she was the one who refused to sign the annulment papers.

When she offers to help with his younger brother, a sweet preacher's daughter seems like an answered prayer. But he soon realizes that she wants a second chance. At everything. And he has a hell of a time resisting her... which is exactly what got him into trouble last time.

# CHAPTER
## ONE

KEVIN CAMPBELL HAD the best reason ever for wanting to fall madly in love and get married—to shut his friends up.

If he was happily, completely committed to a woman, his friends would stop talking about his love—and sex—life.

Or lack thereof.

"I just personally think you can swear off one-night stands and meaningless hook-ups but still get blow jobs." Doug Miller, affectionately known as Dooley, looked around at the other three men who made up their ambulance crew. "That would at least take the edge off."

Kevin Campbell closed his eyes and groaned. They used to talk about *their* sex lives. All the time. In gory detail.

He missed those days.

Ever since all of his friends had committed themselves to monogamous relationships and family life, these kinds of conversations seemed to focus on Kevin. Apparently, his playboy friends had moral standards after all, and one of them was not talking publicly about having sex with their wives and fiancées.

"It's like somebody made chocolate chip cookies and you can see and smell them but you can't even lick the *batter*," Dooley went on. "It's cruel."

"Women are like chocolate chip cookies?" Sam Bradford asked. "Or blow jobs are like chocolate chip cookies?"

"The blow jobs are like chocolate chip cookie *batter*," Dooley said. "Just a taste of the real thing. Sex is the cookies."

"That's a little on the nose, even for you," Mac said.

Dooley grinned.

"Besides, sex isn't like chocolate chip cookies," Mac said, with clear appreciation of the topic. "Sex is like chocolate fudge brownies." It was clear from the emphasis put on the words that Mac was a huge fan of chocolate fudge brownies.

"The not being able to have sex when there are gorgeous women around is like having the temptation of sweet treats around all the time and not being able to even taste them," Dooley insisted. "And I still say blow jobs aren't really sex. I don't see why Kevin can't at least mess around but not break this only-when-I'm-serious-with-someone rule he's got now."

"It's not like he's never had it before. Maybe…licking spoons isn't his thing," Sam said with a smirk, before he tipped his head back and tossed five M&Ms into the air one right after the other, catching all but one in his mouth. "Four," he said, grinning at Mac as the fifth candy bounced and rolled across the floor.

Mac tipped his head back and tossed five more M&M's into the air, catching all five. "I'm up by one."

Kevin rolled his eyes. This could go on all night.

"Then he has *not* licked the right spoons. Or licked them right." Dooley stirred his coffee then tossed the plastic spoon in the garbage before taking his seat on the end of the dilapidated couch in the ER break room. "That's always your thing if you're doing it right."

He had a point. And Kevin didn't want to talk about it. Not that it was stopping his friends from talking about it—and *him*, with him sitting right there—anyway.

"Hey, Campbell." Dan Morris strolled into the break room and headed for the coffee pot. "We just responded to a domestic disturbance call."

"Yeah?" Kevin wasn't sure why Dan felt the urge to tell him that. Kevin and the crew did domestic disturbance calls all the time. But Dan was interrupting a conversation Kevin definitely wanted interrupted—giving up 'licking spoons' had been even harder than giving up alcohol when he'd decided he'd needed to straighten his life out—so he turned to Dan. "Something interesting?"

"A woman stabbed man in the back of the hand with a fork at Spaghetti Works."

"The one in the Old Market?" Mac asked. "No shit?"

"Yeah," Dan said, leaning against the counter and looking like he was eagerly anticipating the retelling of this story. "Apparently, this man and woman were having dinner and suddenly this other woman walks in with a kid. She tells the guy the kid's his and he has to take him. Guy clearly knows the woman and is shocked to see her there. Guy's wife knows nothing about it but immediately freaks out. A plate gets thrown, the wife ducks and it hits the guy in the eye. Then when he tries to step between the women, the younger one stabs him in the hand with the fork to get him to let go of her. Cops are called, we're called because of the black eye and the hand. It was quite the scene."

"Wow, more exciting than our night," Kevin commented, because he felt like he needed to say something since Dan had made a point of addressing him.

"Oh, I haven't told you the best part," Dan said.

"What do you mean?"

"The guy's name is Steve Campbell. His wife is Janice."

Kevin's entire body went cold.

No way. There could be another Steve Campbell in the area. Another Steve Campbell married to a Janice. Another Steve

Campbell who took his wife Janice to Spaghetti Works every Monday.

But tonight was Monday and Kevin knew exactly which Steve and Janice Campbell had been there.

Oh…crap.

Kevin focused on Dooley, Sam and Mac. They were all staring at him.

Crap.

He stood swiftly and headed for the exam rooms. "Which room?"

"Four," Dan called out. "But the girls are in the waiting room."

Kevin immediately changed directions. He felt Dooley right on his heels.

"Calm down, Kev. There's probably a good explanation."

"Yeah? If so, I'm gonna get it."

When he stepped into the ER waiting room he felt like he'd been dropped into the middle of a daytime tabloid talk show. A bad one. Two women faced off—one held a Styrofoam cup of coffee high, as if preparing to hurl it at any moment, and the other held a three-inch heel in a similar pose.

"Go ahead," the one with the coffee said. "Do it. I dare you."

"You think I'm stupid?" the younger woman sneered.

"Yes," the other said. "I think you're stupid. What did you think would happen? You thought he'd smile and say 'fine', buy the kid a Shirley Temple and everything would be good?"

"I think that it's about damned time that he did something right. He doesn't really have a choice, you know. He's the father. He has to take him."

"Hey, Sam!" Dooley called through the door leading to the back of the ER. "Get up here. And bring the popcorn."

Kevin scowled at him.

The two women seemed not to notice anyone but each other. They were glaring at one another, neither willing to back down, or even blink.

"Bullshit," the older of the two snorted. "He doesn't have to do anything. Hasn't he made that clear for the past ten years? If he wanted either of you, he'd have been there."

"He's been there," the younger woman spat. "He's given us money and—"

The older woman snarled and flung the coffee cup at the girl. Even off-balanced by wearing only one high heel, the girl moved in time to only have coffee splashed on her left thigh. Still, it clearly infuriated her because her shoe went sailing, clipping the other woman in the shoulder.

Just as Sam and Mac stepped into the waiting room.

Then it really got ugly. The women both lurched forward, claws drawn, insults flying. The older woman grabbed for the girl's hair, yanking hard enough the girl yelped. But she had the benefit of youth and more flexibility. She bent at the waist and drove her head into the older woman's stomach. The woman didn't let go of the girl's hair though, so together they stumbled and ended up on the floor.

"Bitch!"

"Tramp!"

"Pathetic!"

"Liar!"

Dooley, Sam and Mac had settled onto the nearest couch with, sure enough, a bag of popcorn. They were grinning widely as they watched the scene.

Kevin, on the other hand, had seen enough. He stepped forward with a sigh and yanked the girl off of the woman. She squirmed and fought but he outweighed her by at least one hundred pounds and he'd fought off defensive linemen who were even bigger than that. And madder.

The woman on the floor stared up at him, her eyes wide with fury and shock.

Kevin sighed again. "Hi, Mom."

Janice Campbell scrambled to her feet and Kevin pushed the girl behind him. Thankfully, Dooley stood and took hold of her upper arms, keeping her back from Kevin's mother. The girl was still spitting mad and Dooley had to hold on tight.

"What is going on?" Kevin demanded.

His mother had never been what he'd call particularly feminine or dainty. She was thin and wiry and strong. She and his father owned and operated a landscaping business, and even at age fifty-five she dug holes, carried big bags of fertilizer and worked in the sun and heat ten hours a day in the summer. Most of the time her fingernails were dirty, her hands had calluses and she had the tanned, leathery skin of someone who worked outside. Practicality called for her to wear her hair short and to dress in denim and T-shirts. She only wore make-up to weddings and funerals and she drank beer and swore. She was tough. The other girl had to be crazy to take her on.

In contrast, the younger woman—and it was clear she was much younger—wore a sundress and high-heeled sandals in spite of the fact that it was well into October. Her fingernails were manicured, her long hair hung loose and her lipstick looked intact.

His mother ran a hand through her hair and glared at the other woman. "That tramp came to the restaurant. She's claiming that her son is your father's."

"I'm not claiming it," the girl growled, wiggling hard in Dooley's hold. "It's true. He knows it. Ask him."

This was bad. Really bad. But none of this scene was making anything better.

Janice stepped forward and Kevin held up a hand. "Don't make me hold you back, Mom," he said. He'd do it, but that would be even more humiliating for them both.

"I suspected something back then, but he swore to me it was nothing. He promised me nothing had happened." Janice tore her gaze from the girl and focused on Kevin. "I believed him. I let him talk me into believing that."

Kevin didn't know what to say to her. His mother might be tough physically, but she was a woman who had been married to the same man for thirty-seven years. An affair was going to hurt badly. If it was true. He swung to face the other woman instead. "Who are you?"

She stared at him. "Heather. Hansen."

The name made Kevin frown and look closer. "Heather?" She'd graduated a year ahead of him in high school.

Wow. This was really, really bad.

"And you…" He couldn't say it.

"Had an affair with your father. Yeah," she said bluntly.

Janice made a choking noise behind him and he moved closer, in case he needed to grab her. "Mom," he said warningly.

"You can ask your father," Heather said, lifting her chin. "We did the whole DNA thing ten years ago. Drew's his. He knows it."

"Fuck you!"

Before Kevin knew what was happening a plastic brochure holder flew past his shoulder, straight for Heather. With Dooley holding her, she couldn't duck and it hit her in the nose.

The bleeding started immediately. Dooley swore and turned the girl toward the door leading to the exam rooms. "Kayla!" he barked. "Some help here!"

But as Kayla opened the door for him, Heather jerked out of his hold and sprinted at Janice. She pulled her hand back and slapped the older woman as hard as she could.

Janice grabbed the arm of a chair and yanked it forward— right into Heather's shins. Heather yelled and shoved the chair back at Janice, catching her in one knee. The knee gave and Janice went to the floor, but on her way down, somehow, she managed to rake her stubby nails down Heather's arm.

"Knock it off, both of you!" Kevin roared. This was ridiculous. Kevin grabbed his mother's upper arm, jerking her to her feet. "For God's sake!"

Ready to blast them further, he started to turn…as Heather's fist connected with his jaw. It didn't even jerk his head back, but it didn't feel great.

Dooley grabbed her and Kevin glared, rubbing his face. "What the hell?" he demanded.

"I'll fight whoever I have to!" she declared. "Steve has to do this! It's what's right!"

"Do what?" Kevin asked, giving her a scowl that had made NCAA offensive linemen tremble. "What's this all about? The kid?"

"He has to take him. There isn't anyone else," Heather said. And just like that she started sobbing. "What am I going to do? He can't go to foster care!"

Dooley shook her gently. "Calm down. Tell us what's going on."

"She claims," Janice said, experimentally tugging on the arm Kevin held. But she wasn't going anywhere. She sighed. "She says Steve has to take care of the kid. That he owes them."

Kevin frowned at her. "Does he?" he asked.

Janice shook her head quickly. "No. It can't be. The kid's ten. Why hasn't she come before this? Why would he lie to me?"

Kevin rolled his eyes, looking from Heather's nose—which Dooley had covered with a bloody cloth at the moment—then to the claw marks on her arm. "I don't know why he would have lied. Clearly you'd be completely understanding and supportive about it when you found out."

Not that he was feeling either of those things—at all—toward his father at the moment. If any of this was true, then…

He couldn't think about it. Heather was twenty-five years younger than his dad. She'd been drinking cheap wine coolers and kissing boys for the first time down by the river while his dad had been at home watching TV and eating meatloaf with his wife…Kevin's mom. His dad was married. To his mom. The way it was supposed to be. They were a normal family. He'd grown up with a white picket fence—literally. He couldn't imagine anything tainting that, anything ruining that picture of the all-American family.

Okay, so maybe perfect wasn't fair. They weren't perfect, of course. There had been problems with the business at times and fights about money. His dad had been extremely attentive to Kevin, the boy and the star athlete, and that had caused issues with his older sister. His mom loved them both but she wasn't the cuddly, maternal type. She was much more comfortable yelling from the bleachers at a football game than she was reading bedtime stories in a rocking chair. Which had also been a problem for his sister—the non-athlete.

But they were a family. They were secure and stable. Supposedly.

Now his mother had gotten into a catfight in a nice restaurant and a hospital waiting room with his father's much-younger mistress over his illegitimate child.

Secure and stable were relative terms.

He looked at Heather. The tears were still streaming. "What do you want? Steve? More money?"

She shook her head. "He has to take him."

"Who? Dad?" Kevin looked at his mother but she was stubbornly looking the other direction. "What do you want Dad, I mean Steve, to do?"

"I'm going to jail!" Heather wailed. "For six months! Steve has to take care of Drew. What else am I supposed to do?"

"Jail?" Dooley broke in. His wide eyes met Kevin's. "Seriously?"

Kevin wondered briefly if he was asleep and dreaming. Or maybe this was a practical joke.

But the blood on Heather's shirt front and the rage in his mother's eyes were very, very real.

He shook his head. "What are you going to jail for?"

Two security guards showed up before she could answer. Of course. Now that the girls were calming down.

"You need help, Kevin?" one of them asked.

"No, Brad, thanks. But," he added as they turned to go, "maybe stay close, just in case."

He started to ask Heather again about jail, but movement in

the corner of the waiting room caught his eye. He leaned to get a better look… and then stared, his hold on his mom's arm going slack.

Crouched behind a chair in the corner was a little boy.

Heather's little boy, he'd bet.

Dan had said the woman went into the restaurant with the kid, now that he thought about it.

"You're doing this with him here?" Kevin demanded, anger coursing through him at both of the women who were acting like idiots. "Here." He thrust his mother at one of the security guys and stalked across the waiting room. He made himself draw a deep breath and shorten his steps as he got closer to the boy, trying to at least seem calm.

"Hey, buddy," he said when he was within a few feet of the child. "What's your name?"

The kid stood up behind the chair and met Kevin's gaze evenly. "Drew."

He didn't seem scared. "You okay, Drew?"

If one of these women—his mother or not—had hit the kid with even a drop of coffee, Kevin was going to have security lock them up somewhere.

"Yeah."

"You're not hurt?"

"Nope."

"You scared?"

"Nah. Didn't want to get hit in the head." Ah. Hiding behind the chair was practical.

"Good idea."

Drew shrugged like he wasn't all that impressed with any of it. "I thought we were going to Arby's."

Kevin took a deep breath and forced himself not to look at the two women behind him. "I like Arby's too."

"I don't like spaghetti," Drew said. "That other place only has spaghetti."

Kevin was certain Spaghetti Works had more than spaghetti

but if that was all that stood out in Drew's mind about the restaurant at this point, that was fine. "Are you hungry? 'Cause I really am." He wasn't. At all. But he had to get out of that waiting room and he suspected the same would be good for Drew. He was mortified by his mother's actions. And, quite possibly, his father's.

Again, Drew might be feeling similarly.

Drew slid out from behind the chair and came to stand right in front of Kevin, looking up. Way up. Kevin was six-four and a big guy. He'd played Division I football for Nebraska for four years and had spent two years in the pros with the Kansas City Chiefs. He knew his size was the first thing people noticed about him.

"You got any coffee?" Drew asked.

Kevin looked down at the boy. He knew that most child experts said to get on eye level with kids when you talked to them, to make them feel comfortable. But, strangely, he could tell that it wouldn't matter with Drew. The kid was sizing him up—figuratively and literally—and seemed perfectly comfortable. In fact, for some reason, Kevin thought that if he tried to get on Drew's level, the boy would know exactly what he was trying to do and it might have the opposite effect. "We have coffee in the break room."

"That will do."

Trying not to show his surprise, Kevin started for the back room. He didn't even spare a glance at his mother, Heather, Dooley or anyone else.

"You take cream and sugar?" Kevin asked, crossing to the coffee pot. He'd play along with this. A little coffee wouldn't hurt the kid, and if it made him feel grown-up maybe that was what he needed right now. Thankfully, Sam, Mac and Dan all stayed out of the break room. They might be helping up front—or taking bets on who would win if they let the women go at one another.

Heather was younger and clearly was motivated by something to do with her son, but Kevin knew his mom. She was tough. And she was clearly pissed off.

He wasn't sure who he'd go with, frankly.

"Do you have French vanilla creamer?" Drew asked. "That's my favorite."

Kevin fought a smile. "Nope, sorry, just plain."

Drew sighed. "Okay. Two sugars."

If having the wrong kind of creamer was the worst thing to happen in his mind, then this night might be salvageable. As he mixed cream and sugar into a half cup of coffee, Kevin thought about that...and felt his frown deepen. Maybe this kind of stuff was normal in Drew's life. Maybe Heather did crap like this all the time.

Terrific.

He set the cup down in front of Drew, who immediately picked it up and drank. He swallowed without a wince and Kevin had to wonder if he did, indeed, drink coffee on a regular basis.

"Kevin?"

He turned to find Danika Bradford, Sam's wife, coming through the door. She was a social worker at the hospital and she was the first female he'd encountered in the past hour that he was happy to see. "Hey."

"Exciting night," she said. She smiled at Drew. "Hi, I'm Dani."

"I'm Drew. Want some coffee?"

She raised an eyebrow at Kevin, who shrugged. "He prefers French vanilla creamer but he's putting up with our plain stuff."

"I like hazelnut best," Danika said, taking a seat next to Drew.

"What do you know?" Kevin asked nonchalantly, also pulling out a chair.

Clearly Sam had called her, probably the minute he'd heard Kevin's dad had been stabbed in the hand by a fork. But she might be able to get to the bottom of what was going on. If nothing else, she could be a resource. She knew more about custody situations and what happened when single moms went to jail than he did. Besides, Kevin had way too many emotions swirling to make any sense out of anything right now.

"What I know is that I'm going to challenge Drew to a game of Gin Rummy and that your dad is in exam room four," she said, pulling a deck of cards from her purse. "You play?" she asked Drew.

"I know poker," he said. "But I can learn Gin Rummy."

She smiled. "Great. Because I'm not very good at poker."

"It takes practice," Drew said sagely, as if he'd been playing for years.

She started dealing, but nudged Kevin's foot with hers. "Room four."

He sighed and slid his chair back. Might as well get this over with. His dad was clearly the best one to talk to if he wanted answers. But he was also the last person Kevin wanted to see right now. No matter what was true or not true at the moment, his dad had done something that had resulted in this fiasco.

This stuff didn't happen in Kevin's life. His life was calm, normal, boring even. His buddies had the drama and the chaos. At least until recently when they'd all ended up in love and things had gotten a lot more…stable for all of them.

They were going to really enjoy this.

"Dad?" Kevin pushed the door open, half hoping the room was full of medical staff and half hoping his dad was alone. He really did want to know what was going on but he really didn't want to hate his father.

He was afraid that latter was a distinct possibility.

"Hey, Kev."

His dad was sitting propped up on the exam table. His hand was wrapped with a thick bandage and his eye was already turning dark.

"What the hell is going on?"

Kevin was so worked up he didn't even feel bad about the

swearing. It was one of the many things he'd worked at cleaning up in his life—and was one of many things that often proved difficult for him.

"I screwed up," Steve Campbell said simply.

"So you did have an affair? With Heather?"

Steve nodded, then grimaced. Kevin suspected he had a killer headache. "It was brief. And a long time ago."

"About eleven years ago?" Kevin said dryly. "I met Drew."

Steve swallowed hard. "Yeah."

Kevin shoved his hands into his pockets. "Have you ever met Drew?"

He wasn't sure what he wanted the answer to be. If his dad hadn't been involved, that made him an asshole. But if he had, it made him a liar. He'd been keeping this from them anyway. If he'd been involved, being a father to Drew, then he'd really been sneaky.

"No." Steve closed his eyes and leaned his head back against the pillow. "I've been giving her money every month. I gave her a hair sample to prove paternity. That's it."

Well, and a successful sperm donation, Kevin thought before he could stop it.

"And now?"

Steve opened his eyes and focused on his son. "Now I get to choose between taking care of my son or keeping my wife."

Kevin felt a cold lump settle in his chest, then slide to his gut. "You think Mom would leave you?"

"I know she would. She told me ten years ago when she suspected something was going on and she told me twenty minutes ago. She's leaving for Arizona and I either go with her or I don't. Ever again."

His parents had started spending the winter in Arizona ten Christmases ago. Now he wondered if Heather had something to do with his father choosing to go that year.

"When is she leaving?"

"Friday."

Four days. Kevin couldn't blame her. It was way early to avoid the snow and cold, and there was still some yard cleanup business happening, but they could get their extra guys to handle that. Getting away from all of this would be a welcome relief, Kevin was sure.

"What are you going to do?"

Steve didn't answer at first but finally swung his legs around to sit up on the edge of the bed. "I've been thinking about that since I got here."

"Good." At least he was taking it seriously. Kevin would deal with the reality of what was going on, what all of this meant, later. Right now, he needed to know what was happening with his family.

"I have to go with her, Kevin. I don't want this to break up our marriage. I didn't let it ten years ago and I don't want it to now."

Kevin was glad to hear that. At the same time he was disappointed. The man he'd known for the past thirty-two years was not the kind of guy to turn his back on a little boy who needed him. Especially one he really should be completely responsible for.

"What about Drew?" Kevin asked.

"I have the perfect solution." Steve managed a small smile.

"I can't wait to hear it." Kevin knew perfect might well mean something different to Steve than it would to Kevin. Or Heather. Or Drew.

"I want you to take care of him."

Kevin blinked at him. "What do you mean?"

"Drew needs someone to stay with while Heather serves her time."

"Her time?" Kevin repeated sharply. "How much time? For what?"

"DUI. It's her third offense and the judge is fed up. She's volunteered to go into rehab but it's a three-month program followed by three months in jail."

"Six months?" Kevin said. "You want Drew to stay with me for six months?"

"If you don't do it, he'll go to foster care. She doesn't have any family."

"What about you?" Kevin demanded. "He's your son."

Steve looked pained. "I can't. Your mom won't do it. She'll never forgive me if I choose him over her."

"Maybe you should have thought of that when you had sex with another woman," Kevin snapped. He paced away from his father, shoving his hand through his hair.

"I should have thought of a lot of things," Steve said quietly. "It was a mistake. A huge mistake. It was…wrong on every level. But I want to be with your mom. And she wants to be with me. And she doesn't want anything to do with Drew."

Kevin faced him again. "None of this is that little boy's fault."

"Of course it's not." Steve sighed. "It's temporary, Kevin. It's a few months. If it was bigger than that, permanent, I'd fight harder, but…it's not like Heather and I were ever in love or anything. She doesn't want to be with me. She doesn't want me in Drew's life. We decided that a long time ago. I help financially because she needs that, but she made it clear in the beginning that I wasn't going to be a father to him."

"She sure seems like she wants you to be in his life now," Kevin said, thinking back to the waiting room.

"She's desperate. She has no other options. I can guarantee she ran through every other possibility before she came to me."

"The restaurant was really the first you'd heard from her?"

Steve had the decency to look embarrassed. "She called a couple of times. But I didn't know what to say. Or do."

"So you ignored it and hoped it would go away?" Unbelievable. Kevin shook his head. He couldn't quite wrap his head around how his parents—his parents—were acting.

"No, I was trying to come up with options. I didn't know the timeline."

"The timeline?"

"She goes to jail on Monday."

Of course she did.

Kevin sighed. "And you think the best option is for him to stay with me?"

Steve nodded. "I do. Hang on, hear me out," he said when Kevin started to argue that the idea was ridiculous. "Look at you. You take care of people all the time—the Center and Dooley's dad and Katherine and the others."

The Center was the Bradford Youth Center, a place for at risk teens, founded by his friends' father. Kevin and the rest of his friends spent several hours a week there. Then there was Doug Sr., Dooley's dad. He'd had a stroke several years ago and needed help with general, day to day things. Kevin filled in when others couldn't be there, but he also genuinely liked hanging out with Dooley and his family, so often showed up even if his help wasn't needed. And Katherine was one of three older ladies who Kevin, Sam, Mac and Dooley took care of by helping with the general upkeep of their homes and cars, allowing them to stay independent but safe.

He couldn't argue that his life seemed filled with people who needed him.

But that didn't mean that adding a ten-year-old boy to his routine was a good idea.

"I don't even know Drew, though," he protested. What kid wanted to move in with a total stranger for six months? "Doesn't she have any friends?"

"Sure, if he needed a place for a couple of days," Steve said, sliding off the bed and pacing toward him. "This is six months. This is something family does."

"He's your family," Kevin said.

"He's your little brother. Like it or not."

Kevin felt like someone had kicked him in the chest with a steel-toed shoe.

His dad was right. Drew was his brother.

He'd never had a brother. Had never been the big brother to anyone.

"Yeah, but…" The protest was weak, but he felt like he had to make it. "What about Jill?" Kevin asked of his sister.

"Jill's too far away. We can't just ship the kid off," Steve said. "And you're a terrific choice," Steve said. "You're successful, stable, caring, responsible. You'd be a great role model for a kid Drew's age." Clearly Steve had spent a lot of time thinking about this and preparing his speech.

"I've been watching you," Steve said, pacing back to the bed but facing Kevin without sitting down. "You're a new man in the last few years."

He was, of course. He'd given up drinking, women, the wild lifestyle. But Steve had always been into Kevin, the football player, and he'd looked the other way when it came to everything that had come with it. The parties and women and public spectacle.

"I'm so proud of the man you've become," Steve said. "I can't give Drew much—or really anything—but you can. And I can give him to you. That is probably the best thing I can do for him."

Kevin stared at his father for nearly twenty seconds. Then he slumped into the blue plastic chair by the door.

The last time his father had said he was proud of him had been after they'd won against Florida in the National Championship game his senior year at the University of Nebraska. Up to that point, every other time had been about sports too.

"What about Heather? What does she say? Have you even talked to her?"

He nodded. "The cops showed up to question all of us and said she wouldn't talk to them until she talked to me so they brought her in. I told her about you. She agreed."

"She hasn't seen me since high school."

Steve shrugged. "She doesn't have a lot of choices."

"That's kind of crappy, don't you think? She's going to turn her son over to me because she doesn't have a lot of choices?"

Steve's expression hardened. "Look, she should have thought of that before she drove drunk. If he was going to foster care, she wouldn't know those people either. She's lucky the judge gave her a few days to try to get things arranged for him."

Kevin couldn't really argue with that. She'd made some bad choices and these were the consequences. But Drew was still an innocent victim.

He scrubbed a hand over his tired eyes. He knew about guardianships and custody issues because of the things he'd seen in the ER. Abuse cases, neglect, parents killed in accidents leaving children behind, all kinds of messes. This was temporary. And this was his brother.

Kevin felt a sudden warmth fill his chest.

Like a switch had been turned on that said *yes*.

Yes?

Yes to what, exactly?

Drew needed someone. Drew needed him. A little boy he'd never met, never even heard of, needed him.

Stepping in to help with little notice and no more motive than someone needing help wasn't uncommon for Kevin. Still, this felt different. This was a lot more personal.

Yes.

It was all he could think.

His dad was essentially telling him that he believed Kevin could do this. His dad had always believed he could make the tackle, hit the home run, score the points, stop the play, but he'd never believed Kevin could do anything else. At least not that he'd ever said.

"Okay, I'll take Drew."

"You'll move back to Grover, right?" Steve asked. "You can stay in our house. Heather lives in a dumpy house with two other girls."

Kevin frowned. "Grover? No, I…"

"He's in school, Kev. You have to keep him there, keep his routine as normal as possible. He'll need to be with his friends."

Kevin tried to quickly wrap his mind around the fact that his father seemed genuinely concerned about the boy. "You're acting kind of fatherly," he commented.

Steve blew out a long breath. "I feel like shit about all of this. This whole situation sucks. I knew it in the back of my mind, but I could ignore it. That doesn't make me a good guy, I know, but I didn't let myself spend a lot of time thinking about everything. Now that it's right here in my face I want to be sure I do what I can."

"He needs a father, Dad," Kevin said quietly. "He needs a house and school and stuff too, but he needs a father."

Steve looked seriously pained. "I know. I… How can I do that to your mother?"

Kevin didn't know. He certainly didn't want his parents to break up, but what about the ten-year-old in the other room? Didn't he matter?

Kevin could only hope that his mom would come around, would see that Drew wasn't a threat, but for now it seemed the only person who could really do anything for Drew was him.

"Fine. I'll figure it out."

"I'm paying for everything," Steve interjected. "Stay in the house, I'll pay the bills online. Put groceries and gas on our accounts in town."

Kevin couldn't help but smile at his father's earnestness. "I'm not worried about the money, Dad." His NFL career had been short but he'd invested and saved and had no financial worries.

"And I'll pay for your rent while you're out of your apartment."

"That won't be necessary," Kevin said.

"Kevin?"

They both turned toward Danika as she poked her head into the room. "Yeah?"

"I need to talk to you."

"Okay." He turned to his dad. "We'll talk more."

Steve nodded. "Thanks, son." The look of relief on his face was real.

"Sure thing."

Sure thing. He'd take over as a fill-in father to a ten-year-old he'd met ten minutes ago. He'd turn his whole life upside down and inside out because the kid had two parents who had made a series of the worst decisions ever.

At least he wouldn't have to figure out what ten-year-old boys were into—he hung out with Dooley, who was really an overgrown kid. Dooley and Drew were probably on exactly the same wavelength.

"What's up?" Kevin asked Dani as soon as the door shut behind him.

"There's a caseworker with the state here," Dani said, heading for the break room. She was walking a little different now that her pregnant belly was more obvious. "It's pretty routine when a kid's involved in a scene like tonight, especially when someone ends up in the ER. But Heather told her that you were taking over as Drew's guardian?"

"I am," Kevin said. "I have no idea what I'm doing, but I'm his best option."

Dani smiled up at him. "Oh, I'd say you're the perfect option, Kev."

"Yeah?" He wasn't so sure about that. He could make maca-roni and cheese, play any video game and build model airplanes, but beyond that he wasn't sure what he had to offer. Dooley's nieces loved when he danced with them because he could lift them up over his head and twirl. He didn't think Drew would be in to that. His friends, Jessica and Ben, had a daughter but Ava was still little and thought the fact that he could talk like Cookie Monster was impressive. He wasn't sure Drew would agree.

"Of course," Danika said, pushing the door to the break room open. "You're one of the best guys I know."

Kevin walked through, still feeling a little dizzy. Or something. That was the second time today—within an hour—that someone had said that to him.

A woman was seated at the round table in the middle of the room with a laptop computer open. Drew was nowhere to be found.

"He's with his mom in the waiting room. They have TV and hot chocolate," Danika said before he could ask.

He must have looked concerned because she smiled. "The cops are letting her stay here until we know for sure you're on board. There's some paperwork." She gestured toward the woman at the table. "But there are cops with both Heather and your mom so there won't be any more bloodshed tonight."

Kevin shook his head. He still couldn't believe what had gone down.

"Kevin, this is Linda Rosner. She's with Nebraska Health and Human Services. Mrs. Rosner, this is Kevin Campbell. He's the brother and who the mother chose as guardian."

The other woman was at least sixty and didn't smile as she rose and extended her hand. "Mr. Campbell."

"Hi." He shook her hand, then took the seat across from her. "What do I need to do?"

"Because you are family and the mother has specifically chosen you to care for Drew, it's relatively easy," Mrs. Rosner told him. "I will be conducting a complete background check and home evaluation, but from what I understand, financially this won't be a problem for you?"

Kevin shook his head. "Not at all."

"And you're willing and physically and mentally capable of caring for Drew?"

"Yes."

"There are no other children in your household?"

"That's right."

Mrs. Rosner nodded. "Fine. The preliminaries look good. I'll come to the house tonight to check that you can meet his basic needs, then we'll start proceedings to make you the temporary legal guardian. Because Ms. Hansen is agreeing to this, it should be no problem, but it will take a little time to get the information I need and to the get the hearing scheduled."

"Hearing?"

"To become his legal guardian you have to appear before a judge who makes it official," Danika explained.

"Okay. When can he move in?" Kevin needed to get things figured out at work too. A week or so wouldn't be a bad idea.

"He can leave with you tonight," Mrs. Rosner said.

"Tonight?" Kevin repeated. "Seriously?"

"His mother is to be taken into custody as soon as we get this straightened out, Mr. Campbell. This is considered an emergency placement."

"I thought she had 'til next Monday," he said weakly.

"She did, until she decided to cause that little scene tonight. She has alcohol in her system. They're taking her in as soon as possible."

"She has alcohol in her system?" he repeated, feeling a surge of anger. "Right now? She drove up here with Drew and she's been drinking?"

Mrs. Rosner looked grim as she nodded. "I think the sooner she starts her rehab the better."

Absolutely. For her and for Drew. But now Kevin would need to take Drew tonight.

"I'm not really prepared for this," he said.

Danika gave him a reassuring smile. "It will be okay, Kevin. We're all here to help."

He knew that. And appreciated it. Danika and Sam, Mac and Sara, Dooley and Morgan, Jess and Ben…they'd all be there for him and pitch in to do whatever needed done. He took a deep breath. "Okay, then."

"You'll be taking him back to Grover tonight then?" Mrs. Rosner said. "He has school tomorrow."

Right. School. "You bet." He could get Conner to come in for the rest of the shift and they were off tomorrow anyway. By Thursday he could get someone in place…

"I'll need to do a background check on anyone who will be involved with caring for Drew and then I'll be in touch to complete the Home Approval Study. I'll come to the house so I can do the home assessment and talk with you and your wife. I can answer more questions then and I'll have more information back."

Kevin nodded. "Fine. And it will be even easier—I don't have a wife."

Mrs. Rosner frowned. "I'm sorry?"

Surely he didn't need to be married to take over custody of Drew? "I'm not married. You'll only need to interview me. And we'll be living in my parents' house in Grover." If his mother wanted to avoid Drew it looked like they'd be finding a hotel room tonight and then packing up and hitting the road to Arizona even sooner than they'd planned.

"The State of Nebraska believes you are," Mrs. Rosner said.

"I am what?" Kevin's thoughts were spinning so fast he'd lost track of what they were talking about.

"Married."

He frowned. "Well, I'm not."

"You're not married to Eve Donnelly Campbell of Grover, Nebraska?"

Holy shit.

He couldn't stop the thought.

Holy shit.

He hadn't heard the name Eve Campbell in years and it still nearly knocked him over. He hadn't seen the woman who bore the name in nine years—not since the time he'd seen her across the square in downtown Grover for about ten seconds.

Being hit with his father's affair, a long-lost little brother and his ex-wife in the same day? What were the odds?

And Eve was so much more than just an ex. She wasn't just the girl he'd married.

She was the only girl he'd ever loved.

Even to this day. She'd made him happier and more miserable than anything or anyone in all of his thirty-two years.

Kevin glanced at Danika, who was watching him with wide eyes. He shifted on his seat. "I, um, was married to Eve. Briefly." Yeah, thirty-one hours was definitely brief. "But not anymore. It was annulled several years ago."

Twelve years to be exact.

Wow, twelve years and he still wasn't over her.

"No, it wasn't," Mrs. Rosner said.

Kevin's eyebrows rose. "Yes, it was." He remembered it distinctly. It had been the worst time of his life.

"No, Mr. Campbell," Mrs. Rosner said firmly. "It wasn't. You are still married to Eve Elizabeth Donnelly Campbell."

"No, I'm not." His heart was pounding and he felt his palms begin to sweat. He wasn't married to Eve. He couldn't be. If he was that meant…

"According to the state of Nebraska you are."

"What does that mm?" *She's still mine.*

The thought appeared suddenly and wouldn't leave. His pulse was racing so hard that he couldn't hear well. He wiped his hands on the thighs of his jeans.

"It means that the only paperwork officially on file is the marriage license."

"But… I…signed the annulment papers." He felt stupid arguing this. Shouldn't he know if he was married or not? Again his mind flew to *she's still mine*, but he quickly squashed that thought. It was a mix-up, a clerical error. There was a lot more to being married than a piece of paper filed with the state and over the past twelve years he'd been as un-married to Eve as he had to anyone.

"That may be," Mrs. Rosner conceded. "But even if so, an annulment was never filed. Your marriage was never legally ended."

He stared at her. Was that possible? How was that possible?

He'd had an attorney. Yes, it had been a friend's dad who done it for free in between his real work obligations, but still, wasn't an attorney supposed to make sure things like that got taken care of?

"I don't know what to say."

Mrs. Rosner closed the file and tapped the folder on the table before sliding it back into her bag. "You don't have to say anything to me. This is a temporary custody situation and the mother picked you. As long as everything checks out in your background check and the home assessment, you're better and easier for Drew than foster care, so I'm happy."

Kevin breathed a sigh of relief.

"But," she went on, "the judge will heavily weigh my recommendations and I have very high standards."

His sense of relief disappeared. "Meaning?"

"I take my job and the safety and well-being of the children in my care seriously. I'm also extremely thorough. I want to know everything that's happening in Drew's life and I want to make sure it's all for the best."

"I understand." In fact, he respected it completely.

"Your marital status is in your file now, Mr. Campbell. Until it changes, the state will assume you're married. If you don't live together and she won't have anything to do with caring for Drew, your statement to that effect might be enough."

"And if it's not?"

"I'll need to talk to her."

His relief was short-lived. "She has nothing to do with this."

"No chance at reconciliation?"

Another stupid, random, shocking thought hit him. I wish. "It's been twelve years. I don't think so."

"Then it shouldn't matter." Mrs. Rosner stood and pulled her briefcase strap up over her shoulder. "But if I was you I know what I'd do."

He looked up, still feeling dazed. "What's that?"

"Find out how I'm still married without knowing it and then do something about it."

Yeah, that wasn't a bad idea. "How do I do that?"

"I suggest you start by talking to your wife."

His wife. His wife. Eve.

And he'd thought breaking up a catfight between his mother and his father's fling was going to be the hardest part of all of this.

"Right." They hadn't lived in the same town in years. They hadn't spoken in years for that matter. They'd just graduated high school when they'd eloped. They'd never shared an address except for the few hours they'd spent in the hotel room after they were officially husband and wife.

Kevin shifted, the memories not any easier to bear all these years later. He'd pushed it all to the back of his mind but it had never left him. He certainly had never gotten over it. Or her.

"I'll be in touch about our next steps," Mrs. Rosner said.

Kevin glanced at Danika, who thankfully said nothing, then back to Mrs. Rosner who was already moving toward the door. "All right. When?"

"As soon as possible."

Which was definitely not the "tomorrow" he'd been hoping for. He could really use some guidance here.

"Then I guess I'll take Drew to Grover tonight."

"Yes, that would be good."

Okay. No big deal. He'd pack up his things and move an hour and a half away from home and work and his support system. Tonight. Great.

His whole life had turned upside down in the space of two hours.

He took another deep breath. This wasn't about him. Someone needed him.

That wasn't new. Lots of people needed him every day—work, his friends and their families.

But this was all his. And in the space of the past sixty minutes, Kevin had embraced the idea fully.

He sighed. "Okay, we'll leave as soon as my replacement gets here." He couldn't really expect the kid to stay here until seven a.m. when his shift was done and then drive to Grover and go to school tomorrow.

"Sam will come as soon as they're off," Danika was quick to say.

"Yeah." He was pretty sure that all of his friends were going to come to Grover.

They wouldn't miss this for the world.

# CHAPTER
# TWO

"SO HOW LONG'S it been since you've seen Kevin Campbell?"

Two glasses crashed to the floor in the kitchen of Sherry's Restaurant as Eve Donnelly swung to face her best friend and business partner. "What?" she demanded.

Monica blinked innocently. "Kevin Campbell? You remember him?"

She wasn't innocent at all.

"Why would you ask me something like that?" Eve glared at her. She had successfully not thought about Kevin in three weeks and four days.

Well, that wasn't strictly true. She'd thought of him when Ed Sterham asked for pumpkin pie last week. Pumpkin pie was Kevin's favorite. But that didn't really count. She hadn't really thought of him since his dad had come in for lunch three weeks and four days ago.

"Obviously the rumors got me thinking about him." Monica whacked a potato into little pieces and dumped them in a pan.

"There are rumors about him?"

"Just one."

"When did these start?" It was hard to believe that she would have been able to avoid hearing rumors about Kevin. Grover, Nebraska was a town of eight hundred and twenty-six people. And she ran the only restaurant in town. If it happened in or around Grover—or even if it maybe happened in or around Grover—she heard about it. And if Kevin Campbell was mentioned, she definitely paid attention.

"This morning. Breakfast rush."

Ah, rush had been the key word there. Monica handled the kitchen and counter since Eve couldn't even make a good ham sandwich. That left Eve to manage the books and staff and to fill in waiting tables when needed. Heather Hansen, their main waitress had quit yesterday—not really her fault, jail sentences did get in the way of work, after all—and so Eve had been running around crazy all morning. She'd barely had time to serve food and keep the coffee hot. She hadn't had time for chatting. Of course, most of her customers would have rather chatted and spread gossip than eaten, but Eve had fed them anyway.

"Do I want to know?" she asked as she retrieved the broom and dustpan to clean up the glass. Really, Monica should know better than to toss his name out there like that. Monica was the only person in town—in the world—besides her and Kevin to know everything about their relationship. Unless of course he'd told a bunch of people. Still she was certain no one in Grover knew because she would have definitely heard about that.

"Absolutely not," Monica said, whacking three more potatoes into bite sized squares. "But I have to see your reaction."

Absolutely not. Great. She couldn't wait to hear it.

"What is it?"

"They're saying Kevin is Drew Hansen's father."

Everything seemed to freeze. Including Eve's blood.

She couldn't hear anything—not the clock ticking, not the hiss of the water boiling on the stove, not the clink of glassware —nothing. Everything had gone totally silent.

The only thing registering was one word that kept repeating in her mind, over and over.

No.

She saw Monica's lips moving and saw her friend's concerned frown. Monica put her knife down and came around the corner of the island where she was preparing the potatoes. When she reached Eve she grasped her upper arms and shook.

"Eve?"

Her voice came through the haze and Eve stared at her. "Yeah?" she whispered.

"You okay?"

Eve shook her head. No. If Kevin was Drew's dad... If he'd slept with Heather... If he was...

No. She couldn't handle it. She'd have to sell the restaurant. She'd have to move.

She knew Heather. Heather had worked for her for three years. They were even sort of friends, kind of. And she knew Drew. Drew came with Heather for the morning shift every day and ate breakfast before Heather walked him over to school. He was a great kid. Bright, too mature for his age, a little quiet, but always polite and...quiet. Especially compared to most of the other kids who came in. She really liked that about him.

She'd asked him a few questions here and there but his nose was always buried in a book. And they were thick books. She didn't know much about ten-year-old kids but she didn't think most of them spent their free time reading about the World Wars.

But genius or not, cute or not, he could not be Kevin's son.

She could not deal with that.

He did look like him, though, now that she thought about it...

"Eve!" Monica shook her hard. "Breathe!"

Eve took a deep breath in through her nose and let it out as instructed. Then she focused on her friend. "No way," she finally said.

"No way? Kevin's not Drew's dad?"

"No. No way." Maybe if she kept saying it over and over it would magically be true. "When would that have happened anyway? He's never here. He hasn't been back here in nine years." Nine years, five months and seventeen days.

"You sure?" Monica was evidently convinced that Eve wasn't going to fall over and let go of her. "How do you know?"

Her grandmother told her every time he came home to visit, because he'd stop in the restaurant to see her. Grandma Sherry had loved Kevin. She was the only one in Eve's family who did. She was also the only one in Eve's family who knew how much Eve had loved him.

She felt a sharp jab of pain in her chest. As usual when she thought of Kevin. Really thought of him.

He'd been The One. Even at age eighteen she'd known. And she'd messed up. And he'd walked away.

Grandma Sherry had been gone for a year now, but now that Eve was here at the restaurant every day she would have definitely noticed him stopping in.

"You really don't think it's possible?" Monica's tone indicated that she, on the other hand, thought it was completely possible.

Eve started to shake her head, then she pressed her lips together. Of course it was possible. Heather and Kevin knew each other. They were about the same age. Heather was beautiful and Kevin was hot—he always had been.

Nine years ago was the last time she'd seen him in person—and he had been hot even from across the town square—but she'd seen pictures in the paper and on TV from time to time after that.

He was six-four, two hundred and fifty pounds of pure muscle. He had looked like a star football player when he'd been seventeen and he certainly hadn't gotten smaller or less sculpted as he'd matured. He had dark hair that he had always worn short and dark eyes that were somewhere between coffee colored and dark chocolate colored. What had always made her really tingle, though, were his hands. They were huge and rough from hard work and football, but he'd been gentle with them. Especially with her. He'd always touched her as if she was fragile and needed special care.

She shivered just remembering it.

He was a big-time Nebraska football player. In this state, and particularly in the small town he called home, that put him on par with someone like Ryan Reynolds—famous enough that people of all ages and backgrounds knew who he was. Kevin was a celebrity in Nebraska, having been the leading defensive player on a two-time National Championship team. That meant charity golf tournaments, visits to kids in the hospital, donations to the athletic department at both the University and Grover High. It was safe to say that he made it into the papers on a fairly regular basis.

Sure, it was possible that Heather and Kevin had hooked up.

But even as she admitted that, she knew that Drew couldn't be his kid. Drew's dad hadn't been around. That couldn't be Kevin. He'd never do something like that.

He might charm a young girl into trusting him, he might make that girl fall completely in love with him, he might convince her to elope with him. He might also turn his back at the first sign of adversity, break her heart and then sleep with every other female in the county. But he'd never abandon his kid.

Then again, what the hell did she know? It had been twelve years and she still wasn't over him. Clearly she wasn't very bright.

"Drew's not his kid," she said, partly because she really did believe that and partly because it was a much better than curling up into a fetal position in the corner and crying for the next couple of months.

"Well, there's only one way to know for sure," Monica said, returning to her potatoes.

"What's that?"

"Ask him."

Eve let out a snort. "Sure, you bet. I'll do that the next time I see him." Then she headed for the dining room.

"I think there's an important piece of information that is not getting the proper attention here," Dooley said.

No one looked up from their menus.

Kevin was filled with gratitude that his friends were here... with a touch of trepidation thrown in.

This morning wasn't going to be easier or less crazy than last night had been.

The night before seemed like a blur. They'd been called out to a possible heart attack before anyone could come in to cover him, so, surprisingly, Kevin's mom and dad had gone back to Grover to show Mrs. Rosner the house so she could do the preliminary home assessment and recommend the emergency placement. They had then packed up and hit the road, not intending to come back until long after things with Heather and Drew were settled.

By the time the crew made it back to St. Anthony's, Dani had Drew curled up with her on the couch in the break room, fast asleep. She described the heart-breaking scene in which Heather had said goodbye and Kevin couldn't help but feel relieved he'd missed it. Sam had comforted Dani and Kevin had awkwardly settled down next to Drew.

Before he could get comfortable, they were then called out again to a nursing home where a patient had coded. When they got back, Morgan, Dooley's fiancé, was curled up with Drew.

"Dang, your little brother has slept with more women tonight than you have in years," Sam said, slapping him on the back.

Kevin was grateful that Drew was wiped out. He slept through the rest of the shift and through Kevin carrying him to the car and driving him to Grover. He'd put Drew in his old room with the twin bed before he'd finally crashed for a few hours in the guest room. He'd slept restlessly but at least wasn't functioning on no sleep now the next morning.

He'd awakened and realized that not only did he not have any idea what Drew ate or if he had any food allergies, but his parents had no kid food in the house anyway.

Then he'd heard the knock on the door.

Sam, Mac and Dooley stood on the porch and a pickup full of his stuff sat in the driveway.

He'd actually teared up. They'd gone to his house, packed as much as they could—they'd loaded his entire dresser into the truck rather than touching his underwear—and then driven over an hour to bring it to him.

And they'd brought donuts.

After feeding Drew, the kid brushed his teeth and hair—with no help wanted or needed apparently—and dressed. Kevin was also thankful that Heather had intended to drop Drew off with Steve, because he had a suitcase with him full of clothes, books and a stuffed frog.

Now Drew was at school and Kevin and the guys were seated in a booth at the restaurant for a real breakfast. Kevin needed to see Eve more than he needed eggs and pancakes, but he needed those too. He was hunched down with a cap on his head and was carefully avoiding talking too loud or making eye contact with anyone until the waitress came over.

He was a minor celebrity in Grover because of his football days. In Nebraska, once a Husker, always a hero. And he really didn't want to get into conversation with any of the old guys on the contrasts between Coach Osborn and Coach Frost. He also didn't want to sign any autographs. Mostly because the guys always thought that was hilarious and razzed him unmercifully, but also because he wanted to find Eve and have this conversation as soon as possible.

The more football fans who knew he was in town, the longer it would be before he could get to Eve. Rehashing old games from the glory days was always on the table as possible Grover conversation, but rehashing old games with one of the players was a not-to-be-missed event. The last time he'd gone out in public in Grover, they'd clogged up the bank lobby for over an hour as people came and no one left.

"Okay, I realize that it was dramatic last night," Dooley said. "But come on… Now we can talk about it, right?"

"The Kevin has an illegitimate kid part or the Kevin is married part?" Mac asked, turning the menu to the burger section even though it was nine a.m.

"Keep your voices down," Kevin warned. He was less worried about someone hearing illegitimate kid or married and more worried they'd hear his name. "And I don't have an illegitimate kid," he added. Like it would do any good.

He knew they were amused. Of the group at the table, he was the least likely to suddenly turn up with a wife and kid out of the blue. But he hadn't really. Not really.

Dooley grinned. "The part where Kevin, the good, upstanding boy who tries to go to church regularly and always do the right thing, is secretly married to a girl named Eve."

Kevin rolled his eyes. He had been waiting for this. He was proud of Dooley for holding off this long.

But…even his friends in high school had found this funny. Eve had been the preacher's daughter and he'd gone to church just to prove to her that he'd do anything for her. His friends had teased him about finding paradise and him being willing to follow her into Hell.

Sam leaned back in the booth. "I'm not sure what I'm more stunned by—Kevin having a not-quite-ex-wife or you knowing something about the Bible."

"Har, har," Dooley returned.

Sam finally grinned. "But I'll give you that it's pretty funny."

"It is," Dooley agreed. "It really is."

Mac was smirking too. "I have to admit that it seems a little hard to believe. And perfect at the same time."

Kevin rolled his eyes. The whole story—his dad, Heather, jail, rehab, Drew, temporary guardianship—didn't faze them. They were focusing on Eve.

"You know what this means," Sam said stretching his arms out along the back of the booth. "It means you've been going without sex all this time when you had a wife you could have been with every single night. Too bad, man."

Of course they were focusing on Eve. She was a woman.

They were all great guys—taking care of the sick, the elderly, parents, kids and each other—but nothing got their attention like women.

The rest of the guys nodded with clear sympathy while Kevin tried to block out the truth of what Sam had said. But there was something about the word wife that made a man's mind wander into that territory. And he was no exception.

He shook his head. That wasn't going to do him any good. He had to face Eve with calm and charm. He needed to tell her about the mix-up, the little detail that they were still married and the question about what they were going to do about it. Then they needed to do whatever it was as quickly and easily as possible.

Quick and easy being the key. He had a lot going on. He was in over his head with Drew already. He hadn't even really let himself think about his dad's cheating, his mom's over-the-top reaction and the health and future of their marriage. He needed to figure something out with work. He needed to think about the interview with Mrs. Rosner so that the guardianship would be official. He needed to decide who needed to know about their temporary situation...and who did not. He needed to forward his mail.

He definitely didn't need any drama with Eve. He didn't want to hurt her or open up old wounds or stir things up in either of their lives. They needed to figure this out quickly and quietly. It was nothing more than straightening out a miscommunication. There was no need for any strong emotions.

How he was going to pull that off, he didn't know. All of his emotions for Eve had always been strong.

"Kevin and Eve," Dooley said. "It has a ring to it, doesn't it?"

Mac chuckled. "It does. So, Kev, let me guess... She loves apples and hates snakes right?"

"Oh, I would never love another story more than if she had a pet snake," Dooley chimed in.

"Shouldn't she hate apples?" Sam asked. "I mean, that was what caused the whole problem."

"True," Mac agreed. "But it would be hilarious is she made the best apple pie in the state or something."

Eve couldn't cook. But Kevin didn't share that with them. In fact, he needed to be careful with what he did share with them. So far they'd been caught up in the current events, but eventually they'd want the whole story. How he knew Eve, when and how they'd gotten married, what had happened.

Frankly, he wasn't sure he could tell the story. It made him sick and angry and hurt all over again thinking about it. Saying it all out loud wouldn't be good for his blood pressure at all.

"Well, I can't blame Adam for falling for her."

"You mean Kevin?" Sam asked, chuckling.

"Him too," Dooley said, his eyes on something over Kevin's shoulder. "After all, he might have left one paradise, but maybe he got another one."

"What do you mean?" Mac, who was seated next to Kevin, asked.

"There's a gal with Eve on her name tag coming right for us. And, I wouldn't mind seeing her in nothing but a fig leaf."

*Dang, who are the four big guys in the corner?*

Eve approached the table of newcomers with four glasses of water.

She didn't recognize the two she could see, though both

seemed to be studying her with interest. They were really good-looking. And obviously new. Good-looking guys didn't go nameless long in Grover.

"Hi, I'm Eve. Welcome to Sherry's." She set water down in front of the two guys facing the door first, then turned toward the other two. She got one glass down before she looked at them. The other glass was only halfway to the table when the fourth guy slid out and stretched to his feet. As her eyes followed him up, the water glass in her fingers wobbled, water splashing on the tabletop.

"Whoa, there." Someone grabbed the glass from her hand before it did more damage.

She didn't care as she looked up at Kevin Campbell.

*The* Kevin Campbell. *Her* Kevin Campbell.

"Hi, Eve."

She remembered his voice perfectly. She'd imagined it, dreamed it even, so many times that she wasn't sure it was real for a moment.

But then he smiled.

That smile. The smile that had made her heart pound from the church choir loft, the smile that had made her say yes to that first secret meeting—which had led to so many more—the smile that had made her say yes to that first kiss, that first taste of liquor, that first time skinny dipping. The smile that had made her say yes to marrying him.

There had been a lot of yeses in their past.

Her mind spun as she thought of them all and she couldn't find one that she regretted.

She'd expected that being up close and personal with him again would make her feel flustered or even sad thinking of all the things they'd missed, the ways she'd messed things up.

And she did feel jittery and hot and excited, but not tongue-tied or awkward. She definitely wasn't sad.

Kevin was here. Right in front of her. Smiling that smile.

"Wow," she said softly.

"What?" he asked.

"I didn't expect that to be quite so strong."

His pupils seemed to dilate as he watched her. "You didn't expect what to be so strong?"

"The impulse to kiss you."

His pupils dilated for sure then. It felt like he leaned closer. "You have the urge to kiss me? Now? Just like that?"

She lifted a shoulder. She should probably be embarrassed by that. Or her pride should dictate that she not admit it. Or perhaps her pride should make it so it wasn't true. He'd walked away. Less than thirty-six hours after professing in front of God and witnesses that he would love, honor and protect her until death parted them, to be exact.

But it was true.

"It doesn't feel sudden," she said.

"We're seeing each other again after twelve years apart. That seems sudden." His voice was soft and a little hoarse.

"It doesn't feel sudden because it never stopped being true." She gave him a smile. "But I didn't expect it to be so strong."

"Damn," came a muttered response from one of his friends.

She didn't bother looking at which. But Kevin did. It pulled his attention from her to them and broke the spell.

Damn indeed.

"I, um, need to talk to you," he said.

She sighed. Damn again. When they'd first broken up she would have done anything to get him to talk to her. She would have called, camped out on his porch, shown up at his work place, begged… Anything.

But he'd served her with annulment papers and left town. She knew he'd gone to Lincoln, but wasn't sure how to find him. She hadn't gotten to know his parents well enough to ask them. His friends weren't talking. He'd just been gone.

And now he was back and wanting to talk to her. Terrific.

It had to be something big. Something like being Drew Hansen's father.

Nothing she wanted to hear.

"Can we pretend that you simply came in for coffee and breakfast?" she asked. "I'll take your order and fill your cup, like nothing's weird or awkward, okay?" But she would still have to sell the restaurant and move to Siberia so she didn't have to watch Kevin raise his son with another woman.

One corner of his mouth curled up, but he shook his head. "I need to tell you something."

"You really don't." It was one thing for him to be with another woman, even have a kid, but for it to be in her own backyard—that wasn't fair. But if he didn't say it, she could try to ignore it, try to fake it, tell herself that everything was normal and fine.

"I really do," he said firmly. "It's important."

"Nothing's been this important in twelve years," she said, trying to sound flippant. "I'm sure you'll realize that this is the same—"

"We're still married."

She stared at him.

Oh, that.

He knew. Okay. No wonder he wanted to talk.

Which meant he was getting married. That was the only reason the annulment—or lack thereof—could have come up. In Nebraska, they wouldn't give a marriage license to someone who already had one. In most states probably.

Eve tried to ignore the fact that her heart was trying to turn inside out at the idea of him marrying someone else.

Talking was exactly what she'd been going for when she'd refused to sign the annulment. She'd wanted him to come to her and ask her why. She'd wanted a chance to change his mind. She'd wanted him to have to face her before he gave his heart and life to someone else. Someone who would never love him the way she did, someone who had no right to the man she was supposed to be with.

"Did you hear me?" he asked.

Eve swallowed hard and nodded.

"The annulment was never official," he clarified.

"Yeah. I, um… I really thought this would come up before now." She realized too late how that sounded.

Kevin's eyebrows drew together. "You knew?"

Did she confess? Did she lie? Did she fake a heart attack?

"Yeah, I knew. Know."

"How long have you known?" he demanded.

She hadn't signed because she didn't want the annulment and she'd hoped he'd find out and come to her about it. Well, she was getting her wish. "All along."

His eyes flashed. "You've known all along that we were still married?"

"Maybe we should leave you two alone…" one of the guys in the booth said.

"Not necessary," Kevin said. He grabbed Eve's wrist and started for the kitchen door.

There wasn't really any chance they weren't going to talk about this. Still being married probably meant he was entitled to a conversation at the very least.

But she needed a few minutes to gather her thoughts.

"Wow, guys, did you see that Kevin Campbell's home?" she called as they passed the counter.

Six old farmers swiveled on their stools as if it had been choreographed.

She heard Kevin groan as their faces lit up.

"Kevin!"

"Kevin!"

They climbed off their stools faster than their arthritic knees should have allowed and quickly surrounded him.

Eve slipped her arm from his hand and carefully resisted looking at him.

Kevin Campbell didn't give up when he wanted something.

Even after her father had said no to him taking her out, he'd come to Youth Group events at church and Sunday morning services every week to see her. When that failed he showed up after her piano lessons to walk her home—or at least to the corner where her father couldn't see them. When that didn't result in a date, he started eating breakfast at her grandmother's restaurant every day where Eve worked the early morning shift until school.

He'd never given up. He'd plotted and schemed and found a way to see her in any way he could.

If Kevin Campbell wanted something from her, he always got it.

He'd come after her. They would have to talk.

She just needed a minute.

The second the kitchen door swung shut behind her she breathed deeply, her hand to her heart. She'd missed him. She was so happy to see him. She definitely wanted to kiss him.

"Everything okay up front?" Monica asked.

Eve's attention flew to Monica who was calmly stirring a big pot. Looking at her friend in that moment, everything seemed so normal, so routine, so boring.

What a bunch of crap.

"Kevin's here."

Monica looked up, clearly startled. "Here? In the restaurant?"

"Yes. Trying to untangle himself from his adoring fans and on his way in here right now."

Monica put her spoon down—a sure sign that this was serious. "He's here to see you?"

Eve swallowed hard. The idea of Kevin being here for her gave her tingles, even if she was pretty sure she didn't want to hear what he had to say. "Yeah."

"Why? Is the rumor true?"

Eve's stomach dipped. "I don't know. We didn't get that far."

Monica came around the end of the counter. Now things were beyond serious. "How far did you get?"

"He knows we're still married."

Monica crossed her arms. "And?"

Monica had never been a big fan of Eve keeping that information to herself.

"He seems…unhappy about it." Which made her strangely sad. She'd been living without the guy for twelve years. They'd been about as un-married as two people could be. Yet, she was sad about the idea that he didn't want to be married to her.

Stupid.

"Imagine that," Monica said dryly. "I can't believe someone might be upset about something like that."

Eve frowned. They'd been over this before. "I wanted to talk to him. It's not my fault he didn't follow up on the paperwork until now."

It wasn't like she'd intended to keep it from him for over a decade. She'd wanted a chance to tell him what had happened that morning after their wedding. And that she still loved him. She'd thought it would take a couple of weeks, maybe a month, for him to find out things weren't finished between them and come to see her.

Monica looked at her closely. "You really have been hanging on to him all this time, haven't you?"

Eve had really tried to cover that up. "Not exactly." It wasn't like she was sitting at home on Saturday nights, her and her nine cats, because she could never love another man like she loved Kevin.

She didn't have even one cat.

"But you haven't completely let him go," Monica pointed out.

"I haven't seen him or talked to him," Eve replied. "I don't know what I could have done to get *more* rid of him."

"You could have signed the papers, or called him and told him that you needed new papers, or you could have actually moved on and needed the annulment because you were involved with someone else."

Eve frowned. Of course, she could have done one—or more

—of those things. But all of those ideas made her stomach hurt. As crazy as that was.

"I never had any closure. I never *wanted* to be without him so it makes sense that I haven't gotten over him."

"And now he's here," Monica said. "Time to do something."

"I know," Eve agreed, "this is my chance to finally finish this."

"Good."

"Or to see if we still have feelings for each other." Her toes literally tingled at that.

Monica sighed. "I knew you were going to say that."

"You think I'm crazy?"

"Yes," Monica said without hesitation. "Also slightly delusional and hopelessly romantic."

Eve nodded. "Probably. But it doesn't feel crazy." Or hopeless.

It should. Especially considering Kevin was likely here because he was Drew's father and he was planning to marry Heather.

Which meant delusional was the best term of any of them.

"It should," Monica said.

"But if Kevin's The One? Then it makes sense I'm still in love with him, right?"

"You're still in love with me?"

She turned to find Kevin staring at her, a strange mix of shock, concern and…was that hope?

There was no way he was going to believe that Eve was still in love with him.

No way.

Unless she proved it somehow…

Kevin shook his head. That was stupid. It had been too long.

And she'd made it very clear that she'd made a mistake marrying him. Painfully clear.

"It's probably more like the way I love Ashton Kutcher."

Her tone was surprisingly reasonable, considering the topic.

"Ashton Kutcher?"

"You know, from afar, based only on his good looks and his sense of humor in interviews and stuff."

"Oh," Kevin said with a frown. So her feelings for him weren't serious. Or even real. Great.

And why did that piss him off?

"Then again," she said, "it's got to be more real than that, right? I mean, we've known each other really well. And we've slept together. I haven't done that with Ashton."

Kevin closed his eyes and ran his hand through his hair. "This is not how I thought this conversation would go."

He'd honestly thought he'd show up, probably notice how great she looked, feel a few pangs of the old heartbreak, tell her they were still married, share in her shock, then sign the papers and move on. Or *pretend* to move on, as he had ever since the day she broke every promise she'd made to him.

"I suppose you found out about the annulment thing when you and Heather went to get your marriage license."

He dropped his hand from his head and sighed. He wasn't surprised by her assumption. He knew the news that he was taking Drew in had already circulated. He was a smart guy and knew how it looked, or sounded, or whatever.

"Drew's not mine. I'm just helping out."

Eve crossed her arms across her stomach. "That seems strange, you know."

"Almost as strange as being married without knowing it."

"Are you involved with Heather?"

"No. I haven't seen her since high school. Until last night when I met Drew for the first time."

"But why—"

"None of this is Drew's fault. He needs someone. That's

all I'm focusing on." It was all he was *supposed to be* focusing on, anyway. But there was a willowy brunette with big brown eyes that was making it hard to focus on anything except the fact that she claimed to want to kiss him.

His body couldn't ignore something like that. Not to mention his heart. He'd wanted her since she'd first smiled at him when they were seventeen.

Eve had always seemed small to him. She was five-eight with legs that went on and on, but she was thin and lanky. Not that she would have appreciated either term. She'd always called herself awkward and skinny. She didn't have much for curves, it was true, but he'd found plenty to appreciate. Her breasts were perfect, her hips just right. Her long dark hair, her big brown eyes, her creamy skin made him want to touch everything—and never stop.

This was bad.

She frowned. "How did you get involved with this whole thing then?"

He blew out a long breath. "I'm asking for temporary guardianship of Drew."

"Oh." She frowned. "While Heather's in jail?"

He nodded.

"That's really nice. But…*why*?"

He didn't see a way around the truth here. Yeah, it wouldn't make Heather or his father look real good, but hey, they were grownups who should have known better. "Because Drew's my…little brother."

The sound of stainless steel clattering against the tile floor came from where Monica was still working, but Kevin couldn't take his eyes off of Eve.

She stared at him. She swallowed. She opened her mouth, then shut it. Finally she managed, "He's your *brother*?"

Kevin nodded.

"Oh. *Wow*." It was clear she was calculating the fact that

Drew was ten and Kevin was thirty and that all of this would have to mean…

"Your *dad*… and Heather?"

There it was. He nodded, feeling the surge of anger he'd been periodically tamping down over the past several hours. "My dad and Heather."

Eve huffed out a long breath. "Holy crap."

"Yeah."

"And you're helping Drew out," she said. "That's really cool of you."

He shrugged. He didn't feel cool about it. He felt a driving desire to do *something* to make some good come out of all of this.

"Seriously, Kevin, that's great."

He pushed a hand through his hair again. "Yeah, it would be great. If I had any clue about what I was doing."

Suddenly Eve smiled and he had to force his feet to stay put. He couldn't cave into her sweetness. He'd done that far too many times. He'd been tricked into thinking that sweetness was all there was.

He'd been wrong.

Still, she managed to make him feel lighter when she said, "He's ten. What's to know? Vegetables, not too much TV, decent bedtime. You can do it."

You can do it.

Those four words made his heart thump. His dad, Heather, Danika, the guys—they'd all said or shown with their actions that they believed in him and in what he was doing. But damn if it didn't make him almost grin like a dumbass when Eve said it.

"Nothing to it, huh?"

"No problem," she assured him.

He sighed, the reality once again pressing in. "Oh, there's lots of problems."

"Drew's a really well-adjusted kid," Eve said. "I don't think you'll have any issues with him. And it's not like he's an infant. There aren't any diapers to worry about."

"No, Drew's not a problem. It's complicated." What an understatement. "I haven't had time to get anything really organized."

"You should keep him here in Grover," Eve said. "This is his home. That will be easier on him than anything else. And then you don't need to organize anything."

He frowned. "I know. I intend to keep him here. But I still have to worry about my other responsibilities."

Eve frowned back at him. "He's a ten-year-old kid whose mom is in rehab. I think maybe he's a little bigger priority than… whatever else you have going on, don't you?"

Kevin's frown deepened. "Of course he's the bigger priority. But there are other people who depend on me too. I have to figure out how to not leave anyone hanging."

"I guess your girlfriend is just going to have to deal with it," Eve said, her eyes narrow.

"My…"

Ah. His girlfriend. Eve thought there was a woman. Was Eve annoyed on Drew's behalf or was she annoyed that there might be a woman who wanted Kevin around on a daily—or nightly—basis?

He liked the jealousy theory. Which was stupid.

"No girlfriend. But I work three twelve-hour shifts a week from seven p.m. to seven a.m." He ran a hand over his face, feeling tired even thinking about it. "My days off are no problem, and even the days I work I can be there for him until about five-thirty, but I have no idea what to do about the overnight thing."

He didn't know why he was dumping this all out there. Maybe because all of the thoughts had been nagging at him since last night and he'd realized that this was going to be a major juggling act—and it was very likely he was going to drop some balls.

"We can ask around," Monica volunteered from over by the oven. "Surely we can find someone who can stay with him."

Kevin gave her a small smile. "Thanks, I'd appreciate it." He'd figure something out. He could take some time off, of course, but that meant finding a replacement for the crew. It was a lot to think about. He turned to Eve, intent on dealing with one thing at a time. "Anyway, we'll need to go talk to the lawyer in the next few days. After that, I'm not sure when I'll be able to do it. Things will be crazy."

She said nothing. She looked at him, her bottom lip pulled between her lips. She seemed thoughtful.

"Can you do it tomorrow?" he asked.

"No. Sorry."

Well, crap. They needed to get it over with. Not only because he needed to concentrate on everything with Drew, but because, frankly, it was still painful even with having had twelve years to get used to the idea. It wasn't as if they'd been living like a married couple, but for some reason the idea of signing those papers again made him want to get drunk and hit something. Again.

And getting drunk and hitting things were two things he'd been working on *not* doing in the past several years.

"Okay, how about Friday afternoon, before I have to go back to Omaha?"

Eve drew herself up tall. "Yeah, okay. Maybe."

"Sounds good." But it didn't. Not at all.

"I guess at least we're not fighting over custody of the dog or splitting up our dishes and furniture, right?" she said with a small smile.

Something inside of Kevin ached—he would have loved to have a dog and dishes with Eve. "Right," he said, not bothering to try to force a smile.

Her brows drew together. "We're not going to fight over anything, are we?"

"Nope, I've given up fighting."

The corner of her mouth curled up. "On the straight and narrow now, huh?"

He swallowed. "Yep."

She gave him a full smile then. "I guess things do change in twelve years. Are you obeying speed limits and drinking Shirley Temples too?"

She was kidding around. He knew that. He had to remember that he was the one who had constantly bent the rules and pushed the boundaries—even where she was concerned. Maybe especially where she was concerned. Tempting the sweet preacher's daughter had been fun, particularly once he realized that he was the only person in the world who made her morals wobble. She clearly found the idea of him now being well-behaved amusing.

He looked down at her. This was the woman who had made him want to be a better man, the reason he'd ever set foot in a church, the one person who's opinion mattered enough to make him want to change.

Speed limits and Shirley Temples were only the beginning of the changes Eve had wanted…and that he'd been willing to give her.

But she hadn't stayed with him long enough to see it.

Did he want her to know about the man he'd become without her, even in spite of her?

Damn, right.

It might not be particularly noble, but he wanted her to know that he was even better now than when she'd been—supposedly —madly in love with him.

"Oh yeah, Eve. That and so much more," he finally said with a little smirk.

She frowned. "What do you mean?"

"It means I'm finally someone you could take home to Daddy. You wouldn't even have to tie my tie for me. Or remind me which fork to use." Okay, so he hadn't kept *all* the bitterness out of his voice. But he was happy with the changes he'd made. And he hadn't done it for her. He'd done it for himself. Just because he thought of her and what she'd think of it once in a while didn't mean anything.

She swallowed hard. "Kevin, I never—"

He cut her off. "I don't drink anymore. I don't fight. I haven't been arrested in...a long time."

She was staring at him, with her lips pressed together.

"And, I'm celibate now."

Her eyes widened. "Cel...celibate?" she finally choked out.

"Yep."

She finally shook her head, clearly stunned. "You've got to be frickin' kidding me."

He couldn't help his grin as he turned and started for the front of the restaurant. That was exactly the reaction he'd wanted from her. Shock and awe—two of the best things to see on the face of your ex no matter who you were.

"See ya for our divorce on Friday, Eve," he said as he pushed through the swinging door.

Eve turned slowly to face Monica.

"Did he say he's *celibate*?"

"Yep. Sounds like he's a good boy now." Monica was scraping burnt pieces of something into the garbage. Monica never burned stuff. More proof that the world was suddenly upside down.

"Holy crap," Eve breathed.

When Monica turned back to Eve, she looked concerned. "So that's...interesting."

Eve ran a hand through her hair. Kevin Campbell was a new man. A *completely* new man.

About as different as she was now.

Eve tipped her head back, staring at the kitchen's light fixtures. "Yeah, really interesting."

"Of course, you do realize how funny this is too, right?"

Monica asked, a big grin stretching her mouth when Eve focused on her.

"*Funny*?" That was so not the right word.

"Sure. He's the good boy that you always wanted and now you're the bad girl that he always wanted."

Dammit. Eve slumped onto one of the tall stools near the prep table. "That's not fair. We loved each other just the way we were back then."

Monica's expression softened. "I know honey. But your differences were a…complication."

"Yeah." That was an understatement. "But we were kids."

"And now?"

Eve lifted a shoulder. "I guess it could be nothing. We're getting divorced on Friday."

"Are you?"

Eve looked up. "When I saw him out front it took about five seconds for me to think *second chance*. I thought maybe we were gonna get a do-over."

Monica leaned a hip against the counter and crossed her arms. "And now all those feelings are suddenly gone?"

Eve sighed. "He doesn't drink. And he's…celibate." She groaned.

Monica laughed and pointed a finger at Eve's nose. "You are *so naughty!*"

Eve looked at her with wide eyes. "I don't know what you're talking about."

"You are *so* thinking about being the one who ruins his celibacy!"

"I am not!"

"Liar!"

Eve felt her cheeks flush and she slapped a hand over her mouth to hide her grin from her best friend.

"Eve Donnelly!" But Monica was laughing.

"I'm just curious about why!" She was *really* curious about why.

"And you're wondering if you still have the same power over that man," Monica accused.

"Power?" Eve asked, trying to seem innocent.

"Yes, power. You got Grover's bad boy to *go to church* as a teenager. Now you're wondering if you can get this new good boy to do bad things with you."

Eve couldn't hide her grin fast enough this time. "I just want to know what caused these changes! He's my *husband*," she said with a laugh. "I just have a few *questions*."

"Well, you should definitely ask him," Monica said with a nod.

"You think so?"

"Is he still the guy that makes your skin flush or not?"

Eve's eyes widened. "You remember that?"

Monica grinned. "Of course."

Eve hadn't even known that her throat would flush dark pink when she was aroused until the first time Kevin turned his dark brown eyes on her, hot with desire.

He was the only one who'd ever caused that reaction in her.

"Aren't *you* still the woman who called me crazy for thinking I might still love him?"

Monica smiled. "Yeah. But I like you hopelessly romantic."

"That's because you're in love," Eve pointed out.

"Maybe." The smile on Monica's face said it all. She was head over heels.

Something in Eve said, *I want that*. She groaned. "Why can't Kevin and I get on the same page at the same time?" she asked, kind of rhetorically.

Monica answered anyway. "Maybe it's not meant to be between you."

And her answer sucked.

It had been a really long time since Eve and Kevin had even been in the same room together. But it had been equally as long since a man made her heart pound and her toes tingle like Kevin did. That had to mean something.

WHY YOU SHOULD NEVER KISS YOUR EX-HUSBAND   55

They were still married. He was here, practically on her doorstep, and was staying for six months. And he'd been as affected by seeing her as she had by seeing him. That had to mean something.

"I think I have to find out what—if anything—is still between us."

"He wants to meet with the lawyer about the divorce on Friday," Monica reminded her.

"Then I'd better get to work."

"How?"

"I'll offer to help Kevin with Drew."

Monica's jaw dropped. "What?"

"I get the impression Kevin is in a little over his head here," Eve said, her thoughts whirling. "I know Drew and I can be the one to stay with him when Kevin works overnight. I can help ease the transition, and spend time with Kevin in the process. See if there's anything still there."

"Are you sure—" Monica started.

"Why not? My schedule fits perfectly with the hours they need. I don't have any reason not to." Eve felt a surge of excitement. This would be perfect. A win-win.

"Well, just be careful," Monica said.

"Careful?"

"While you're debauching this good boy."

"This good boy debauched me first."

Monica nodded. "But you broke his heart."

Eve felt her heart squeeze. Yeah, she had. But she was going to make that up to him. If he'd let her.

# CHAPTER
# THREE

"SO SHOULD we unpack his stuff and make it look like home or let him move it in how he wants to?" Kevin asked the guys.

All of Drew's stuff had been moved from the tiny house Heather shared with two roommates to the middle of the guest room across from Kevin's childhood bedroom.

Drew didn't have a ton of stuff, but in the middle of the room at Janice and Steve's house it seemed even more limited.

Dooley shrugged. "Tell him you'll give him a hundred bucks to buy whatever else he wants or needs and he won't care either way."

Kevin slid his hands into his back pockets. That wasn't a bad idea. Was it? Drew was ten. A hundred bucks had to sound like a fortune. He could buy...

Kevin wasn't sure. When he was ten, ninety-percent of the time he was playing, watching, reading about or thinking about football. The other ten percent of the time it was baseball or basketball.

Drew clearly wasn't into sports. He had a ton of books, comic books and video games but not a single ball, glove or helmet. Not a poster or trading card in sight.

"What in the world are we going to talk about?"

"You play video games," Sam pointed out.

"Yeah, football and baseball games."

"Hell, I can catch you up on most of these," Dooley said, lifting the box with Drew's games and the PlayStation.

Kevin suspected the expensive game system had come from his father's guilt money. He rolled his eyes at his friend but grinned. "I knew you'd prove useful."

"Oh, and that's not even including my knowledge of comic books," Dooley said, unoffended. "Let's hook this baby up."

Kevin knew Dooley really wanted to play—educating Kevin would be a side effect only—but he'd take it. He should go to the grocery store, but thought maybe Drew should go to pick out his favorites too. Or they could go to Eve's restaurant today instead. Or every day.

It shouldn't surprise him how easily his thoughts went to her. It had been that way ever since he'd walked into that classroom at Grover High.

He was lost in thought—like how to avoid Eve over the next six months in Grover and if he really *wanted* to avoid her—so didn't notice the conversation around him until Sam nudged his foot, "She's the one, right? The one you're always thinking about?"

Kevin cleared his throat and straightened, then tried to look unaffected. "Um, yeah."

"And you're getting the annulment fixed up?" Mac asked.

"Yep. On Friday." He hoped. He had to call the lawyer before he'd know for sure.

"It's a long time until Friday." Sam leaned back with a wide grin, draping an arm across the back of the couch.

Kevin frowned. It really wasn't. Three days. There wasn't much chance of anything happening between now and then.

Especially if he avoided her like the plague. Which seemed…unlikely.

He didn't say a word though. With these guys, the best options were staying quiet or duct taping their mouths.

"Hey, Dooley, how long did it take you to get wrapped around Morgan's finger?" Sam asked.

Dooley looked like he was concentrating hard on the video game, but he answered, "Looking back now? Probably an hour."

Sam chuckled. "Yeah, it took Danika one night to make me nuts."

"It was about five minutes for me," Mac said. "The second Sara climbed on my lap at Sam's wedding and laid that kiss on me I knew—"

"No one asked you," Sam said with a frown. He turned to Kevin. "So, three days is like an eternity for her to get under your skin."

"Not gonna happen." Kevin tipped his soda can back for a nonchalant drink. "I'm probably not even going to see her until the meeting with the lawyer," he said after he'd swallowed— also nonchalantly. "And even if I did, it wouldn't matter."

Dooley glanced over from his game. "Dude, we were there, remember? We saw how you looked at her. You're a goner if she so much as smiles within ten feet of you."

"So I'll have to stay more than ten feet away from her." How hard could that be?

"It's gonna be hard to kiss her from more than ten feet away," Sam said, watching Dooley maneuver his way through some maze of buildings and cars on screen.

"Kiss her?" Kevin frowned at him. "Why the hell would I kiss her?"

He should go in the other room. He should avoid this conversation entirely. Because deep down he was hoping his buddies could give him a really good reason to do just that.

"Do you remember what underwear she was wearing the first time you went far enough to see it?" Mac asked.

The question seemed out of left field but Kevin knew these guys—Mac was leading up to something. He shouldn't answer. He should go into the kitchen. Or leave the house entirely. Or kick their asses out. He should not be thinking about Eve's underwear.

Instead, he said, "Cotton panties. White with blue flowers."

Mac smiled and nodded. "Nice."

Kevin sighed. "So?"

"So, how many women have there been since Eve?"

He didn't have an exact number. "Lots." Too many.

"I'll bet you've seen your share of panties."

"Um, yeah." They knew he'd seen his more than his share of all of it.

"Do you remember any details about them? Or which woman wore what?" Mac asked.

Kevin sighed. "No. What's your point?" But he was pretty sure he knew.

"That this woman matters. Still. More than any other ever has."

Kevin slumped back into the couch cushions. Dammit. Still he said, "So?"

"So, that's worth at least finding out if her panties are still sweet cotton or if she's got some silk and lace going on now."

Kevin started to push himself up off the couch. Yeah, this conversation was not where he should be right now.

"I'll tell you right now that I'm gonna start saying grace at all my meals since I've seen how good boys are rewarded," Sam said.

Kevin paused with his ass two inches off the cushion. "What do you mean?"

Sam glanced over. "You've been minding your manners, right? You gave up all the trouble-making. And now, dude, karma is being *so* good to you. Suddenly, right in front of you, is the love of your life, and she still wants you too." He chuckled. "You keep saying no sex until you're really serious about someone, right? Well, it doesn't get much more serious than marriage. And you've been married for *twelve years*."

Kevin plopped himself back down. He didn't need this. He really didn't need this. Seeing Eve again had him all mixed up. And he absolutely did not need to be thinking about the fact that he could have her. Technically anyway.

"First of all," he said, "you're already married to the love of your life. You don't need to be rewarded with another one."

Sam shrugged and grinned. "I'm thinking an equivalent reward for me would be winning the lottery or something."

Yeah, being married to Eve was exactly like winning the lottery, Kevin thought wryly. But right on the heels of that thought was yeah, maybe it was. For most people, the lottery meant access to everything they'd ever wanted. Being married to Eve really could be a lot like that for him…

He shook his head and frowned. "Second of all, I haven't been celibate that whole time."

Sex—or the lack of sex—was, by far, the hardest part about the life changes he'd made. He wasn't a sex addict, he wasn't into porn—well, any more than the next guy—and he'd never been a playboy like Sam or into the sexier stuff like Mac. But he'd been offered a little bit of everything. Threesomes—two girls, a girl and another guy—but that had never gotten him going. He wasn't against toys and lickable body oil, but he didn't need them either.

He just loved women. Loved touching them, making them moan, making them crazy about him. Giving that up had been his biggest challenge for sure. The drinking had been tough to give up. Moreso the partying—the socializing where he was treated like a big star. The fighting had also been difficult. He'd been quick to swing when someone piqued his temper and his fuse was short. But women were a temptation he had to consciously deal with every time. A pregnancy scare with a woman he didn't even remember when she'd come to him seven weeks after their one drunken night together had been his wake up call.

Ironic consider the situation he was now in with his dad and Heather and Drew.

But now there was one—Eve, The One—that he could have by all legal and moral standards.

It seemed too good to be true.

"Third of all," he went on, "I can't sleep with her whether we're married or not. It's been too long. We barely know each other anymore. That's not the kind of serious, committed relationship I'm talking about."

There was a pause as all the guys looked at him. Then Sam asked, "Is there a fourth of all coming?"

Kevin frowned. "No. Why?"

"Because the third of all kind of sucks."

Dooley and Mac nodded. Kevin's scowl got deeper. "Why does that suck? Just because a piece of paper says we're married, doesn't mean we're *married*."

"Don't you want to be?" Sam asked. "Don't you want to find the right girl and live happily ever after?"

Kevin opened his mouth but immediately realized there was only one thing he could say. He saw his friends living happily-ever-after every day. Did he want what they had?

"Yeah," he admitted. "Of course I do."

"Then doesn't it make sense to at least see how it goes with the woman you're already married to?" Mac asked. "This girl is the one that got away. The one you still think about. The one who about knocked you on your ass when you saw her again. You're both single, you're here, there's still chemistry…why not find out what it means, if anything? The lawyer's office and those papers will still be there down the road if you need them."

That all sounded damned good to him. Too good. Too easy. Too…risky.

Kevin groaned and covered his face with his hands. How

could he be expected to not want to do all the things the guys were saying he could, and even should, do?

He might be a different guy now than he had been twelve years ago, but he was still a guy. And it was still Eve they were talking about.

"It's like I haven't had candy in eight years and now someone threw open the door to the candy shop and said 'it's all yours'. I could make myself really sick doing that. Just because I can, doesn't mean I should."

"I disagree," Dooley said, pushing himself up from the floor and tossing one of the game controllers to Mac. "I think you're going to stand outside that shop staring, drooling, dreaming about it, distracted from everything else until you have a taste. You should march in there and eat until you can't move. Then you'll be able to tell if your cravings are because you haven't been inside any candy store in so long or because you really want this candy."

That sounded like a really good idea. A really, really tempting good idea. Which could lead to a major stomach ache. Or heartache.

The new game blipped on and Mac settled onto the floor.

"I..." Kevin started.

"I'm confused."

They all swung toward the living room doorway. Eve stood holding a cardboard box with a paper bag balanced on top of it.

"Am I the candy or the whole shop?"

"I think you're the whole shop, sweetheart," Dooley said without missing a beat. "A variety of treats wrapped up in one tempting package."

Though he couldn't see him, Kevin was sure Dooley winked at her.

Eve laughed. "Nice analogy," she said, coming into the room. "The front door was propped open, and I couldn't really knock."

Kevin stood quickly and headed for her. They'd propped the front door open when they were carrying stuff in from the truck and had obviously forgotten it. He took the armload from her in one sweep, intent on getting her into another room before his friends started in with a bunch of stuff he was sure he didn't want Eve to hear.

"What are you doing here?" he asked.

"I was thinking about things. I have a proposition for you." She smiled up at him.

He'd seen her four hours earlier and had been thinking about her non-stop since. He should have been prepared for what it was like to look into her eyes.

He wasn't. The impact almost knocked him over.

Then her words hit his consciousness. A proposition.

His first instinct was to say yes, without even knowing what she wanted.

She smelled fantastic and Kevin wanted to sweep her off her feet and carry her upstairs. It didn't help that *what's stopping you?* followed quickly on that heels of the thought.

Nothing was stopping him.

She was his wife.

He felt want wash through his body as he thought about licorice and chocolate covered peanuts and peppermints and his favorite, jelly beans. Eve was most definitely like a candy store with everything he loved best inside. In fact, he could combine the two ideas. He could cover her in candy, he could put a jelly bean in her belly button and suck it out on his way…

"Kevin?" Her voice was soft and husky and she was staring at him with wide eyes. "You okay?" It was obvious she was reading the heat and desire in his gaze. She swallowed hard and moved closer. "I was…"

Heat—and not the Eve kind—registered on his palms where he held the box and he managed to pull his eyes from her face. "Yeah, I'm fine. What's all this?"

"There's a pan of mac and cheese from Monica in the box. And some other snacks."

"Just out of the oven?" he asked, heading for the kitchen

quickly before she—or the guys—noticed the erection he was suddenly sporting.

"Yeah. Monica said Drew loves her mac and cheese and I thought, first night and all, maybe it would be nice for you to have something he really likes for dinner," she said following him. "You can warm it up later."

"Great idea." And it was. It wasn't quite enough to get his thoughts away from Eve covered in jelly beans, but it was helping.

He set the box and bag on the center island, keeping it all between him and Eve.

"There's also a pan of brownies, some popcorn and some jelly beans."

His eyes flew to her. "What?"

"For snacks."

"Did you say jelly beans?" Or was he dreaming it?

"Yeah." She smiled. "Those are for you. You always liked them best."

He groaned. He braced his hands on the island and dropped his head. He needed strength here. They were going to *talk*. About getting a *divorce*. They were not going to strip down and break open the jelly beans.

At least, they shouldn't.

He lifted his head, looking anywhere but at her. Mac and cheese. She'd also brought mac and cheese. That was awesome. He was nervous when he thought about getting Drew home, trying to do dinner, help with homework and, of course, helping the kid adjust to the fact that his mom was gone for six months and he wouldn't see her. Drew was stuck with a big brother he didn't know and…that was that. There wasn't really anything either of them could do.

But for one night he'd at least be feeding the kid something he liked.

"What's in the bag?" he asked, reaching for the paper sack she'd also brought.

"Books."

He pulled one out. "*An Encyclopedia of the Presidents*?" he read aloud. The next was about World War II and the third was about the assassination of JFK. "You thought he'd need some extra reading material?" he asked, looking up at Eve.

"Those are for you," she said with a grin. "He's already read them."

Kevin looked back down at the JFK book, weighing it in his hand. It was heavy. Thick. Not a fairy tale.

"Thought you might wonder what to talk about with a ten-year-old who's not into sports," Eve said.

He'd been wondering exactly that. Tonight he'd have Dooley as a buffer even after Sam and Mac headed back for Omaha. Dooley was going to stay until tomorrow night and drive back with Kevin for work. Dooley could talk video games and comics. But Kevin couldn't keep him here for six months. If nothing else, Morgan would likely protest. Then there were all the other people Dooley took care of—his dad, his sisters, the kids at the Youth Center where the guys all volunteered, the three older ladies who fed the guys cookies and pie and TLC in exchange for home and car repairs. In fact, Kevin was going to miss all of that too.

He looked at Eve. She smiled and he decided maybe he wouldn't miss it as much as he thought.

"Thanks. This is all great," he said sincerely. "But how do you know what Drew reads?"

"I talked to his teacher."

"You did?" That was a great idea. That would have never occurred to Kevin.

"His teacher is Jennifer Albert. She used to be Jennifer McPherson."

Kevin remembered her. She'd been a grade ahead of them in school.

"Sure, I know Jennifer."

"I went up during her lunch break and asked her some questions. Who would be better tuned in to his needs and likes, right?" Eve started unpacking the box as she talked.

Cereal, pudding, milk, orange juice, fruit and those damned jelly beans joined a pan of brownies, a pan of macaroni and cheese and a box of microwave popcorn.

"She said he's into eating fruit and veggies and stuff since he saw a thing on TV about kids who play video games being overweight and unhealthy."

She put the pudding in the fridge and found a bowl for the bananas, grapes, and apples.

Kevin was having a hard time pulling his attention from the jelly beans.

"He's into history, especially World War II and U.S. Presidents. His best friends are Tanner and Matthew—they're into gaming too."

She spun, realized she'd missed the milk and OJ and stored them in the fridge too. She seemed to take a quick inventory of the other contents.

"Can you make eggs?" she asked leaning on the door. "I know he likes eggs. But you might want to bring him to Sherry's for breakfast. That's what he's used to and Monica makes great eggs. We'll have to come up with something for lunch though. Unless he eats at school. I should have asked Jennifer about that. I'll e-mail her." She shut the fridge and looked around. "Oh, and I was thinking maybe you should invite Tanner and Matthew over for dinner. Show they're welcome here, help smooth this first evening in a new place with new people a little?"

Kevin knew he was staring and barely breathing, but…wow. This woman was making things a whole lot easier and it was very sexy. He certainly didn't need another reason to think she was sexy but there was something about the way she was jumping in to help him that made him hot.

None of these things were her problems to solve and yet here she was.

He moved around the island quickly, before he could think

better of it, grasped her by the upper arms and pulled her up onto her tiptoes.

"Thank you, Eve."

Then he kissed her.

It was a sweet, affectionate kiss for exactly five seconds. Then it turned hot. It was still plenty sweet though. The candy store analogy fit even better when he fully tasted her, tongue on tongue, breath to breath. Not jelly beans. They were hard and cold. This was more like hot fudge.

He loved hot fudge.

He turned her so her waist was against the island, and he pressed close as her fingers tangled in his hair. She was tall enough that between the heels on her boots and her tiptoes the fly of his jeans was right against the fly of hers, and everything behind and below that point.

She gasped, then groaned. He felt the same way but couldn't bring enough air into his lungs to make a sound. Which was fine. He preferred her sounds anyway. Especially when he dropped his hands to her ass. He wanted to touch her everywhere at once, he wanted to make her crazy, he wanted to possess her. Again.

He'd felt this before. Felt like he'd never get enough. And losing that, losing her, had almost ruined him. His health, his career, his chance at anything good.

Kevin pulled back, sucking in air and common sense.

"That got a little carried away," he said, taking a step back— way back—and shoving his hands into his pockets.

"In case you didn't notice, I was okay with that," she said breathlessly, hanging on to the counter behind her.

"I'm going to be blunt here." He had to be. For his own sake.

"I'm okay with that too." Her fingers gripped the edge of the counter, like she was holding herself back.

"I'm not sure I can do this again."

"This?"

"You."

"You're not sure you can do me again?" she clarified.

Of course, when she said it like *that*…

"You broke my heart, Eve. I went into a tailspin. I almost… did a lot of things that could have turned out really ugly."

He'd immediately started screwing around and partying because he was trying to prove to himself that there were people who still wanted him around, people he could please, people who appreciated what he had to offer, people—okay, women— who could help him forget about Eve.

It hadn't worked. But he'd given it his all.

So much so that it had landed him in the hospital more than once. There had been a couple of trips to detox, a couple of cracked ribs and several stitches from fights, a scare with an STD.

He'd also landed in jail a couple of times.

He'd almost failed his freshman year of college, had almost been kicked off the football team.

It had gotten bad.

"I've got my life together now. I'm not perfect, but I…I can't go back to that and I'm sure that if you mess with me again I'll be right back there or worse."

She bit her bottom lip, staring at him.

He wanted her. He wanted her to say he was crazy for thinking any of those things. That of course this would work.

But how could she say that? It had been too long. So much had happened. They were different people now. She couldn't possibly promise not to break his heart again.

"I understand," she finally said, "but I'm not going anywhere. I'm here, you're here, and there's obviously still… something…between us. So, it's all your call. Whatever you want. You want to just be friends?" She let go of the counter and moved forward. "We can try that." She stepped forward again. "Or we can go back to not seeing each other at all."

*No.* Without input from his brain at all, his first reaction, from the gut was no. Now that he'd seen her again, staying away wouldn't last a day.

"Friends, huh?" he asked. Not that he believed that was going to work either.

"We can try," she said, taking another tiny step, bringing her right in front of him. "But based on that kiss we just had I'm not optimistic."

Yeah, there was no way they were going to be able to be just friends.

"And there's something about *me* you should know," she said.

Oh, boy. He wasn't sure how many more surprises he could take. "Yeah? What's that?"

"I don't want to sign the papers on Friday."

Kevin had to try twice to swallow. "Why not?"

"For the same reason I didn't sign them before."

"Wait, you *purposely* didn't sign the papers before?" he asked.

"Right."

"*Why?*"

"Because I wanted to be married to you."

Kevin couldn't believe his system could still produce adrenaline. So much had been made and used over the past several hours that he was sure he was becoming immune to it. But a jolt hit his bloodstream and went straight to his ticker.

"No, you didn't," he said with a quick shake of his head. "*You* were the one who denied the whole thing. *You* changed your mind the minute we got home."

They'd headed out of town right after the graduation reception at her house was over. They'd gone straight to the Justice of the Peace and had been married before her parents had finished picking up the folding chairs in their backyard.

After they'd become husband and wife they'd gone to the nicest hotel he could afford—a Holiday Inn—and spent the rest of the evening and night making love, talking, laughing, basking in their love and their plans.

The next morning they'd driven back to Grover and right to

her father's church. They'd walked into that sanctuary together for the first time. Hand in hand.

The plan was that when her father asked for announcements and prayer requests from the congregation, Eve was going to get up and announce their marriage to her family and their community.

But she hadn't done it.

She'd sat beside him, hands folded in her lap, knuckles white, throughout the service. Then after everything was over and her father came straight at them, demanding to know where she'd been all night, she'd denied that she'd even been with Kevin. According to her account, she'd spent the night at Monica's and Kevin had shown up that morning to come to church with her.

After her father, still looking angry and suspicious, left them, Kevin had demanded to know what was going on.

She'd changed her mind.

Those had been her exact words. He could still remember the way she said them, the color of her lip-gloss, the fact that the ring was shoved in her pocket instead of on her finger.

"I know I messed up," Eve said. "I panicked once I got there, facing them all." She moved closer. "I'm so sorry. I *wanted* you, Kevin. But I didn't want to tell my dad."

Yeah, her dad had been a piece of work. Still was, Kevin was sure. She'd been eighteen, ready to leave home, in love. Yet, face to face with her dad none of that had mattered. "You said you changed your mind," he repeated.

Now, though, he knew it wasn't what she'd said or hadn't said—it had been the look in her eyes that had torn his heart in two. She'd looked guilty. And ashamed.

Guilty about and ashamed of *him*.

"I was *eighteen*," she said. "I freaked out."

His chest ached. The elopement had been completely spontaneous, his over-the-top attempt to bind her to him. He'd wanted her forever and knew he wasn't good enough for her. But he also knew that a girl like Eve would never take marriage lightly. If she said vows to him, she'd be his forever, whether he deserved her or not.

He'd been sure during the drive to the Justice of the Peace, through the wedding service, through the drive to the hotel and through the night, that she'd change her mind. So the moment she'd said the words *he'd* freaked out.

"I'd changed my mind about telling them right then, like that," she said, exasperation in her tone. "Not about you. Not about us." She looked completely frustrated, "I haven't practiced this speech in like eight years."

"Speech?" he asked with a frown.

"The one I was going to give you when you came to me to get the papers signed." She frowned back.

"There's a speech?" He couldn't help it—he was curious. What had Eve wanted to say to him so badly that she refused to sign annulment papers for twelve years? And she'd practiced the speech? For a few *years* after the fact?

"There's a speech."

"That you practiced?"

She shrugged. "Once in a while I'd imagine running into you or drinking and dialing and I wanted to be prepared."

"It was all a long time ago," he finally said softly.

"Yeah," she agreed. "But love isn't supposed to change with time, or mistakes." She looked at him directly, her chin up. "I was determined to prove that to you. I wanted to show you that even if you ignored me, wouldn't speak to me, slept with a million girls, my feelings wouldn't change."

He was having trouble breathing. "Eve, I…" He had no idea what he meant to say.

"And, of course, there was also spite," she finally said, her tone lighter. She slid her hands into her back pockets. "I figured at least I was getting revenge because every time you slept with someone else you were committing adultery."

He blinked several times, surprise rippling through him as

the urge to smile overcame the what-am-I-supposed-to-do-with-these-feelings confusion he was trying to sort out. She was still the preacher's daughter deep down it seemed. "So, when you go for revenge it's soul-burning-in-hell-for-all-eternity revenge?"

She laughed. "Yep."

The sound of her laughter washed over him. "I'll keep that in mind," he said, the corner of his mouth curling. "And I think I need to hear this speech."

"Oh, yeah? Feeling less good about yourself with the twenty-six counts of adultery against you?"

Telling her that twenty-six was way too low would do nothing good for him, he was sure. "Come on, let's hear it," he said.

"You need an ego stroke that bad?"

"Would this do it?"

She chuckled softly. "If hearing how someone can't live without you, how they're sorry for everything, how they'd do anything to get you back and how much they love you makes you feel good then…yeah, this would do it." She sighed, but was still smiling. "I was a heartbroken eighteen-year-old girl. The speech was plenty sappy and pathetic."

He cleared his throat again. "Then I gotta hear it." His voice was still a little hoarse and he took a step closer, unable to help himself.

She certainly didn't move back. "I started off with how I was sorry for breaking my promise to you and that I still thought of you all the time. Then there was a bunch of dramatic teenage girl stuff about how I should have loved you no matter who was trying to break us up and I should have been willing to face my father's anger to be with you, that our love should have been enough to overcome all of that."

That was at the base of all the hurt he'd felt. She'd promised to love him, to honor him, to forsake all others. He'd believed all of those things. He'd pledged the same things back to her, readily and happily.

She'd blown all of those within twenty-four hours of getting home from their wedding.

"Good premise," he said gruffly.

"Yeah?" There was definite warmth in her eyes. It was bordering on heat. "Would it have worked?"

That was a really good question.

Kevin blew out a long breath. "I don't know. I would have liked hearing it." He liked hearing it even now. A lot. Something about Eve semi-groveling, declaring her feelings and apologizing felt really good. But… "I don't know if I would have believed you."

She'd said vows and backed out. Could he trust even a simple apology?

"I would have been very persuasive."

*I would have liked to see that.* He couldn't stop the thought. In their entire history together, he had always been the pursuer, the one who made sacrifices and took risks to be with her.

He'd shown up at church—her father's church—twice a week for months, proving how he felt about her. He'd been alone in the pew every time. He'd been uncomfortable, knowing people were wondering why he was there, knowing he didn't really belong. The kid who had been hailed a hometown star for as long as he could remember was out of place for the first time in his life.

Still, in spite of his discomfort, he'd shown up and he'd stayed. For Eve.

Who had then denied him in that very place after promising to love him for better or worse.

Yeah, it would have been a nice change for her to come after him.

"What if it would have taken more than a speech?" he asked. He almost regretted it the moment he'd said it. Something flared in her eyes and she moved closer. And he knew he would have been a goner if she'd been truly determined to get him back. He'd been a sucker for Eve since he'd walked into Algebra II.

"I would have done anything."

"Oh?" He shouldn't be encouraging this. It didn't matter now. It had been too long. He should be bitter and angry and should *not* want to run his fingers through her hair or see if that spot on her inner elbow was still sensitive or see if her throat still flushed when she was turned on.

She moved an inch closer and her gaze dropped to his mouth.

It turned out that righteous indignation was hard to hang on to in the face of Eve looking at him like her speech had an X-rated addendum.

"After all those girls, I knew I would have to remind you of how things were with us."

She was close enough now that he got the answer to his last question—her throat did still get pink when she was turned on.

"I'm not sure this is a good idea," he choked out, knowing exactly what she intended.

He'd already kissed her, spontaneously, without thinking. But *this* was deliberate, with purpose, both of them knowing exactly what was coming.

"Oh, come on, Kevin," she said with a little smile, "it's just a kiss."

He pulled in a quick breath, recognizing those four words immediately. They were the ones he'd said to her before their very first kiss ever.

He'd known even then, even before it happened, that it was going to change his life.

He felt the same way now.

With a touch of panic thrown in this time.

That, however, was forgotten as their lips met.

It was just as kiss like Niagara Falls was just a waterfall.

Eve tilted her head to one side as Kevin moved the other way so their mouths were able to meet fully. They groaned together and she stretched up at the same time he bent his knees to fit their bodies more fully against the other. Their mouths opened, tongues met, breaths mingled and Kevin's hand lifted to the back of her head at the same time she grabbed the front of his sweatshirt, attempting to pull him even closer.

As he tangled his fingers in her hair he thought about how the heavy silkiness felt softer and smelled different than he remembered, which led him to wonder what else had changed. Then her hands dropped to his butt and she urged him closer. And it really hit him.

A lot of things had changed. Twelve years worth.

He pulled back, looking down at her. Her cheeks were pink, she was breathing hard and her eyes were unfocused as she opened them. But he couldn't escape one thought—she'd never kissed him like that before.

They'd gotten carried away on the couch at Justin Thompson's Halloween party, on a blanket by the river and in the front seat of Kevin's car and she'd been eager, but sweet. Now she was bold, clearly confident, obviously knew what she was doing in arousing him.

There had been someone else. Maybe more than one someone else.

It had been a long time after all and he'd very definitely not been celibate. Could he expect that she had been?

Maybe not rationally, but yes, part of him really thought she should have been saving herself for him all this time.

He did not, however, let himself wonder how not-virtuous she had been.

Staring down at his wife, he wanted to dive right back in to that kiss.

Instead he took a big step back.

His *wife*. *His* wife.

There was something about that term that made him feel possessive even while he was trying to remind himself that he needed to stay away from her.

For some reason.

"I knew it would still be like this," Eve said breathlessly, tucking her hair behind her ear and looking at him with wonder.

Yeah. He felt it—exactly like before. Her ability to suck him in and take him over completely was still intact.

He wasn't over her. That was clear. If he was honest, he'd always known it. But getting close to her again couldn't be good.

"We're still *us*. Now I know for sure," she said.

Yes, they were. That was exactly what he needed to remember.

Almost grateful to her for the reminder, he said, "Right. You're still the woman who said marriage vows to me and then forgot all about them the moment you realized things were complicated."

She sucked in a quick, hurt breath and he almost regretted his words. But they were true.

"I don't want to sign the papers, Kevin," she said softly, her eyes sad. "Not yet. I want to show you that I've…changed. I know what I want and I'm willing to fight for it. You're going to be here for the next six months. Can't we…try?"

She wanted him back. Or thought she did. Or thought she might.

Kevin took in the brightness in her eyes and the plump pinkness of her lips from his kiss. He'd done that to her. He was the one who'd put that look on her face. He'd always been the one. And now he was even more what she'd always wanted, always needed. He'd still have her if her father had approved of him and the man he was today would have gotten her father's consent without question.

And *now* she wanted him back. What a coincidence.

He took a steadying breath, then cleared his throat. "We'd better cool it. The guys won't stay out of here forever. I can't believe they're not in here already."

"Wait—" She caught his arm.

That kiss had been a bad idea. Not that her touching his arm should have anything to do with the kiss, but it brought her close enough he could smell her and that's all it took for him to want it all over again.

Aw, hell.

"I haven't told you my proposition yet."

No. Whatever it was, it was a bad idea. "I need to get ready for Drew—"

"It's about Drew. I thought I'd stay for dinner and help with his first night at your place."

"You know Drew that well?" He hadn't expected that.

"Heather works for me," Eve said. "Drew's at the restaurant every day."

A familiar face. Someone Drew knew and could talk to. Someone who knew something about the kid.

That could be really, really good. And it had nothing to do with Kevin wanting to kiss her again. Nothing at all.

"Fine. Dinner tonight," he said reluctantly. "That will be nice for Drew."

She smiled. "You'll need more help than that."

He sighed and looked around the kitchen, noting the bowl of fruit and books...and ignoring the jelly beans...that she'd brought.

Yeah, he needed help all right.

"Your proposition is for more than dinner tonight?" he guessed.

"I can be the one that stays with Drew when you work," she said, grinning proudly as if she hadn't given him the perfect, horrible situation to love and hate at the same time.

That would mean she would be here. A lot. "That's a big commitment."

"But it makes sense. My schedule can be flexible and he already knows me."

"I work seven p.m. to seven a.m."

"You said that."

"I don't have a backup plan."

"You won't need one."

"Drew might get attached to you."

"Fine. Great. He can. No worries."

"He's a kid, Eve. You can't change your mind partway into this."

Again, she took a quick breath as hurt flashed in her eyes. Kevin steeled himself against the urge to apologize.

"I'm not changing my mind," she said firmly, chin up, meeting his gaze directly.

He looked at her for several seconds. He needed someone to help him, there was no way around it. He might be able to switch some shifts, but nothing on a regular basis. All the guys who worked days now did so because of their own families. And he had no other options. Taking Drew back and forth to Omaha wouldn't give the kid the stability he needed and even though his friends and their wives would make the drive, Kevin couldn't ask them to do that.

Besides, Eve was here and, apparently, willing.

And, dammit, part of him wanted to see her do this for him, *with* him and stick with it.

He was in trouble.

"Okay, fine," he finally said. "Three nights a week you can come stay with Drew."

She seemed to be pondering that. "How about I have dinner with you every night, so that it doesn't feel like I'm a babysitter?" she said. "But I'll spend the night only when you need me to."

He knew that she'd said it that way on purpose. Only when he needed her to? He'd needed her to spend the night every damn night for the past twelve years. For a start.

He reigned in the thoughts that were part desire and part frustration. This was about Drew. She was offering to help with Drew. He needed to focus on *Drew*.

And there was something else Eve Donnelly could help with besides macaroni and cheese.

"I know six months isn't a long time overall, but I want to be a good influence on him here while we're together. I could really use help with that."

Eve smiled up at him. "Whatever you need. I'm your girl."

Why did everything sound so temping and sexual?

Oh yeah, because he really wanted to take her to bed.

He cleared his throat. Focus. He needed focus. "My friends are great with kids," he said.

"The guys drinking root beer, playing video games and belching and swearing in your living room right now?"

He nodded, trying not to smile. "My best friends. They'll give me lots of advice, help out whenever they can, but I could really use someone who's a...."

Eve's eyes widened for a split second, then she wet her lips and smiled. "A...what?"

"Stable influence," he filled in after a moment's though. "A good role model. When things got out of hand in my life, I realized I needed something that would be solid and stable. Obviously, things are crazy in Drew's life. I want to give him something he can depend on."

"I was thinking more along the lines of helping with his math homework and doing some laundry."

Kevin shrugged. "That would be great too."

"Too?" She swallowed and gave a little laugh. "What else are you thinking?"

"Someone who can answer the hard questions?" He didn't mean to say it as a question. But damn...he was new at this good guy stuff compared to Eve. She'd been raised with a moral compass that pointed due north. She had very solid convictions. She'd been a rule-follower all her life. "Someone who will help him through the tough times. All of this with his mom, and my...his...our...dad. An affair. His mom's drinking. Jail." Kevin shoved a hand through his hair. "He's probably going to have questions, right?"

"Why can't *you* be who helps him with the hard questions?" she asked. "I thought you had changed all your bad boy ways."

He rubbed the back of his neck. "I'll do my best. But you've got a lot more practice with knowing what's right and how to explain it."

She blew out a breath. "We should talk about what we're going to tell people. And Drew," she said, changing the subject a bit. "What should we tell them about why we're always together and why we're kissing and stuff?"

"We're going to be kissing and *stuff*?" he asked. No. No, no, *no*. She was going to be here for *Drew*, not for him. And what kind of stuff exactly?

"I don't see how we can possibly avoid it."

He cleared his throat and shifted, suddenly uncomfortable in his jeans. She had a point. Even Sam had said it—if Eve was within ten feet of him, he was going to have a hell of a time keeping his hands to himself.

"Should we tell them we're dating?" she suggested.

And who said he had to keep his hands to himself? She was his *wife*. If he was married to her, he wouldn't be putting his hands on anyone else. And surely he wasn't expected to live like a monk while he was *married*. He'd meant every word of the vows he'd said to her and she was the one who didn't want to sign the divorce papers. It stood to reason that, of all the times in his life when he should be putting his hands on a woman, it was now. And it should be Eve.

He was practically *required* to put his hands on her.

Made complete sense.

"Sure. Dating. Okay."

"Are we dating exclusively?" she asked, leaning against the counter again.

Only then did he think to ask, "Why? Are you dating someone?"

"There's a guy I've—"

"Yes, *exclusively*." The surge of jealousy was surprisingly strong. Of course she was dating someone. The men in Grover weren't complete idiots. "And tell people it's getting serious. I'm the only one you're doing *anything* with."

Her grin grew and he knew she'd been messing with him. She'd been looking for a reaction and he'd apparently given her the one she'd wanted.

"And by *anything* I assume you're talking about sex," she went on.

Want slammed into him. Hell yes, he was talking about sex. Okay, she wanted to rile him up? He'd show her riled up. "You're my *wife*. And as long as that's true, I'm talking about everything from laughing at jokes, to touching someone's shoulder, to dancing at a town dance." He frowned at her to show he was serious, but she was practically beaming at him.

"No one else knows I'm your wife."

"*You* know it and I know it. That's enough to keep you from…"

"Laughing at other people's jokes?"

He knew that sounded ridiculous. For some reason, he didn't care. "Right."

"Even if they're funny?" She was clearly teasing him.

"Yes."

She grinned. "What if a woman tells the joke?"

"Even then." He felt the corner of his mouth twitch though. "The only person you act interested in or amused or impressed by is me."

"And turned on by, right?" she asked, her smile turning from entertained to seductive. "You're the only one I get turned on by."

"Yes." He couldn't help it—he had to touch her. He moved forward and stroked his hand up and down her bare arm.

"And, to be clear," she said, "this forsaking all others that we both managed to mess up goes both ways."

Oh, he really liked the jealousy from her.

"There won't be any other women, Eve." Hell, there hadn't

really been in all this time. Now that he was here with her, how could there possibly be anyone else?

"You're right about that," she said firmly. Then she took his face in her hands. "I know what I gave up when I gave you up. I'm not doing that again. If I say it's only you, then it's only you."

"You said it was only me before." God, the hurt was still there and still surprisingly strong.

"I was stupid. And chicken. And wrong. Give me a chance to prove I'm sorry."

He wanted her to. He wanted her to be sorry and he wanted her to prove it. Maybe it wasn't the most chivalrous attitude, but at least he was giving her chance. That had to count for something. "Okay."

"Okay, what?"

"Prove it."

Her eyes brightened. "Yay."

"You're excited about that?" This might be really, really bad.

She brought his hand up to her mouth and placed a kiss on his knuckles. "Of course. I've always wanted to seduce somebody."

Yep. Really, really bad.

Or very, very good.

She was a natural. A simple touch of her lips to his hand and he was practically panting.

"Seduce, huh?" Kevin was proud of how normal his voice sounded, even as his heart pounded so hard he felt it in the bottom of his feet.

"Oh, yeah." She said it with a huskiness he wasn't sure he'd ever heard from her. "And I think I'll be pretty good at it."

"How—" He had to stop and clear his throat. "How so?"

"Well, I was seduced by the best." She leaned in closer.

His hands went to her hips, partly so he could touch her and partly because he needed to control how close she got. "Is that right?" One thing he was sure of was that he did not want to hear anything about the other men that had been in her life.

She looked up from where she had her hand on his chest to his eyes. "You, Kevin." She laughed lightly. "I was talking about you."

Okay, that was better. Then he asked, "The way I seduced you was the best?" He remembered it being awkward and fumbling.

She was still smiling. "Definitely." She tipped her head to one side. "Seduction is about more than kissing and touching and undressing, you know."

He drew in a deep breath. She was probably right. But he was having a hard time not focusing on, and imagining, all three of those things at the moment.

"You were seducing me every time you were waiting by my locker with a Hershey's kiss, every time I found a note in my Algebra book when I sat down to study at night, every time you held my hand, and every time I looked up in church and saw you standing there singing along to the hymns."

Kevin smiled too. "I wasn't thinking about having sex with you every single minute of the day." He made a little circle on her hip with his palm. "Every other minute, sure, but not every Hershey's kiss was about trying to get a real kiss."

He'd been a teenage guy. He'd thought about getting Eve naked plenty. But he'd wanted to spend time with her, wanted to make her smile, wanted to know he was thinking of her too.

"I know." She moved a little closer, sincerity in her eyes. "And *that* was what was seductive," she said softly. "I knew that you wanted more than sex. I knew that you really cared about me too. And that's what I need to do for you now."

She was already doing it. The thought hit him square in the chest. She'd bought him jelly beans instead of chocolate kisses, but she was here, with macaroni and cheese, making him smile, encouraging him, offering her help and it was all making him want to keep her around indefinitely—both dressed and naked.

"Okay," he finally said.

"Okay?" She seemed surprised, but that quickly melted into a huge smile.

He groaned. He was already a goner.

"Yeah," he finally said. "Let's see what you've got."

He was in trouble. But watching the sparkle in her eyes go from surprised to pleased to mischievous made him positive he wouldn't mind losing this battle.

Having Eve do the seducing would be a nice change—for the entire ten minutes it took her to talk him into doing pretty much whatever she wanted.

# CHAPTER
## FOUR

"EVE CAN TAKE you for breakfast and get you to school,"
Kevin told Drew as Eve dished a second helping of mac and
cheese for Tanner and refilled Drew's salad bowl. "Then I'll be
home when you get home from school and we'll be able to hang
out and have dinner before I leave for Omaha at five-thirty. I'll
be gone while you sleep so you won't even know I'm not here
and Eve will stay here with you on those nights."

Drew chewed and watched Kevin. He'd already explained
that they were brothers, had the same dad, and that he intended
to stay until Heather got back home. He'd even told the kid that
they could still hang out after his mom was back. He'd put it out
there for the other boys too, assuming it was important for
Drew's friends to understand their connection as well.

None of them seemed overly impressed or concerned.

"I only work three days a week though," Kevin went on since
he didn't know what else to talk about, "the days I'm off I'll be
here the whole time. We can do more those evenings. Maybe go
to a movie or a ballgame."

That was the wrong thing to say. And he'd known it. Kevin

watched Drew's eyes go to his plate at the mention of the ballgame.

"What kind of movies do you guys like?" Eve asked, including Tanner and Matthew.

"I like all of the *Avengers* movies," Tanner said.

"Yeah, really cool," Matthew agreed. "And *The Fast and the Furious*."

"*Star Wars* kicks all of those movies' butts," Dooley said.

"New *Star Wars* or old?" Eve asked.

"New as in the most recent made or the most recent chronologically?" Dooley asked.

"Any."

"The old ones, as in the ones made first, are by far the best. By far. But I think all of them beat out *Avengers*. What do you think, guys?" he asked, pointing his fork at the boys.

"Never seen *Star Wars*," Tanner said.

Dooley looked at Matthew. "Please tell me you have."

"I saw one of the old ones. I like that big bear that walks around."

Dooley's fork clattered against his plate. "No." He shook his head. "No. You're ten years old, right?"

Tanner and Matthew both nodded.

"Then it is not okay that you haven't seen all the *Star Wars* and it is *unacceptable* that you think Chewbacca is a bear." He looked at Kevin and Eve. "We're going to have to fix this."

Eve grinned. "Agreed. How about you, Drew? Have you seen *Star Wars*?"

Drew shrugged.

"Drew doesn't watch movies much," Tanner said, reaching for his milk. "His mom makes him do educational stuff." He rolled his eyes and drank.

"Yeah, his mom doesn't like guns and fighting and stuff. But he sometimes watches stuff at my house," Matthew said. "We saw *Goonies*. Have you ever seen that one? It's old."

"I love that movie," Eve said. She winked at Kevin. "Movies like that never get old. Treasure hunts and pirates? Come on!"

Kevin couldn't help but smile. She and Dooley were a great team. Awkward silences were not an issue and they were even getting information about Drew in spite of the fact that his little brother wasn't saying a word.

"*Pirates of the Carribean* was good too," Matthew said.

"Yeah," Dooley agreed. "All of 'em. Except number three How about *The Mummy?*"

"Kind of scary, maybe?" Eve said. "But Brendan Fraser? Yes, please."

"And Rachel Weisz," Dooley said with a nod.

"Are you Drew's brother too?" Tanner asked Dooley.

"Nope. I'm Kevin's best friend."

"Is Eve your sister?" Tanner asked.

Kevin looked over to find him addressing Drew. He held his breath. Would Drew talk to his own friends?

Drew shook his head though and Kevin's heart felt heavy.

"She's Kevin's girlfriend," Matthew said, his tone making it clear that Tanner was stupid.

"So Kevin kisses Eve?" Tanner asked.

Dooley laughed. "Oh, yeah, Kevin kisses Eve."

"Dool—" Kevin started.

"Eve kisses Kevin too," Eve said.

He turned to her quickly. "Eve—"

Dooley laughed. "I'll bet she does."

"Like my mom kisses my dad?" Tanner asked, his nose wrinkled.

"Well, I don't know how your mom and dad kiss," Dooley said. "But I'm pretty sure she's going to kiss him the way my girl kisses me."

"There's different kinds of kissing," Matthew said wisely to Tanner and Drew.

Not that Drew looked any more interested in this than he had the movie discussion.

"Duh," Tanner said.

Kevin was getting a headache. They weren't talking about anything blatantly inappropriate but the first night of having the boys over for dinner might not be the best time for them to go home and announce they'd talked about boys and girls kissing.

"Maybe we should change the subject," he said.

"What are big brothers for if not to teach their younger brothers important things?" Dooley asked.

Having Dooley here was a mistake if they were going for positive role models. No doubt about it.

"You're right, Dooley," Eve said.

Great. The last thing Kevin needed was for Eve and Dooley to be on the same page with anything other than *Star Wars*.

"I think Kevin is the perfect guy to teach Drew and his friends all kinds of things."

"Like what?" Matthew asked.

*Yeah, like what?* Kevin prepared himself to stop anything R-rated. But surely Eve wouldn't do something bad for the boys. He could trust her with them.

And that was nice.

He wanted to trust her. With something. And this was a really good place to start.

"Like kissing isn't the only way to show someone you care about them." Eve picked up two of the dinner plates and turned toward the sink.

"That's true," Dooley said. "There's lots of ways of showing someone how you feel."

"You can give them flowers," Tanner said.

"Sure," Eve agreed, picking up two more plates. "And you can say nice things to them, tell them you like their smile or that you think they're funny."

"My mom makes my dad cookies," Matthew added.

"Cookies are a great way to show someone you love them," Eve said nodding.

"So's lingerie," Dooley said, draining his tea glass.

Kevin kicked him under the table, but Eve caught his eye and gave him a wink.

"Yep, dressing up in special ways can show someone that you're excited to spend time with them," Eve said, covering Dooley's comment smoothly.

She was awesome. This was probably one of the most unconventional seductions ever, but she was doing it to him by doing dishes.

Sam had been right. Three days was more than enough time for her to get under his skin. It had been only about eight hours at this point.

Kevin stood and grabbed a bowl and a plate and met her at the sink. "You can also help people to show them you care," he said rinsing and putting the dishes in the dishwasher.

"Right. Like scrubbing their toilets," Eve said with a smile, "that's a sure sign of adoration."

Adoration. Now there was a good word.

He had to touch her. It couldn't wait. "You can hold their hand." He linked their fingers and tugged her close.

"My mom holds my hand when we go to the mall," Tanner said.

"Because she wants to keep you close," Kevin said, keeping his gaze locked on Eve's.

"Yeah. Because I get into trouble."

Kevin's mouth curled at the same time Eve's did. Was she thinking about all the fun trouble he used to get her into?

She had been the quintessential good girl. Even with his influence, which he could honestly say had been significant, she'd resisted drinking—other than that first taste of schnapps—smoking, swearing and sex. Yes, he'd talked her into skinny dipping that one time, but she hadn't taken her bra or underwear off. Yes, he'd talked her into reading those erotic stories he'd found online, but she hadn't gone further than the first page of the first one. Yes, he'd talked her into swiping the garden gnome from their principal's house, but she'd felt horrible, cried and snuck it back into his yard before morning and no one but Kevin was ever the wiser.

"You going to keep me out of trouble?" he whispered.

"Oh, absolutely not," she replied quietly.

He laughed. Sure she would. She always had. He wrapped his arms around her and pulled her up against him. "And of course," he said, raising his voice again, "there's good old hugging."

"Hugging's really good," she agreed, melting into him and wrapping her arms around his waist.

He loved how easily she came into his arms, how she was totally fine with the display of affection. In fact, in the next moment she pressed in and rubbed just right and Kevin had to quickly make the choice between what he wanted—to back her up against the counter—and what he should do—let her go.

He did, but he looked down at her. "I might like your type of trouble," he said for her ears only.

She grinned and he felt like grabbing her and giving the boys a real-life, up-close-and-personal lesson in kissing a girl.

Instead, he let her step around him—somehow—and finished clearing the dishes with her. As he did, Dooley kept talking to the boys. Whether he sensed that Kevin had nothing to say or he really did relate to them well, Kevin was grateful. He felt himself relax a little. Dooley and Eve were here for him. Tanner and Matthew were here for Drew. That was what friends were for—to make life a little easier.

Kevin grabbed some glasses and followed Eve to the sink.

No question having Eve here made him feel better. But was she his friend? She had been at one time. She'd been his best friend. They'd told each other secrets and plans and dreams they hadn't told anyone else. She was the only person from Grover he'd ever told that he didn't want to play professional football. It seemed the path everyone had put him on, especially his father, but Kevin hadn't really wanted it. No one else would have understood that, but he'd been able to tell Eve.

He hadn't been friends with any of the other girls he'd ever dated. Or slept with. Most of them had been flings, fun, nothing serious. Some had been fans, or women looking to hook up with a football player for the parties and glory. None had been friends.

Being friends with women wasn't completely foreign to him, though. Jessica, Sara, Danika and more recently Morgan were all a part of his inner circle. He enjoyed them, trusted them.

But he didn't tell them secrets.

"Can I tell you a secret?" he asked, moving in behind Eve and dropping his voice.

The boys were daring each other to finish off the brownies and Dooley was telling them about the more infamous Mac and Sam eating contests, so Kevin could talk low to Eve without being overheard.

She was rinsing a bowl and started to turn only to find herself caged in between the countertop and Kevin's body. She looked over her shoulder. "I love secrets."

She smelled so good he wanted to lick her. "I'm not proud of it, but with Drew not talking, this is a little easier. He's not asking hard questions or saying things like 'our father is a major asshole and I want nothing to do with him or you'."

Eve chuckled and he pressed closer, almost without thought.

"I'm not sure that's exactly how he'd put it." She sounded a little breathless.

Kevin wanted to pull her more firmly against him but resisted, reaching around her to put the glasses in the sink and using it as an excuse to press his chest against her back. "Well, even though I agree with the sentiment about my dad and this situation, I'm not disappointed that we haven't jumped right into that discussion."

He took his time pulling his arm back from the sink and she suddenly turned putting her front right against his front.

"You don't have to feel bad about that," she said, gripping his chin in her hand, making him look at her.

At the moment, he had no idea what they were talking about. He was completely distracted by her.

"You got dumped into this situation as much as Drew did," she continued. "You don't have to have all the right answers or perform miracles here, Kevin."

Miracles. Yeah, that'd be nice. Even a little one.

He studied her face and breathed deep. Looking at her he felt calmer, he felt like maybe he wasn't going to completely screw this up. "Tell me it's going to be okay."

She tipped her head to the side a little puzzled, but said, "It's going to be okay."

Maybe he already had all the miracle he needed right here.

He breathed again. "Now what?"

"We make out? At least that's what I'm feeling inclined to do right now."

He sucked in a quick breath. She had never been this bold before. It took some getting used to, though he certainly liked it.

"Whatever you say."

She glanced at the clock, then behind him at the kids, seemed to do some mental calculations and then said, "Living room couch, two hours from now."

"Two hours?" That seemed like a year.

"We have to get Tanner and Matthew home, get homework done, bath, bedtime—"

"Tanner, Matthew," Kevin said, turning away and looking at the boys. He clapped his hands together. "Time to go."

He heard Eve stifle a giggle behind him.

# CHAPTER
# FIVE

WHEN EVE HEARD the front door open and shut, her heart sped up. Kevin was back from dropping the boys off.

"Okay, last one," she told Drew pointing to the blank spots on his science worksheet. "Name the two types of vertebrates that are warm-blooded."

"Birds and mammals," Drew told her.

"You got it." She watched him write the answers in.

She knew it was bugging Kevin that Drew wasn't talking to him, or even around him, but she was grateful that his teacher had explained that since he was being raised by a single mom with two female roommates, he'd likely be more comfortable around Eve than Kevin. Otherwise she might have fallen off her chair when he spoke to her.

"Anything else we need to work on?"

"Nah. I need to read another chapter in my book for reading but I always do that in bed before I turn off the light."

Wow, complete sentences and everything.

Drew stored the completed worksheet and his pencil in his backpack and zipped it up as Kevin came into the room.

"Hey."

"Hi." She gave him a bright smile to make up for the fact that Drew didn't even look in his direction. "We've got homework done. Heading upstairs for a bath. Right, Drew?"

She assumed he needed to bathe at some point. Unless he did it in the morning.

Drew nodded.

"Kevin will have to show you where the towels and stuff are," she said, informing them both. If the kid needed help washing his hair or something that was all on Kevin too.

Drew didn't say anything and still didn't look at Kevin, but he headed for the steps.

Kevin sighed as he watched him go. He'd shown Drew and his friends around the house earlier, including which room was Drew's. Tanner and Matthew had instructed Kevin and Dooley where to put all his stuff and then the adults had left the kids to really settle in. After about an hour, Dooley had gotten them interested in the PlayStation and they'd played until dinner.

"He talked to you," Kevin said.

"Yeah."

"I guess that's good. Is he okay?"

She stretched to her feet. "We talked about fish, amphibians, reptiles, birds and mammals. Nothing deep or personal." He'd only been gone about fifteen minutes. Grover wasn't big enough for it to take any longer than that to drop two kids off at their houses.

"Bath time now, huh?"

She smiled. "Heck if I know. Seemed like it made sense. Teeth brushing and stuff like that goes well before bedtime."

It was a little after eight. That seemed like a good bedtime too. But what did she know?

"I'll head up and see if he can find everything he needs." Kevin seemed hesitant.

"Okay."

"You're not going to leave?"

"We have a date," she said. Drew was on his way to bed and Dooley had headed downtown—she figured to give her and Kevin some alone time.

She wasn't going anywhere and Kevin needed to figure that out. When she said they were going to be on that couch together at eight-thirty, then he could count on her being on that middle cushion at eight-twenty seven. If she said she'd be there for Drew after school, she'd be there after school for Drew. And when she said she wanted another chance to be Kevin's wife, that meant she was going to perform every wifely duty she knew of, including several that most husbands *wished* their wives would perform.

He looked at the couch, then back to her. "I'll be back as soon as I can."

He took the stairs two at a time and Eve let her grin loose.

Okay, she was going to seduce him. So how to go about this? She couldn't slip a note into his locker, she couldn't wait for him in the parking lot after school or show up week after week at church to prove that she was willing to try whatever was important to him.

She headed for the kitchen.

Wine. That was a good answer to nearly any question.

She searched the kitchen and pantry but couldn't find anything other than vodka and beer. Okay, so much for that. They didn't need alcohol.

Instead, she made cocoa.

They could sit on the couch together, drink hot chocolate and talk.

Just talk.

No matter how much she wanted to make out.

The way he'd kissed her earlier made her think that he might not protest that idea, but she was determined to show him that there was more to what she was feeling than that.

Even if she had to drink her weight in non-alcoholic beverages to prove it.

Fortunately, however, in searching for the marshmallows, she found some peppermint schnapps. She added it to the cocoa before she could think better of it.

As she picked up the mugs, she realized her palms were sweating.

Ridiculous. This was Kevin. He was as excited as she was. They were just going to talk anyway. Find out who the other person was. Date.

But when she stepped into the living room and saw him sitting on the couch, his arm stretched out across the back, waiting for her, she nearly dropped everything. Lord, he looked good.

"Done already?" she asked, setting the cups on the coffee table.

"I'm not sure he scrubbed everywhere he was supposed to," Kevin said. "But at least the water ran on him, right? He won't be filthy anyway. Then he hightailed it into his bedroom and shut the door." He leaned forward, resting his elbows on his knees. "Should I check on him or do you think he's okay?"

"He's fine, I'm sure," she said. "He told me he had some reading to do."

Kevin gave a heavy sigh. "I don't know what I'm doing."

"Well..." she shrugged. "Yeah. How would you know?"

He frowned. "That doesn't help me, Eve."

She tried not to laugh. He was so cute. "Come on. It's gonna take some time. Don't beat yourself up." She took a seat beside him on the couch and tucked her feet up under her, facing him.

"He hasn't said a word to me since I picked him up. He doesn't want to be here."

Kevin looked miserable and she couldn't help but rub a hand up and down his back.

"Of course he doesn't. This isn't his home. He doesn't know you. His mom isn't here. Of course he doesn't want to be here.

But that isn't your fault. It's nothing you've done wrong. And it doesn't mean it's going to last."

"Maybe. It's sinking in how hard this might be."

"And you know what?" she went on. "It doesn't matter if he never wants to be here. This is where he needs to be. This is what's best for him. You're what's best for him."

Kevin turned, captured her hand and pulled her closer. She, of course, went willingly. "I think it's you," he said, looking into her eyes.

"What's me?" She felt breathless, which wasn't unusual around him, but he hadn't really done anything yet.

"You're what I can do for him. I can't do anything but buy him groceries and give him you." He stroked his thumb across the back of her knuckles.

"You're giving him *me*? How's that work?" And why did it make her majorly nervous?

"I'm not what's best for him. I mean, I can keep him safe, make sure he does his homework, all of that, but he needs you."

Her stomach flipped and it wasn't in a good, Kevin-might-kiss-me way. It was in the oh-shit-what-have-I-gotten-into way. "What do you mean?"

"You're the best one to be a positive role model."

She almost snorted at that. Almost. Instead, she wiped her hand over her mouth. "No pressure."

"This is second nature for you. I still have to *try* at it." He brushed a fingertip along her jaw. "You kept *me* out of trouble, you made me want to be a better person. I know you can be good for a kid like Drew."

She swallowed hard.

As far as Kevin knew, she was still a good girl, the perfect person to help him have a positive influence on Drew…and she wasn't quite ready to tell him any different.

Why couldn't she be in charge of after school snacks?

"Maybe you should go check on him," Kevin suggested. "He'll talk to you. He'll tell you if he's really okay."

"I could do that. But maybe we should give him some space." The kid didn't need her hovering over him. And she wasn't sure she'd be very good at hovering anyway.

Dinner had been fine, fun even. But Dooley and Tanner and Matthew had been a part of that. It wouldn't always be that way. In fact, tomorrow night she was going to be on her own with Drew. That should be interesting.

"Maybe," Kevin said. "But not too much, right? I mean he can't go for six months without talking to me."

"What's the worst thing that happens? He doesn't talk. He's still safe. He's still getting fed, going to school. Then his mom comes home and things get back to normal. You don't have to be his best friend."

But she could tell he wanted to be.

"I want to do more than that, Eve." Kevin sat back against the couch, letting his head fall back on the cushion behind him. "I'm his brother. His only one. Surely, I can do better."

She ran her fingers through his hair, wanting to comfort him. Somehow, some way. Kevin was a great guy, he put all of himself into the things he did. Of course he would want to do that for Drew.

How the little boy could resist wanting to be close to Kevin, to hear him talk and laugh, to spend time with him, was beyond her.

Kevin rolled his head to look at her as she stroked her fingers through his hair from forehead to crown. "He likes you," he said. "Or at least, he's more comfortable with you. Maybe if you build a relationship with him, and he sees that you like me and are close to me, that will help him trust me."

"I don't mind getting as close to you as you'll let me," she said, leaning in. He looked so vulnerable like this. His hands lay relaxed against the cushion next to his thighs, his head rested back, his hair mussed from her fingers. "And I won't have any trouble showing him that I like you."

"Just having you here helps," he said quietly, "I think it helps both of us."

"I'll do whatever I can to make this easier on both of you."

His eyes focused on her mouth and she started to lean in.

"Will you go check on him?" he asked.

She stopped and held back her sigh. "Of course."

A minute later she knocked on Drew's bedroom door. "Drew?" She pushed the door open a few inches. "Can I come in for a second?"

"Yeah." He didn't sound enthusiastic but he hadn't said no.

"How's it going in here?" she asked.

Kevin and the guys had brought everything of Drew's, including his own bed and bedding. That had to be a little better than sleeping in a strange room and strange bed.

"I'm almost done with my chapter."

She moved further into the room. Drew's hair was still damp from his shower and he was in his pajamas and tucked under his navy blue comforter. Like this he looked…not all that intimidating. She didn't know much about kids, and her interactions with this one in particular were really important, but in the soft light from his bedside lamp, with the big book resting in his lap he looked almost sweet.

"What are you reading?" She stopped by his bed and looked at the thick book with small print and no pictures.

"The Penderwicks," he said, with a grimace.

Her eyebrows went up. "Oh, I love that book. You don't like it?" She'd personally loved it. And this was something they could talk about. Unless he hated it.

"It's fiction," he said as if it was complete trash.

"You're not a big fan of fiction, I take it." She decided to take a risk and settled down on the side of his bed next to his feet.

He scooted over a little to give her room. "I like comic books," he said. "Those are fictitious. But I prefer non-fiction to novels."

Was it just her or was he talking like he was thirty instead of ten? "So you decided to give this a try?"

"Mrs. Albert is making us read fiction." It was clear that he felt this was a huge mistake on her part. "I think it's dumb. Nonfiction is about stuff that really happened. That's more important to know about."

"It's for entertainment," Eve said.

He shrugged.

Wow, this kid needed to have more fun.

"What I like about fiction is getting to do things and go places I can't go in real life and…it's often about the world the way we wish it was. And people acting the way we wish they would. Things working out happily ever after." She hadn't really thought that out before speaking, but it was true.

"But it's not real," Drew grumbled.

"It's…" She started to say that no, it could be real. That if people could imagine it and fall in love with the ideas, then it could really happen.

But she couldn't say that with the absolute certainty a lost and sad child needed to hear.

In her life, the people she'd trusted to always do the right thing had not stood by her when she'd needed them. In fact, her father had been very clear when he'd said that he not only didn't understand her choices, but he did not support them or even acknowledge them. As far as he was concerned, he 'no longer had any obligation or motivation to be involved in her life'.

No motivation.

That was her favorite part.

She did, however, like the *idea* that you could count on people. That even if it meant risk to them, they'd be there beside you until the bitter end, and she'd read a lot of books like that.

She swallowed hard and concentrated on Drew. "The books aren't real," she said. "But the ideas, the hopes inside are. We're supposed to take those ideas and hopes and do what we can to make them real."

He was staring down at the book. He shook his head. "My mom is in jail. That's not someone acting the way they should. And it's not happy."

Ah, a moment of truth. She'd really thought it would take longer to get to something like that. And she'd definitely hoped it would be when Kevin was here to handle it.

"Yes, your mom is in jail, but do you know why?"

"Drunk driving."

"Yes, but…" She reached over and put her hand in front of the book, causing him to look her. "It *is* someone acting the way she should. She took responsibility. She's in jail, because she pled guilty, because then the judge would let her go into treatment. She did that for you, Drew. She knew that she had to suck it up and do that or she might never get you back. And even though it's going to be really tough on her, she's going to get cleaned up and then be able to come back and be a great mom again."

"She shouldn't have had those drinks in the first place." His words were angry, but Eve could see something in his eyes that told her he really wanted to believe what she was saying.

"No, she shouldn't. But making mistakes doesn't mean that you don't care or that you're a bad person." A thought came to her. "It's like with me and pie."

Drew looked up and Eve knew she had to keep going with the analogy. "I'm not a good cook, especially pies. I mess them up all the time, but I keep trying because someday I want someone to say 'wow, you did a great job with this pie'. I keep making mistakes but not because I don't care or don't try my best, but because it's hard for me. But every mess-up makes me better at it next time."

"So being my mom is hard?"

Eve felt her heart squeeze. She didn't really know anything about being a mom except that it looked like a hell of a lot of work. "It's easier for some people than others. But yeah, being really good at it and doing it perfectly is hard. You know what, though?" she asked giving him a smile, "I'm guessing it's also like pie in that even when it's not perfect, if you're doing it because you like it, it's still pretty good."

Drew's eyes dropped to the book in his lap, but she could tell he wasn't seeing the words.

"You could give up on the pie and do something easier," he said quietly.

Eve looked at him with surprise. Was it possible for a kid his age to really get a metaphor like that? "No way," she said firmly. "When something really matters, you don't give up."

"My mom won't give up then?" he asked, his eyes back on Eve's. "She'll get better and come back?"

In that moment, Drew seemed like the little boy he really was.

Eve forced herself not to cry. "Oh, honey, everything that's going on right now is her way of getting better at the mom-thing," she said sincerely. "And everything she did to arrange for you to stay with Kevin so that you're safe and taken care of is her loving you even when she's not here."

"She wanted my dad, Steve, to take care of me. But he didn't want to."

Oh, boy. Eve really didn't want to do this part. But she wanted to hug him more than she wanted to run.

"You know what?" Eve touched Drew's foot and he didn't pull it away. "I know both Steve and Kevin. I'd say you ended up with the much better deal. Kevin really cares about you and he wants you to be happy."

"Maybe." Drew didn't sound completely convinced but he also didn't sound mad anymore.

"You ready for sleep now?" she asked, gently removing the book and laying it on his bedside table.

"Okay." He scooted down under the covers. "I guess."

"And in the morning, Kevin's going to bring you to Sherry's for breakfast. I'll see you then."

"Okay."

She stood and looked down at him awkwardly. "You need a hug or anything?"

"That would be okay."

Surprised, she leaned in. He wrapped his arms around her neck for a quick second, then lay back.

She shifted back, pressing her lips together. It was really stupid to be choked up by that barely-there hug.

"Night, D," she said, clicking off the light before he could see the shininess in her eyes.

"Night, Eve."

She padded to the door with the light from a plain old white nightlight in the outlet. The kid didn't even have a fun nightlight. How could he not like Sponge Bob or something? That nightlight was her final straw. The kid was going to watch cartoons with her. Period.

She was mostly composed as she stepped into the hallway and pulled his door halfway shut. Then she turned and nearly plowed into Kevin.

"What the hell?" she hissed as she straightened away from him. He'd scared the crap out of her.

"Is he okay?" Kevin whispered.

"Yeah, he's fine." She glanced at the doorway, then frowned at Kevin. "What are you doing up here?"

"Eavesdropping." He didn't seem the least bit apologetic about it either.

She rolled her eyes and headed for the stairs. She didn't want to talk right outside Drew's room.

As soon as his foot hit the first floor, he grabbed her arm and swung her to face him. "That was great, Eve." His smile was huge.

For a moment she blinked at him. Wow, that smile did stuff to her. "It was?"

Kevin nodded. "I knew this would be really natural to you."

"This?"

"Helping Drew, making him feel secure and cared for."

Well, Drew mattered to her. At first, her heart had gone out to a little boy who was suffering the consequences of the bad decisions the adults around him had made. Then she'd been pulled further in because Kevin needed her help. But now, Drew had gotten to her too. If she could help him sleep better at night and smile some during the day, she'd do whatever it took.

And if it put that look—a combination of relief and affection and desire—on Kevin's face she'd take that bonus and enjoy the hell out of it.

Taking his hand, she led him to the couch.

"Cocoa?" she asked, pushing him to sit.

"Um..."

She lifted a cup and held it out. As she met his eyes, she hesitated. And had to take a deep breath. He was looking at her with an expression that made her feel like she'd downed the whole cup of cocoa and half the bottle of schnapps—warm and tingly from the inside out.

"You're going to have to stop looking at me like that," she said.

"Like what?"

"Like you want to take over the seduction."

"Ah, right, okay." He glanced at and finally accepted the cup.

She settled down on the couch next to him with her own cup, again tucking her feet up and facing him. "Yep. Relaxing, talking, being together."

Sure, relaxing. That was going to take a lot of schnapps. Every nerve in her body seemed to be humming and jumping.

"Hmm." Kevin sipped, the swallowed and licked his lips. Then he turned toward her. "Maybe we could fast track some of that."

She smiled. "How would we do that?" She wrapped both hands around the cup to keep them off of him and sipped. The peppermint was perfect. Not a substitute for the taste of Kevin but not a bad way to keep her mouth busy.

"We each get five questions. The most important ones, the ones we really want answered."

Oh, boy. This could be dangerous. "And then?"

"I'll be honest," he said. "You've been seducing me all night."

"I haven't done anything yet."

But there was definite heat in his eyes.

"You've been here, you've made me smile, you've made Drew smile. You talked to his teacher, you gave Dooley a hard time, you didn't even blink when Tanner got cheese on the sleeve of your shirt."

She looked at the spot where she'd wiped cheese from the plum colored polyester. She shrugged. Cheese was no big deal. "I thought having the boys here was good."

"It was good. And it was your idea."

She leaned deeper into the cushions. "And that tempted you a little?"

He spread his palm out on her knee. "Definitely. You were great."

The heat from his hand soaked through her jeans quickly, heating the skin underneath. "I was planning to buy you a bunch of stuff and take you on a romantic picnic and impress you with all of the football stats I've memorized."

"See," he said, sliding his hand up and down the thigh of her jeans, "we can fast track for sure then. You already bought me jelly beans and I think this is pretty much like a picnic."

"Drinking cocoa on the couch is like a picnic?" she asked as his hand stroked up and down again, making the skin underneath tingle. She loved having him touch her so she shifted and stretched her leg out to rest it across his lap.

"We could sit on the floor if it would help," he said, running his hand down her calf and over the top of her bare foot.

Why would she *not* agree to fast-tracking?

She shivered. "Sure, this is a picnic. Okay, what's your first question?"

He didn't move his hand, but his gaze went from her face to

his cup. He took a deep breath. "You seem so sure that you want me back."

"I am," she said firmly.

"But why now? It's been a long time, Eve."

She sipped, taking time to form her words carefully. It was a great question. Why had she waited to get him back? Why hadn't she gone after him before now if she wanted to be married to him so badly?

Swallowing the now cold cocoa, she leaned over and set her cup on the table. "Okay." She took a deep breath. "I did try, at first," she started, "but you wouldn't talk to me. So then I spent quite a bit of time angry, then ashamed. Then I tried to forget you. Then I tried to move on. I've been working on that one for awhile."

He still wasn't looking at her, but he was still touching her, so she went on, "I think I knew a long time ago that I wasn't going to get over you, but I was trying to ignore it because…it made me sad, and hopeless and lonely. I felt pretty pathetic, frankly, but I couldn't help that no guy ever measured up to you. Then, seeing you again, talking to you again, I realized that I was getting a second chance. You're here and I can't let you leave again without trying."

There. That hadn't been so bad.

She wasn't sure Kevin was breathing.

"Okay," he finally said hoarsely.

"Okay?"

He looked up at her. His eyes held a heart-wrenching combination of regret, relief and want. She leaned closer.

"So let's hear some stats."

She blinked. Then smiled. "College or pro?"

He wrinkled his nose. "College." He hadn't wanted to go pro. At least at one time.

Eve had been surprised when he'd entered the draft, but things had changed drastically in her life by that time too, so she couldn't question his decisions. He'd seen a little playing time that first year and impressed everyone. His second year with the Chiefs had been outstanding and things had looked promising. She'd seen every televised game of his college and pro career. Including the game that had ended it all.

She'd watched the slow-motion replay of the hit that had torn up his knee over and over. She could still feel the way her stomach had roiled and her heart had squeezed. She didn't necessarily mourn his career so much as she felt sick about him being injured and the slow, frustrating, painful rehab process.

"Do you miss playing?" she asked.

He dragged his hand down her leg to her foot, pressing his thumb into the arch. She moaned and he sucked in a quick breath. But he pressed again, massaging.

"Is that your first question?" he asked. "Because I'm thinking that maybe five questions each is too many."

She flexed her foot against his hand and grinned. "You're the one that wanted me to prove that I wanted you back."

"I didn't know you'd be so good at it."

She raised her eyebrows. "Is that right?"

He chuckled. "If I'd thought for even three seconds about it, I would have realized what I was getting into. But all I could think was that I've always been too easy for you. Before I do that again, I want to be sure you're really in this."

She started to say something smartass about him being easy, but suddenly she couldn't. The thing was, he had been easy for her. But not because he wanted in her pants. Even as a naïve teen she'd felt the difference between the boys that flirted because they wanted in her pants and Kevin. Kevin had truly cared about her. He'd fallen in love with her. He would have done anything for her.

She'd made him work at it because she'd thought that's what she should do. She'd been raised knowing right and wrong, good and bad. Even more than those black and white ideas, she'd also been taught about consequences—that bad things happened when you made the wrong choices.

Yeah, well, that may be true, but bad things could happen even if you made the right choices so all of that seemed like a lot of crap to her now.

She'd honored her father's beliefs and the church's teachings about love and sex and marriage and had waited—and made Kevin wait. Then she'd done it the right way. She'd married him. And from there her whole world fell apart.

Kevin didn't know that after she'd lied to her father about where she'd spent their wedding night, she'd finally gone and confessed. He didn't know that even though she'd essentially rejected him, her father had still asked her to leave their house. For good.

She still remembered how calmly he'd made the request. There had been no yelling, no accusations, no recitation of the Ten Commandments. He'd asked her to leave and she had.

She'd followed the ideas of right and wrong, good and bad, and it seemed that she was screwed either way. She'd been miserable doing the right thing and miserable doing the wrong thing. And it had cost her this man. This man who had taken in a little boy whose parents had messed everything up, who had no one else, who was a complete stranger and who wouldn't even make eye contact with him. He was looking past his father's mistake, Heather's mistake, even Drew's own behaviors, and was doing something good.

He wasn't getting away again.

Eve met Kevin's gaze directly. "No, my first question is how do you feel about forgiveness?"

He looked at her without a word for a moment. Then he moved and set his cup beside hers. When he leaned back, he rested his elbow on the back of the couch and took a deep breath. "I think most people are really bad at forgiving. I think a lot of people who say the words, don't *actually* do it."

She stared at him. "I, um…"

"It's the most difficult thing someone who's wronged us can

ask of us," he went on, "especially when it's for something that can't be changed."

She swallowed hard.

"Even saying the words are hard enough sometimes, but really *feeling* it is something else. But…" He took another deep breath, "when we really do it, then it's amazing. It's a fucking gift. It makes *everybody* involved better."

Tears stung the back of her eyes and her throat felt thick. He'd been back in town for less than twenty-four hours, but she knew that her life had changed.

"So question two," she said, her voice scratchy, "is can you forgive me? For not telling my dad, and everyone, that we'd gotten married? For making you feel like I was ashamed of it, or of you? For not confessing to the world how much I loved you?"

His gaze roamed over her face, touching every centimeter from her forehead to her chin, ear to ear. Finally he said, "I want to. Can we start with that?"

Her heart stopped for a moment. He hadn't said yes. It was way too soon for that. But he wanted to.

They could definitely start with that. She couldn't have stopped the grin on her face for anything. She was going to deserve this man this time.

Moving quickly, she shifted and slid onto his lap, straddling his thighs to face him. "You hold Nebraska's school record for tackles with loss at sixty," she said, putting a hand on his chest and leaning in to kiss him.

She pulled back after only a moment. "You are second in school history for quarterback sacks with twenty-eight." She tipped her head and kissed him again.

Kevin's hands went to her hips and he held her close as the second kiss lasted longer. He groaned in protest when she lifted her head.

"You also had seven fumble recoveries." This kiss lasted even longer and Kevin opened his mouth under hers, curling his fingers into her hips and shifting his thighs restlessly against her, but she still pulled back.

"And you scored two touchdowns from those recoveries. Oh, and blocked three kicks—"

"Yeah, yeah. Very nice. I'm officially seduced. Now kiss me," he demanded.

"I am kissing you," she said with a grin.

"Like you mean it."

Her smile died and she looked him directly in the eyes. "Oh, I mean it," she said softly.

*Finally.* He was hungry for her, the ever-present desire fueled by a strange combination of the crimson-colored polish on her toes, the smudge of chocolate frosting on her shoulder from the brownies—that had been there before the cheese—and the fact that she knew how many fumble recoveries he had. As soon as their lips met, Kevin spread his hand over her middle back holding her in place. He needed her right where she was for a very long time.

The strength of the hunger in her kiss took him aback though. Her hands slid from his jaw to his hair, her fingertips flat against his scalp, holding *him* in place. Their lips opened simultaneously and Kevin's tongue stroked deep. She moaned—or he moaned—or they both moaned—it didn't really matter. All that mattered was Eve was here, in his arms, where she belonged.

She wiggled closer, her pelvis pressing against his cock. He lifted against her, wanting some relief to the pressure behind his zipper. That seemed to flip her switch from high to frenzied.

She moaned and ran her hands up under his shirt, her palms hot against his skin. He shuddered, his body straining toward her. Her thumbs brushed over his nipples and heat streaked through him.

"Eve," he groaned.

"Yes. God, I want you," she panted.

She'd never ever said that before. All the times they'd made out she was always the one pulling back, reminding him—albeit breathlessly—that she couldn't go further. Even on their wedding night, she'd followed his lead. She'd been curious, sweet, even greedy at times, but never the aggressor.

"I want to strip you down and lick every inch of you, feel every—"

The sound of the back door opening stopped her words and they heard Dooley tramping in—likely on purpose to alert them to his presence.

Kevin tipped his head back, breathing and listening to the sound of Dooley banging cupboard doors in the kitchen.

At his age and with his experience, he should not feel so out of control, so desperate, so willing to do anything to be inside of her again.

His friend had never had better timing. Kevin started to shift Eve off of his lap, when she leaned in and put her mouth to his ear.

"Part of making out on the living room couch is the risk of being caught." She licked the spot on his neck below his ear and he groaned. "I don't even have my bra off yet. Nothing to worry about."

He heard Dooley's footsteps approaching, then treading across the floor leading to the stairs.

"'Night kids. Remember to wrap it up," Dooley called.

Eve giggled. "'Night, Dooley."

He headed up the stairs and Eve pressed her hips against Kevin's.

"Did you ever fantasize about having me on this couch?" she asked huskily, lifting her hips slightly and pressing forward. They'd never made out in either of their parents' houses. They hadn't even watched a movie together here. "Did you think about fucking me here? Or up in your bed?"

Had he? Was snow cold? And had Eve Donnelly just said the

word *fuck* to him? "And a million other places," he admitted gruffly.

"What did you do about it?"

"Me and my hand got to be good friends while we were dating," he told her without really thinking.

She pulled back and looked down at him. "Yeah?" Her pupils were dilated and her mouth dark pink from kissing.

Oh, yeah. "I thought of you every single night before I went to sleep. Sometimes twice." He'd been seventeen when they'd gotten together. By then he'd read and seen and done more than enough to have several fantasies going about Eve. Many involved his childhood bedroom, but he hadn't limited them to one setting.

Her attention dropped to his lap, then she looked back to his face. "Me too."

He had to swallow hard before he could answer that. "You're telling me that you touched yourself while thinking of me?"

"Every night." She gave him a naughty smile. "Sometimes twice."

He wanted to see that.

His eyes narrowed and he made himself breathe. He'd had no idea sweet innocent little Eve knew how to pleasure herself back then. And that she'd done it.

Or even now.

He hadn't thought about that, actually, until that moment. Now he couldn't stop thinking about it. She was thirty. She'd obviously become more confident in her sexuality. It was quite possible, likely even, that she had toys and everything.

His cock strained against his fly.

"Did you make yourself come?" he asked gruffly. "Back then? Thinking of me?"

She nodded.

"How about now?"

"Definitely. And still thinking of you."

She had to be lying about that, but he didn't care. His body certainly didn't care. The image was too fantastic.

"Do you use your fingers?" he asked, running his hands up and down her thighs. "Or do you have a vibrator?"

"Yes. Either. Both." She was breathing even more rapidly now, and she shifted on his lap as if she was also aching.

"How about tonight?"

She groaned and leaned in to rest her forehead on his shoulder. "You're killing me here."

"What about tonight, Eve?" he repeated, giving no mercy. "I want to imagine you like that. Tonight. Tell me how you're going to lie in bed and touch yourself."

Her head came up quickly.

"And give me lots of details to work with," he added, with a smile that made her suck in a quick breath.

She looked at him as her tongue darted out to wet her lips. She pulled in a long breath and said, "In this fantasy, are you watching or are you involved? I don't want to miss describing anything important."

Kevin felt his cock twitch and his hands tightened on her hips. She really was going to talk him through this? Right here? Out loud?

Damn. He liked this. He was absolutely, positively not going to think about how she'd gotten more sexually confident. He was just going to enjoy it.

"Yes, I'll be involved." He so wanted to hear her describe all of this. He shifted under her, loving the feel of her against him even with clothes between them. "With my fingers, my tongue and my cock. In that order," he told her, relishing the way her eyes widened.

He would have never talked to the Eve he used to know like that. He would have never used the word cock with her. She had been a girl. Now she was a woman. And no matter who or what had happened over the past twelve years, he was here now and he was going to be everything she'd ever wanted. He could tell she liked him talking like that. Her cheeks were flushed but it wasn't embarrassment. It was good old-fashioned lust.

"But first," he said, sliding his hands down her sides, lightly skimming over her breasts. "I would want to watch you do it. Tell me how you like it, how to make you moan."

"Holy crap," she breathed, "you've gotten…way…hotter over the years."

He grinned. Exactly what he wanted to hear.

She looked at his mouth, then his fly. She pressed against it, clearly reveling in his quick intake of air. "You sure you don't want to go up to your bedroom and make this more than a story?"

Of course he did. But it was the first night they'd been back together in years. They couldn't sleep together this fast. Probably. "When I take you to bed, it will be to stay all night," he said, pulling his thumb across her lips. "I think it's too soon for that—for Drew and the neighbors."

Her eyes flew to the staircase. He could read her thoughts. Drew was right upstairs.

"I'm sure he's asleep," he said. "Even if he isn't, he thinks you went home and his head would have to be on fire for him to come down here and find me," he said, hating that but admitting it was convenient right now. "And Dooley's up there. I guarantee he checked in on him and if he hears Drew for any reason he'll be there."

Eve met his gaze again. "Okay then."

She scooted off his lap and turned to lie back along the cushion next to him.

"What are you doing?" He reached for her. He wanted to touch her, kiss her, while she told him this sexy bedtime story.

"If you want to use just your imagination, say the word. But I thought I'd help with some visual aids." That naughty smile he was quickly getting used to was on her lips again.

She started inching her top up. It was a silky material in a deep purple and slid easily up her torso, revealing the pale creamy skin of her stomach and ribs, then finally the same dark purple color of her bra.

"Visual…" He groaned as her intention sunk in. "Here? Now?" He wasn't exactly protesting. He wasn't stupid. Just a little surprised.

But if Eve Donnelly wanted to show him…well, anything… he would be a rapt audience.

"Yes. Here. Now."

Her voice was husky and Kevin knew he wasn't moving from this spot for anything.

With the staircase behind the high backed couch no one would be able to see her until long after Kevin heard them coming.

Her head lay against the pillowed armrest of the couch, her legs still stretched across his thighs from mid-calf to her feet. He turned to face her and swallowed hard. This was going to be the perfect view.

The bra was low cut, showing off the inner curves of her breasts. Her nipples were already hard, pressing the soft material into two points.

He longed to lean over and suck one into his mouth, but he held back, gripping the back couch cushion where he rested his arm.

The bra was also front clasp. She flicked it open with her fingers, the cups falling away. Her breasts were exactly as he'd remembered them all this time. She was a B cup, maybe, and her nipples were a pretty dark pink color and amazingly sensitive.

Eve was watching him watch her and he wanted to see her eyes when she touched herself, but he couldn't pull his attention away from her breasts. She lifted a hand, running it over her breast, cupping it, then lightly rolling the nipple. Her breath hitched and then she tugged the tip harder, moaning softly as she did it.

She played with the other side, pinching and tugging until he thought he was going to explode. She must have felt similarly because she dropped her hands to her jeans. Quickly unsnapping and unzipping, she pushed the denim down past her knees.

This was exactly as it would have been too, Kevin realized. Making out generally meant not having the opportunity—or courage—to fully undress. If he'd had her here back in high school, he would have only pushed her clothes enough out of the way to reach what he needed to.

Her panties didn't match her bra and he smiled. She hadn't expected this to turn out this way either. Not that they weren't sexy anyway. They were black silk, with a butterfly cut out right in front.

Which told him something he hadn't even realized he'd been wondering about subconsciously—she was bare.

Unable to stop himself, he reached for her, running his thumb back and forth across the butterfly and the skin underneath.

Her breath hissed out and when he looked up he saw that she had her bottom lip pulled between her teeth and a hand back on her breast. Hotter still, her eyes were locked on his thumb on top of her panties.

"Down about a centimeter and you'll be my favorite person today," she said huskily when she saw him watching her.

"I'm already your favorite person today," he said with a half-smile. "I'm the only person to talk dirty to you." Then he frowned. "Right?"

She laughed softly. "Right. Or if you're not, I've completely forgotten about whoever else it was."

"That works too." He moved his thumb back and forth, feeling the heat emanating from her body. "And you like it, don't you?"

She glanced at his hand. "Um, yeah."

"I mean the dirty talk."

She licked her lips. "Yeah. I do. Does that shock you?"

It didn't shock him, he realized. She'd been eager and curious in bed and he'd known with experience she'd be a firecracker.

That she was a little naughty too seemed to fit. "Surprised maybe," he said. "But I'm a fan."

She said nothing but she slipped her thumbs into either side of her panties and started to inch them down. He moved his hand to allow the silk to move out of the way as she bared herself to him.

"You're gorgeous," he choked out.

"So are you," she said. "You can put your hand back."

He wanted to. He ached with the need to touch her. He wanted to spread her open and simply look for a few hours. He wanted to touch and taste.

But he had a fantasy going here and he thought she was getting into it as much as he was. He shook his head. "I'm a spectator this time."

"You're not a spectator," she said, running her hand over her lower stomach. "You not only play all your favorite sports but you play hard."

He coughed, then said, "And I'm the best at what I play."

She nodded. "Right."

"Do you know what it takes to be the best?" he asked, running his hand up and down her calf, then bending her knee.

"What?"

"Knowledge and a commitment to learning." He bent her other knee. "Help me learn your body. Show me what works for you, what you like, how to be the best."

She whimpered as he parted her knees. She let them fall open, and he couldn't have looked away if the house suddenly collapsed around them.

She was all wet, pink sweetness. Her desire was impossible to hide in this position and he again had to hold back from touching. Or better yet, leaning in with his tongue.

"Show me," he said hoarsely.

Eve ran her hand down her stomach and over her mound. Then she spread herself open. Her other hand's middle finger skimmed over her clit and she breathed harder. She circled there for a moment, then dipped lower, spreading her wetness up and over the tender bud as if she'd done it hundreds of times.

Kevin felt his mouth go dry and his cock swell. She was more gorgeous, more confident and more in tune with her body than he'd even imagined.

Slowly she pushed a finger in where he so wanted to be buried. She slid in and out, then added another. Her hips were lifting slightly with each finger thrust and he quickly glanced up to find her eyes on him. Her mouth was open though and she was breathing hard and moaning.

"Kevin."

His name. She was moaning his name.

She withdrew to circle her clit again, this time faster and with more pressure. She alternated between quick thrusts inside and circles on the outside, her rhythm increasing. He knew that with a vibrator she'd only have to concentrate on one area and she'd already be there. Or with his fingers. Or tongue. Or cock.

But he wanted to watch her the whole way through. He wanted to know if she came with her fingers inside or if she needed her clit stroked. He needed to know how to get her there when he was inside her.

Her breathing was erratic and she arched as if trying to get closer to something. Finally, he had to help. He reached up and took a nipple between his thumb and forefinger. He squeezed then tugged as she had done. "Come for me, Eve," he said huskily. "Let me watch you lose it right here, right now."

And she came apart.

"Kevin!" she gasped as the orgasm overtook her.

He watched as the waves subsided and she slumped into the cushions, her hands sliding to rest on her stomach. Still leaning over her, he lifted her hand and closed his mouth around the fingers that had been inside her. Her eyes flew open and she watched as he sucked, then dragged his tongue up and down each finger. After he'd tasted all he could, he linked his fingers with hers.

"Anything else you need to know?" she asked breathlessly.

"Oh, there's a whole lot I need to know," he told her sincerely. "How you taste directly on my tongue, how you looking riding me, how it feels on my cock when you come like that."

Her eyes widened and she shook her head. "Wow, if you'd talked like that back in high school I would have never been able to—" She stopped abruptly and looked at the ceiling. "Never mind."

He sat back and watched as she pulled her panties and jeans up and adjusted her bra and top.

When she was done fiddling he said, "You would have never been able to what?"

He knew what she'd almost said. And he was as dazed by it as she was.

"Nothing. I didn't mean it." She sat up and pushed her hair back from her face. Then she tried to smile. It didn't quite work.

"If I'd talked like that back then you would have never been able to walk away?" he asked, trying to keep the bite out of his tone. Her denial of him hadn't been about their sex life. It had been about her father, and Eve feeling she had to choose between the man she admired and looked up to, and the man she loved.

Kevin hadn't deserved admiration or being looked up to back then. He'd been a kid. Before Eve, he'd been a trouble-making kid. If he hadn't been good at football, he would have gotten into even more trouble. But as the star of the State Championship team he got a lot of passes and favors.

She'd loved him. He knew that. She had loved him as much as an eighteen-year-old girl could love an eighteen-year-old boy who wasn't living up to his potential. But she'd respected her father.

Respect had won out over love when they came head to head.

"I didn't mean it," she said softly.

No, she hadn't walked away because he hadn't talked dirty to her. But she had walked away.

He reached for her hand and when she put hers in his he tugged her onto his lap. She snuggled close and he closed his eyes as a different kind of wanting washed over him.

"Just in case," he said lightly, in spite of the intense emotions coursing through him. "I'm going to talk dirty to you every chance I have. I'll teach you every filthy word I know."

"You think there are some I don't know?"

"Let's be sure."

# CHAPTER
# SIX

EVE WATCHED Kevin and Dooley back out of the driveway and head for Omaha. Then she turned and faced the front door with trepidation. On the other side was the ten-year-old boy she was supposed to positively influence.

Staying out here would be a lot easier.

She was exhausted. She'd stayed here, snuggling and talking with Kevin after the couch make out session until well past midnight. They hadn't talked about anything too serious. He'd told her about the Youth Center where he and his friends volunteered, the three older ladies they helped out, about Dooley and his family and then about all of his friends and their wives and fiancées.

Hearing about his life, how full it was, how many people he had loving him, made her ache. She'd missed so much. *They'd* missed so much. She wanted to know the people who were important to him, see the Youth Center and the hospital where he worked.

Eve made herself breathe. He was here now. She had him for six months. She intended to make the most of that time.

Which brought her thoughts to the other reason for her lack of sleep.

She pressed her hands to her cheeks, feeling them heat as she remembered the night before. Wow. She couldn't believe she'd done what she'd done right in front of him. It was too fast. It had been their first night back together. But thinking of it now made her bones feel like they were melting. He had barely touched her and her orgasm had been surprisingly intense. For that alone she'd crawl across the desert on hands and knees.

"I'm not really into knowing about people being impaled by the steering columns on their cars or being extricated from under semi-trucks," Drew said as they sat together at the kitchen island, him working on homework and her reading.

Eve looked up with wide eyes. "I'm not really into that either."

"That's what Kevin does, right? Pulls people out of wrecks and things. He's a paramedic."

Oh, okay, now she was following. Eve closed her book and nodded. "Yes. That's right. And I suppose he does do those things. Or things like that. Did he tell you that?"

Drew shook his head. "I was doing some research."

Eve gave a little shudder. "What Kevin and Dooley and the other guys do is really brave and super important, but I do *not* think researching that on the internet is a great idea. If you want to know more about it, you can ask them though."

Drew shook his head. "I really don't want to know a lot about it."

"Okay. That's okay too."

"Do you think he knows which two Presidents died on July fourth?"

"Um…I don't know. But I'm going to guess no."

"What *does* he know?" Drew asked. "Anything besides blood and guts?"

She grinned. Oh, some interest in his big brother. This was good. "Football."

Drew didn't say anything to that.

"Do you like football?"

"I don't know anything about it."

"You don't…" She gaped at him. "You don't know anything about it? What do you mean?"

"I don't know football."

She shut her book. "You've spent ten years in this town and you don't know anything about football? How is that possible?"

He raised an eyebrow. "I live with three single women. I know a lot about shoes and PMS."

"PMS?" she repeated. "As in period PMS?"

He shrugged. "It's a normal bodily function. It's not a big deal."

Right.

"Okay, so you know nothing about football and tons about PMS." She took a deep breath and nodded. "We can fix that. You're with the right girl if you want to know football."

Drew studied her for a moment and she let him. It was going to take time for them to get to know each other, but she thought maybe, just maybe, he liked her. Or wanted to anyway.

"Fix it? Do you get PMS?"

He was so matter-of-fact about all of this. She could be too. "You know, I'm lucky. Not too bad. I do crave a lot of salt for a couple of days before. But I was talking about fixing your lack of knowledge about the greatest game ever invented."

Drew sighed. "I brought this on myself, didn't I?"

She grinned. "Good news, the football lessons come with football *food*."

"Football food? Like what?"

"Nachos, pigs-in-a-blanket, barbecue meatballs, seven-layer dip. We spread it all out on the coffee table, get comfy on the couch, and scream at the TV for a few hours on Sunday."

"This kind of sounds like period week at our house," Drew said. "Since we've lived with Libby and Lacey for so long, they are synced up with mom. The snacks and the couch are similar. But they scream at reality TV."

Eve laughed. This kid was...unexpected.

But if he liked to pig out on snacks while lying on the couch, they were going to get along just fine.

"How's the wife and kid, Kev?" Sam asked as he came into the locker room and dropped his duffle on the bench.

"Let's just say that I totally see the draw to the marriage thing," Kevin answered, unable to help his grin.

Mac turned from his locker. "Yeah?"

"Totally."

Sam slammed his locker, his eyes on Kevin. "You've got to be kidding."

"What?" Kevin tied his shoe. "You like being married."

"You got lucky," Sam said, his eyes wide. "The first night?" He shook his head. "I underestimated you, man. Good job."

"Who said that?" Kevin asked, his mind flooding with images of Eve on his couch.

"Your face and that I-got-lucky grin," Mac said, pointing a finger at him.

"I'm lucky," Kevin agreed. And left it at that. Or tried to anyway.

"But the first night... That's so...unlike you," Sam said.

"He's had a lot of time for the lust to build up," Mac said. "I can kind of relate."

It had been several years between the time Mac was first attracted to his wife Sara and when they finally got together.

Sam glared at Mac. "Oh, yeah? I suppose it was the first night when you and Sara got together?"

Mac turned his body to fully face Sam. "No, it wasn't. Not that it's your business."

Kevin sighed and rose, shrugging into his button up shirt. "I saw her naked." That would distract them from their stupid, ongoing argument.

They both swung to face him.

"I knew it."

"Naked?"

It had been a bit more than naked. It had been hot, amazing, the sexiest thing he'd ever seen. It had tugged at his heart as hard as it had squeezed other parts of his body.

"And?"

"We talked the rest of the night."

There was a beat of silence. Then they said in unison, "You *talked* the rest of the night?"

Kevin finished the last button on his shirt. "You never talk to your wives?"

"Hey, I get it, man," Sam said, patting Kevin on the shoulder, then reaching for his shoes. "It's been a long time. Nothing to be embarrassed about."

Kevin's eyes narrowed suspiciously. "Wait, what's nothing to be embarrassed about?"

"Yeah. I mean I haven't played Pac Man in years. I probably wouldn't be that good at it without a little practice first," Mac said.

"What is it you don't think I'm good at anymore?" Kevin asked. To no avail.

"But you'd remember *how* to play," Sam said to Mac. "You wouldn't panic about it and end up talking instead of stepping up to the joystick."

"Good point," Mac agreed with a laugh.

They were on one of their rolls. Kevin crossed his arms and leaned back against his locker, waiting for them to finish their conversation about him in front of him.

And who knew? Maybe he'd pick up something useful. It was a stretch, but not completely impossible. Somehow these guys had gotten amazing women to fall in love with them.

But…he hadn't talked to Eve because he'd *forgotten* what else to do. He'd touched women, kissed women, made out and had to pull back before it went too far. And he'd definitely wanted it to go too far a few times.

But the heat had never been so intense so fast. This even beat the way he'd felt as a horny teenager with Eve herself.

And maybe that's all this was—heat and temptation and nothing to hold them back—that made it more seductive.

Going without sex as a virgin wasn't nearly as hard as having had a taste and then deciding to say no. And he'd had a taste. Not just of women and sex in general, but of Eve. Even now he could remember it. They'd been young and nervous. He'd been with two girls before Eve, but with her it had truly mattered for the first time. It had made his hands shake and what little technique he might have acquired completely abandon him. They'd bumbled their way through it. It hadn't been the best sex ever from a physical standpoint, but his heart remembered what it had been like. And it wanted more.

The only thing saving him from going crazy without her—especially as woman after woman failed to give him the same feelings she had—was the anger and hurt he'd held toward her for the past twelve years.

Now seeing her again, he was feeling that let up a little. Okay, a lot.

Because of everything from her attempts to make Drew feel good to the fact that she liked *Star Wars* and dirty talk. And the kisses. And the way she'd touched herself. Everything about last night. The hot, intense, too-soon, I've-never-felt-this-with-anyone-else night.

It was definitely making him more forgiving.

Then what if they were completely mismatched in every other way? What if he couldn't trust her again? Would he walk away? Or would he make up excuses and overlook problems so he could stay in her bed?

That would be pathetic, but he was seriously concerned.

He was lost in thought, barely aware that Sam and Mac had

headed into the break room for food, until Dooley asked, "So how long is the list you made of all the reasons you shouldn't sleep with her?"

Kevin wasn't particularly surprised that Dooley knew what he'd been thinking. "Why would I make a list like that?"

"Because you're trying to convince yourself that sex with Eve is frosting on the cake."

"The cake?"

"The relationship. You've convinced yourself that the frosting, the sex, just makes it better, it's just extra. You can have cake without frosting and you think you can have a relationship without sex."

Kevin had heard nearly every theory about women and sex that any of his friends—especially Dooley—had. They were entertaining at least.

"And you're telling me I can't? That sex is integral?"

Dooley finished buckling his belt. "Sex isn't the frosting on the cake, man. It's the sugar in the batter—a key ingredient."

"You can have sex without a relationship," Kevin pointed out. Both of them had proven that several times.

"Sure. By itself, it's great, lots of ways to use it, but it's just sugar. But if you want cake, you have to mix the sugar in with a bunch of other stuff. Like a relationship."

Kevin wasn't sure he wanted to hear the rest of this. But he wasn't sure he could resist.

"And you can't have a cake without sugar," Kevin said. "I'm with you so far."

"Well, you can try it, but it won't be any good," Dooley said. "And if you try a relationship with Eve without the sex, it won't be as good as it can be either."

"That sounds like a really good excuse to have sex." But he was listening.

"It's a good *reason*," Dooley said, unapologetically. "If you love her, sex isn't just a nice way to spend some time. It's—more than that. It connects you in a way that you can't connect with anyone else. It's a way of expressing emotions that are too big to say sometimes."

Kevin's heart thumped.

Whether or not his friend was incredibly eloquent about it or not, Dooley was right. He'd been there. Kevin knew he felt closer to Eve than he ever had to anyone and that being as close as possible physically seemed almost *necessary*. Like he couldn't have held anything back, including every part of his body, and he wanted to be close to every part of her, every inch of her physically. It was different with her than with other women.

But…

"Sex complicates things. It scrambles your brain," Kevin said, looking pointedly at Dooley, knowing his friend would agree. He'd been scrambled by Morgan. "I need to make sure that what I'm feeling for Eve is more than leftover lust and the fact that it's been a really long time."

"Why else would you have just talked to a naked girl that you've been in love with forever?" Dooley asked, leading the way into the break room.

"So you really don't ever talk to Morgan?" Kevin asked, knowing it wasn't true.

"Not when she's naked. Unless it's dirty." Dooley opened the fridge and took out two Cokes. "Did you talk dirty?"

Kevin thought about changing the subject. It would be easier. But instead he said, "Yes."

Mac's eyes widened and he totally missed the can of Coke Dooley tossed to him. Sam dropped a donut.

"You did not," Sam said.

"*You* talked dirty?" Mac asked.

"I did."

"No way."

"I did," he insisted.

"Give me an example," Sam said, hands on his hips, clearly not believing Kevin capable of dirty talk.

"I'm not talking dirty to you, Sam."

"You wouldn't be the first."

Kevin smiled. "Saying these things to a guy would be a first for me."

"You don't know dirty words," Sam decided, picking up his donut.

"You've heard me swear," Kevin pointed out. He'd known these guys a long time.

"Yeah, but a well-placed 'fuck' when you're mad or frustrated is different from a 'fuck yeah' or 'oh fuck' during sex," Mac said.

Kevin laughed. "Thanks for explaining that. Okay, I used the word cock. More than once."

Sam stared at him.

"To Eve?" Mac asked.

"Yes."

"You said cock to the preacher's daughter?" Mac asked again.

Kevin grinned. "Yes."

"What did she think of that?"

"She liked it." He had to swallow hard remembering how much she'd liked it.

"Then we definitely need to help you remember how to do this," Sam said. "You've gotta keep this one around and happy."

Kevin sighed. "I don't need help—"

"We can get you pictures, videos, whatever you need," Sam interrupted.

Kevin smiled and rolled his eyes. "Gee, really? They make pictures and videos of sex? Who knew? And what will Dani and Sara think of that?"

Sam scoffed and Mac chuckled.

"For you?" Sam asked. "You can get away with anything with our girls."

They were all finally in their uniforms and had food and drink so they headed for the couches. The ER was quiet at the moment. That could change in a heartbeat, so eating right away was important.

"So what's the deal with you?" Sam asked as he chewed.

"The deal?" Kevin asked.

"With you and Eve. Your history. Like what happened with you?"

"It's a long story."

"We've got twelve hours if everyone out there behaves tonight," Mac said, propping his feet on the coffee table.

This was how and where they spent a lot of their time. Unless, of course, people drove recklessly or decided to shoot each other.

"You really want to hear this?" Kevin asked.

"Of course. It's about damned time a woman's crazy about you and you can do something about it," Sam said.

"A woman who likes the word cock," Mac had to add.

"Eve's dad got assigned to the church in Grover and they moved to town our junior year," Kevin said quickly. He didn't need them talking about Eve and the dirty talk any more. It was hard enough to keep his mind off of the couch last night. "I didn't really notice her at first. She wasn't in any of my classes and we didn't exactly hang with the same social crowd. I wasn't about to seek out the minister's daughter, no matter how cute the guys said she was. Me and my friends skipped a lot of class, drank a lot of beer and kissed a lot of girls."

"No Bible studies for you?" Mac said with a grin.

"Not exactly," Kevin agreed. "My life was all about football, baseball and having fun. But then, senior year, I walked into Algebra II and there she was. She was way too good for me but once she smiled at me, I was a goner."

The guys knew exactly what he was talking about. They'd all gone down hard for their girls.

"I couldn't stop thinking about her. I started sitting next to her, walking with her after class. She was sweet and a little shy and it was obvious she had no idea what to do with attention from a guy like me."

"That doesn't sound like the girl we met in the restaurant who said she couldn't believe how much she wanted to kiss you," Sam said.

"Yeah, she...didn't stay shy," Kevin said.

That was an understatement. Eve had blossomed with his attention, his flirting, his compliments. It was clear that no one had ever thought she walked on water—probably because her family had been so focused on the guy who'd literally walked on water—and that being adored was exactly what Eve needed.

"You were her first?" Sam asked.

Absolutely. He'd been her first everything. "She wasn't allowed to date," he said. "She could only go to church youth group functions and school dances with boys from church. Nothing else. So, I started showing up at church. I figured maybe I could put some time in before Homecoming. But her dad still said no. I showed up at the dance alone and monopolized her time and attention all night, but it wasn't enough."

It had seemed that he could never get enough of her. It drove him crazy that her father didn't see how much he cared, how much he wanted to take care of her.

"So then I started going to youth group meetings, thinking that I could get a date for the Christmas dance. But her dad didn't like me and still said no." He'd always suspected it had to do with his parents not going to church too. Eve's dad had wanted a good boy from a good family, not some kid who showed up and took up space in the pew which, admittedly, was what Kevin had been doing.

He liked to think that some of it had sunk in. He'd heard the sermons. But that wasn't the same thing as really getting it, really feeling it and believing.

"Then I started doing charity work looking toward Prom. I helped with food drives, community service, all that stuff. But the cool thing was, all the time in youth group and with the charities, Eve got to know me. She started sneaking out to see me, spending time with me when she was supposed to be doing other things. We were totally in love and when her dad said no to Prom, I proposed. And she said yes. Secretly, of course."

"Wow. You were, what, eighteen?" Mac asked.

"Yep. And crazy about her. Couldn't live without her. Willing to do anything to have her with me." He took a deep breath, staring into his coffee cup. "I was so afraid that she'd wake up one morning and believe her dad instead of me. That she'd realize she was way too good for me."

"So you eloped?" Sam asked. "That took balls."

"The night of graduation. The minute we were free."

Several moments went by and finally Sam asked, "And then what?"

Kevin looked up. "We went back to Grover, planning to tell everyone. But when she was face to face with her dad she chickened out."

"And you walked away," Mac said.

He knew it sounded like an over-reaction but he could still feel that knife of betrayal and hurt. And the realization that when it came right down to it…he really wasn't good enough. Not good enough to fight her father for, anyway.

"I told myself that if she didn't want me, I didn't want her."

"We know the stories about college and those years in the NFL," Sam said. "You went crazy, I guess."

"Yep. Football, booze and women took up the next few years."

"What she'd do?"

"Went to college in Kearney. I didn't hear her name or see her again for years. But I thought about her all the time."

"What makes you think those feelings can still be real this long after the fact?" Mac asked.

He'd been thinking of little else so he was ready for this. "Because Eve is one of those people who doesn't change. She's more mature and has life experience now, but she's a steady soul. She knows what she believes and knows who she is. I can count on that," Kevin said.

"But you couldn't count on her right after you married her," Mac said. "She backed out of the whole thing. Doesn't that make you a little…cautious now? Like maybe playing house on the first day together is a little fast?"

"Yes," Kevin admitted. "But…I'm better now."

"Better?" Mac said with a frown. "What's that mean?"

"I'm not messing around anymore," Kevin said, pushing to his feet and pacing a few strides before turning. "I save lives for a living. I work at the Youth Center and…everything I do is for the right reasons now."

Sam was scowling. "You don't have to convince us, Kevin. We know you're a great guy."

"It's that I…" Kevin really wanted to explain this to them. Because then maybe he'd understand it too. "I'm not doing it *for her* now. I wanted to be the right guy. The perfect guy. I wanted to be the guy who would deserve Eve."

"But you're—"

He held up his hand, stopping Dooley. "Now I'm a guy Eve would want to be with, but I didn't do it for her. I don't have to prove myself anymore. And I don't have to pretend to be better than I really am."

"What are you talking about?" Now Dooley was frowning as hard as Sam was.

Kevin worked through the words as he paced from one end of the room to the other. These feelings, these realizations had been bubbling below the surface since he'd first faced Eve in the restaurant. He had felt the old urge to stand up straighter and smooth down his cowlick. But he didn't need to do that anymore.

"I know what it feels like to be important and wanted and admired. I spent all those years as the big star because I could knock other guys down and could hit the ball over the outfield fence. But that was never hard. That was never something I had to work at. And there wasn't a purpose, really. I wasn't useful unless I was in uniform. And then, really only if the bases were loaded or the other team was inside the ten yard line."

He sighed. It sounded like he was whining when there were hundreds of guys who would have given anything to play ball like he had. His athletic ability had paid for his college degree, it had allowed him to have a healthy chunk of money in the bank and he'd gotten to travel and meet some great people. And he'd enjoyed it.

Still, the work he'd done with the at-risk teens, who may or may not remember his name in ten years, felt like more than anything he'd ever done on the field. For sure helping out and getting to know Dooley's family meant more. As did the time he spent with Barb, Katherine and Dorothy, the older women he and the guys looked after.

"I married Eve because she was the best person, the best actual person *inside*, that I'd ever met. She was the first girl who had standards and whose father wanted more from me than my football stats. I felt like if I could be important to her, then it would really mean something. And I thought if I could bind her to me forever, really make her *mine*, then the rest of the world would see something in me besides a means to a championship trophy."

Mac looked concerned as he leaned forward. "And now? Do you still feel like you need Eve to prove that you're a good guy?"

Kevin let the question sink in. He made himself really think about it. Because this was big. He couldn't stay married to Eve for any reason other than love and wanting to spend his life with her.

Finally, he shook his head. "No. I made something of myself on my own."

"You sure as hell did," Sam agreed.

Kevin settled back in the chair, letting his thoughts quiet and a smile emerge.

Mac sat back, still frowning, but less tense. "So you want to be with her because of real feelings? Not because you're trying to prove something?"

"Yeah."

They all seemed to relax and breathe.

"Real feelings are good," Sam finally said, toasting with his cup. "But don't underestimate the fact that she likes dirty talk either."

Kevin laughed, feeling lighter and…free. Free to explore his feelings for Eve and what was really between them.

# CHAPTER
## SEVEN

KEVIN DROPPED his bag on the foyer of the house with a loud thump.

The eighty-seven minute drive to Grover after his twelve-hour shift was going to be tough.

He wanted to go to Sherry's, he wanted to call Eve, he wanted to ask her to come over. But he was exhausted. The shift had been quiet for the first two hours. The following ten, not so much.

He needed sleep before Drew was out of school. Of course, then he wouldn't be able to get Eve naked—at least not totally naked and loud like he wanted to. And he didn't know how much longer he could wait to do that. He was aching for her as if...they'd been apart for twelve years.

Sighing, torn between horniness and fatigue, he headed for the kitchen.

And froze in the doorway.

There was a huge sign on the center island, black marker on red construction paper, that said *Welcome Home*. It was clearly Drew's handwriting, but the little heart and xoxo at the bottom were obviously from Eve.

There was a piece of yellow construction paper underneath it with an arrow pointing to the fridge. It said Breakfast. On the bottom shelf was the pitcher for the blender, full of something orange. He sniffed it, recognizing orange and peach. A smoothie. No way.

There was also a green note that said *Oven*.

In the oven was a pan of blueberry muffins. He assumed from a mix, knowing Eve, but he didn't care. Grabbing one, he put the blender jar on the base and mixed the smoothie, then dumped it in the glass already sitting ready with a twisty straw.

He usually came home to an empty apartment where no one else lived. In fact, he rarely spent time there. He was more often at Dooley's house or at Sam and Danika's house. When he went home it was alone to a space he didn't share with anyone.

This was way better.

Sipping and chewing he made his way upstairs. In his room he found another note—

*Sleep well*—with an eye mask—which was a little girlie but he didn't care—and some ear plugs.

Smiling, he finished the muffin and smoothie, then pulled the comforter back.

On the sheet underneath was another note: *I hope you sleep naked. I'll be over later.*

And suddenly sleep was the last thing on his mind.

It was probably the vitamins in the smoothie, but he had a surge of energy.

Or it was Eve.

She was seducing him and it was completely working.

He looked from the pillow to the empty smoothie glass then to the note where she'd written the word "naked". He should sleep. He needed to sleep.

But he needed her more.

He headed back down the steps and yanked the front door

open, determined to take her in the back room of her grand-mother's restaurant if needed.

Eve had just stepped onto the porch.

"Hi."

He loved how her eyes lit up when she saw him.

"Hi."

"I thought you'd go to bed."

"I will. But not without you." The moment she was close enough, her grabbed her wrist and pulled her inside.

"I should leave you alone to sleep." Her hands went to the bottom of his T-shirt and she started tugging it up. "But I can't. I promise I'll be quick."

He pulled the shirt off and tossed it away as he slammed the door behind her. His fingers went to the buttons on her shirt. "You better not be quick."

Her shirt came open and he pushed it from her shoulders.

"I don't think I'll be able to help the quick thing," she said, reaching behind and unhooking her bra, tossing it on the growing pile of clothes.

"Then we'll have to do it more than once." He was surprised he could speak. The sight of her bare breasts, hard nipples and huge smile was enough to suck the oxygen from his lungs.

"Darn." She started for the stairs, unhooking and unzipping her jeans.

He was right on her heels. "You sure you can leave the restaurant?"

She was on the third step and he was on the first when she turned, slid the denim over her hips and wiggled out of her jeans. She kicked them to the bottom of the stairs. "Monica agreed that I'd be way nicer to be around if I was getting some."

He put his hands on her waist, stroking his open palms from hip to breast on either side. Goose bumps erupted on her skin and she sighed.

"I think she's right," she said happily. "I feel better already."

He couldn't help it. She was standing above him on the steps, her breasts nearly at eye level, wearing nothing but a pair of skimpy white panties. He dipped his knees and took a nipple into his mouth.

Her hand went to the back of his head and she arched into him. "*Yes.*"

"I need you, Eve," he said huskily. "I'm keeping you here awhile. You sure they don't need you downtown?"

"The only people there are the retired farmers and all they need is coffee. They know where the pot is." She leaned closer. "Now where were you?"

He took her other nipple into his mouth and brought her hips closer.

"Yep, right there," she breathed. After a moment though, she pulled away. "I want to see more of you," she said. "You got an eyeful the other night but I haven't seen anything but pecs and abs. Not that I'm complaining." She ran her hand over his chest and then down his stomach.

He sucked in a quick breath. "No arguments from me."

She walked backward up the steps as he followed, unzipping and shedding his jeans along the way until they entered his bedroom in underwear only, hands everywhere.

"Let me look for a minute," she said, pushing him down onto the bed. "I've been watching you on TV for years, remembering that awesome ass and those thighs. Now I'm up close and personal and I want to enjoy it."

She straddled his thighs, but he caught her wrists before she could run them over his stomach again. "You've been watching me on TV? What do you mean?"

"Football," she said. "I saw every game that was televised."

"College or pro?"

"Both."

He stared at her. She'd been watching him play football? Even in college? That was right after they'd broken up. "You don't like football."

"I do too," she said. "I'd never really seen or understood it before I dated you. I love it now. And I know a lot about it."

"So those stats you knew? You didn't look them up?" He'd never imagined she might see him play, or pay attention or want to understand it because of him.

"I knew them," she confirmed. "My college roommate's boyfriend was a huge football fan and explained a lot to me, and then I read some stuff and picked a lot up by watching."

"Wow."

She smiled. "I think I like surprising you."

He smiled back, flattered by her interest in his football career, but there was a little niggle of unease. He didn't want her to surprise him. At least not too much. He wanted Eve. The Eve he'd always known, the girl he'd always loved.

"What else have you learned since I knew you?" he asked. It was so easy to forget that they hadn't been together for more than a decade. In some ways it seemed that they'd never been apart.

Her grin grew mischievous. "Let me show you." She pulled her wrists free from his hold and spread her palms on his stomach, running them up and down over the muscles and ribs. "You feel so good," she said, watching where her hands touched.

"You too." He held her hips, watching her watch him. Then his eyes were drawn again to her breasts, then her stomach, then the dip of the silky panties below her belly button. He needed more. He flipped her to her back, the movement bouncing her breasts softly, and stretched out beside her. "I want to see you again," he said, running the tip of his finger along the top edge of her panties.

"Good. And ditto."

She lifted her hips off the mattress and he quickly pulled the white silk down her legs and off over her feet.

He gazed at her, completely bare, his cock and heart both throbbing. She was his. She was here, they were together. All his.

"You too," she urged, tugging at the top of his boxers.

He whisked them off, tossing them somewhere near the foot of the bed.

"Lie back. I want to look."

She pushed against his chest and he rolled back. Paper crinkled underneath him and he reached to pull her note from underneath him.

"I sleep in boxers," he said, showing her the note before tossing it toward the bedside table.

She smiled looking up from where she'd been studying his body. "Unless I wear you out to the point you can't even pull them on afterward."

He pulled her down for a kiss. The hunger was intense and it was unquestionably on both sides. She ran her hands over his face, his shoulders, chest and ribs, then over his naked hips and the sides of his thighs. It was as if they couldn't touch each other enough.

"Let me look," she said, pulling back, breathless, from the kiss. Her gaze traveled over him eagerly, seemingly taking in every inch. "Holy cow. You haven't played in years. You can't tell me you still workout that hard?"

"I'm at the gym regularly. My job requires me to be in good shape."

"But wow." Her eyes found his. "I would really appreciate it if you would walk around naked all the time. In fact, every woman in the world would appreciate that. But you're all mine." She leaned in and kissed his sternum.

Other women had complimented him, ogled him, lusted over him. But it had never felt like this. The fact that he turned her on, that she wanted him as much as he did her, that she sounded possessive of him thrilled him beyond any prior seduction or experience.

She was the only one who mattered. Her happiness and her pleasure were the only ones he would ever care about again.

Then she wrapped her hand around his cock and all sweet thoughts vanished as lust took over.

He gasped. "Damn, Eve."

"I like how I can make you lose your mind," she said, stroking up and down his length.

"You have no idea." He flipped her to her back again. "My turn."

She didn't move to cover herself at all, letting him look his fill, then run his hands up and down her legs, over her stomach to cup her breasts. He played with her nipples enough to get her writhing underneath him. Then he parted her knees and ran his hand up the inside of her thigh. She let her legs spread wide and he had to swallow hard.

"You're gorgeous. I've been thinking about this all night."

"Me too."

He lifted his gaze to her face. "Yeah?"

"Of course." She wiggled again. "Last night was fun and all but I want you touching me this time."

"Well, if you insist." He ran his finger over her mound, then the slick cleft beneath.

She lifted her hips. "More."

"Anything you want," he said sincerely. He parted her folds and stroked her, over her clit and through the sweet wetness. He stared, unable to believe he finally had Eve, his wife, spread out on his bed, begging him to touch her.

"More," she said, her voice definitely rougher.

He watched her face as he slipped his finger into her, slowly. Her legs parted further and she seemed to be holding her breath. "So hot and tight," he said softly. "Perfect."

"Kevin." Her eyes had drifted shut and she was biting her bottom lip.

He loved how he could affect her, occupy her mind as he touched her body.

He slid his finger in fully, then added a second, stretching her.

She moaned and lifted her hips. He slid in and out, watching her body react, then leaned over and flicked his tongue over her clit.

"Oh!" It was definitely louder than the panting she'd been doing.

He licked again, then sucked as he stroked his fingers in and out.

"Kevin!" Even louder this time. Almost a cry.

He reached for the drawer in his nightstand, retrieved, opened and donned a condom all with one hand and his teeth, his other hand continuing to work Eve to the breaking point.

He finally slid his fingers free and shifted over her.

"Oh, finally," she breathed, opening her legs for his hips and grabbing his ass.

He laughed.

Right in the middle of sex. Sex with Eve.

Shaking his head he said, "Sorry to hold things up."

She grinned. "Make it up to me now. I need you."

He braced his hands on the mattress and pressed forward. "I know the feeling."

He entered her slowly, wanting to savor it, wanting to be sure she could take him, but she did. Completely. His body took over quickly and halfway home he thrust, burying himself deep.

"Yes," she encouraged, wrapping her legs around him. "Yes, yes."

He paused a moment, soaking in the feel, scent and sound of her. But she squeezed her inner muscles and he groaned. "Eve, I want this to last more than two minutes."

"Why?" She squeezed again. "This is amazing."

It was. It was incredible.

Then she reached between them, finding her clit with her finger and circling.

The sight, the sexy hitch in her breathing, the way she looked down at her finger and where they were joined, the feel of her inner walls beginning to ripple all combined and Kevin began to stroke, long and deep.

She moved with him, her hips meeting his. Both moaning and gasping, the heat and friction building between them steadily.

"More," she whimpered.

She shifted under him, moving her right leg and he paused as she wiggled, then stretched it up, hooking her knee over his shoulder.

"Holy…" he trailed off as he sank deep. He was a big guy, in all ways. She shouldn't be able to take him like that. He might hurt…

"*Yes.*" Her moan was loud and heartfelt. Using her leg against his shoulder she moved against him even harder.

"Eve, I don't—"

"So good," she panted. "Just like that."

As her walls squeezed him, he couldn't have held back if he tried. The thrusts were deep and hard, the rhythm increased and soon the bed was rocking, knocking the headboard against the wall in hard, loud thumps.

"Kevin!" she called out as her orgasm hit, her body drawing his deep.

He was right behind her. His climax swept over him and he felt wave after wave of pleasure race through him.

For several moments afterward he was able to hold himself up on his arms, but when Eve moved her leg off his shoulder and slumped, spent, beneath him, he lowered himself to her side and let his whole body fully relax.

He sank into the mattress, feeling heat and satisfaction and fatigue all cover him at once.

Eve lay breathing hard next to him until she finally could slow the rhythm and she rolled into him. Spreading her hand out over his heart she sighed.

"That was totally worth waiting ten years for," she said.

Puzzled he looked down at her, brushing her hair back from her face. "Ten?" he asked. "We've been apart for twelve."

She grinned up at him. "Yeah. If I'd been on top it would have been worth twelve."

"Hey." He chuckled and gently smacked her butt. "Be good or I'll keep trying for the twelve without *letting* you on top."

Though he knew he wouldn't. He wanted her on top. He wanted to see what she'd do with the control. In fact, the idea of it was already causing parts of his body to react.

"You need to sleep," she said with a giggle, clearly noticing his response.

"I do." He wanted to do a lot more of what they'd been doing, but he needed sleep before Drew was out of school. "Stay, oka—?" He yawned before he got all of the question out.

She snuggled close. "I was hoping you'd say that."

He closed his eyes, loving the feel of her head on his chest, his arm around her. They'd only spent one night like this ever. He could still remember how it felt to sleep with Eve in his arms. Right. That was the only word. It felt *right*.

They needed to talk some too, before Drew was home. He wanted to know how everything had gone the night before.

And there was at least one other question he needed to ask her. Was it about sex? Maybe about a guy? Something having to do with…

He couldn't remember and he couldn't fight sleep any longer.

He'd think of it later.

Probably.

If it was important.

Kevin fell into a deep sleep quickly, but Eve lay thinking. Worrying.

She should have held back more. She shouldn't have been that bold their first time back together. She shouldn't have done what she'd done on the couch the other night either, but he hadn't seemed bothered by that. She grinned. No, definitely not bothered.

But surely he was going to wonder how she'd learned some of the things she'd learned. Throwing her leg over his shoulder had not been particularly brilliant. And that bit about being on top? Geez, nothing like giving it all up at once.

When they'd last been together, they'd made love exactly four times, all in the same night. Their wedding night. The first time with him had been her first time ever. It had been the first time she'd seen or touched a penis in person without his jeans barely pulled out of the way with only the car's dashboard lights illuminating things. They'd used the same position—the traditional, with him on top—all four times.

It wouldn't take him long to realize that either she'd been watching porn or had some experience with an erection other than his.

Or, in actuality, both. At the same time once or twice.

What was she ready for him to know?

Maybe more importantly, what was Kevin ready to know?

Okay, so she was probably going to have to hold back a bit. It wasn't like sex with him would ever be less than amazing. She knew he had experience—probably more than *she* wanted to know—so maybe she'd let him lead things and keep her mouth shut.

At least about the things that Kevin didn't want to know. She knew that he didn't want to know about the time she and Zach got naked on the not-exactly-a-nude-beach, or the time she and Andy gave some college guys an eyeful at a Green Day concert, or the time she and Tom…

Anyway.

The other guys didn't matter. She could leave those parts out. Because she was very okay with him leaving out the exact number of blow jobs he'd had before her. Among other things.

She could probably also leave out the three months she'd smoked. She didn't need to tell him about her unfortunate relationship with peach schnapps because that was *definitely* over. Forever. And he probably didn't need to know about the nights when she said "what the hell" when the marijuana was passed around.

But otherwise—there were a few little details he should probably know about. Like her arrest, for instance. She hadn't been convicted. She hadn't done anything wrong—other than pick a roommate out of the classifieds—but it was on her record.

She rolled toward him, reaching to put her hand on his back. She absorbed the warmth of his skin, the rise and fall as he breathed and she finally dozed and then fell into an actual sleep, the late nights and the crazy tornado of emotions combining with the big, hot body next to her and the rip-roaring orgasm to create the perfect recipe for a deep, contented sleep.

At three thirty-seven the ringing phone woke them.

Eve jerked upright as Kevin blindly reached for the bedside table where his cell phone lay. But it wasn't until after he answered, "Hello?" that they both realized the ringing phone was hers.

She grabbed it right before it went to voice mail. "Hello?"

"Eve?"

Crap. Drew. School was out. "We're on the way, buddy. Wait by—"

"Can I go to a friend's house to play and stay for dinner?" he interrupted.

Relief washed over her. He wasn't sitting in the school office panicking about them not being there. "Sure. There will be adults there?" she thought to ask.

"Yeah. Of course."

"Okay. Great." They hadn't screwed up too badly. "Call us when you're ready to get picked up."

"'Kay, bye." He disconnected before she could say goodbye.

She slumped back onto the pillow. "Drew's going to a friend's house to play and eat dinner and will call us to pick him up later."

Kevin rubbed a hand over his face. "I can't believe I did that."

"It's no problem," she assured him. "He wasn't freaked out or anything."

"Still, I messed up."

Though her own guilt was plenty thick, she propped herself up on her elbow. "Kevin, we're ten blocks from the school. Everyone knows him and vice versa. It's not like it's forty below and he's standing out on the corner. He'd be fine if he had to wait for a few minutes. No harm done."

"Still..."

She put her hand on his chest. "Still you're not perfect and no one expects you to be. You're not used to having a little boy to think about picking up from school. It doesn't mean you don't care."

He sighed. "You're right. Okay. It's fine."

"It's completely fine," she agreed. "In fact, it's fantastic."

"It is?"

"Yeah, he gets to have fun and we have more time alone." She rubbed her hand over his chest, then slid lower. "Any idea how to kill some time?"

"Only fifty," he said, rolling toward her. He pulled her close and kissed her.

Her arms went around his neck and she arched into his body, wanting to touch every centimeter at once.

As she started to throw her leg over his hip to roll him to his back, she stopped herself. She needed to let him lead. What good would it do to demonstrate how much she'd experimented and learned since they'd been apart? Kevin seemed to have some pretty specific ideas of how things should go and he seemed to like the idea that she was the same sweet girl he'd known in high school. The same sweet girl he'd married.

Yeah, he wanted her to be the same.

Fine. People changed for the ones they loved, why couldn't

she stay the same if that's what he needed and wanted? That wasn't going to hurt anyone.

"Come here," he said, turning onto his back and pulling her on top of his body. "Let's see what you've got."

She paused in the midst of rubbing her whole body against all of his.

She had plenty to show him. But no, that's not how he meant it. Was it?

"What do you want to see?"

"All of you. Moving on me. Taking me deep," he said hoarsely, cupping her breasts as she braced herself with her hands on his chest.

She loved when he talked like that. "This is a side of you I haven't seen before," she said, venturing cautiously into the subject of changes.

"Underneath you?" he asked, pressing his hips up against her.

She dragged in a deep breath. "Yeah, that," she admitted. It was a nice side to see too. "And the dirty talk."

"You like it though." He rolled her nipple between thumb and finger.

"Hell yeah I do." In fact, she was holding herself back from begging him to fuck her. In those exact words.

"If I keep it up will you slide back and take my cock?"

She groaned. She'd take it all right. She could shock the hell out of Kevin Campbell by using her mouth on his aforementioned cock. And she could tell him exactly what she intended to do with it in graphic detail.

According to a couple of experts, she was pretty good with her mouth.

But she didn't think that was a recommendation Kevin would appreciate.

Damn. This was going to get complicated.

"I'll do whatever you want," she told him, shifting back, feeling the head of his erection against her.

"You sure you're ready for that?" he asked, lifting his hips and pressing down on hers.

It wasn't the exact angle they needed but it still made her catch her breath.

And why was it okay for him to say things that more than hinted at the experiences *he'd* had? She didn't want to hear or think about the other women. Then again, he hadn't been the virgin on their wedding night. He had hardly been a playboy at that point, but hers wasn't the first bra he'd unhooked, that was for sure.

"I'm ready for whatever you've got," she told him, leaning over and licking at one of his nipples.

He cupped the back of her head with a groan. "I want to do *everything* to you, with you, on you, in you."

"We'd better get started then," she said, sliding back without warning and tipping her pelvis so that when she pushed herself up to extended elbows, he slid in.

He lifted and thrust to get deep as they gasped together.

"Perfect," he groaned, "so tight. So good."

She flexed her inner muscles again, then started to move, pulling and squeezing him as she did it. If she got him caught up in the moment and the heat, then he wouldn't notice—or care—what she knew or didn't know.

"I've imagined you like this so many times," he rasped.

"Ditto." She loved this position. It was one of her favorites. He was certainly her pick for bottom too.

His big hands moved to cup her butt, lifting and lowering her, thrusting up to meet her as he did.

Eve lifted her hands to her breasts, pinching her nipples and wresting a groan from Kevin. She liked that sound. She wanted more of it. Leaning back, she braced one hand on his thigh, changing the angle of his thrusts. She pushed with one foot against the mattress, moving just enough for him to hit her g-spot perfectly.

She gasped and threw her head back. Her body took the

rhythm over from Kevin. She was in a much better position to lift, lower and grind and soon his hands fell away, limp on the mattress.

"Eve," he groaned.

She opened her eyes to watch him. His face showed it all. His jaw was tight, his eyes were on her, though, as his chest rose and fell as he breathed hard.

A surge of power, a deep satisfaction at making him look that way, rushed through her. "Hang on," she told him with grin.

She increased the tempo, squeezing him tightly each time, and finally reached behind with the hand that wasn't holding her up and cupped his balls.

His hips surged upward as she played with him and she could feel his climax building.

"You're coming with me," he said through gritted teeth as he brought his thumb to her clit.

He pressed and circled and almost the moment she felt her orgasm begin, it rose, grew and crashed over her quickly.

A moment later, Kevin thrust up with a groan, holding her hips tight against his as he came.

They stayed still, only breathing for nearly a minute before she slumped forward, her forehead on his shoulder.

"Okay. That was pretty darned good," he said, running his hands up and down her back. "What do you think? Worth twelve years?"

She laughed and lifted her head. "Honestly, it makes me mad that we haven't been doing that twice a day for the past twelve years."

He met her gaze and she saw a mix of emotions—heat, regret, and, yes, love.

"I know what you mean."

His voice sounded like maybe he was choked up and she had to clear her throat to say, "I guess we'll have to do it four times a day for the next twelve to make up for it."

He drew a deep breath and gave her a smile that made her

heart ache. Twelve years she'd been without that smile, his voice, his touch.

"I think that's a fantastic idea," he said, pulling her close and kissing her forehead.

Twelve years. Twelve years she could have been with him, talking, laughing, watching TV, going on vacation…so many things. Twelve years was a long time in a married couple's life. They could have remodeled a kitchen, bought two or three cars and—she felt tears prickle and she had to blink rapidly—they could have a child celebrating double digit birthdays by now.

A child.

After twelve years they would definitely have had kids.

She lifted her head and stared at him. Kids. She wanted kids. Correction, she wanted Kevin's kids.

Then she realized… They hadn't used a condom. She glanced at the nightstand. It hadn't even occurred to her.

"We didn't use a condom," he said.

Oh, so he'd realized that too. "Yeah, I was just thinking of that."

The corner of his mouth curled. "You're supposed to think of it *before* climbing on."

She climbed *off* and arched an eyebrow. "I didn't hear you screaming at me to stop and wait."

"The minute I kissed you I wasn't thinking of anything else," he admitted.

"And I was trying to keep myself from going down on you so I wasn't thinking about condoms."

Too late—far, far too late—she realized what she'd admitted.

Kevin made a strange choking sound.

She frowned. "You okay?"

"Did you say 'going down on you'?"

She bit her bottom lip but nodded.

"As in…"

"Blow job," she clarified. It looked like Kevin was going to learn at least one thing about her past experience.

"Blow j…" he started to repeat, as if in awe. "You were trying to *keep* from doing that?"

"Yeah."

"Was it difficult?"

"Extremely."

He stared at her, then pushed himself up to sitting. "You *wanted* to give me a blow job and held yourself back?"

"Yes."

"Why?"

"I…" Oh, boy. Why was this so hard? He'd been with other women. It had been a long time since they'd been together. Did he really think she hadn't been with anyone else? There was one way to find out.

"I wasn't sure how you'd feel about it."

He blinked three times. "Okay. For the record, I'm very much in favor of blow jobs."

She couldn't help it—she laughed. "I meant, I wasn't sure how you'd feel about me knowing how to do that."

"Oh." He looked stunned.

It seemed that he hadn't really given that much thought.

"I thought maybe you wouldn't want to know…"

"Yeah," he interrupted, "you're right. I don't want to know."

"You don't?"

"No. I don't want to know that just like I'm not going to think about how well you did up on top for your first time."

"But that wasn't…" She trailed off as she realized what he was doing. He wanted to pretend that was her first time in that position. Oooo-k-a-y. If that worked for him, great. "That wasn't that hard to figure out," she said instead. "I followed my instincts. And you were great about showing me what to do."

"Right," he said, slowly nodding his head. "I showed you. Okay, tell you what. How about I tell you how to give me a blow job and you follow my instructions."

She thought about that. Pretend she didn't know how? Let him pretend it was a first for her? That could actually be really hot. Hearing Kevin tell her what he liked, how and where he wanted her tongue, how deep to go, how much suction he liked, where to put her hands. Oh yeah, this could work out really well.

"Let's start now," she said eagerly, bouncing on the mattress. "I've always really been curious about those."

He grinned. "I think I can help you out with that."

Sure enough, it looked like he was recovering quickly.

She turned so she was kneeling beside him. "How do I start?"

"Wrap your hand around me."

She started to reach, then decided she was going to really play this up. "Are you sure?" she asked. "You're so big."

He chuckled and reached for her hand. "It's okay, you can do it." He guided her hand to his waiting cock and wrapped her fingers around his shaft. "Like that," he said. "Firm but gentle."

She squeezed slightly and he breathed in. "Yeah."

"Now what?"

"Move your hand up and down. Like this." His hand cupped the back of hers and slid it up and down in a long stroke.

"Maybe you should do it and I'll watch," she suggested, her voice a little breathy. She'd love to watch Kevin touch himself. She pulled her hand away and he did as she asked, gliding along his length with long, sure strokes.

His eyes were on her as he did it.

"Keep going," she urged when he slowed.

"I can't get my mouth down there," he said. Then he smiled. "If I could, I might never leave my house."

She snorted. "You and every other man on the planet."

"That's why we need girls. Why I need you."

"That's the only reason?" she teased before wetting her lips.

"No. But at the moment I can't think of any of the others." His attention was on her mouth.

"Then we'd better take care of this before you lose any more oxygen to your brain. What do I do next?"

"Come here."

She leaned in and he lifted his middle finger to her mouth. "Suck."

She let him slide his finger past her lips, their gazes locked. She closed her lips around his finger, pressed her tongue against it and sucked. He slid his finger in and out, slowly, the heat in his eyes holding her mesmerized.

"Like that," he said roughly.

When he pulled his finger free, she grabbed his wrist and dragged her tongue up and down the length of his wet finger. Then she swirled her tongue around the tip.

"Can I do that too?" she asked.

He cleared his throat. "Sure. That would work."

His other hand was still on his cock, though unmoving. As she leaned back from his finger, he held his erection up proud. "Try it."

She leaned over, trying to go slow, trying to play it up for him. Really she wanted to go to town, make him squirm and cry out her name. Anything she could do to pleasure Kevin, she was more than happy to oblige.

She swirled her tongue around the head and he sucked in a lungful of air.

Then she ran her tongue down the front, like she'd done on his finger. Air hissed out between his teeth.

"Is that okay?" she asked, looking up at him.

He nodded. "Now do it again, but put your hand here."

He guided her hand to his balls. Smiling to herself, she repeated the action twice more, then a third while cupping and massaging. He was breathing hard, his hips trying to thrust upward. But he was fighting for control.

"Now what?" she asked.

"Take me in your mouth."

Hearing him instruct her made heat wash over her. She wrapped her hand around the base of his erection and put her mouth to the top, letting the tip slide between her lips.

"Eve," he breathed.

Oh, she definitely liked this. This was going on the twice-a-day-list too.

"I'm doing okay?" she asked.

"Yes. More. Take more."

She let him slide further into her mouth.

"Now suck me." His fingers were in her hair, holding it back away from her face, so he could watch what she was doing.

She sucked once, reveled in his moan, then sucked harder on the tip.

"More. Take me in."

She did. Kevin was a big guy so there was no way she could take him all, but she gave it her best.

"*Yes.*"

He arched and she relaxed, letting him in further.

"*Damn.*"

She loved doing this to him. Kevin didn't lose control often and she guessed it was even rarer now in adulthood. In fact... he'd been celibate...it had probably been a really long time since anyone had done this to him. She loved it even more with that realization. The idea that other woman had been like this, had put their mouths here, had drawn those groans and sighs from him, stuck a knife of jealousy deep in her chest and she sucked harder.

"Yes. Now faster," he urged, his hand cupping the back of her head.

She increased the tempo with both her hand and her mouth, caressing his full length each time. She took him deep, stroked him hard, until finally he said, "Enough."

She looked up in surprise. He hadn't come. It wasn't enough.

"Eve, enough," he repeated when he saw she was going to argue.

"But—"

"Come here."

He pulled her up his body, nudged her onto her back, and

spread her legs. His fingers slid into her body without any warning and she cried out. She was wet and swollen and ready for him, her nerves dancing.

"You really do like doing that, don't you?" he asked, pumping his fingers deep, feeling how much he'd turned her on.

"Yes, yes," she gasped.

He remembered to reach for a condom this time, sheathed himself and then, still on his side facing her, drew her leg up and over his hip, then thrust forward, sinking deep.

It was a vulnerable position for her, spread open, on her back with him at her side. But it allowed him to see everything he wanted to see, which seemed to be *everything*.

His finger found her clit and he watched himself circle and rub until she came apart with an orgasm that seemed to thunder from the depths of her body.

Then he thrust harder and deeper and faster until his climax took him over the edge too.

When he caught his breath he cuddled her close, burying his face in her hair. "You're a fast learner," he said near her ear.

She laughed lightly. "Good instructions."

He was quiet for a moment. Then he said, "Maybe we should talk about a few things."

Oh, boy. She didn't try to shift or turn. "Like what?"

"As much as I'd love to believe that there's been no one else, and while I *really* don't need a lot of details, I suppose it makes sense that we talk about some things."

"Some guys?" she asked.

"I guess." He didn't sound excited about it. "There have been some?"

"Yes," she said softly.

"More than one?"

"Yes."

"Less than…forty?"

She laughed in surprise. "Um, yes."

"Okay, so we'll go with two."

She laughed again. "Two, huh?"

"That's more than one and less than forty."

She cuddled in closer but neither made a move to make eye contact. "Okay."

"Anybody serious?" he asked, running his hand over her hip.

"Serious?" She thought about that. "Kind of. Maybe. I guess."

"You fell for someone?"

She took a deep breath. "No. Not that." She'd never been in love with anyone else. At least, not compared to what she felt for Kevin. "But almost that."

"How many?"

"Two. One and a half," she corrected. "I was serious about Zach at the time. We were together for a long time—two years—but looking back it was a lot more about wanting to be with someone rather than really wanting to be with him."

"When was that?"

This was weird. Things were intense between them and they were talking about the future as if it was definitely going to happen with comments like making love four times a day for the next twelve years. But were they solid? She was. For sure. She wanted Kevin, for good, no matter what. But where was he? Was he feeling the strength of emotion between them? Was it enough to make him care less about the changes in her and focus on the things that were the same… or better?

"I met Zach at the end of my sophomore year." That would have been almost two years after Kevin had left. Two years after they'd gotten married.

She didn't mention that he was at least the twelfth guy she'd dated and slept with by that time. She'd also drank, smoked, partied, nearly flunked out and spent some time in jail. She'd also stolen money from her father, practically starved herself and nearly ruined her life. She'd tried it all. Tried to find a thrill, a good feeling again. Supposedly.

Now, looking back, she knew exactly what she'd really been doing. She'd been pushing and pushing, wondering how far she had to go until someone, *anyone*, stepped in and pulled her back. How gone did she have to be before someone cared enough to find her?

Ultimately, she'd had to find herself.

"Zach, huh?" Kevin asked, nudging her gently.

She'd been so lost in thought that she'd forgotten the question. "Zach? Oh, yeah. He was…pretty serious."

Zach had been the first guy she'd dated who wasn't a complete fuck-up, frankly. He didn't do drugs, had a college degree and a real job. He looked fantastic next to the guys she'd been hanging out with—and the guys who her crazy roommates had dated.

Sure, he'd enabled her partying—he was right there beside her. He had never been concerned about her eating disorder—he liked skinny girls. He had even been okay with sharing her with his best friend—which *she'd* said no to. But overall he'd been nice, didn't cheat on her and remembered her birthday.

But he'd had a final straw—like everyone. He'd dumped her when she got arrested. He didn't even wait around to see the final verdict.

"But you didn't love him?"

Hell, no. She shrugged. "I wasn't too worried about that."

"Why?"

"I'd already been crazy in love. I didn't really want it again."

Kevin pulled in a deep breath. "Why?"

"Because having it with you…" It had been the one thing that was special, the one thing she'd only given to him. She'd regretted all the craziness, the sex, the…everything after she'd cleaned up. After that the only thing that Kevin had that no one else had was her heart. "I never expected it to get better with anyone else than it had been with you. So what was the point?"

He breathed deep again. She wanted to see his face. Yet, she didn't. She wasn't sure what she wanted to see in his expression —regret, apology, love?

"Wait," she said, as a thought occurred. She pushed up onto

her elbow wanting to see his face now. "What about you? Someone serious in your past? Did you fall in love with someone?"

Her stomach cramped at the thought, nausea threatening.

"I um…" He focused on her shoulder instead of her eyes. "I tried to."

Ugh. Another cramp. "You did? What do you mean?"

He sighed. "I wanted to. I wanted to be in love. Especially since my friends have started getting married and having families. I want that. So I tried to be in love. With more than one girl. But…"

"But?" she asked, nudging him. "But what?"

"It hasn't worked. No one's been right."

Relief poured over her. "Good."

He smiled. "I'm glad you feel that way."

"How did you try to be in love?" she asked, thinking that sounded odd.

"I focused on all the reasons I *should* love them. Tried to convince myself that I felt things that I didn't really feel. I tried to tell myself that they were good enough, that they didn't have to be *perfect*, just close."

She frowned, the stomach cramp suddenly back. "What reasons did you think you should love them for?"

"They were beautiful, intelligent, wanted the same things in life, got along with my friends."

Eve curled her legs up a little, trying to relieve the feeling in her gut. "What was the problem?"

He frowned. "I don't know. It's been driving me nuts. They should have been perfect. They had everything I wanted. But—" he squeezed her hip and gave her a smile, "—now I know why. It's because of you. I was only supposed to be with you."

"*Supposed to*, huh?" she asked weakly.

"You have to admit that there has to have been some divine intervention or something here," he said, rubbing her hip. "What are the chances that all of this—my dad, Drew, Heather, everything—would line up like this? That our feelings would still be so strong? That we would still be *married*?"

She sighed. Terrific. Not only did Kevin think that the universe had brought them back together, but that she was *perfect* for him. Based on the girl he'd known twelve years ago.

This would be a great time to tell him about all the ways she'd changed.

All her mistakes.

All the ways she was very much not perfect at all.

But then he kissed her again. And she decided that all of that was tomorrow Eve's problem.

And then he pulled her naked body over on top of his naked body and she decided it was all the day after tomorrow Eve's problem.

# CHAPTER
# EIGHT

THEY FINALLY GOT out of bed, showered and made it to the kitchen to eat. But it took awhile. The shower was another first for them.

It was fortunate that Kevin had been a bachelor for so long because that meant he could cook. Kind of. It was true that he spent a lot of meals with his friends, at their houses. But if he needed to make an omelet, grill a cheese sandwich or throw together some chili, he could do it.

He made chicken salad sandwiches for Eve.

"So what's your dad going to think?" he asked as he served her sandwich and passed the barbecue potato chips. The question had been pressing on him. Her mom and dad didn't live here anymore, and if her father had reservations about them being together, Kevin would have a hard time demonstrating how he'd changed.

"Think about what?" she asked, taking the first bite.

"Me. Us. The fact that we're married."

She stopped chewing. "Oh."

"You haven't told your parents, have you?"

She shook her head quickly. "No. Definitely not."

"Definitely not?" He frowned. So she still didn't want Daddy to know? Was she going to keep it a secret until their fiftieth wedding anniversary? Or forever?

He made himself take a deep breath. They'd been back together, aware of their marriage, for three days. Maybe that wasn't enough time for her to call them. He hadn't told his parents either. Though that had everything to do with being mad at them and not wanting to open the whole can of worms surrounding Drew yet, and nothing to do with Eve and his feelings for her.

"I don't…talk to my parents much," she said, pushing chips around on her plate with her finger.

"What?" The parents who had been her conscience, her moral compass, whose expectations outweighed everything else? The parents whose approval—or lack thereof—had been the whole reason they'd broken up?

"We, um, don't talk much." She sighed. "Or at all."

Kevin grabbed her plate and pulled it out of her reach. "Eve, what are you talking about?"

Her father and his influence over her had changed Kevin's life. He'd been without her because of the man. And now she didn't even talk to him?

She looked so sad when she looked up that he wanted to pull her onto his lap. But that passed when she blinked, the sadness replaced by a hard glint of anger. "We…broke up."

He couldn't help it. He smiled at the strange phrasing. "You broke up with your parents?"

She slumped on the tall stool. "Yeah. Once I told them about us eloping they got pretty upset. Then I left for college and went through a rebellious stage. Then he got reassigned and left Grover. They're in Arkansas right now. They don't call me and I don't call them."

He knew he was staring, but he couldn't quite wrap his mind

around everything she was telling him. "So your dad knows we got married? You told him?"

"Yes."

"What did he do?"

She took a deep breath. "Told me how disappointed he was and…"

She stopped and Kevin felt his heart lodge in his throat. It was pure instinct, but he felt a surge of protectiveness brought on by nothing more than the down turn of her mouth.

"And?" he prodded.

"He asked me for an apology."

"*Apology*?" he repeated, anger surging. "What the hell were you supposed to be sorry for?"

She lifted a shoulder. "All of it. Mostly not doing things his way."

"Did you apologize?" He could feel the tension in every inch of his body and he gripped the edge of the table.

She shook her head. "No. And then he asked me to leave."

"Leave?" Kevin felt shock rush through him. "What did you do?"

"I left."

He didn't know what to say to that.

She sighed. "I wasn't sorry. And I was so angry and hurt and disillusioned about everything—him, you, my plans, what I wanted—that I didn't come home until Christmas." She stared into her glass of water. "And then it was pretty obvious that I'd changed. I was drinking and swearing." She looked up. "I was as far from their angel daughter as I could get. I'd cut my hair and dyed it. I lit up a cigarette in my mom's kitchen. Basically, I was trying to shock him." She laughed humorlessly. "But it was pretty blatant. Cliché even. I was playing the angry, rebellious teenager but it was a few years later than most."

He tried to picture her with short hair and a cigarette. "I didn't know any of that," he said quietly.

"Why would you have known?"

He'd come home for that first Christmas from college. He'd remembered dreading and hoping to see her at the same time.

He'd even rehearsed what he'd say if he saw her.

Now, knowing what she'd been going through he felt a sharp stab of regret and pain. If he'd seen her he would have known immediately something was wrong. He'd known her better than anyone. One look in her eyes and he would have known she was hurting—and he would have cracked. His own hurt wouldn't have mattered. He would have swept her up and taken her far away.

Kevin forced himself to unclench his hands. It was his fault she'd gone through that, his fault she'd been alone to face it.

But he was here now.

Freaking out and wrapping her in cashmere and tucking her away someplace where nothing could ever hurt her again, then driving overnight to Arkansas to tell her father what he thought of him would be too much. Probably.

But dammit, he'd missed *years* of being there for her, of holding her when she cried, of telling her that her father was an asshole who didn't deserve her respect.

Kevin swallowed. He couldn't act on any of these emotions—mostly because he couldn't even name them all.

Finally he said, as lightly as he could, "Eve Donnelly with a short skirt and swearing like a sailor? Someone would have noticed and the gossips would have gone crazy."

She shook her head. "I was home for an hour before Dad told me to get out. He didn't want anyone else to see me like that, of course. I should have marched up and down Main Street but, after getting up my nerve to walk into their house like that and then the emotions of fighting with them, I didn't have the energy. I drove back to Kearney that same afternoon. I didn't come home again after that for a couple of years."

Kevin stood up, unable to sit with the emotions coursing through him, and paced to the fridge. He pulled it open without a clue as to what he wanted. "What about your mom?"

Eve sniffed and he gripped the fridge door, wanting to grab her and strangle her parents at the same time.

"She never stood up to Dad," she said quietly. "His was the final say, in all things, all the time. She never argued with him. I'm not saying she *wanted* me to leave, but if came down to picking sides, Dad would always win."

Kevin stared into the fridge, seeing nothing but a red cloud of anger and resentment. "And he didn't come to you? Didn't call? Didn't try to reach out or anything?"

"Nope. His ideas weren't going to change. He was never going to think what I was doing was okay and if I was going to keep doing it, then he didn't have anything else to say. I knew what his expectations were and if I wasn't going to meet them, then he didn't see the point in fighting."

Kevin finally pulled a soda that he didn't want from the fridge and slammed the door. He'd let her go? Said "see ya' later" to his only daughter, his only *child*?

He turned to face her again. "But then you did finally talk to them again?" he asked. He wanted to feel better about this. He wanted to know that they'd at least *tried*.

She nodded. "That really crazy stage lasted about two years, then I was with Zach—and still not living a life my dad would have been proud of—for another two. But then I..." She bit her bottom lip, running her finger up and down the side of her glass, clearly thinking. "Finally I got into trouble where I really needed some help and I swallowed my pride and called him."

He wanted to know what trouble. He wanted to know everything. Instead, he gripped the edge of the counter and made his voice calm when he said, "What happened?"

The sadness was back in her eyes. "He said I needed to live with my choices. I'd purposefully followed a path I knew he didn't approve of. He told me that he'd taught me right and wrong for eighteen years and he didn't really know what else he could add that hadn't already been said." She stopped and swallowed, blinking rapidly. "He said that if I was going to ignore everything I knew and then cry when it turned out badly, he was no longer obligated or motivated to be involved in my life."

Kevin stared at her. What the fuck was that? What kind of father said something like that to their child? And this was a guy who Kevin had listened to on Sunday mornings, whose words had come back in later years when he was trying to get his life straight?

"That was it? He didn't help? And you don't see them anymore?"

"He's proven that he had nothing else to say. Mom's never gone against him. It's been ten years since I talked to either of them."

Kevin couldn't imagine. Even as disappointed as he was in his dad, he couldn't imagine not having him around, not talking to him. Especially by his father's choice. He slumped onto his stool. "Eve, I don't know what to say."

She shook her head. "You don't have to say anything. There's nothing to say." She shrugged. "It is what it is."

"No, it's not what it is," he said reaching for her hand. "It all started because of us. Because of me you're cut off from your family."

She let him hold her hand, but she shook her head. "I'm cut off because my father, the guy who literally preached unconditional love, cut himself off from me. It's his fault, Kevin, and it's his loss."

It was clear that she was sad and hurt, in spite of her tough words. And there was something else underneath it—a distrust or a cynicism that he wasn't used to from her. She'd said something similar in her get-Kevin-back speech—about how real love didn't change with time or mistakes.

Yet, she'd been let down in that department by two men who meant the most to her—her father and *him*.

Kevin felt like he'd swallowed a ball of cement. It sat heavy and hard in his gut.

"It doesn't matter what he thinks about us now," she said.

"But I'm thinking of writing to let them know. I want them to know. And I want to prove to you that I want everyone to know."

He tugged on her hand, bringing her around the corner of the island to him. She stepped between his knees and he enfolded her in a hug.

"I have a few things to prove to you too," he said softly.

"Like what?"

"Like the fact that being with you is absolutely where I want to be." He slid his hand into her hair, keeping her cheek against his heart. "And that I'll be here every single day. And that I don't want anything more than I want you just like this."

She cuddled close. "You can have me however you want me."

It turned out he wanted her on the kitchen island and on the living room couch.

As they lay with their limbs tangled on the sofa, Kevin rolled and glanced at the clock.

"What time did Drew say he'd call?" he asked.

"When he was ready to come home." Eve also looked over at the clock. It was after seven. "I wonder if he has homework."

"We should probably go get him," Kevin said. He wasn't proud of it, but he'd enjoyed the time while Drew was at his friend's. And not because he'd spent most of that time naked with Eve. It was because Drew was somewhere he was happy and Kevin could feel good about that, rather than worrying about things or being frustrated because Drew wouldn't talk to him.

"Probably." Eve pushed herself off of his chest, then off of the couch. Then she paused. "Did I say which friend he was with?"

Kevin sat up and reached for his underwear and jeans. "No, I don't think so."

She frowned. "I don't remember him telling me. But it has to be Matt or Tanner, right?"

She called Tanner's house first. Drew wasn't there. He wasn't at Matthew's either.

"Is there any chance Drew mentioned where he was going after school to Matt?" Eve asked Matt's mom.

She reported he'd gone home for dinner.

"Home?" Eve repeated. "But he isn't here."

"Oh," she said a moment later. "Really? Why would he think of that?"

She paused to listen. Then, "Oh, okay. That helps, thanks."

"Well?" Kevin demanded as soon as she disconnected.

"He went home. To his house. With Libby and Lacey, the roommates."

"Libby and Lacey?" Kevin repeated. "Seriously?"

Eve pulled her clothes on. "Yeah, Heather's been taking a class on Thursday nights so he hangs with the girls. They get pizza and watch reality TV. I guess he missed it."

Terrific. Reality TV and pizza with two twenty-somethings. For a guy ten years older it would be his idea of heaven. But Drew was ten. And Kevin's responsibility.

"Let's go," he said grimly, grabbing his keys off the table by the door.

Five minutes later they pulled up in front of a tiny house with two cars parked out front and seemingly every light in the place on.

As they approached the door, they heard a female shriek and then laughter.

Eve put a hand on his arm as he reached for the door. "Hey, take it easy here, okay? Nobody really did anything wrong." He was clearly tense.

"They shouldn't assume he can come over and hang out anytime he wants to."

"They didn't really have a reason to think that he couldn't

come over," Eve said. "This is the routine. He lives with them, Kevin. They're more normal for him than we are."

He didn't reply as he raised his fist and pounded on the door.

The door swung open almost immediately.

"Hi."

The young girl who greeted them in a tank top and cut off sweat pants was breathing hard. Her blonde hair was pulled up into a ponytail and she was barefoot, her toes painted neon blue. She could have passed for sixteen. And she was covered in silly string.

"Are you Libby or Lacey?" Kevin asked.

"Lacey," she said with a big smile.

"Great." Kevin sighed. "Is Drew here?"

"Of course he is." She tipped her head. "You're his brother, huh?"

"Yep."

Lacey looked at Eve. "Hi, Eve."

"Hi, Lacey."

"Come on in." Lacey stepped back. "Here, you might need this." She handed him a can of string.

Kevin looked at it and sighed again.

Eve followed him into the house. "We were—"

Drew came thundering through the room, chased by another girl with silly string.

He was shrieking and laughing and Libby quickly caught him, pulled him to the floor and covered his face in bright pink sticky string.

Eve looked from the little boy to Kevin. Kevin's mouth was literally hanging open.

She stifled a grin. It was great for Kevin to see Drew as a kid who laughed and had fun. Who was comfortable and happy.

"I think everything looks fine here," she said.

"Hey, Drew, your brother's here," Lacey said.

He and Libby both rolled to look up at Eve and Kevin.

"Hi," Libby said, tickling Drew's ribs.

"Um, hi." Kevin looked and sounded stunned.

Libby pushed herself to her feet. "He doesn't have to go until after DETAI does he?"

"DETAI?" Kevin asked.

"Don't Even Think About It," Libby said.

"Don't even think about what?" Kevin asked, frowning.

"The TV show. Don't Even Think About It is a reality show where—"

"Never mind," Kevin cut her off.

"Do you have homework?" Eve asked Drew, to cover Kevin's rudeness.

"Nope." Drew wasn't even looking at Kevin. A minute ago he was laughing and enjoying, now he looked embarrassed.

"Did you have supper?" she asked.

"Yeah. Pizza and Oreos."

"That's it? What about vegetables, milk?" Kevin asked.

Eve rolled her eyes.

Libby said, "We always have carrot sticks and apples too." She nudged Drew with her foot.

"We dip the apples in peanut butter," Drew said, seemingly just to be contrary. "And sometimes we put chocolate chips in the peanut butter."

"Peanut butter is good for you," Eve felt the need to point out.

"I dip mine in marshmallow cream," Lacey said, clearly not overly concerned about Kevin's disapproval.

"They're still apples," Eve interjected.

"Sometimes I just eat the marshmallow cream with a spoon," Lacey said. She crossed her arms, clearly challenging Kevin.

Libby crossed to her and nudged her with her elbow. "Heather gave us Thursdays as a free night. We hang out and have fun, eat junk. It's not like he does it all the time."

"Fine." Kevin's jaw was tight. "He needs to come home now."

Libby glanced at Drew. "We were hoping maybe he could stay over tonight."

"No," Kevin said quickly and firmly, "it's a school night."

"We finished his math homework when he first got here," Libby said.

"He doesn't even have a bed here anymore," Kevin said, "that's at my place."

Eve watched Kevin's face. He seemed almost…jealous. And protective.

"We'll camp out here in the living room," Lacey said. "We've done it lots of times, even when his bed was here."

"He has school tomorrow."

Eve started to jump in, but Lacey gave Kevin a look that clearly said *you're an idiot* and Eve settled back to watch. It was probably better for Kevin to hear that he was overreacting from more than just her.

"It would be *such* a hardship, but I guess I could take him with me when I leave for work in the morning and drop him off *way* across town."

In reality, they lived about three blocks from the school. Which had been one consideration when Heather had chosen the house.

Kevin frowned at her. "You work?"

Lacey drew herself up tall and frowned right back. "Yeah, my hooker corner is right across from the school."

Libby grabbed Lacey's arm and pulled her back. "She's the receptionist at the medical clinic," she told Kevin.

"What about you?" Kevin asked.

"I'm still going to school," Libby said, her eyes wide at the way he snapped. "I'll be applying to law school in the spring."

Kevin looked at her, then to Lacey. "He needs to come home."

Lacey started to respond, but Libby squeezed her arm. "Okay. Fine. How about next week we do this again though and we plan to have him overnight? That way everyone knows what's gonna happen ahead of time."

Kevin didn't respond right away, but he glanced at Drew.

Eve followed his eyes.

Drew was sitting in the middle of the floor, his eyes on the carpet. He looked completely dejected.

"Fine," Kevin finally answered. "And I'll send an extra jar of marshmallow cream with him."

Eve grinned at that. Libby smiled.

Lacey lifted a shoulder, unimpressed by his peace offering. "Get the brand name stuff. The generic sucks."

Kevin rolled his eyes then said to Drew, "Let's go, bud. Time to get home."

Drew got to his feet slowly, trudged to the mat by the door, put his shoes on—slowly—and finally shrugged into his coat. The whole process took five times longer than it should have.

The muscle in Kevin's cheek was jumping by the time they opened the door to leave, but he said nothing.

Eve put her arm around Drew's shoulders and pulled him up against her as they walked down the sidewalk to the car. "You ever heard of Nutella?"

"Maybe." He sounded like someone had told him that there would be no Christmas.

"I'll get you some. It's the best for apples."

None of them spoke on the way back to the house. The boys because they were both pouting, Eve because she was pretty much on Drew's side but didn't think she should say that in front of him. Or at all. That would surely start a fight with Kevin.

As soon as they walked through the door, Drew threw his coat on the floor, stomped up the stairs and slammed the bedroom door.

Kevin sighed heavily and pushed his fingers through his hair. "Dammit."

"I'm on Drew's side, by the way," she said.

Kevin frowned. "What about, exactly? Me being an ass, that Lacey and Libby are way more fun that I am, or that sleeping on the couch at his own house is better than sleeping in his bed at my house?"

She went straight to him and wrapped her arms around him. "Well, when you put it that way...all of the above." She hugged him tight.

He wrapped his arms around her and sighed. "I told my dad and Heather that *I* would take care of him. They agreed. If Libby and Lacey were best for him, they would have asked them, right?"

"Right." She pulled back. "There's no question that when it comes to taking care of him overall, you're the best choice. But that doesn't mean that they can't see him at all or help out once in awhile or that when he's with them it's bad for him."

"But I'm already passing off some of the responsibility to you."

"So?"

"I need to do... the rest."

"Why? You're not his father, Kevin. You're his big brother. And you don't have to be perfect at this."

"You keep saying that." He let go of her and stepped back.

"Because it's true. Lacey and Libby don't have to be perfect either. Is marshmallow cream the best thing for him to eat? No. But it won't hurt him. Is watching *Don't Even Think About It* the most intellectually stimulating thing they could do? No. But it also won't hurt him. Stop worrying about doing everything right every second."

"Someone has to do everything right every second for him, Eve." Kevin turned away and paced to the window. "Or at least, someone should try."

Her heart melted a little even as she worried. *Perfect.* There was that word again. Kevin was trying so hard to be perfect and he clearly expected everyone else to do the same. That was a sure way to set himself up for disappointment. Because no one was perfect and they all screwed up and broke other people's hearts.

"Good intentions are great, Kevin," she said carefully, "but give yourself a break. You're going to make some mistakes."

"Like tonight?"

"What do you mean?"

"You think that pulling him away from the good time girls was the wrong thing to do?"

She quirked an eyebrow. "The good time girls?" She waited until he turned to face her. "Don't you think that's a little harsh?"

"Really? You think Lacey and Libby are good influences?"

She decided not to mention how much Drew knew about PMS or what he did with the girls and his mom during 'period week'. "I think they're fun and clearly care about him."

"Kids have fun on their own. They can't help it," Kevin said. "The adults around him are supposed to be the ones who are teaching him things and showing him a good example."

"It was pizza and silly string," Eve said, "it's not like they were playing strip poker and holding up liquor stores." She swallowed hard. What would he think about her influence on Drew if he knew all about her past? She was afraid she knew exactly what he would think.

"If they'd been playing strip poker, Drew would have won easily. Neither of them were wearing much to work with."

She swallowed her first retort about him noticing so much about what Lacey and Libby had not been wearing. "Maybe instead of rules and dress codes, pizza and silly string would help him open up to you."

Kevin's frown deepened. "I'm not worried about that. As long as I'm taking care of him, he doesn't have to like me."

Uh-huh. Sure. Having Drew like him wasn't important. "Right. As long as you follow all the rules, you can't go wrong."

This was not the Kevin she'd known in high school. He certainly hadn't worried much about rules and what others thought of him.

"Right." He didn't look totally convinced. Thank God.

"But you are going to let him hang out with the girls next week?" she asked. "Even if it's all marshmallow cream and fun?"

"I guess it's too much to ask that they do Bible study instead," he said wryly.

"That's the only way to be a good influence?" she asked, trying to keep her tone light.

"Of course not. You think they might make blankets for the homeless?"

He was joking. Surely he was joking. He had to be joking. Or she was in deep trouble.

"Are *you* going to make blankets for the homeless with him?" she asked.

"It was an example. But yes, I'm going to do things with him that teach him things—how to be responsible, how to be giving, how to make a difference."

"What kind of things are you going to do?"

That seemed to throw him off and he was clearly thinking fast. "I can take him to the Youth Center I volunteer at."

"That would be great," she agreed. "What else?"

"Maybe we'll find a community service project here in town to help with."

"Okay. Sure. That's great too."

"Maybe we'll…find a stray dog and adopt him."

Wow, he was clearly reaching. "Dogs are great. I think Drew would love to have a dog."

"Yeah, great." Kevin looked less than convinced.

That was exactly what he needed—something else to feel guilty about when he didn't throw the stick far enough or didn't get the thing's favorite dog food.

She looked at him, seeing his frustration, his concern. "If we hadn't been having sex while Drew was with Libby and Lacey would you be feeling this bad about it?"

"I wasn't being completely responsible and available, was I?"

"He didn't need you to be responsible or available. He was

with them."

"But if you hadn't been lying naked next to me I would have at least asked where he was going and he wouldn't have ended up over there in the first place."

Ah. She straightened. "So, you're actually upset with me because I didn't ask where he was going to be."

"It makes sense to ask that, doesn't it?"

"Of course it does. But I also trusted Drew to know what was okay and what wasn't."

"He's ten."

"Why would he think it wasn't okay to be with them? He *lives* with them, Kevin."

"Not right now, he doesn't," he said stubbornly. "Heather needs them to help make her house payment. But I don't."

"They were just having fun," she tried again, "and fun is a good thing."

"Well, everything he's going to have for the next six months is going to come from someone he can really look up to!"

"You?" she asked.

"Us."

That probably should have made her happy. They were an *us* in Kevin's mind. And she recognized that he was feeling inadequate. He wanted to be a positive role model to a kid who had yet to say three words to him, but who would talk and laugh with Lacey and Libby.

But she couldn't pull out a lot of sympathy for him. He was judging Libby and Lacey based on a jar of marshmallow cream for God's sake. That was hardly rational or fair. "You're being ridiculous," she told him. "You're jealous of two girls that he's been around so much that he knows about their PMS."

"He knows about their *what*?" Kevin demanded.

Dammit.

"Did you say PMS?"

"So?" she shot back. "It's a normal bodily function."

"Jesus, Eve." Kevin pushed his hand through his hair. "He's

ten. He shouldn't know a damned thing about PMS."

"Argh!" She stomped to the table and grabbed her purse. "I had no idea you were this judgmental."

"Where are you going?" He started for her as she yanked the front door open.

"I'm leaving."

"No, wait. What about Drew?"

She turned and planted a hand on her hip. "What about him? You're here. You're the great and amazing responsible influence."

"He won't talk to me."

"Yeah, well, you better figure that out because you don't want him hanging out with me anymore."

Kevin frowned and stalked forward. "Of course I do. You're wonderful with him."

"If you don't want him spending time with Libby and Lacey —two intelligent, fun and sweet girls—you definitely don't want him with me."

Kevin was really going to have to get over this idea of perfection if he wanted to hang out with her. Otherwise he was going to be really disappointed.

"Eve, I need you."

He sounded so worried that she almost caved. Almost.

He did need her. And not only for help with Drew. She was surer of that every time they were together. He also needed to figure out that what he thought he needed, and what he really needed, weren't exactly the same thing.

He needed her because no one else would ever love him as much as she did.

Even when he was being an ass.

"Yes, you do need me," she said sweetly. "Isn't irony a bitch?"

"What's ironic about that?" Kevin asked, his eyebrows drawn together tightly.

"That you need me, but that you don't want Drew around

someone like me."

"What does that mean?" Kevin demanded.

"Well, I can't imagine that, with the way you feel about silly string, that you'd tolerate someone with an felony arrest record around Drew."

He stared at her. "*What*?"

"That's right. Me. The one you're going to be really missing here in about ten seconds."

She took a small bit of satisfaction in his look of shock before she turned and stomped down the front steps, the door slamming behind her.

Kevin yanked the door open and started after her, but she was already in her car. He stared after her until her car disappeared at the end of the block. Fuck. And he didn't use that word mildly.

What the hell had just happened?

Eve had left, that's what had happened. Angry.

And a felon?

What was that all about?

She'd said she had some wild years, some times her father had adamantly not approved of. But an arrest? For what?

He didn't think going after her and demanding to know was the best move at the moment. That's what he wanted to do though.

But Drew was here.

Dammit.

Kevin headed back into the house and stood at the bottom of the stairs staring up. Drew was up there and Kevin was here alone with him.

Did her trouble with the law matter? At the moment, not at all.

Sighing, he made himself ask the question seriously. Did it

matter what she'd done in the past?

He thought about the woman he'd made love to and held as he slept. He thought about the woman who had rescheduled her life and reordered her priorities for him and his little brother, the woman who made Drew so obviously feel better. He thought about the woman who had faced the start of her adulthood and the last ten years without the family that had been her foundation. And he thought about that sweet girl who had looked up at him as she said "I do" all those years ago.

He'd seen his future in her eyes.

He'd known that those were the eyes he wanted to look into at the happiest moments—their child's first day of school, his retirement, their fiftieth wedding anniversary—and the darkest moments—the illnesses, the hard financial times, the funerals—that would make up their life.

They'd missed happy and hard times already. She wasn't there when he'd graduated as an Academic All American or when his knee rehab made him sweat and cuss and almost cry. He hadn't been there for twelve birthdays or when her grandmother died.

He wasn't going to lose any more moments.

No matter what she'd done.

He trusted and wanted her sweetness, her intelligence, her humor, her sense of right and wrong. He'd always been able to count on that.

But what about now? She'd clearly changed. Her rebellions and partying had caused a rift with her father. And an *arrest*?

This was getting complicated. And confusing. Definitely confusing.

He was in love with one version of Eve. But was it the real version?

He was pulled from his thoughts by the sound of footsteps upstairs. Drew was up there.

Sighing, he headed up. Drew had school tomorrow, so he needed to get in bed.

Kevin knocked and then pushed the door open when there was no answer.

"Hey."

Drew was already in bed. His pajamas were on and his hair brushed. Kevin figured he'd brushed his teeth too.

"You okay?" he asked.

Drew stared at the book in his lap.

"Eve had to go home. But she'll be here tomorrow." Kevin hoped to hell she would be anyway. He had to head back to work at five-thirty.

Nothing. Not a smile or even a glance up.

Kevin sighed and stood. He felt like he'd been sighing a lot today.

He'd reached the door when he heard, "Eve said that she likes fiction books because they tell us stories about the world the way we wish it could be. And that if we can enjoy those stories, it means there's hope for us to help make the world like those stories."

Kevin turned back. "I like that idea. It makes sense."

Drew nodded. "What's your favorite book?"

Kevin thought about that. "When I was your age, I didn't read a lot. I was all about sports," he admitted.

Drew looked up. "Okay. What do you like about football so much?"

Kevin straightened. Drew was talking to him. And actually asking him questions. About *him*.

"Well, probably when I was your age, it was just about having fun. I loved being outside and playing with my friends. But then I started loving the game itself. The strategy of designing plays and stuff. But then..." He thought about it. "Actually, all along, my favorite part was the teamwork. The feeling that when you were out there on the field, you had this job to do but you could also count on the ten other guys to do their job and that all together you were doing an even bigger job. And then when the defense, my half of the team, was on the sidelines, we could depend on the eleven guys on the offense to go out there and do their jobs. It was this cool feeling of being part of something bigger."

Drew was watching him and Kevin just let that all sink in. He hoped it made sense.

"Is that how you feel with the guys you work with too?"

Kevin was surprised by the question, and that Drew had given his job any thought, but he nodded. "Yeah. Very much so."

"You go out and save people from accidents right?"

"Sometimes. Other times we go when someone gets sick at home. Or if they're involved in an incident at work, or maybe at a concert, or at a restaurant or something. Medical emergencies can happen in lots of places."

"And you all have a certain job to do."

"Yep. And we're just part of that team too. We get the person to the hospital and turn them over to the next part of the team in the emergency department."

Drew was quiet for a long moment. "It must feel good to know that there are people who you know will do what they're supposed to do."

Kevin had to clear his throat as emotion tightened it. He nodded. "It's the most important thing in my life." He wasn't sure he'd really *fully* realized it until that moment. But the most pivotal times in his life had been when people had been there for him as they'd promised. And when they hadn't.

"I can understand that," his little brother said quietly.

Yeah, Kevin bet he could. Unfortunately, Drew was learning how much it could hurt when someone didn't have your back much younger than he should have to.

"I'll be right downstairs," Kevin said. *He* was going to be there for Drew. No matter what.

"Thanks," Drew said.

"Of course."

"'Night, Kevin."

"Goodnight, Drew."

# CHAPTER
# NINE

KEVIN NEEDED to leave for work at five thirty. Eve showed up at five twenty-two.

"You're here," he said with equal parts relief and frustration. They didn't have time to talk now. He'd looked all over town for her earlier with no success and she hadn't answered her phone or returned any of his messages.

"I told you I would be here whenever you needed to work," she said with a frown.

"But you're mad at me."

"Yes, I am. But that doesn't mean I'm not going to show up." She held up a jar of Nutella and an old DVD of *Star Wars*. "And you're just going to have to deal with this," she told him.

He sighed. "No Bible study or blankets for the homeless for you tonight either, huh?"

"No. But if I see any stray dogs, I'm going to let them have your bed."

He leaned in. "*You* better be in my bed."

"I'm couchin' it," she said, stepping back. "I don't want to get convict cooties on your sheets."

He frowned. "Yeah, speaking of that—"

"You'd better get going," she said, turning toward the kitchen. "Don't want anybody in Omaha dying 'cause you're not there."

Damn. She was right. He was already running late.

"I'm calling you later," he said as he shouldered his bag and pushed the screen door open. "And you better answer. We have some things to talk about."

"Well, call after nine. I'll have the joints rolled by then, but the orgy won't have started yet." She disappeared around the corner.

*Hilarious.* Kevin stomped to his truck. She was absolutely hilarious.

💋

"Kev! Someone to see you!"

He and all the guys swiveled to find Kayla escorting Mrs. Rosner, the caseworker for Drew, into the ER break room. He quickly got to his feet. "Mrs. Rosner." He extended his hand.

She took it. "Mr. Campbell. How is everything going with Drew?"

That was a great question. "Fine. It's been an adjustment for us all."

"I can imagine." She looked around. "Can we chat? I'd like to do a follow up and figured it was easiest to catch you here at work."

"Sure. It's slow right now. If you don't mind the chance of being interrupted."

"It's fine."

He gestured toward the round table to one side. "Is here all right?"

Mrs. Rosner glanced at the other men seated on the couches around the TV. None of them were looking at the screen of course.

"I don't mind if they're here," Kevin said before she could ask. "They know everything anyway."

"That's up to you," she said, moving toward the table.

He sat across from her. He'd forgotten about the follow up interview. And the hearing. What about that? He still wasn't legally Drew's guardian.

How had all of this slipped his mind?

"Things are going well with Drew then?" she asked, pulling a file from her bag.

"For the most part," he said. He wasn't going to mention the not talking to him, the marshmallow cream or the fact that he'd pretty much blown off picking Drew up from school because he was sleeping off a major orgasm. He shifted on his chair. "I know he isn't thrilled with the situation, but his teacher thinks he's managing well in class."

"You spoke with his teacher?"

"Yes. I wanted her opinion."

Mrs. Rosner made a notation. "And you're living in your mom and dad's house?"

"Yes."

"Tell me about the routine so far. Anything consistent?"

He swallowed. Eve was the most consistent thing so far. "I'm going to be working three nights a week, not consecutive. Those days, I'll leave after dinner with Drew. He'll be sleeping while I work. When I get home he'll be at school, so I can sleep. Then I'll be there to pick him up from school and get to spend that evening and night with him, take him to school the next day, all of that."

"And who's staying with Drew while you're here at work?"

"Um…" A woman with an arrest on her record. An arrest for something he still knew nothing about. Shit.

"You know," he said conversationally. "I thought about bringing him to Omaha with me those nights and having him stay with some friends, but obviously that will mess with his school schedule too much. And I didn't want to move him to Omaha for good...or for the six months."

"I would agree that seems best. Who is with Drew when you work?"

His thoughts swirled. He couldn't tell her about Eve, could he? She'd do an instant background check, Eve would fail it and then he'd not only be in trouble for having her as a caregiver, but it could ruin *his* chances of being Drew's guardian. He had to give her a name though. Something. Someone who would not only appease Mrs. Rosner, but who might actually need to be Drew's caregiver going forward. Drew and his secure placement with Kevin had to be the priority here.

He really only had one option and it irritated the hell out of him. Still he made himself say, "I think keeping the routine as stable as possible is best, so I think the two women he and his mother have been living with are the best options to help out."

He tried to sound mature and confident. And not at all like he was making stuff up as he went. He hadn't asked Lacey and Libby to help with Drew, but somehow he knew they would say yes. They were clearly a big part of his life, and, they'd probably do better on their background check than Eve would.

Mrs. Rosner nodded. "Good. I have their names right here. I'll run the checks on them tonight."

He swallowed hard and nodded.

"And how's your wife?"

Ah, so she did remember that detail. Kevin worked on not choking or stammering. "Fine. We've...talked." Visions of Eve in the shower, soap bubbles clinging to her nipples, water sluicing over her skin assaulted him. That's what happened when you went eight years without sex, he supposed. But they *had* talked. Too.

"Are you working on reconciling?" Mrs. Rosner asked, watching him closely.

Until last night they certainly had been.

He still wanted to. He needed her. Not just for Drew. That

was awesome, but temporary. However, in less than a week with her back in his life, he knew that he wanted it all—going home to a house where he'd find love notes with his breakfast and her little pink razor next to his big black one in the shower, the smell of her perfume lingering in his car after he took her out for dinner and strands of her hair on his pillow from where he'd made love to her the night before.

But dammit, could he really risk Drew going into foster care because he wanted to share toothpaste with Eve?

That was selfish. He couldn't screw this up for Drew. He and Eve would have to figure it out *around* the little boy who needed them even more than he needed Eve in his bed every night. And that was saying a lot.

Kevin locked the rambling thoughts down. He'd had the whole drive to Omaha to think and stew and all it had accomplished was giving him a pounding headache. This wasn't going to do him any good right now.

"No, I wouldn't say that we were reconciling," he told the caseworker. At least not at the moment. She was way too mad for any reconciling right now. "That's, um…"

"Complicated?" Dooley suggested.

"Yes, a *complicated* subject," Kevin answered, shooting his friend a grateful glance.

"I imagine it is," Mrs. Rosner said. She made a note in the file.

Kevin resisted the urge to rip it from her hands and see what she'd written.

"To be clear, Mr. Campbell," she said when her pen stopped moving, "if you do reconcile and your wife assumes a caregiving role with Drew on a regular basis and/or you live together, I'll need to include her in interviews and so on."

"I'm clear." He was crystal clear on the fact that this was a damned mess.

He looked at Mrs. Rosner. The woman seemed nice enough

but he could tell that she took her job seriously. He didn't think she would like the arrest record. Whatever it was for.

Ten minutes later, Mrs. Rosner was satisfied with the interview. "I'll need to come do a home visit to finish up the assessment," she said, "then we can get the hearing scheduled."

"Great." He walked her to the door. "Thanks."

When he turned back to face his friends, he knew what he would find.

"Are you *insane*?" Sam asked. "You lied about being involved with Eve?"

"You're dead," Dooley told him.

"That was cold, man," Mac agreed.

"What the fuck was I supposed to do?" he asked.

They all stared. He never said fuck. Well, almost never.

"You might be the only guy I know who thinks clearer when he's *not* getting laid," Sam commented.

Kevin frowned at him. "This isn't about getting laid. Or not getting laid."

It wasn't *exactly* about getting laid. But as Dooley had said just days before, sex wasn't frosting on the cake. It was part of the cake, one of the main ingredients, and with Eve that was especially true.

And now he'd had a taste.

He was so screwed.

"So, what's it about?" Dooley asked.

He hadn't told them anything about Eve and Lacey and Libby. Where should he even start? Especially when he had a suspicion that he wasn't handling it well.

"Eve and I had a fight."

Mac tried to hide his grin behind his coffee cup, but he wasn't fast enough. Kevin frowned at him. "What?"

"It's nice to have you in the club, man," Mac said.

"The club?"

"The married guys club. Don't worry—make-up sex really is great."

"Like you and Sara ever have make-up sex," Dooley said. "You always let her have her way and everyone's happy."

Mac grinned again. "Sometimes we fight so we can make up."

"You could buy her flowers," Sam muttered, instantly shifting into big brother mode.

"Do you buy Dani flowers after you fight?" Mac asked.

Sam didn't answer and they all laughed. Flowers *instead* of make-up sex? Not in Sam Bradford's world.

"Besides, if I'm gonna spend money on something to get me on her good side, I'd better go to Tease or order from Scandalous," Mac went on, naming a local adult toy and costume shop and an online erotic boutique.

Sam groaned and covered his ears. And that made Mac happy since he'd mentioned it only to torture Sam. It was especially funny though considering Sam and Dani were regulars at Tease too.

"What did you do, man?" Dooley asked Kevin. "We can help you pick out something appropriate at Tease but the gift should fit the crime."

"*I* didn't do anything," he said. "It was Eve."

The guys all sat looking at him.

"What?" he asked.

"You think it was her fault?"

"It was," Kevin said. "No question."

"Uh-huh," Mac said.

"Let's hear what you think she did," Sam said, crossing his ankle over his knee.

"Did she run up the credit cards?" Mac asked Kevin.

"I know—she forbid you from ever seeing Dooley again, right?" Sam tossed out with a grin. "Said she could never be with a guy who had friends like him?"

"Fuck you," Dooley shot back, but he was smiling too. "She loved me."

"She got arrested," Kevin blurted out.

God help him, but he couldn't listen to them joking around when he really was feeling lost here.

All three of his friends turned to stare at him.

"Who got arrested?" Sam said, suspicious.

"Eve."

"Last night?" Dooley demanded.

"For what?" Mac asked.

Kevin slumped into the closest chair and laid his head back. "Not last night."

"Well, when?" Dooley asked.

"I...don't know."

"For *what*?" Mac repeated.

Kevin groaned. "I don't know."

"So you don't really know anything?" Dooley asked. "But you're pissed at her."

"I'm not *pissed*. I'm...concerned." Though that didn't seem quite strong enough to describe his emotions.

"Dude, you're suddenly married and raising a kid. You should totally be concerned. And I'm not talking about the arrest."

Kevin opened his eyes and looked at Sam. "And the arrest shouldn't make me *more* concerned?"

He lifted a shoulder. "You don't know anything about it."

That wasn't true. "She was arrested as an accessory to a felony."

Mac frowned at him. "Well, that's...something."

"Yeah, but..."

"What. Did. She. *Do*?" Sam asked.

"She was *arrested*. And she's helping me with Drew," Kevin said.

"It's not like she was arrested yesterday while Drew was driving the get-away car," Dooley said.

"I know but—"

"I have an arrest record," Mac said, stretching his arms out along the back of the couch. Mac was a big guy and sitting like

WHY YOU SHOULD NEVER KISS YOUR EX-HUSBAND  191

that he seemed to be challenging Kevin to question his good influence.

"I have an arrest record too," Dooley said. "So does Ben."

"You'd let any of us hang out with Drew, wouldn't you?" Sam asked.

He would. Of course he would. These men were some of the best people he knew. They would protect what was important to Kevin simply because it was important to Kevin.

*So would Eve.*

He wasn't questioning her loyalty. He was mad…at himself. He hadn't asked any questions. He'd assumed because he so wanted her to be the same girl he'd always loved, that there was nothing to talk about or be concerned with. And now Drew might be at risk.

"Yes."

"So, the arrest doesn't automatically mean that she's bad for Drew," Dooley said. "Why are your panties in such a wad?"

"I know about your arrest records." Hell, he'd bailed two of them out himself.

"You're mad she didn't tell you?" Mac asked.

"Maybe a little."

"That's not why you're mad," Dooley said.

No, it wasn't. Hell, he couldn't even be mad at her correctly.

Kevin sighed. "Then why am I mad?"

"Because she's not the sweet, innocent, perfect little preacher's daughter she used to be."

Yep, that was absolutely it. And he was way more stressed than he was mad.

The clock on the wall in the break room ticked thirty times. Finally Kevin said, "She's changed."

"People tend to do that over the course of twelve years," Mac said.

Kevin sighed. "I'm trying to bare my soul here."

Mac grinned. "I don't expect this will take long. Your soul's been pretty clean for quite awhile."

He loved these guys. He really did. He couldn't remember why at the moment, but he was sure he did.

"What you're saying is that now you know Eve isn't perfect, she's not as attractive to you," Sam said with a nod. "She's tainted."

Kevin scowled at his friend. "She's not tainted. Don't be an idiot."

"So, what's the problem here?" Sam asked.

"She's…changed."

"So have you."

"Yeah, for the better."

Three wide-eyed stares met his.

"Wow," Sam said.

"Really cold," Mac said with some wonder.

Kevin puffed out a breath. "I know. I sound like a dick. But I'm…scared." There, he'd admitted it.

"Scared?" Dooley said. "Of little Eve?"

Yes, definitely. Of the changes in her. Of the idea that maybe he wasn't the right guy for her now. Or she wasn't the right girl for him. Of the idea that maybe nothing in life was absolute and steadfast.

Her father had turned out not to be. His father had turned out not to be. His relationship with Eve, his football career, even his body—the thing that he'd always depended on to make him popular and noteworthy and to make his dad proud—had ended up being unstable.

If Eve Donnelly couldn't be counted on, nothing could.

He shrugged. "She's changed," he said again, not able to explain it better than that.

"Lots of things have changed," Dooley pointed out.

"Yes. Exactly." Kevin leaned forward with his elbows on his knees and dropped his head, staring at the floor. "You guys have all changed. Your girls are awesome, but things are different. Things with my parents have changed. I have Drew. Eve is back in my life. I…I want something to be the way I'm used to, the way it's always been. I'd hoped that would be *her*."

"You've changed too, buddy," Sam said, his voice gentler now. "You've changed more than any of us, probably."

"I know. And that shook my life most of all," he said. It was true. He'd changed. But it hadn't been easy and there were lots of times that he found himself tempted to go back to how things used to be.

Having a beer with the guys was easier than always ordering soda and water. Doing whatever he wanted to do was far easier than examining his intentions, and who might get hurt, and what the long-term consequences might be of every fucking decision. Flirting—and more—with women was far easier than resisting the temptation.

"So you were hoping Eve would be predictable and steady?" Dooley said.

"Right." And it was more than knowing what he could expect from and with her. It was also about her choices. She'd always known who she was, what she believed, what was important.

That stuff wasn't supposed to change.

Now, he wondered—she was obviously more sexually expe-rienced, she had gotten into some trouble with the cops—what else was different? What other choices had she made?

"I'm scared to find out what else might have changed."

No one answered him for a moment—not even sarcastically.

"You know, Kev," Dooley finally said, "it's possible that you're scaring her too."

He looked at his friend with surprise. "What do you mean?"

"You're different too and maybe she's worried, especially with her changes, that it's too much."

Kevin felt his stomach churn with trepidation. "You think?"

Dooley looked at the other guys. "Has that bothered you at all that as our lives have changed, as new people have come into our lives and we've had new experiences and worries and problems and challenges, has it worried you at all that *we* might change?"

Kevin opened his mouth to reply but then realized he couldn't answer that quickly.

Yes. As his friends had fallen in love, he'd worried how it would change their relationships with one another. And with him. How it might affect the team. How it might change their dynamic in the field. And personally.

But, they hadn't changed on him. Mac, Dooley and Sam were essentially the same guys they'd always been. They were more mellow, happier, less self-absorbed because of their wives and almost-wife. But it was more their lives that had changed versus the people they *were*. They had anniversaries and monogamy now, but they were still there for him, they still gave him opinions whether he wanted them or not and they still had his back whether it was on a call for work or when he was feeling his way through a new relationship.

Loving them, depending on them, trusting them wasn't hard.

Could he love and trust Eve even if she wasn't the same person deep down, underneath all the experiences and challenges?

Was he capable of loving her through major changes in her life?

He thought of his father and the disappointment of learning that his son's football career had been so important to him, then the disappointment of finding out about his infidelity. His feelings for his dad were shaky at the moment for sure. And his mom—she'd made Kevin's dad choose between her and his ten-year-old son. Could he forgive her for that? Get past it? Love her in the same way?

Kevin squeezed his eyes shut.

It was quite possible that all of this with Eve was very much *his* problem and his need for stability from the people in his life.

"I want her to be able to tell me anything," he finally answered honestly.

"But you're not sure," Dooley said.

"I guess not."

"Then you need to find out. Find out what changes there are and see how you feel about them."

"And keep in mind, we're all different. But I have to say that I think in every case we're *better*," Sam said.

Mac nodded. "Absolutely."

Dooley propped his feet up on the table. "Yep, change can be good."

But it was change. "I guess."

"For instance," Sam said, "sounds like you would have never taken the old Eve to Tease. What about the new Eve?"

"She's probably already been there," he muttered.

Sam laughed. "See, change isn't all bad."

"How about elevator sex?" Dooley asked. "Never with the old Eve, right?"

Definitely not. But the new Eve... Kevin's thoughts went immediately to how she'd touched herself on the couch. Elevators might be a possibility.

"What about being yourself?" Mac asked.

Kevin was surprised to find the topic off of sex already. "What do you mean?"

"Sounds like the old Eve was damned near perfect. And sweet. It's hard to be yourself with someone who's perfect." He glanced at Sam. "I should know. When you have a girl up on a pedestal, it's hard to realize she's real. And it's hard to be real yourself."

Kevin thought about that. He'd always been trying to be *good* with Eve. He'd worked on being who he thought he needed to be—who her father wanted him to be—instead of who he really was.

Damn, Mac had something there. "So..." he prompted, hoping for more insight.

"So, now that she's not quite perfect, it'll be easier to be your not-quite-perfect self. It'll be more real. And trust me, real is better. Finding someone you can be yourself with is the best thing there is."

Kevin thought about that. He wanted to get home and be real with Eve right then and there.

"Okay, since Mac is showing off with all his knowledge and deep thoughts," Dooley said. "*I'll* tell you something too."

Kevin could use all the help he could get. "Okay."

"You need to go home tonight. You need to talk to Eve. Then you need to make love to her until neither of you can move."

The heat hit him hard. He wanted her in his arms, moving with him, making those sounds…

"Be sure you do the talking first," Dooley said, clearly reading Kevin's thoughts.

"That would be great. But I'm working."

"Hey, guys, what's up?" Conner Dixon walked in as if it had been scripted.

"About time," Mac muttered at him.

"I came right over." Conner looked at Mac with a frown.

Conner clearly wanted Mac's approval, but Kevin—and everyone else—knew that the kid was going to have to work his ass off to get it. Eventually Mac would let up and mentor the younger guy who so obviously admired him, but he wouldn't make it easy. Conner should have never told Sara she smelled like cotton candy…and that he really liked cotton candy.

"Good thing you're here, Dixon," Sam said, getting to his feet. "Kevin here is heading home."

"I am?"

"You are," Dooley said.

Someone had texted Conner to come in for him. So Kevin could go home and talk to Eve.

He wasn't going to argue with the three best friends a guy could have. "Okay, I'll see you guys in a couple of days," he said, heading for his locker.

"And remember…make-up, *then* make-up sex," Sam called.

"Or make-up sex, make-up and then make-up sex again," Mac called. "That's how Sara, Sam's little sister, and I do it."

"You're an ass," Sam said to him.

"An ass your sister is crazy about," Mac reminded him. "Not that her ass doesn't make me a little crazy too."

"She could have done so much better," Sam muttered.

Mac's laughter was the last thing Kevin heard as the door shut behind him.

And these were the men giving him advice on women?

But he was grinning as he changed out of his uniform in record time and jogged to the parking lot.

# CHAPTER
# TEN

EVE EYED THE COUCH. Part of her wanted to sleep there. To make a point. If Kevin was going to be judgmental and unaccepting, then she wasn't so sure she wanted to be in his bed.

Of course, she knew that she definitely *should* refuse to be in his bed if he was going to be like that. But definitely refusing Kevin seemed an unlikely undertaking.

Besides, the point was going to be wasted. He wasn't here tonight and wouldn't be here until after she'd gone into work in the morning. So he wouldn't know where she'd slept anyway.

And she really wanted to sleep in his bed.

For years she'd dreamed of it. When she'd first fallen for him in high school, she'd imagined him in that bed and wished she could be there with him, in his arms all night. It had been more than a heated teenage fantasy. It had been a longing to be with him. Then, since their wedding night, it had been an even more painful desire.

Without him there, his bed still tempted her. It smelled like him and it was as close to him as she could get tonight.

Angry or not, she always wanted to be close to him.

So after she was sure Drew was asleep, she showered and crawled between Kevin's sheets.

Heat and need woke her a few hours later.

"I'm home."

The thick whisper swept over the skin of her neck and shoulder.

She became conscious of the room slowly, but kept her eyes closed, reveling in the sensation of a heavy hot hand on her stomach, rubbing back and forth over the skin between the top of her cotton drawstring pajama pants and the short T-shirt she wore.

"I know I shouldn't wake you up," he said against her shoulder blade.

She lay on her side and when she leaned back the solid form behind her didn't move.

Kevin's voice was husky against her ear. "But please let me touch you."

It wasn't a dream. He was here. "Work?" she asked, still climbing out of the cobwebs of sleep.

"Got someone to cover. Had to come home."

"You okay?" she asked.

He pressed closer and she realized he had on only boxers. His chest was bare and heat soaked through the thin cotton of her top and spread down her spine, the backs of her legs and to her feet. He was also hard. His erection pressed against her butt.

"I'm okay," he said. "And I know we need to talk, but I need you. Seeing you in my bed does something to me."

"Being in your bed does something to me, so that works out." She tried to roll back, but he didn't let her.

"I think this is nice, just like this," he said, his hand stealing down over the front of her pajama pants. "I'm wide awake. Let me wake you up," he breathed against her neck as she arched into his hand.

Every nerve in her body seemed be suddenly alive and jumping. "I don't think that's going to take long," she said breathlessly.

"Good. Wouldn't want you to miss the first orgasm."

He was only using one hand, but he easily undid the tie below her belly button, loosened the waistband and slipped his big hand into the front of her pants.

She wasn't wearing underwear—she never did at night—and he groaned as he discovered that fact. "It's like you were waiting for me," he said.

"I've been waiting for you for years," she said softly, without thinking.

His hand paused, his palm over her mound. She froze, wondering if she'd said something wrong, to jerk him out of the moment.

But his voice was even thicker as he said, "I need you to know that when I said those marriage vows to you, I meant them, Eve."

He ran his hand down, over her, the pad of his middle finger skimming over her clit, but not sliding inside.

"When I said that I wanted to love, honor and cherish you forever, I meant it." This time his finger nudged inside slightly, stroking up and down through her wetness.

She pulled in a breath. "I know."

"Do you?" he asked. "I screwed it up."

She felt tears prick in her eyes.

At one time, he would have fought any foe for her. But he wouldn't have—hadn't—fought *her*.

"I screwed it up too. First," she said.

She felt him breathe against her shoulder.

"It shouldn't have mattered," he said. "I should have been there. I should have fought harder."

But he wouldn't have pushed her for something she didn't want. That morning, standing in her father's church, she knew that Kevin believed she'd changed her mind, that she didn't want him. Or at least, that she didn't want him *enough*.

"You walked away because you were hurt, but also because *I* hadn't honored *you*, Kevin. You didn't know how much I needed you. You knew that I loved you, but you didn't know that..." She had to swallow to keep from crying.

His finger pressed in further, rubbing gently over her clit and making fire lick out and down her legs.

She gasped and her fist tightened on the sheet.

"I didn't know what?"

His touch made her want to do anything, tell him anything he wanted to hear. But it didn't feel manipulative. It felt intimate. Talking while letting him touch her like that, telling him things that she'd carried with her, in her soul, for so long, felt more intimate than she could ever be with anyone else.

"You didn't know that getting out of bed every morning after that was the hardest thing I'd ever had to do, that the sight or smell of Juicy Fruit gum made me want to cry for almost two years." That had been his favorite gum and he'd chewed it every time they were together so it reminded her of the taste of his kisses. "That I bought a Nebraska football jersey with your number and slept in it every night, that I drove with two girl-friends to Kansas City thinking I'd camp outside the stadium and somehow find you. Twice."

His finger, just one, pressed into her. He stroked deep as she gasped. Then he stopped, his finger deep inside her.

"More," he said roughly. "What else don't I know?"

"You don't know that I kept messing up—getting drunk, not eating, flunking classes—because I kept hoping that you would hear about it and come save me. If my dad didn't give a shit, I kept thinking that you would and it would prove to me that I had been right to marry you, to give you my life instead of him."

He stroked his finger in and out twice, deep and firm, not rough, but not gentle. Then he added a second finger, curling them both to rub over her g-spot when he stroked. But again he stopped.

"And I fucked up. I didn't come to you," he said against her shoulder. "I kept the hurt inside, wallowed, said that you'd rejected me and that was that. I didn't fight, I didn't try."

She felt tears stream over her cheeks. There had been plenty of tears after he'd left, but as far as he'd known she was happy with her decision, that she was relieved that he *hadn't* fought and made things harder and worse with her father.

"You wouldn't have fought with me. You would have never pushed or argued with me. You never would have made me cry…not on purpose."

She felt his forehead rest against her shoulder. He stroked his fingers deep again and she shifted, parting her legs, arching closer.

"I want to tell you about the arrest," she said quietly, even as she felt her body winding tighter. "I want to tell you everything."

"No," he said softly. "I don't need to know."

She struggled to concentrate, but his hand was making magic. "But, I—"

"I only wanted to make you happy, Eve. I want you to feel good now, to know how amazing you are, to know that I love you. No matter what's happened."

He pressed his fingers deep, then slid them out and over her clit, circling.

"I know," she told him, then caught her breath as he pressed her clit just right. "I know," she said again raggedly.

"Well, I'm not quite through showing you," he said.

He shifted and she rolled to her back, though his fingers slid inside her again. In the light that glowed from the streetlight outside the window, their eyes locked. He looked serious, intent. Not playful. There wasn't even a hint of a smile. He watched her as he stroked her. She felt the tension, the desire, that incredible coil of need that Kevin inspired, begin deep in her gut. She arched closer, but he pulled his hand away.

"No, I—" she started, but he shifted so he could use both

hands to whisk her pants off. He tossed them to the side and then took a knee in each hand and spread her legs.

He knelt between them and she felt exposed, vulnerable and incredibly turned on.

"Kevin," she breathed.

He met her eyes, that intense, determined look still in place, before he dipped his head and kissed her inner thigh. Then he licked. And moved his way up the curve of her right thigh to her mound then to her clit. His tongue dragged over her clit three times and Eve thought she was going to float off the bed. She was so close to orgasm already but she wanted to drag this out. She wanted his mouth, tongue, hands, body on her and in her for as long as they could both take it.

His tongue slid lower, licking over her, his tongue dipping inside, then sliding up and over her clit again. He sucked softly and she cried out, her hands tangling in his hair. Her legs slid further apart, her heels digging into the mattress as he feasted on her. He'd suck, lick and swirl, then start over.

Eve felt the coil tightening in her belly and hoped she didn't pass out before she orgasmed.

That was not a problem. Ten seconds later, the coil of desire pulled tight then let go all at once and her release crashed over her. She cried his name as she arched off the bed, pressing closer and closer to his mouth.

He stayed between her legs as her body's tremors quieted. When she finally sighed and let herself sink into the mattress he moved to lay against her side again.

He stroked his hand up and down her arm.

"Sorry I woke you up," he said after almost two minutes. "I couldn't help it."

She turned toward him. "I'm glad you did."

"We need to talk but we can do that later. I took the next couple days off."

He still looked far too serious. She put her hand to his cheek and waited for him to look at her. "Be honest, Kevin. Are you worried about me being with Drew?"

He shook his head. "I don't think so." Then he sighed. "The time off is about you and me. Not Drew."

"You and me?" That sounded a little ominous.

"I need you to get to know me. I want to show you my life, show you the ways I've changed."

"And vice versa?" she asked. He had a right to know who she was. But the idea made her feel like she'd swallowed a lump of clay that had lodged in her throat.

"Yes." He stroked his fingers through her hair. "I want to know about your life too, the changes. But I... You need..." He stopped and took a deep breath. "When we were together before I was focused on being the right guy, the perfect guy, showing you the good things, trying to impress you and your dad. I was pretty careful not to tell or show you anything that would make me look bad."

Eve felt a flutter in her chest. "What do you mean? There were bad things?"

"A few," he confessed. "I got a B in science because my football coach asked the teacher to throw out the two tests I'd flunked. I failed one because he had me reviewing game films the night before and I didn't study. I failed the other because I was hanging out and had too much to drink the night before, and fell asleep halfway through the test."

She looked up. "I didn't know that."

"Exactly."

She smiled. "Okay, what else?"

"I wanted Mike Carsen to go out with me one night but he had to babysit his two younger brothers. So we ended up taking them to a party with us and the twelve-year-old drank beer when we weren't looking and the fourteen-year-old made out with a seventeen-year-old girl."

Eve was sure her eyes were comically round, but...wow. "Made out?"

"Felt naked boobs for the first time and learned to French kiss."

"But—no one got hurt?"

"Not until the younger one started puking," Kevin said with a sigh. "He confessed the whole thing to their parents and Mike was forbidden to see me for almost three months."

Eve pushed up onto her elbow. "More. What else?"

"You're clearly horrified and shocked," he said wryly.

"I'm pretty shocked," she said. "I mean, you were such a *nice* guy with me. But maybe my father heard some of these stories and that's why he didn't want you around?"

"Very likely. The test scores and speeding tickets and stuff that I got out of were pretty secret, but whenever someone else got in trouble because of or with me, everyone knew. But, they all tolerated it. I was the football star."

He sighed and she got the definite impression that the memories weren't exactly good or welcome.

"You didn't enjoy the perks that went with being a local celebrity?" she asked.

"I can't deny that I did," he said. "I took advantage of it. But I guess I always felt…a little empty about it all. I mean, even as a teenager I knew that people liked me and did me favors because I helped the team win. It wasn't about me, who I was."

"And then with me, it wasn't about you either. It was about doing and saying the right things to impress me and my father."

He nodded. "I didn't lie to you, but I did a lot of things to be with you. I was never in church because I wanted to be, I didn't help at the shelter because it was the right thing to do. I did it to get a date."

"What about when we were together? That was never real?" That made her sad. He'd been her prince charming, and it hadn't even been real?

"When we were together it was as close as I ever got with anyone," he said. "I told you things I didn't tell anyone else. But I was careful to keep it all positive and good. I told you about things I wanted to do, places I wanted to visit, about my family and friends and books and movies I liked. Do you remember? We never talked about being sad or scared or mad."

She did remember, now. She had, admittedly, grown up in a world of hope and faith with the idea that the good guys always won and if you did the right thing, you'd always be happy. Children's church stories were about overcoming obstacles and the underdog coming out on top—the little guy felling the giant, big walls tumbling down because of trust and persistence, seas parting to allow the believers to escape.

"There's no way I would have noticed that though," she said out loud as she pondered it. "I would've chalked that up to you being a great guy who had the same life outlook that I did."

He nodded. "Yep. You were Suzy Sunshine. And I loved that. It made me happy to be around you. So, I never tried to change it or bring clouds to your sunny days."

She smiled even as she realized that he had a point with all of this. "I don't really know you that well then?" she asked. That lump that had been sitting in her throat earlier was back.

"But I want you to. I want to be real with you. I want to show you my life."

"What does that entail?" she asked, snuggling closer, as if she could paste herself against him and pretend that they would never be apart.

"Going to Omaha. For the weekend. I want you to see my apartment, see the Youth Center, hospital, all of it."

"Great." She wanted that too. He was transplanted here right now. She'd love to observe him in his natural habitat. "It will be good for Drew to see your world too. The Youth Center and stuff could make a good impression on him."

Kevin shifted and cleared his throat. "Yeah, about that. I…" He cleared it again. "I think so too and I want to do that sometime but…this trip I want it to be the two of us. I think we have a lot to work out. Some talking to do that maybe he shouldn't hear, for one thing."

"Like about my criminal record?" she asked.

He grimaced. "Maybe."

"Okay. But where will he go then?"

Kevin wouldn't look at her and he wiggled as if uncomfortable for a few seconds.

"Kevin? Where is Drew going to be while we're in Omaha for the weekend?"

He sighed. "I thought I might call Libby and Lacey."

Surprise silenced her for a few seconds. Then she asked, "You mean the good time girls?"

"I think I might have overreacted," he said sheepishly. "He clearly wants to be with them and I know I should give them the chance to do this before I ask anyone else."

She hooted with laughter—though quietly because Drew was asleep across the hall. "You realize you'll have to admit you were wrong and apologize. Big time."

"Yeah, I know."

"Well," Eve said, still chuckling and feeling a ridiculous surge of optimism. "I think a big spoonful of marshmallow cream might make it go down easier when you swallow your pride."

"And, in case I put my foot in my mouth over anything else," he said, "I'll get an extra-large jar."

When Kevin came through the back door after dropping Drew at Libby and Lacey's the next morning, Eve spoke before he could even say hi.

"Do you want to hear about the arrest now?"

He froze for a second. Then he carefully set his keys on the counter before turning to look at her. He studied her for a moment. Then shook his head. "No, I don't, actually."

"You sure?"

He sighed. "Okay, I kind of do. Of course. But there are

things about me I want you to know first. I want you to see what you're getting into too."

"You know what I really want to know, don't you?" She poured him a cup of coffee and grabbed her cup.

"What?"

"Why you gave up the drinking and women and everything." She slid onto the stool.

"Ah." He nodded. "Okay. But it's not a long or complicated story."

"Great. Let's hear it."

"It was the Christmas after I blew my knee out." He stared down into his cup. "My body and pride were hurting, my career was over, and I decided that coming home for Christmas sounded really comforting. But Mom and Dad decided to go to Florida for Christmas." He took a deep breath, then let it out. "I knew it was because Dad didn't know what to say to me. He hated the idea of me being here with nothing for us to talk about. Football was our bond and it was, apparently, over."

Eve felt the scowl on her face. "Are you fricking kidding me?" she demanded. "He didn't want to see you for Christmas because you got hurt and couldn't play football?"

Kevin gave her a half smile. "It might have also been because I was being a major asshole to everyone I knew."

"That's understandable," Eve said, furious on Kevin's behalf. "It's no reason for your dad to avoid you."

"And now you know why I want to beat your dad's ass for how he treated you," Kevin said mildly.

She looked into his eyes and saw the hurt that his dad's actions had caused. "I guess so. I'd love to have a few words with your dad at least."

Kevin chuckled. "I appreciate it."

She took his hand. "So you were alone for Christmas?"

"Yeah, lying on the couch, drinking, hating everything and everyone," he said ruefully. "I was pissed because things weren't going my way, but even more I was scared."

"Scared of how to make a living?"

"Scared of what else was going to go to crap. It seemed like I couldn't count on anything or anyone. Nothing was staying the same and I remember thinking how much I wanted to have something, one thing, that wouldn't change on me."

Her heart tripped at his words. She knew that feeling well too.

"So, I was flipping through the channels and I realized that everywhere I turned it was Christmas. Every channel—cartoons, the History channel, the Food Network—every time zone, all over the world. And I thought, hell, at least that's the same every year, year after year, no matter where I am."

Her throat tightened. "That's nice." And it was. It really was.

He grinned. "I kept thinking and my mind kept going to other things like that. Like how in your dad's church all those Sundays when I sat there, you all sang the same hymns, read the same stories, over and over."

"Oh." She barely made a sound with the word.

"So, I finally pushed myself up off the couch and…went to church. On Christmas Eve."

She stared at him. "No way."

"Yep. When I was at my lowest, I went to church." He laughed. "I, of course, was afraid of being struck by lightning the whole time." He gave her a wink. "But I thought of you the entire time too. And I just… I don't know. I just thought about how I'd been living this wild life, trying to feel happy and none of it was working and how, maybe I needed to try something *else*. Something *totally* different. My knee was shot. My career was over. So it was time for something equally drastic to change things up."

Eve wet her lips, shifted on the stool and swallowed hard. "That's…" But she didn't have a word for it. "Did you keep going?"

He shrugged. "Once in a while. I just mostly realized that I was sick of being hungover, and fighting with people, and feeling pissed off, and not remembering the names of the people I…hung out with. Being there took me back to a time when I was happy and hopeful. I liked that feeling."

She lifted a brow. The women. She knew that's who he meant when he said he didn't remember the "people" he hung out with.

"So I decided to make a one-eighty and see if that was any better."

"And?"

"Yeah. It's been better," he said with a nod. "Not perfect. But becoming a paramedic, taking care of myself, taking care of *other* people…yeah. It's definitely better."

Kevin had a lot on his mind as he and Eve drove to Omaha.

Lacey and Libby had been happy to have Drew spend the weekend with them and they didn't even make Kevin grovel much. Especially when he showed up with ingredients for s'mores, hot chocolate mix and his passwords for *all* of the streaming services for their Saturday night.

They had the whole schedule worked out within minutes. Lacey had a yoga class, but Libby could take Drew on the hike she'd planned, then while Libby was studying for a few hours, Lacey and Drew were going to clean the house. Drew wasn't overly excited about that part of the plan, but when Lacey said she'd give him his usual allowance for the job, he perked up.

Kevin made a note to give Drew some chores and an allowance at his place too.

And then there was Eve. She had changed. Her major life influence—her father and his church—were out of her life. She'd lost faith, in her dad at least, and it was clear that was where the edge of cynicism he sensed in her came from. He couldn't say he blamed her.

And he still wanted to kick Pastor Donnelly's ass.

Oh, and she still had an arrest record that could screw everything up with his guardianship of Drew.

And he didn't want to let her go, even temporarily, even if it would appease the state of Nebraska.

"This feels like a date," Eve said from the passenger seat.

Pulling his thoughts from the complications that he had no idea how to solve, he focused on the fact that she was here with him right now. Kevin smiled at her. "It does?"

What was she going to think of everything? His life was a hodge-podge of people and activities.

"Yeah, we never did this," she said with a grin.

They hadn't. They'd driven together a few times when she'd snuck out and met him a few blocks away to go to a party or drive around and talk. But they'd never gone out together without worrying about someone seeing them or getting caught.

He linked his fingers with hers. "No more sneaking." He pressed his lips to her hand.

It was Saturday and the guys weren't working tonight which meant they'd all be at the Bradford Youth Center. But that wouldn't be until later, after they'd slept off last night's shift, so Kevin started by taking her to the hospital.

On the way to St. Anthony's, Kevin told Eve about some of the staff that she'd probably meet. He obviously worked a different shift most of the time, but he still knew all the nurses and physicians because of Sam's sister, Jessica, a nurse and head of the ER, and her husband, Ben, a trauma surgeon. He also knew most of the lab techs, radiology techs, front desk receptionists and everyone else who wandered through the ER.

It was an amazing place. They were like a big family when it came to messing in each other's business and giving each other a hard time, but they all came together as a team—the best in the city—when that ambulance pulled into the bay. Even though he was a part of it and had been for years, he was still in awe of the things the ER at St. Anthony's saw and dealt with. There wasn't anything they couldn't do.

"Wow, sounds impressive," Eve commented. "I'm not really going to fit in."

He took her hand and squeezed. "No worries. You're with me. You're automatically in."

They would be quite enthusiastic about meeting her, in fact. He was one of the family and they would all be curious, if not downright thrilled, that he was with a woman who wasn't a co-worker and wasn't on a gurney in the back of an ambulance.

A few minutes later they walked through the sliding doors into the emergency department. It was a fairly quiet time and it didn't take long for someone to notice him. Everyone greeted him with huge smiles and a little ribbing about bailing the night before and making "poor Conner" work with Mac.

"I had things to take care of," he told John Parker. He knew his grin was huge.

John laughed and looked Eve up and down. "Amen, brother."

Chuckling, Kevin led her to the nurses' station. "Hey, Tara," he said enthusiastically when he saw the cute redhead in nurse's scrubs. "How's your mom?"

Tara's face broke into a huge smile when she looked up. "Kevin!" She came around the counter and hugged him tight. When she pulled back, she had tears in her eyes, but was still smiling. "She's better. Scared, of course, but the doctor said they got it all. She's going to do chemo for awhile, and she's really weak right now, but she's home and doing okay."

"Great," he said, feeling relieved. "But you know where to find me if you need anything."

She nodded. "I can't believe you answered your phone at two a.m. on your night off."

"Doesn't matter," he said sincerely. "I'm glad I did."

"Me too." Tara sniffed a little, then glanced at Eve.

Kevin grabbed Eve's hand and tugged her forward. "This is Eve."

"Hi, Tara. I'm sorry about your mom," Eve said.

Tara smiled and shook her hand. "Thanks. And if you were with Kevin when I called and talked to him for over an hour at two a.m., I'm really sorry."

She hadn't been and Kevin wondered if that bugged Eve. Tara's mom's cancer diagnosis and Tara's middle-of-the-night meltdown had happened about a week before all of the drama with Drew and Eve. But he'd told the nurse that he'd be happy to talk anytime she needed to and was flattered that she'd taken him up on it.

He often offered that to co-workers going through a tough time. Some called, some didn't.

"I'm glad you called him," Eve said to Tara. "It's good to have people you can really talk to."

"It is." Tara grinned at him and then gave Eve a wink. "It's good to have people you can do other stuff with too. Right, Kevin?"

He chuckled and looked at Eve. He pulled her close. "Definitely."

He introduced Eve around the rest of the ER, showed her a couple of the trauma rooms, the break room, the locker room. He hoped she didn't mind. It seemed silly, but he wanted her to see where he spent so much of his time and energy. This place affected him—sometimes for the better, sometimes the worst—and he wanted her to know a little about it.

"That's it," he said when the tour was complete.

"Wow."

He looked down at her. "Really?"

"Yeah. Most of my ideas about hospitals and ERs are from TV and movies, but…this is real. You all save lives here."

He smiled at that. "Yeah." He felt a surge of pride. "We do."

"I'm impressed. Thanks for bringing me here."

Something in her eyes begged him to kiss her. He leaned in as someone called, "Kevin!"

Sighing he lifted his head and focused on Jason Anderson

jogging toward him. "Hey, man, here's your book back. Finished it the other night. I liked it."

He handed over the book Kevin had loaned him.

"Keep it," Kevin said. "Pass it on to someone else who might need it sometime."

"Really?" John asked. "You sure?"

"Of course. You'll come across someone at some point."

John nodded. "Okay, thanks. I'll do that."

Kevin turned Eve toward the exit. "Let's head to the Center."

"What was the book?" she asked as they walked.

"The Calvin and Hobbes Tenth Anniversary Book." It was his all-time favorite cartoon strip and he'd bought every collection there was after the author stopped doing it.

"Seriously?" she asked.

"What were you expecting?" Kevin asked, glancing at her.

"Something…deep. Inspirational, I guess," she said.

"He's not ready for that," Kevin told her. He'd just wanted to lighten the kid up. He was taking one trauma from the week before particularly hard. "We see a lot of bad stuff here in the ER and John's a new resident. I could tell it was wearing on him, so I gave him something to make him smile. I didn't know if he'd think it was stupid or not, but I'm glad he liked it." He glanced back at John who was heading in the other direction. "It's hard to know what to say sometimes, so I let Calvin cheer him up."

Eve pressed against his side as they walked. "It isn't about what you say or do, it's about caring enough to say or do something at all."

They didn't talk about anything too deep on the way to the Center and Kevin tried to ignore that the nerves were back. This was the Center. A place he'd spent hours of his life. Full of people he genuinely cared about and who cared about him. Why was he nervous about bringing her here?

They walked through the front doors and found the entryway empty. That was unusual. The place was generally loud and fun, teeming with teenagers and volunteers. Pool games, basketball games, video games, conversation and laughter, homework and food—that was normal. The front lobby was usually piled with shoes, jackets, bags and anything else the kids shed when they stepped inside.

Confused, Kevin took Eve's hand and headed for the double doors that led into the main rec room. Surely someone was…

"I told you to watch your damn mouths!" Sam roared as Kevin pulled the door open.

He and Eve pulled up short in the doorway as six scuffing teenage boys came to a stop and turned to stare at Sam and Mac, who were standing with their backs to the door—and to Kevin and Eve.

"They'll be here any minute. Stop jacking around," Mac added firmly.

Mac and Sam had their hands on their hips, legs spread and —Kevin had no doubt—stern looks on their faces as they reprimanded the boys.

Three turned and scattered, but the older boys, who had been around the Center longer, stayed, facing off with the men.

In the ER and on calls, no one messed with their crew. They were all big guys, who could be intimidating when they needed to be. They also took their jobs and their reputation as the best paramedics in the area seriously.

They had a lot of fun, flirting and giving everyone a hard time, but when they were working, no one pushed their buttons.

Except the kids at the Center.

The kids knew the guys were all big softies who would do anything for any one of the kids.

They were grinning at Sam and Mac now.

"So, to be clear, this is the preacher's daughter he's bringing over, right?" Lucas, the oldest and tallest of the boys, asked.

Kevin knew Lucas saw him standing behind Mac. This would be interesting. He leaned a shoulder against the doorjamb and pulled Eve against his side, signaling her to stay quiet and giving her a wink.

"Right," Sam said. "A nice girl who prefers to think that the youth of tomorrow are polite and respectful."

Oh, this was great. Kevin couldn't help but grin at Sam Bradford—one of the biggest playboys of all—giving lectures about anything polite or respectful.

"So, we're not supposed to say hell or damn, right?" Eli, a stocky kid who was never without a baseball cap on, asked.

"Right," Mac confirmed. "Or any others."

The kids were supposed to watch their mouths all the time really—house rules—but Sam and the other guys generally let a lot slide. If that was the worst any of these kids did, they were happy. In a neighborhood where fighting, drugs and school drop outs were common, swearing seemed a minor offense. As long as it wasn't *at* anyone. Treating everyone at the Center with respect was also house rules.

"Others like what?" Juan, the most easy-going of the three, asked with a big grin.

"You know the words," Mac said. "No swearing, period."

"Hell, damn, shit, Jesus, Jesus Christ, God, God damn it," Eli recited. "Right. Got it."

Mac gave a little growl. "Yes, all of those. And fuck. Seriously, kid, you say that one way too much even when there's not a nice lady around."

"Fuck. Right." Eli nodded solemnly. "I won't say fuck. You won't hear fuck from me, Mac."

"Great," Mac muttered.

"Anything else?" Lucas asked.

"Only sports video games, no shooting," Sam said.

"Jessica took the shooting games away anyway," Juan said. He clearly thought that was an extreme action.

"She took them away in part because you failed your last geography test," Sam reminded him.

"Yeah, yeah."

"What else? That it?" Lucas wanted to know, his eyes skipping to Kevin.

"Don't chew with your mouth open, say 'excuse me', don't belch," Sam said. "All the basics, guys."

"And no kissing Kayla," Mac added.

"Oh, come on, man," Lucas moaned. "It's just kissing."

Uh, huh. Kevin knew all about "just kissing".

"You and Kayla do not just kiss," Sam said. "Dani told me she found you two in the supply closet last week. Not cool."

"I found Dooley and Morgan doing more than kissing in the kitchen two days ago," Lucas said.

Mac rubbed a hand over his face. "Can you…be good, okay? No making out, swearing, violent video games or trying to shock Eve with your stories about fights or drugs at school."

"You bet," Eli said. "We'll drink lemonade and watch cartoons and hold hands the whole time she's here."

The boys all laughed, elbowing each other and heading toward a pool table.

"And no gambling," Sam yelled after them.

"Or dirty jokes," Mac called.

"Or mentioning that she's hot," Sam said.

The boys turned as one. "She's hot?" Juan asked.

"Well, um…" Sam sighed. "Yeah, she is. But it's inappropriate for you to say that."

Kevin heard Eve make a little squeak and he squeezed her waist to keep her quiet. He wanted to hear the rest of this.

"Is it inappropriate for *you* to say it?" Eli asked.

"Yes, it is," Mac said resolutely. "Her hotness has nothing to do with her being here, so shut up about it."

"Nothing to do with her being here?" Lucas asked with a grin. "Not even for Kevin?"

Again Eve made a muffled choking sound and Kevin squeezed her again, trying to keep from laughing out loud himself.

"It might have something to do with… That's not why he… or why she's here…" Sam sighed. "Be good. 'Kay? For Kevin?"

All three boys grinned. "Sure. For Kevin."

The boys moved off and Sam glanced at Mac. "We missed some rules."

"Probably." Mac relaxed his stance. "This place is kind of high risk for misbehaving—good and bad misbehaving." He chuckled.

"Yeah, and then there's the kids," Sam joked. Then he counted on his fingers. "Swearing, video games, kissing, dirty jokes…" He shook his head. "I could have sworn there was more on the list Dani and Jess put together."

Kevin almost laughed out loud at that too. Of course the girls were behind the rules.

"Sara told me to be sure the kitchen and bathrooms were clean," Mac said.

"Are they?"

"Hell if I know."

"Maybe next time we should go get the food and let the girls cover the rules," Sam said.

"Yeah, the kids are definitely more scared of the girls," Mac agreed.

"Fuck."

Kevin couldn't hold back any longer. "The bathrooms aren't even clean?"

Mac and Sam jerked up straight and spun. They took in Kevin's casual pose against the doorjamb and Eve's against Kevin. It was clear they'd been there for awhile.

"Damn."

"Hell."

Eve burst out laughing. "Don't worry, Kevin's been working on teaching me all kinds of dirty words."

"So we heard," Sam said, with the grin he simply couldn't turn off when there was a woman within range.

Eve's eyebrows went up and Kevin stepped between her and Sam before his friend could spill any more info. "What's to eat?"

"Fried chicken," Mac answered.

But that didn't keep Eve from leaning around Kevin and asking Sam, "Did he tell you my favorite word?"

Sam winked at Eve. "Cock is one of Danika's favorite words too."

Danika and Sara had come up behind their husbands as they'd been talking, but Kevin didn't say a word. These guys were very likely going to do something at some point to make him regret bringing Eve here, so he'd get what revenge he could even before the fact.

Dani grinned at Kevin and Eve before she frowned and said, "Sam Bradford, did you seriously say cock to the new girl?"

Sam closed his eyes and muttered, "Damn," again before he turned to face his wife.

"I was trying to be good, honest," he said.

Danika rolled her eyes and slid her hand into his. "Maybe next time you guys should go for the food and leave us in charge of welcoming the guests."

Sara grinned at Eve, tucking herself against Mac, who immediately wrapped his arm around her, his big hand on her butt.

"Hi, I'm Sara."

"Hi, Sara." Eve extended her hand. "Nice to meet you."

Sara looked at Eve's hand, then laughed and lunged to catch Eve in a hug. "God, it's so nice to meet you." She jerked back right away though, cheeks pink. "I'm sorry. I mean *gosh* it's nice to meet you."

Mac tugged her back to his side. "Relax, princess. She's cool."

"Yeah, and Lucas ran through the whole list of swear words," Sam said.

Dani sighed, but smiled at Eve. "Sorry about that. I'm Dani. I'm really happy to meet you too."

"No problem at all and me too," Eve said with a warm smile.

Kevin relaxed completely. These were his friends. They truly were happy to meet Eve, simply because it was clear she made *him* happy.

And Eve loved him. He knew that and he knew that she

understood how important these people were to him. She'd love them because they were a part of him.

"So, who's got the most embarrassing Kevin stories?" Eve asked.

Everyone laughed, but Sam was clearly thinking.

"You are hereby forbidden to talk to Sam, Mac or Dooley without supervision," Kevin said, gently pushing her past them and further into the rec room.

Eve grinned up at him. "You mean without editing?"

Kevin nodded. "Sara, Dani and the other girls like to pretend I've always been upstanding and decent. They like to believe some guys are naturally sweet and well-behaved."

Eve tripped and Kevin caught her with a hand on her elbow. She glanced up at him. "Oh, you bet, you've been sweet and well-behaved since you were born."

"Sounds like *you* might have some stories for us," Sam said as they all settled into the couches and love seats clustered around a coffee table in one corner of the big room.

"Nope," Eve said, "no stories about streaking down main street Grover or setting fireworks off at the river—in February— or leaving a shoe behind because he had to sneak out the window only half-dressed when the Chief of Police came home earlier than his daughter expected."

Everyone was staring at her, including Kevin. "You knew about all of that?" he asked, too amazed to blush.

"Of course." She gave him a mischievous smile. "I was equally intrigued and scared of you when you started talking to me."

"But I fooled around with the chief's daughter a year before we even met." No wonder she'd been so shy with him at first. Not only had she never had a boyfriend but she also wasn't used to hanging out with people who had such wild reputations.

"Oh, I knew who you were, Kevin Campbell. Even the preacher's daughter notices the hot bad boys."

And yet she'd still given him a chance. He grinned at her. "Intrigued, huh?"

"Stop!" Sara put her hands over her ears. "This is our sweet, responsible Kevin."

"Yeah, Kevin is what we hope Sam and Mac can be when they grow up," Dani added.

Sam put a possessive hand on her pregnant belly and said, "If you didn't like my naughty side so much, I'd grow up right now."

"Uh-huh," they all said at once.

Eve chuckled.

"Thank goodness Dani and Sara have magical powers over Sam and Mac to help keep them in line," Kevin said.

Sara laughed. "I'll tell you a secret. Those magical powers are called breasts."

"Okay, new topic," Sam said loudly.

"Prude." Dani laughed and put her hand on his thigh.

Sam leaned over and said something for only her to hear, but her giggle assured it was very un-prudish.

Sara fit perfectly next to Mac too, and Kevin found himself pulling Eve closer, his chest a little tight.

This—this thing that was so hard to describe or explain but was obvious when he watched his friends with their wives—this was what he wanted. With Eve.

"Kevin!"

He looked over his shoulder to find a couple of the teenagers he spent the most time with, David and Anthony, coming toward them with a newer kid, Ryan, between them.

"Hey, guys," he greeted warmly as he got to his feet. Both David and Anthony had been struggling with choices like drugs and dropping out of school about a year ago. He'd taken them under his wing and turned them on to helping others. It had worked to keep them out of trouble.

"Ryan almost fought today," Anthony reported, "but he said no."

Kevin looked at the kid in the middle. "Yeah?"

Ryan lifted a shoulder. "Yeah. They were pissing me off, but I walked away."

Kevin felt warmth spread through his chest and he stepped around the couch and put a hand on Ryan's shoulder. "That's hard to do. Good job."

"I really wanted to hit him though," Ryan said. "I can't get rid of that feeling."

"It's not about never feeling stuff," Kevin said. "It's about being stronger than those feelings. Knowing that it's harder to not do that stuff should make you feel powerful."

Ryan sighed. "Maybe. But the other guys don't see it as powerful."

"Deep down they do," Kevin assured him. "Anybody can hit someone. Not everyone can overcome the urge. That's strength."

Ryan nodded. "Okay. I'm working on it."

"I know." Kevin squeezed his shoulder, then let go. He was working on it too.

# CHAPTER
# ELEVEN

"KEVIN?" Eve called, letting herself in the front door. She'd talked to Lacey and Libby and they'd said it was no problem for Drew to stay a little longer.

She didn't know how long soul-baring generally took, but she guessed more than the twenty minutes they had left before the girls were originally supposed to bring Drew home.

"Kevin?"

He came out of the kitchen, his cell phone pressed to his ear. "No, I understand," he said. He held up a finger, asking her to wait.

She propped her shoulder against the doorway to watch him. His faded blue jeans had obviously been worn enough that they were soft and fit his ass perfectly. He wore a simple black T-shirt but it hugged his chest and shoulders outlining his shape and strength, making her shiver remembering how easily he could lift and move her and how big he was—all over. Then he raked his fingers through his hair and the shirt pulled up from the waistband of his jeans, revealing a strip of skin dusted with dark hair and she wanted to push it up further and further, licking every inch of the skin she exposed as she went.

"I'll be there as soon as I can."

She straightened as he disconnected. She couldn't lick anything right now. They needed to talk. And it sounded like he might be leaving.

"I have to go back to Omaha," he said, crossing the foyer.

"Oh." No talking or licking. "I was hoping… Do you have to leave right away? We need to talk."

"I know."

He shoved his fingers through his hair again, but instead of focusing on his abs—though it was difficult—she noticed the strain on his face.

Maybe this wasn't the time to add more strain. Then again, maybe telling him everything would give him some relief. Her arrest wasn't great, but, she hadn't murdered anyone. She'd wanted to after it all went down, but she hadn't. She took a deep breath. "I want to tell you about the arrest."

His gaze flew to her face, his eyes widened and his hand dropped from his head. "I… I want to…" He looked down at the phone in his hand. "Damn. I have to go. Ryan's in trouble."

"Ryan?" Eve said. "The kid from the Center?"

"Yeah." Kevin looked downright pissed off. "He got into a fight on his way home. The cops took him in. They'll let him go, but only if I'm the one to come get him."

Eve frowned. "The kid you talked to about *not* fighting a few hours ago?"

He sighed. "That's the one."

"You're going to help him?" she asked, her frown deepening. "After he did exactly what you told him not to do?"

"Yeah." Kevin lifted a shoulder.

What had the kid been thinking? This amazing man was giving him time and attention, genuinely cared about him and had been praising him. How had Ryan turned around and forgotten all of that within the hour? "Aren't you mad?" she asked.

It was clear he was. "Of course."

"Aren't you disappointed?"

"Yes."

"But you're going anyway?"

Kevin was watching her closely. "Yes. I'm going anyway. I told him that if he ever needed anything he only had to call."

He meant it. She could see it in his eyes. He was angry, but he was going to be there for Ryan anyway. "Wow." He really did walk the walk.

And she suddenly smiled brightly. So brightly that Kevin blinked in surprise.

"My stuff can wait. I'll tell you all about it when you get back." She felt almost giddy. Kevin knew what it meant to care unconditionally. He knew how to forgive. She could tell him anything and he'd still love her. "You should go get Ryan."

"You okay?" he asked, reaching for her.

She went to him, wrapping her arms around him and holding tight. "Absolutely. We'll talk when you get back."

He hugged her for a long moment, then let her go. He searched her face for a moment. "I meant it when I said I don't need to know."

"I need to tell you." She meant what she said too. She wanted him to know everything. And she had to trust that his feelings for her were bigger than everything else.

He leaned in, cupped her cheek and kissed her sweetly. "I'll be back as soon as I can."

As the door closed behind him, Eve took a deep breath. She couldn't deny she was a little nervous and didn't mind the reprieve. She'd once trusted that her father's feelings for her were bigger than everything else too. But comparing Reverend Donnelly and Kevin Campbell now, she could see that her father had always been more comfortable with a pulpit between him and the people he talked to. Of course, people sought out his council outside of Sunday service, but he'd given them Bible verses and clichéd statements about reflecting and praying and turning it all over to God.

Not that those were the wrong things to say. But he'd never really given any honest, heartfelt words that were all his. Not even to his daughter.

She felt guilty thinking those thoughts of her father and wondered if she was coloring the past this way because of her hurt. Possibly. But she really would like to remember some sincere comforting words from Reverend Donnelly. Maybe they'd happened behind closed doors. She was going to try to focus on that.

Then there was Kevin. He gave people Calvin and Hobbes, if that's what they needed. He answered his phone at two a.m. He was steady and there when someone needed him and lived a life that demonstrated things that were very hard to even put into words.

She felt tears sting, but her smile grew. He was definitely the real deal.

Feeling lighter than she had in a long time, Eve took the bag of food from Sherry's and stored it in the fridge for tomorrow. Then she swung through the drive-through on the highway and headed to Lacey and Libby's with burgers and fries.

"Eve!"

As Libby led her into the kitchen, she was surprised to find Drew making a bee-line for her with a huge grin.

"Hi, D," she greeted. She was equally surprised to find that she'd missed him. "How was your day?"

"Good. Except for the cleaning part."

She handed him the food bags and followed him to the table. "But you survived," she pointed out with a smile, "and the place looks great." It did. The kitchen was spotless and smelled great.

Lacey laughed. "He's a perfectionist. Best cleaning partner I've ever had. He doesn't half-ass anything."

"I'll keep that in mind," Eve said, looking at Drew. "I haven't seen evidence of this particular talent."

"Will you hide money?" Drew asked, pulling burgers and fries from the bag eagerly. At least his appetite had improved over the past few days.

"Hide money?" She looked at Lacey.

"We started it awhile ago. He was sloppy with dusting the bookshelves and stuff, so Libby told him she was going to hide quarters all over the house. If he found them, he could keep them. He became much more careful about getting all the nooks and crannies clean."

Eve was impressed. "I could probably find some places to put some quarters."

Drew rolled his eyes and bit into a fry.

They chatted and laughed as they ate, then Eve decided it was time to coax him home. But it didn't take coaxing. Drew hugged Libby and Lacey and then grabbed his bag and was by the door within minutes.

Eve couldn't deny that made her feel good.

"So, it's Saturday night. Seven o'clock. What do you want to do?" she asked as they pulled into the driveway.

"We should finish the Nebraska-Missouri game, shouldn't we?" he asked.

They'd only watched the first quarter of that game from Kevin's senior season. "You bet. Put your stuff away and come on down."

Drew thundered up the stairs and Eve got the TV and DVD player turned on. She wondered when, or if, Drew would ask about Kevin. He should be here tonight.

But Drew didn't ask about his brother when he came back down.

They watched the game for almost an hour and Drew still didn't ask about Kevin.

In fact, he asked a total of seven questions. All were about the game and all showed he was learning the ins and outs of football. But none were about Kevin.

"Kevin will be back tonight," she finally said as she paused the game and rose to get some drinks. "He had to run back to Omaha. It might be late though."

"Okay." Drew shrugged.

Okay. She really wanted Drew to like Kevin, to give him a chance. But in some ways, she supposed this was better than dealing with tears or something because Kevin wasn't here as expected.

As she was returning with two glasses of apple juice, the doorbell rang.

Eve handed the glasses to Drew and headed for the door.

She pulled it open to reveal a woman dressed in a pantsuit and carrying a briefcase.

"Hello," she said with a small smile. "I'm looking for Kevin Campbell."

"Oh, I'm sorry, he's not here." Eve glanced at the clock. It was eight-thirty so Kevin had probably just gotten to Ryan. "It could be a few more hours."

The woman frowned. "I was under the impression he wasn't working tonight."

"No, he's not. A friend needed some help."

The woman extended her hand. "I'm Linda Rosner. I'm Drew's caseworker."

"Oh!" Eve shook her hand. "Nice to meet you."

"Maybe I can get some information for the home assessment anyway," Mrs. Rosner said.

"Of course." Eve stepped back to let the woman in. "How can I help?"

The woman noticed Drew. "Hello, Drew."

"Hi."

He looked concerned. Which was odd.

Eve gave him a smile. "You know Mrs. Rosner?"

"Yeah. From the hospital that night."

That night. The night he came to live with Kevin. The night his mother stabbed his father with a fork. The night Heather went into treatment. "Ah," Eve said.

"How are you?" Mrs. Rosner asked him.

"Okay. Good," he said quickly. "It's like home."

"Is it?" Mrs. Rosner asked.

"Without the vodka, of course," he said. "We have home cooked meals, and she helps with homework, and I do chores, and I'm learning about football."

Mrs. Rosner's eyebrows rose and Eve gave Drew a little frown. Why was he selling this so hard?

"Glad to hear all of that," Mrs. Rosner said. "Especially the vodka part."

Drew got up on his knees on the cushion to look over the back of the couch. "I'm very well-adjusted."

Eve rolled her eyes. A little much, there. But she had to smile. He was well-adjusted. And to hear him trying to convince the caseworker that Eve and Kevin were good for him did make her happy.

"Wonderful," Mrs. Rosner said to Drew. "I don't suppose you have some school papers or tests or anything you could show me so I can see that school's going well?"

"Sure." He bounced off the couch and started for the steps.

"I'm sorry," Mrs. Rosner said, turning to Eve. "Who are you?"

"Oh, I'm Eve."

When the woman frowned, Eve felt her stomach flip. Suddenly she was nervous. But there was nothing to be nervous about, was there? This woman was here to make sure that Drew was doing well and was being cared for and…he was. There was no reason to feel like she was being scrutinized. Except that she really felt like she was being scrutinized.

"Eve?" Mrs. Rosner repeated.

"Yes." Eve smiled. "Eve Donnelly. Or Campbell. I guess."

This was complicated, but probably something the case-worker would need explained.

"I'm kind of…Kevin's wife."

It was hard to get that word out without emotions tumbling through her and threatening her breath.

Mrs. Rosner's eyebrows creased into a deeper frown. "His wife."

"Yes." Eve gave a nervous laugh, not sure why exactly she was nervous. "It's a long story."

"You've been estranged for twelve years."

Okay, maybe the story wasn't that long after all.

Eve blinked at her. "Um, yes. That's true. You knew that?"

"Yes." The other woman didn't look pleased. "Is there somewhere we can sit and talk?"

That didn't sound good. "Of course. We can go in the kitchen. Coffee?"

"I'll take tea if you have it." Mrs. Rosner followed right behind her.

"Of course." Eve started the kettle heating on the stove, then turned and took a deep breath. "I get the impression there's a problem?"

"Not exactly. At least, not for certain." Mrs. Rosner withdrew two folders from her briefcase and then took a seat at the island. "You are, obviously, here caring for Drew tonight while Mr. Campbell is away."

"Yes." Eve slipped her hands into her back pockets and stayed by the stove.

Mrs. Rosner withdrew some paperwork, scanned it and then made a note. "Was this an emergency situation?"

"Kevin's trip to Omaha?" Eve asked. "Yes. It was unexpected." Maybe Mrs. Rosner didn't like the idea of Kevin taking off on Drew and calling someone in at the last minute. "But I was already here. And Drew's used to me. I'm here a lot."

Mrs. Rosner made another note. "I see."

Okay, she wasn't family. Heather hadn't specifically picked

Eve to take care of Drew, but Kevin trusted her. They had a relationship so that should count, shouldn't it? "Heather and I were —are—friends. In fact, Heather works for me. So, I've known Drew. And when Kevin said he wasn't sure what he was going to do with work and everything, I offered to help out."

Mrs. Rosner looked up. "When did you make this arrangement?"

Eve wanted to be sure that Mrs. Rosner knew that Drew being well-adjusted had come partly from her. "From the beginning. Right away. I've been here all along."

Mrs. Rosner's lips thinned and she again bent her head to write.

The teakettle whistled, making Eve jump and she whirled to take care of it, grateful to have something to do. This was crazy. It was clear that Drew was doing well here and Kevin was obviously the right choice for who should care for him. She was sure the interview and home assessment was a formality.

So why did she feel so nervous?

Maybe it was Mrs. Rosner's sunny disposition.

Eve set a cup of hot water with a tea bag in front of the other woman and took a seat across the table from her.

"Mrs. Campbell…" Mrs. Rosner started.

Drew came in just then with a stack of school papers. "I've been keeping up with all of my work and I have straight As," he announced, handing the pile of papers to the caseworker.

Mrs. Rosner took the papers and flipped through them. "Impressive," she said. "I'm happy to hear that you're keeping your priorities straight." She looked Drew in the eye. "I'll be sure to tell your mother that you're doing well."

Drew pressed his lips together and nodded.

"Is there anything else you'd like her to know?"

His eyes widened and Eve watched him, her heart aching. He missed his mom. He didn't let on about it. He'd been happier lately. But, of course, he missed his mom.

She missed hers a little bit in that moment too.

"Yes," he finally said softly.

"If you want to write her a letter, I can see that she gets it," Mrs. Rosner said. "I think it would really make her happy."

"Okay."

Drew nodded, his eyes a little shiny, and Eve couldn't help but reach out and squeeze his hand.

He gave her a wobbly smile, then turned and headed back for his room.

Eve drew a deep breath, then focused back on the caseworker. "He really is doing well."

"I can see that," she said. She lay her pen down and leaned her elbows on the table. "Mrs. Campbell, I'm confused."

Eve felt her heart flip at that second *Mrs. Campbell.*

"Confused about what?"

"I'm confused about your involvement here."

"Oh?" Eve licked her dry lips. Mrs. Rosner seemed more concerned than confused.

"I made it clear to Mr. Campbell that I would need to interview anyone who had a primary caregiving role with Drew."

"Oh, that's fine. You can interview me now."

Mrs. Rosner sighed. "That's not the problem. The problem is that he lied to me."

Eve's eyes went wide. "Kevin lied to you?"

"Yes."

"About what?"

"You."

Eve looked at her. Kevin had *lied* about her? Kevin had lied about *her*? Why?

"What do you mean?"

"He told me that you would not be caring for Drew. He told me there was no chance at reconciliation between the two of you."

Eve sat back in her chair, replaying the words in her head. She crossed her arms. Kevin had said there was no chance at reconciliation? He'd lied about her involvement with Drew? Why?

But the next second, she knew exactly why.

"When did he say this?"

"During our initial interview."

Okay. That wasn't so bad. That was before they'd seen each other again. Before they decided to give it a try. "We—"

"And then again last night. I specifically asked about it."

Last night. Eve hugged her arms harder across her stomach.

Last night Kevin had denied that she was involved with Drew and had said there was no chance of reconciliation.

"I see," she finally said.

"You can see where I'm confused," Mrs. Rosner said.

Eve nodded. She was a little confused herself.

"Is there any reason that Mr. Campbell would have felt the need to lie about this?"

Eve drew in a long breath. Of course there was. She wasn't good enough.

"I assume that everyone caring for Drew has to meet some basic standards?" she said.

"Of course. It's my job to be sure he's safe and cared for."

"And I suppose that if Mr. Campbell chose to involve someone who didn't quite meet your standards, it would be a mark against him as a caregiver as well?" Eve asked smoothly. Calling him Mr. Campbell was easier than using his name. It gave her some distance.

Mrs. Rosner frowned. "Yes. Part of his role for Drew is making decisions for Drew's well-being."

Eve nodded. Right. "Then I guess it's safe to assume that Ke—Mr. Campbell had reason to believe that you would find me lacking if you knew I was involved and it would hurt his chances of being named Drew's guardian."

She pressed her arms in tighter. This hurt.

But she couldn't think about it right now. For one, Drew did need her—worthy or not—at the moment and sliding off her chair into a limp pile of hurt and disappointment wouldn't do him any good. For another, that would *definitely* get written into Mrs. Rosner's file.

The caseworker studied her for a moment. "Any idea what he thought was lacking?"

Eve laughed at that. But it hurt her stomach—and her heart—to do it. There was the arrest, of course. Then there were all the things she'd confessed about her drinking, smoking, the guys, the estrangement from her family, her partying—there was a veritable plethora of reasons that Kevin would find her lacking as a positive influence over Drew. And he didn't even know her feelings about church. Imagine how he'd feel then.

"I suppose it was probably my arrest that made him the most nervous," she finally said.

Mrs. Rosner raised an eyebrow. "Arrest?"

Eve sighed and nodded. "Accessory to felony embezzlement. I was found not guilty, but…" She trailed off and swallowed hard. "Kevin would still find that…lacking."

"I see." Mrs. Rosner made another note, then sighed and put her pen down. "I'll need to look into the arrest. Actually, I'll have to do a full background check."

"That's fine." It made sense. Even though it meant opening up her past and information she'd rather never have *anyone* know, Eve was glad to know that Linda Rosner was so careful about the kids on her caseload. Someone needed to look out for them.

But Eve *hated* that Kevin had hidden this—had hidden *her*. He'd risked lying to the state of Nebraska, and not only getting in trouble if caught, but dealing with his conscience about lying in the first place.

Because she knew this had to be eating at him.

He'd taken a big risk not telling Mrs. Rosner about her. But if he had told Mrs. Rosner, her background check might have kept them from being together.

She got it.

But it still hurt.

She knew, on some level, she was overreacting a little.

Kevin wasn't like her father. He wasn't turning his back on her just because she'd screwed up.

She pulled in a deep breath and watched Mrs. Rosner fill out another form.

Kevin had stood by Ryan, Eve reminded herself. The kid had messed up and Kevin had still been there for him.

He'd still be there for her too.

He just didn't want the world to know it.

He'd sleep with her, let her help him out, take as many orgasms as he could get, just as long as no one knew about it…

Eve made herself stop and breathe again. She was definitely overreacting. Probably.

She wanted to be loved unconditionally. By Kevin.

Maybe that was too much to ask for.

Drew came skidding into the kitchen. "I got it done," he said, thrusting a folded piece of paper toward Mrs. Rosner.

"Wonderful. I'll be sure she gets it right away."

As the woman smiled at Drew, Eve realized she looked kind for the first time. Drew really was her primary concern.

"Do you think, from what I've told you, that there will be problems for Ke—Mr. Campbell?" Eve made herself ask. She didn't want to worry Drew so she tried to keep the question generic.

Mrs. Rosner sighed. "I hope not. This is a good situation in many ways. Drew is clearly doing very well. I don't have a reason to remove him tonight."

Remove him? Eve's gut clenched painfully. She hadn't realized that was a possibility. Drew couldn't be removed. He needed to be here with *them*. With Kevin at least. No matter what was between the two of them, Kevin was the best person to take care of Drew, no question.

"Your—" Mrs. Rosner glanced at Drew and clearly censored

her comment, "—information is only part of this. The…omission of facts is a concern."

Yeah, it sure as hell was, Eve thought. Still, she didn't want Drew to be in the middle of any struggle or stress. "I'll do whatever I can to help."

"I'll be in touch."

Eve walked her to the door and said a final goodbye before closing the front door gently and resting her head against the wood.

She needed to think.

# CHAPTER
# TWELVE

KEVIN CAME through the door to the house at four minutes past midnight He was tired and not happy.

Ryan was out of jail and home with his two big brothers who had personally guaranteed Kevin that they'd be sure he stayed home and out of trouble. He'd also gotten hold of David and Anthony who promised to show up, with at least two other friends—big friends—the next day to be sure Ryan behaved.

Kevin knew Ryan. By Monday, he'd cool off and have control again. Kevin would get a phone call, no doubt with an apology and to set up a time to get together to talk. But right now, Ryan needed some people around to take care of him. He had that. Two brothers and good friends. He'd be okay.

Though Kevin hadn't completely given up on the idea that he, Mac, Sam and Dooley should find the kid who'd jumped Ryan and have a talk with him.

But that would have to wait.

He'd left in the middle of an important time with Eve. He'd been going crazy thinking about how she'd been about to tell him everything.

"Eve?" he called softly, knowing Drew would be in bed.

The house was dark with the exception of the light over the sink glowing from the kitchen and the lamp on the table beside the couch.

Had she gone to bed? He'd certainly had a great time waking her up last night and wouldn't complain about doing that again.

He leaned over the back of the couch to shut off the lamp, then froze. "Lacey?"

The blonde hair on the pillow on the couch was definitely not Eve.

"Lacey?" he said a little louder.

She rolled and blinked up at him. "Oh, hey, Kevin," she said sleepily.

"You okay? What's going on?"

She yawned and said. "Nothing. Yeah, I'm good."

"Why are you here?"

She rubbed a hand over her eyes. "Eve went out so I came over to stay with Drew. He's asleep. Doesn't even know she's gone."

He glanced at the stairs. "Out? Where'd she go?" It was past midnight on a Saturday night. "Everything okay at the restaurant?"

"Yeah. I think so."

"She didn't go down to Sherry's?"

Lacey yawned widely again. "Nope. She's meeting Monica at Tony's."

"She went to the *bar*?" When she was supposed to be here with Drew? And him?

"Can you stay?" he asked Lacey. Drew was fine. He needed to talk to Eve. "Lace?"

But there was no answer. She'd already fallen back to sleep. He didn't miss the irony. He'd assumed she and Libby were party girls and she couldn't even stay up past midnight.

The truth was, the girls had stepped up for Drew more than

once. He'd have to get them something nice. Like a case of silly string.

Lacey's soft snore pulled him back to the situation at hand.

Ten minutes later he strode into Tony's.

Greetings erupted, several hands slapped his back, but he didn't stop or even pause as he waded through the crowd. He'd zeroed in on Eve immediately.

But it wasn't hard. For one thing she'd changed clothes.

He briefly noticed that Monica looked hot too, in tight jeans and a shimmery silver top, but it was Eve who really shone. She wore ass-hugging jeans with pink heels that boosted her another three inches into the air and a pink sequined top that left one shoulder bare, molded to her breasts and waist and, most of all, showed off her cleavage.

And he wasn't the only one noticing.

But more than the shiny top and the cleavage, Eve was drawing attention because she was squared off with another woman in the middle of the bar, encircled by a crowd of spectators.

"You should be careful what you say, Abby. Someone might take offense to the way you're talking about one of their friends." Eve's hands were on her hips, her chest out, chin high, eyes glittering.

Abby, the blonde glaring at Eve from a distance of about two feet, sneered. "Lucky for me she hardly has any friends."

"Unlucky for you, you happened to open your huge mouth in front of one that's in the mood to hit something," Eve took a menacing step forward. "You need to shut up now."

Abby laughed. "If Heather didn't want people talking about her, she should have put down the bottle and picked up a condom."

With a rush, Kevin realized that Abby was talking about Heather Hansen. Drew's mom. Oh, crap. He shouldered past a few more guys as he heard Eve say, "Put your drink down,

Abby. I don't want to break any of Tony's glasses when I hit you."

"Oh, sure, I'll put my drink down," Abby said.

Kevin was almost to Eve, but wasn't in time to prevent the contents of Abby's glass from splashing in Eve's face and down the front of her shirt.

The crowd gasped as Eve wiped her eyes and glared at Abby. "I think you're mistaking me for the sweet girl in high school who would never do something like kick your ass."

"Yeah, if you're hanging with Heather than I'd say drunk and slutty were a lot more accurate than sweet," Abby said.

"You're basing that opinion on the fact that she has a kid she's completely devoted to, a job that she gives a hundred and ten percent to, and that she had the balls to admit she'd made some mistakes and needed help?" Eve asked, taking another step forward.

Abby backed up until her butt hit a table.

Eve kept going. "At least she's trying to do the right thing and be a good person. I'll take a woman who likes men and margaritas and screws up once in awhile over an opinionated, judgmental, whiny bitch who's never done anything worthwhile in her life."

With that, Eve pivoted on her heel and started to march away.

Unfortunately, Abby's exclamation of, "Never done anything?" followed her. "As if working in your crappy diner, ending up in rehab and raising a weird kid were such huge accomplishments."

Eve froze halfway across the circle of space the crowd had provided for the scene.

"Eve." Kevin tried to grab her hand, but she spun away too quickly.

"What did you say about Drew?" she asked Abby.

Oh, boy. Kevin started forward, but Abby made the mistake of repeating what she'd said.

"He's weird."

Eve got right in Abby's face. "Too bad for you I don't go to church anymore, so I've totally forgotten about turning the other cheek and all that bullshit." Then she drew her hand back and slapped Abby so hard that people fifty feet away heard it.

Abby cried out in shock and pain, then stood staring at Eve's enraged face. Five seconds of shocked silence hovered, then Abby lunged forward, claws drawn.

*Not again.* That was all Kevin could think as he stepped between them. His mother and Heather had been bad enough.

"Stop it," he ordered, blocking Eve from Abby's attack.

"Get out of the way, Kevin." Eve tried to push him out of the way, but of course didn't succeed.

When she couldn't get to Eve, Abby shoved the table next to her hard into the next one, sending three glasses crashing to the floor.

"That's it!" Tony grabbed Abby while Kevin picked Eve up and started for the door.

"I can't believe I pulled Eve Donnelly out of a bar fight." Kevin deposited Eve on the sidewalk ten yards from the door to the bar.

"What are you doing here?" she asked, straightening her shirt.

"Protecting Abby seemingly."

Eve didn't smile. Kevin shifted his weight, feeling like he needed to tread lightly with whatever he said or did next, but he had no idea why.

"What are you doing here?" he asked instead.

She didn't look angry—exactly. She seemed sad. Or disappointed. Or something.

"Having a drink with my best friend after a stressful night. We do this. Often. You should probably know that."

Okay. "Stressful night?" he asked. "Did something happen with Drew?"

"Nope. Drew's great. Mrs. Rosner, on the other hand, is a bit confused. And irritated."

Kevin felt shock ripple through him. Oh…shit.

Eve read his reaction on his face. "Yeah. Mrs. Rosner. The woman you lied to about me."

The emotion in her eyes became clear in that second—she was hurt.

He'd denied her. He'd lied about their connection, their relationship, what she meant to him. And she'd found out about it.

"Eve…"

She backed up as he reached for her. "Too soon, Kevin," she said. "Way too soon. I'm really trying not to compare this to my dad telling me he wanted nothing to do with me if I wasn't exactly what he wanted me to be. But I'm still about three beers from being numb enough to *not* lump you together with him. So touching me isn't a good idea."

Before Kevin could respond to that, the door to Tony's banged open, music and voices spilling out, as Wes Mitchell stormed out onto the sidewalk. He saw Eve and Kevin immediately and started in their direction.

*Dammit.* Kevin clenched his jaw. He needed to concentrate on Eve and what she'd thrown at him. She was hurt. She was feeling rejected. She was… But he couldn't concentrate. Wes was bearing down.

"What's your problem, Eve?" he demanded as he approached. "You hit my little sister?"

Abby was right behind him, glaring at Eve.

Eve sighed. "You weren't there," she told Wes. "You didn't hear what a complete bitch she was being."

"Hey!" Abby exclaimed.

Kevin stepped between them. "It's over, Wes. Let it go."

Wes frowned at him. "Let it go? She started it." He jabbed a finger in Eve's direction. "And now Tony's saying Abby has to pay for the stuff that got broken and she can't come back for a month."

Kevin and the guys were often the ones called to domestic situations and he knew that his size was on his side, but he also knew that trying to talk the person down and calm the situation was important.

"I was there. Abby was the one who broke the glasses," he said calmly.

"Of course, you're going to say that. You're fucking Eve."

Kevin winced, but he didn't—couldn't—deny it. "That doesn't have anything to do with it, Wes. Let's not make this worse."

Wes started to move forward. "Pay up, Eve."

Kevin put a hand up. "Stop it, Wes. It's not that big of a deal."

"Abby was embarrassed in front of everyone," Wes said. "She got kicked out of Tony's!"

"Abby embarrassed herself long before I did anything," Eve said, stepping forward.

Without warning, Abby lunged forward and swiped at Eve. She wasn't close enough to make good contact with Eve's cheek but she caught her hair and whipped it across Eve's eyes.

"Take it easy." Kevin caught Abby's wrist and pushed her back as Eve wiped her hair out of her face.

"Don't touch her!" Wes shoved Kevin's shoulder.

Kevin dropped his hold on Abby, but turned to Wes with a frown. "I wouldn't suggest doing that again."

"This?" Wes shoved him again.

Kevin breathed in through his nose, trying to keep his cool. But this night had been crazy. He'd gone to help Ryan, only to find the kid belligerent and still spoiling for a fight. He'd come home to find Eve gone and then to Tony's to find her dressed, talking and acting like the polar opposite of the Eve he'd expected. Then he'd been confronted with the truth that he'd screwed up bigger than anyone.

He and Eve needed to work this out, but instead he was

facing down a mad big brother who was being an ass. And shoving him.

"Knock it off," Kevin said through gritted teeth. "I don't want to have a problem here." He didn't want *another* problem. This thing with Eve was big enough.

"No problem, as long as Eve apologizes and pays for half the damages," Wes said.

"Apologize to Abby?" Eve laughed. "I don't think so."

Wes went to grab for Eve and Kevin saw red.

He put his hands on Wes's chest and pushed. Hard.

Wes went sprawling to the ground.

"Stay there," Kevin ordered. "Or it'll hurt a lot more next time."

Wes, of course, didn't listen. He scrambled to his feet and charged at Kevin.

Kevin sighed. He ducked as Wes swung, then pulled his fist back and hit Wes in the jaw.

Wes slumped to the ground.

Abby screamed as the door to Tony's swung open, people stumbling out onto the sidewalk to see what was going on.

When Wes groaned and lifted his hand to his face, Abby whirled on Eve and grabbed for her again, catching her hair. She yanked and Eve yelled as she brought her hands up and dug her fingernails into Abby's hand to get her to let go.

"You bitch!" Abby cried as Eve spun away.

"You do not want to mess with me tonight," Eve warned.

Abby came at her again anyway and Eve pulled her arm back and connected with Abby's cheek in a fairly impressive right hook.

Screaming and crying, her hand against her face, Abby called Eve several more unflattering names as Kevin grabbed Eve around the waist and held her back.

"Let me go!" Eve told him.

"No way in hell." He started toward his truck, determined to get her away from the scene and calm her down. But as he reached for the door, he heard the sound that ensured he was going to end his night with a blistering headache and in a really horrible mood—police sirens.

💋

Kevin watched Eve pace the tiny holding cell in the Grover police station—and attempt to ignore him—for ten minutes.

She was across the cell, her back to him when he finally couldn't stand it anymore.

"I didn't know Mrs. Rosner was coming over tonight."

He watched her spine straighten and her turn to face him slowly, her eyes wide. "How would it have been different if you'd known?"

That was a very good question.

He sighed and got to his feet. "Eve, I never meant to hurt you."

"I assume you never meant for me to find out at all."

"I…" Okay, maybe that was true. "I want to be Drew's guardian."

"And yet here you are sitting in a jail cell. And, gee, do I smell beer on your breath? I also recall you dropping a few swear words."

"Yeah," he sighed. "Unfortunately that's not all that unusual for me either." He ran a hand through his hair. Hell, he was always on the verge of all of this anyway. It seemed fitting that it would all come boiling over at the worst possible time.

"You know what's the worst part of all of this?" she asked after a moment of silence. "My dad was disappointed in me and my choices and my mistakes, but he told me that upfront to my face. You lied about being with me because of those mistakes and then had no intention of ever telling *me* that it all bothered you so much." She crossed her arms. "With my dad I earned his rejection. I mean, I really did all of the things he hated, knowing he'd hate them. But with you, you say my past mistakes don't matter, then it ends up mattering more than anything else—more than what you *do* know about me."

Kevin just stared at her. He had nothing to say. No idea how to fix this.

He'd screwed things up and hurt her just like her father had.

That was big. Really big.

He felt sick. And desperate. He opened his mouth, but she went on.

"I know you were trying to be supportive, saying my record and past didn't matter. And I went along because I didn't want to tell you all the gory details of my screw-ups or that I've lost faith in a lot of things. But I should have insisted. Because when my father turned his back, it was real. It hurt, but it was based on real things. You wanting me in your life, without knowing about the mistakes, pretending things are perfect, isn't real." She took a deep breath and dropped her hands to her sides. She met his gaze directly. "In high school you were afraid of me finding out who you really were. Well, I've been feeling like that since you came back to Grover. And it's exhausting. It's time for us both to be real—good, bad and ugly—with each other. So…" She took another deep breath, then said, "I was arrested as an accessory to felony embezzlement, but I was found not guilty. I don't go to church anymore, ever. I can drink four beers and not feel even a buzz. I *love* tequila. Straight up. But in any mixed drink too. I like marijuana. I don't use it often and definitely prefer edibles, but yeah, I like it." Before he could respond—as if he had any idea whatsoever how to respond—the door at the end of the hall opened and Libby came through with one of the cops that had brought them in from Tony's.

Eve moved to the side of the cell. "Libby?"

"They're willing to release you since I vouched for you," Libby said, her eyes on Kevin. "Well, that and the bail. But I'm enjoying coming to your rescue more than I should."

Eve smiled and Kevin had to suck in a quick breath. Would he ever see that smile aimed at him again?

"How'd you know what happened?" Eve asked.

"Steve called me."

"Ah."

"Steve?" Kevin asked.

"One of the cops. He and I see each other sometimes. And he knows I'm helping out with Drew. And that you're Drew's big brother." She paused. "Small towns are great. Sometimes."

The officer unlocked their door and Eve stepped through.

"Eve," Kevin said without any idea what he was going to say next.

"I understand, Kevin," she said, without looking at him. "You're right that I could hurt your situation with Drew. But you don't have to worry about what to tell Mrs. Rosner about me now. I'm done."

*No!* Everything in him protested. He stepped forward. "We can't be done."

She did look at him then. And the sadness in her eyes tore him apart. "Really? 'Cause it seems to me that in a lot of ways we never really got started."

It was after two a.m. but Kevin wasn't completely surprised to hear footsteps coming down the stairs. He couldn't explain it except to think that of course his little brother would need something in the middle of the worst night he'd had in a really long time. It would be something big too. Drew was sick or there'd been a nightmare or something. Drew never got out of bed in the night, and if he did Kevin knew he wouldn't come to him without Eve.

Eve.

Even thinking her name made his chest hurt.

He'd failed her. They'd screwed it all up. Again.

He tried to grab onto the fact that she was part of this. She hadn't been upfront and honest with him. She hadn't trusted him, which had led him to not trust her and to—stupidly—lie to Mrs. Rosner.

But, bottom line, *he* was the one who had lied.

Drew came around the end of the couch and stood there looking at Kevin.

Kevin didn't make any sudden movements. He still felt Drew was like a wild squirrel or rabbit and would bolt if he thought Kevin was paying attention.

Instead, he shocked Kevin by leaning closer to look at *An Encyclopedia of the Presidents* Kevin had open in his lap. Kevin had been trying to read it. He really had. But his mind had been wandering and the throbbing in his heart wouldn't stop long enough for him to concentrate on any words.

"That book isn't going to help you much with the problem you have," Drew said.

Kevin lifted his brows. "Which problem is that?" It seemed he had a rather impressive list of them.

Drew flopped into the arm chair that sat at the end of the coffee table. "Maybe I can put this in terms you can understand."

Kevin wasn't about to interrupt this. For one, Drew was talking to him. For another, he could use any advice he could get.

"It's like Eve was the quarterback of the team and her dad was the center on the offensive line. His job was to give her the ball—love and trust—and then block to protect her from the people trying to take that away from her, so she could pass it on to the other people who were on her team."

Kevin knew his mouth was hanging open, but he wouldn't have interrupted this for anything.

"But then she ended up sacked. A bunch of times. Her dad wasn't protecting her. So then she stopped giving the ball away at all. She kept it to herself. But you know it's hard to score any touchdowns that way."

Kevin found himself nodding along to the seemingly ridiculous, yet incredibly insightful, analogy.

"Then you came along, and she started thinking she had a new center, someone who could protect her and help her score."

Kevin's mouth curled up.

"But then she not only got sacked but it was *you* who knocked her down."

His smile died.

"You can understand why it was hard for her to think that she can pass love and trust on, because there's nobody there protecting her when she does."

Drew sounded like he was four times his age.

"Yeah." Kevin had to clear his throat. "I can understand that."

The kid was right. Her dad had hurt her badly. It made sense that she would be careful trusting someone again. Especially when she didn't really know Kevin anymore.

He had felt fear and hesitation in light of the changes in her over the years. Of course that would go both ways.

"You and Eve have been talking a lot," he finally said to Drew.

"Yeah." The kid shrugged. "Mostly about football. And some about families and people we love and trust and want to depend on."

Kevin really looked at his brother. He was dressed in gray cotton shorts and a *Star Wars* T-shirt. His hair stuck up over his right ear and he had a crease from his pillow on his right cheek. But his eyes were bright and he met Kevin's gaze directly.

"You seem to really get it," Kevin said. Both football and relationships.

"I'm exceptionally bright."

Kevin didn't know what to say to that. It was like Drew commenting that the sky was blue. It wasn't like Kevin needed to agree here.

After a long pause, Drew asked, "Are *you*?"

"Am I what?"

Drew rolled his eyes. "Exceptionally bright."

Oh. No, Kevin didn't think he was, actually. "If you were me, what would you do?"

"Talk to Eve. Tell her I'm sorry. And then tell her how I feel about her and that the other stuff doesn't matter. Tell her I would protect her heart and trust, no matter what."

Kevin nodded and sighed.

"And I would *beg* for her forgiveness."

Clearly Drew had gotten his intelligence from his mother, because there wasn't a lot of astuteness with women on the Campbell side of the family.

# CHAPTER
# THIRTEEN

IF SHE WAS GOING to feel like crap in the morning, the night before should at least include rum.

Her head hurt, her heart hurt, she felt fuzzy headed and none of it was from the two beers she'd had—actually, one and two-thirds—last night.

It was all Kevin's fault.

Eve sighed as she looked into her fridge. She'd been spending so much time at Kevin's that she'd sadly neglected her own shopping.

Of course, she did own a restaurant.

Swinging the fridge door shut, she realized that not only was she going to need to go into Sherry's to eat, she needed to work. The pile of paperwork that had accumulated on her desk might keep her mind off of the mess the rest of her life had become and if that didn't work, she could help out front. Sunday after church was a busy time.

Forty minutes later, she was digging in her purse for her car keys when the doorbell rang.

She jumped, her eyes going immediately to the clock. Church

had let out about five minutes ago. She took a deep breath, set her purse down and proceeded calmly to the door.

Then she wrenched it open, convinced Kevin would be on the other side.

He had some major groveling to do after all.

Instead, she blinked into the bright sunlight shining on the heads of the five women on her porch. It looked like they were wearing halos.

"Lacey?" she asked, surprised.

The blonde grinned at her as Libby handed Eve a huge thermos. "Hazelnut cream coffee," she said.

"What's going on?" But she readily took the coffee.

Monica held out a plate of cinnamon rolls with frosting so thick Eve's mouth started watering.

"Breakfast," Monica said.

"Breakfast," Eve repeated, confused.

She looked at each woman, including Beth Reynolds and Connie Fisher, who stood smiling behind Libby. Beth had always been a quiet, mousy girl who liked books better than people and blended into the background, but she had a beautiful, sincere smile that helped ease some tension in Eve's shoulders. Connie, on the other hand, was an energetic older woman who was generally known for being loud and boisterous. This morning, though, she wore a bright smile and a twinkle in her eye that made Eve smile in return.

"Why?" Eve finally asked them.

"You had a late night," Lacey said. "We heard all about it."

Of course they had. It was a *very* small town.

"And because you're awesome," Connie added. "We were talking before church about how you stuck up for Heather last night in front of everyone."

Eve blinked at her. "You heard about that? At church?"

Lacey grinned. "Libby leads the adult Sunday school class. Everyone shows up early to chat and have coffee before we start." Suddenly she stepped forward and grabbed Eve in a hug. "Thank you for being such a good friend to Heather and Drew."

Eve hugged her back, too stunned to do anything else.

"That's really nice," she said as Lacey released her. "But you know I was arrested for that last night, right?" She looked at Connie and Beth. She knew how Lacey and Libby felt about Drew and Heather but she wasn't sure about the rest of the town.

Connie smiled. "You stood up for someone who needed someone to support them."

"I hit her," Eve confessed, to see if anyone flinched.

They didn't.

"We know." Lacey's grin showed that she wasn't a bit offended.

"I would have too."

Everyone turned to look at Beth.

"Except that I don't know how to throw a punch," she added with a little smile.

Eve couldn't help it. She burst out laughing.

"You ladies want to come in for rolls?" she asked, stepping back.

"Nah, you get to keep them all," Monica said. "You earned them."

"And I'm hoping you'll let me bring a casserole or something over tomorrow," Connie said. "We were talking about how you and Kevin have stepped up to help Heather and be there for Drew. Not only defending them in the bar, but truly being there. That's a lot of work and sacrifice. I'd like to help you out somehow if I can."

Eve felt tears well up and she blinked rapidly. "Connie, that's…really nice." That seemed inadequate somehow. It was about more than a casserole that was for sure. She was being admired by someone. That hadn't happened in a long time.

The women said their goodbyes and Eve enjoyed her breakfast. The cinnamon rolls were Monica's—which meant they were amazing—and the coffee was perfect.

When she walked into Sherry's twenty minutes later, she was feeling better. Surprised, but better.

Deep in thought, she was halfway across the restaurant before she realized everyone was quiet and staring at her.

She stopped. Quiet in Sherry's was unheard of.

Had someone died?

She looked around. "What?"

Was this about last night? Was she going to be judged after all? Right here in her own dining room?

She felt her heart start to pound and her eyes narrowed, but before she could say anything she heard a man behind her clear his throat.

Turning, her mouth open to respond to…whatever…she froze.

Kevin stood by the front counter, Drew perched on one of the stools beside him, a plate of half-eaten pancakes in front of him.

Oh, boy. She wasn't quite ready for this.

Focusing on the little boy she wanted to hug instead of the big man she wanted to cling to, she forced herself to smile. "Hey, D."

That was all it took for him to throw himself off the stool and run to grab her in a hug. She squeezed him tight for a moment, pressing her lips together so she wouldn't cry. It was stupid to be sad or feel like she was losing him. He lived here, so did she. She'd seen him every morning since Heather had started working at Sherry's. There was no reason to feel she wasn't going to see him again.

But it wouldn't be the same.

And she already missed it.

Finally, she couldn't avoid Kevin any longer. She lifted her attention to him.

"I have something I need to say," he told her the moment she looked up.

Yeah, she knew he did. "Let's go into the kitchen." She let go of Drew and started forwarding, trying to strategize how to get around Kevin and into the back room without brushing against him—or wanting to.

It was never going to work.

"No. I want everyone to hear this."

She stopped a foot in front of him. Oh, crap. "Why?" She pressed her hand against her stomach as it threatened to reject the cinnamon roll. But he wouldn't tell her he never wanted to see her again in front of the entire town would he?

"Because I haven't done a good job of showing the world how much I love you."

Her stomach definitely pitched then, but in a much better way.

"What do you—" she started hoarsely

But he continued on, his voice easily heard throughout the restaurant. No one even dared click their spoon against their plate.

"When I first saw you in Algebra II, you were sitting in the second chair from the door. You were wearing a yellow top and jeans, your hair was loose and you didn't have any make-up on. When I walked past, you looked up and smiled at me. And I couldn't breathe."

He took a step closer and Eve knew how he felt. At that very moment, in fact. He remembered what she'd *worn* fifteen years ago?

"I'd made a point of avoiding the preacher's daughter, for obvious reasons." He gave a self-deprecating half-grin. "But once I was hooked, I was *really* hooked. And I have been ever since."

She felt the insane urge to giggle. It was adrenaline she knew, but it was completely inappropriate. "Kevin, I—"

"Hang on," he said, stepping forward again and taking her hand. "I'm sorry I hurt you. And I know I did. Of course, I did. Stating that you have nothing to do with my life or Drew's was wrong, and a complete lie and unforgiveable." He squeezed her hand. The warmth from his touch and the warmth in his eyes spread through her.

"And I know that you've had people let you down. But I want to promise you, in front of all these people, that I will not only be your center, I'll be your entire offensive line from here on out."

Her offensive line? She glanced at Drew to find him grinning at her and nodding. "Kevin, I—"

"You have nothing to worry about. You're protected. No one's getting through who can hurt you or ruin your chances of completing every pass."

Now she really felt like giggling. Drew had, somehow, helped Kevin with this football analogy. And she was pretty sure she understood it. Even if she didn't get every detail, it was a nice effort.

"Kevin, I—"

"I'm almost done." He tugged her close. "I'm in love with you, Eve. You are who I want and need. I'm sorry for not showing you every single day, but starting today, you and the whole world will know." He went down on one knee, her hand still in his. "Eve Marie Donnelly Campbell, will you marry me? Again?"

Emotions coursed through her like she'd been hit by a tidal wave. She was warm and cold, shaking, having a hard time keeping her feet. She didn't know why this was so shocking, but it was. Here? Like this? In front of everyone? He was claiming her in public, declaring his feelings. Everyone now knew that he wanted her, in spite of everything.

She stared at him. He was giving her exactly what she wanted. She had to say yes. She had to say of course.

But as she opened her mouth, she looked at Drew.

Drew. The whole reason Kevin was here, the reason he was back in her life. Drew, who she'd also fallen in love with. Drew—who still needed them, needed Kevin, for all of the reasons he'd come back to Grover. She flashed to the moment when Mrs. Rosner told her that Kevin had claimed there was no chance at reconciliation.

The sharp pain jabbed her again, but in its wake she realized how he could have said it. This whole thing, from the beginning, had been about Drew. Their reconciliation could change everything for the boy.

Kevin shouldn't have lied, of course. He should have talked to her about it. They should have figured the solution out together. But the *reasons* he'd done it were still true. Her background check could put them at risk in the eyes of the court that would decide where Drew would spend the next six months. None of that had changed.

She licked her suddenly dry lips and shook her head. "Kevin, I don't know. I don't think that it's…" She glanced at Drew. "It's not a good idea," she finally said.

She and Kevin were married regardless. They would have to deal with that at some point. And she was in love with him. In spite of the hurt, and the fact that no one could ever hurt her like he could, she loved him. And she believed he loved her. He was flawed, imperfect, but that was actually nice to know. She could never be with someone who was perfect.

However, right now the focus needed to be on Drew. In six months, when Heather was back, they could talk about it.

"We should wait. See what happens with the judge. Let's not make that any harder."

"Okay." Kevin got to his feet, his face serious where before it had been open and happy. "I understand. But I swear to you, Eve, I'm going to prove this to you."

"You don't have to prove anything," she assured him. "I don't want to be a complication. You weren't wrong about that."

"You're part of the *solution*, Eve. We need you."

That melted her enough to make her smile. "The judge might not—"

But he leaned in and covered her lips with his.

He kissed her sweetly, but thoroughly and for long enough to not leave a shred of doubt in anyone's mind that they were very reconciled.

She was still trying to catch her breath when he stepped back, put a hand on Drew's head and steered the boy toward the door.

Eve's fingers were against her lips when he turned back and said, loud enough for everyone to hear, "I love you, Eve."

They disappeared through the door with equally satisfied grins.

Ten seconds after the door swung shut, the restaurant erupted. Everyone wanted to know what he meant by *re*-marry and when had that happened and how had no one known. Of course, everyone agreed that she should say yes.

Realizing that she wasn't going to get a word in anyway, Eve headed for her office in a daze.

But the reprieve only lasted thirty minutes. Which was twenty-five more than she'd expected.

"Eve? Felix Potter says he has something for you," Lisa, one of their waitresses, said from her office doorway.

"What is it?"

"He didn't say."

Of course he hadn't. Eve got to her feet. It wasn't like she could stay in her office for the next six months anyway. Her head was a little clearer now though. She loved Kevin, she believed he loved her too and she believed they might have a chance at making a real marriage work, but they couldn't do it now. They had things to work out, things to talk about before recommitting everything. That would be a great way to spend the next few months.

Drew needed them to not be selfish. They'd been apart this long. Another few months was nothing. And it wasn't like they couldn't see each other. She couldn't be one of Drew's primary caregivers but they could still all hang out together.

Feeling better about things she headed out front with a smile.

"Hi, Eve."

"Hi, Felix. Generally people come in here to get things from me, not give them to me."

"This is a special occasion," he said. He handed her a purple envelope.

"What this?" But a moment later her heart thumped. Her name was all that was written on the front but it was clearly Kevin's handwriting. "A love note?" she asked.

They couldn't renew their vows right now, but she wouldn't mind having some romance, for sure.

"Guess you have to open it," Felix teased.

She noted that most of her patrons were watching, but she could easily get used to everyone knowing she and Kevin were together. She ripped the envelope open and pulled out the piece of purple paper.

*I promise to love, honor and cherish you.*

That was all. Those few words. But Eve was choked up anyway.

"Thanks, Felix," she said.

"You're gonna say yes, aren't you?" he asked.

"When it's the right time," she answered, truthfully.

An hour later, Paul Carter came into the restaurant with another envelope.

Eve felt a little giddy. This one said simply, *For better or worse.*

He was giving her his vows anyway.

Sniffing, she smiled at Paul. And the next five messengers. They arrived on the hour. Each note held another vow.

*In sickness and in health.*

*For richer or poorer.*

*Forsaking all others.*

*As long as we both shall live.*

All were in his handwriting. All made her heart trip.

The last one said, *Marry me again tomorrow.*

That was the only one that tripped her up. They couldn't do it tomorrow. They were scheduled to meet with the judge about the guardianship on Friday.

No more messengers came, but Eve wasn't sure what to expect next. She drove home that night and approached her door with trepidation.

But nothing waited. No one waited.

Trying not to be disappointed, she ate two more cinnamon rolls, took a shower and climbed into bed.

She wondered what Kevin and Drew were having for dinner, what they were talking about, if Drew had any homework to catch up on. But she resisted calling. Or going over.

Barely.

She knew if she did contact Kevin, he would want an answer about getting married again tomorrow. And she couldn't say yes. But she also couldn't say no.

She wasn't good at saying no to Kevin.

Instead, she made herself go to bed early, so she could be at the restaurant in the morning to see Drew before school. She knew Kevin would bring him in.

She knew she could try to explain to him why she wanted to wait, but she had a feeling he would just try harder to talk her into it…and frankly, she doubted her ability to resist.

Still she fell asleep imagining all the tactics he might use to persuade her.

💋

Kevin had the best reason ever for being glad he was madly in love and married—it should shut his friends up.

But as it turned out, just because he was happily, completely committed to a woman, his friends would not stop talking about his love—and sex—life.

"Clearly you're going to have to pull out the big guns," Dooley said.

Kevin shook his head. "Short of tying her up and carrying her up the aisle, I don't know what else will work."

"Don't underestimate the use of duct tape in emergency situations," Mac said, tossing a soda bottle into the recycling bin.

"Even duct tape won't work," Kevin said.

Eve was too stubborn. He'd been working on winning her over for the past four days. Every hour for six hours each day she got a note, each with another vow. They were delivered by various people in the community so she'd know that he wanted everyone to know how he felt. Lacey and Libby had each delivered one. Pastor Bryan had even called Kevin and asked why he hadn't gotten to deliver one yet.

But she had yet to say yes to the final note asking her to marry him the next day. Whichever day. It didn't matter. As long as she said yes.

It was Thursday and they were meeting with the judge tomorrow. Drew was sleeping at Libby and Lacey's and then they were bringing him to Omaha to meet at the courthouse.

He needed Eve to say yes tonight. Before that meeting

He wanted Eve to know that he didn't care what the judge or Mrs. Rosner thought or decided. He wanted Eve. They'd figure the rest out.

But she wasn't budging. Every morning he and Drew showed up for breakfast and he'd ask her to re-marry him again. And every morning she smiled, leaned in to kiss him, then said not yet.

Not yet. That was her answer. It wasn't no, but it sure as hell wasn't yes.

"Kev, she has a point," Sam said, also tossing a soda bottle into the bin. He and Mac were seeing who could drink the most Dr. Pepper before their next call.

It was nice to see that settling down hadn't resulted in them completely growing up.

Kevin rolled his eyes as they each opened their third. This couldn't end well.

"I don't care about her point. My point is more important," he said firmly.

"She wants to wait until Heather's home," Sam said. "Then nothing will be in the way."

"But I want to show her that I don't care what's in the way. I want her no matter what. Right now," Kevin said.

He was generally the more patient, gentle one of the group but when he needed to be stubborn, he could go toe to toe with any of them.

"Drew needs you, buddy," Mac said, swallowing a large gulp of soda and grimacing as it went down. "What if the judge says it's Drew or Eve?"

Kevin's heart clenched at the thought. His brother needed him. His father and Heather had trusted him to take care of Drew. But... "I think Eve needs me more."

Dooley lifted an eyebrow. "Yeah? How's an independent adult woman who runs her own business and has lived on her own for over a decade need you more than an innocent ten year old boy who can't cook, drive or take care of himself?"

"Drew and I were talking about that and—"

"You've talked to Drew about all of this?" Dooley interrupted.

Kevin nodded. The kid amazed him, pure and simple. He'd pointed out that cooking, driving and making sure he brushed his teeth at night were basics that could fall to almost anyone.

"Drew feels secure that he has lots of people who care about him. And I can be there, be around for him, even if he doesn't live with me. Same for Eve."

Lacey and Libby had turned into absolute life-savers. And friends. Or rather, they'd always been that and Kevin had finally admitted it. Besides helping out with Drew, they'd showed Kevin that he didn't have to have all the answers or be present twenty-four-seven to be important and influential with Drew.

Plus, Drew had his mother, of course, and Mrs. Rosner who would make sure he was cared for, and dozens of people in Grover who would help out however was needed. Even his own father might come around. Eventually. Maybe.

But no matter who else stepped up—or didn't—Drew had Kevin and Eve. He might not be able to live with them, but he could count on them to do whatever he needed them to do.

Eve on the other hand…

"Eve doesn't have people who care about her?" Mac asked.

"Not that can give her the things I can."

His friends exchanged knowing smiles.

Yeah, okay, that sounded dirty. But he only kind-of meant it that way.

Eve needed someone who would love her unconditionally and be there no matter how hard she pushed him away. She had friends, but there was no one who would love her like Kevin did.

"Drew thinks that this is the perfect chance to show Eve that I'm not walking away again. No matter how tough or complicated things get or what she does, or has done, I'll be there. She needs that."

The guys didn't say anything to that. Which was completely out of character. Kevin frowned at them. "What?"

Sam cleared his throat. "I think we all need that."

"Yeah, go for it, man," Mac said.

"That kid's something, isn't he?" Dooley asked.

"Yes he is." Kevin wasn't sure how he would have handled all of this without Drew being cool and loving Eve and wanting her to be happy.

"So, I'm stupid in love like all of you have been," he said. "What do I do to convince her?"

Sam pushed up from his chair and crossed to the table that sat by the sink in the break room. "We have something to give you," he said, coming back to Kevin and holding out a folder.

"What's this?" He didn't want a copy of Eve's background check, or a letter from the state of Nebraska telling him the guardianship had been turned down.

"It's a gift." Sam reclaimed his seat. "From all of us."

Kevin opened it up. Sure enough, the letterhead read *State of Nebraska*.

"What—"

"Read it," Dooley said, nudging his foot.

He did.

By the time he'd flipped to the last page, his chest and throat were tight. "Really?" he asked gruffly, looking up at each of his friends.

"Really," Sam said, then chugged half his soda.

"But…why? You don't even know him."

"We don't have to know him. We know you and that's more than enough recommendation for us," Mac said.

The guys and their wives—fiancé in Dooley's case—had all submitted applications to the state to become foster parents and written letters to Mrs. Rosner stating that any of them were ready and willing to step in immediately if Drew needed somewhere to go.

Kevin swiped at his eyes, knowing the guys would razz him unmercifully for getting choked up.

But none of them did anything more than meet his gaze when he looked up again. "I don't know what to say."

"We don't think it will be necessary," Sam said. "But Danika said it would be good to have everything in order just in case. This way you and Eve don't have to worry about Drew. Like you said, you'll still be around, with him, all of that. But he can have another place to sleep and eat, if needed."

"It will be out of his school district and away from everything that's familiar," Mac pointed out. "But we're hoping that will work in *your* favor. That they'll prefer to leave him with you."

"But if that doesn't work, maybe this will." Dooley handed him one more letter.

It was from Lacey and Libby stating that they were also willing and able to take care of Drew, with Kevin's support, until Heather was home.

"All of the applications have been approved," Mac said.

"When did you do this?" Kevin asked. He was sure for couples like these—even Ben and Jessica had applied in spite of having a baby of their own at home—it would be a piece of cake to get approved, but it surely hadn't happened just since Sunday.

"We talked about it right from the beginning, actually," Sam said. "Dani came home that night and was telling me about how hard it can be to place kids like Drew and how lucky he was to have you."

"Then me and the guys were talking about how much you do for all of us," Dooley said. "And for everyone. And we realized that we wouldn't mind being more like you." His voice was a little gruff by the time he finished and he had to clear his throat.

Kevin didn't know what to say. Which was okay, since he couldn't speak anyway.

"So even if Drew doesn't need a place to stay, I think Dani and I are going to do the foster parent thing," Sam said.

"Yeah, us too," Mac said.

"Morgan and I are going to talk about it," Dooley said. "With Dad we don't have a ton of room, but we could do the emergency thing where kids can come to us for the night or a couple days until they can be placed more permanently."

Kevin nodded. They were all great people and any kid would be lucky to spend even a few hours with them.

Finally, he coughed and found his voice. "You guys are amazing."

"Right back at 'ya," Sam said, toasting with his fourth Dr. Pepper.

Kevin sat back on the couch, satisfaction seeping through him.

Drew was going to be okay. And Kevin had made an impression. He'd lived a good life, he was an example that others were watching and now repeating. Maybe he was figuring all of this out after all.

He couldn't ask for more than that.

Well, that and Eve.

But that was just a matter of time. Now she had no more excuses.

It was getting more and more difficult to say no to Kevin. Every morning she had to look into Drew's eyes to remind herself that waiting was the right thing to do.

But Friday morning it was really easy to resist saying yes.

Because Kevin didn't ask her to marry him. He didn't even show up. Neither did Drew.

She must have slammed her tray down loudly one too many times because Monica finally snapped, "Can you say yes already? I'm running out of eggs keeping up with the crowd that shows up every morning to see you get proposed to."

"I can't say yes if he doesn't come in and ask me, can I?" she snapped right back at her partner and friend.

Monica frowned at her. "You really think he's changed his mind all of a sudden?"

"He isn't here."

"Eve," Monica said, clearly exasperated, "he's in love with you. That doesn't change that easily."

That stopped Eve. She breathed, then asked softly, "You sure?"

Monica put her whisk down and came around the counter. She put her hands on Eve's face and said gently, "I'm sure. He loves you. You have to trust that. Show him that you trust it."

Eve knew she was right. Kevin wasn't her father. Kevin was a great man. Who loved her. And she remembered— "He worked last night. He stayed in Omaha for the meeting with the judge."

"There you go—"

Eve gasped. "The judge!" She spun toward the door. "Monica, I have to go. I have to be there."

Monica sighed as Eve tossed her apron to the side and grabbed her purse.

"At least pick up more eggs on your way back, okay?" Monica called after her.

Eve had just run into the courthouse, when her cell phone rang.

"Hello?" She was breathless from jogging across the parking lot and up the steps.

"Eve, it's Lacey. I'm at the judge's meeting. I think you should try to get here."

"I'm here."

"Oh, then hustle. Judge Henricks."

Eve headed for the directory, found Judge Henricks in room three twenty-one, then ran for the steps. She was sucking wind by the time she got to the third floor. She found three twenty-one and burst in to find herself face to face with the judge's secretary.

"Can I help you?"

"I need to…" Eve stopped, bent to brace her hands on her knees and wheezed for a moment. Then she straightened. "I need to get into the hearing."

"The hearing?" the woman asked.

"With…" She had to stop and breathe again before she could say, "Kevin Campbell. About Drew Hansen."

"Ah. Room three thirty-two. Go down the hall, take a left."

The hearing was supposed to start at nine and it was already nine sixteen so Eve jogged once she left the Judge's office in spite of the fact she was pretty sure she was on the verge of her lungs exploding. She really needed to get on the treadmill more often.

She heard voices on the other side of the door as she approached the court room and she quietly pushed the door open far enough to see inside. Could she sneak in unnoticed?

The door was at the back of the room and all she saw were the backs of people, so she slipped inside and let the door bump gently shut behind her before moving forward. It was a fairly typical looking court room, though smaller than the ones she'd been in.

It took only a second to realize that Kevin was the voice she'd heard from the hallway. He was standing behind the long table in front of the judge.

"All of these people are here on Drew's behalf, Your Honor," he was saying. "I think you would agree that he's well supported."

"Yes, very impressive Mr. Campbell."

"I understand that there are some concerns about leaving him in my care, but I want to assure you that Drew is happy, healthy and well-adjusted."

"Mrs. Rosner's report suggests the same," Judge Henricks commented.

Eve slipped into the back row.

"And if there was any reason that Drew should *not* be in my care, I would be the first to be looking for a better placement," Kevin said.

"You've done that as well from the looks of it," Judge Henricks said. "I can honestly say that I've never had a case where there were five excellent options for placement and they all showed up at the hearing."

Five options? Eve took a seat and more carefully surveyed the room. The guys she'd been sneaking behind were now familiar. They were Kevin's friends. Including Dooley. Wow. Kevin really did have good friends who would never let him down. They all had women sitting next to them, who she assumed were wives and fiancées, and they all looked serious.

"Yes, sir," Kevin said. "All of these people have submitted applications and been approved. If Drew needs another place to go, any of them would be an excellent choice."

Eve frowned. All of his friends were here to offer Drew an option? Wow.

"I understand there were initial concerns with your wife and her involvement," the judge said.

Eve craned her neck to find Drew. He sat between Kevin and a man in a suit and tie, who sat next to a woman in a suit. Eve had done some research on how this all worked and she assumed one of them was the Guardian Ad Litem, who would have been appointed to be sure that Drew's best interests were represented, and one was the attorney who had been appointed by the Department of Health and Human Services for Kevin. Mrs. Rosner sat at the other end of the long table.

Kevin nodded. "Yes. There were. But I want to go on record as saying that there is no better person for Drew to be around and learn from than Eve. She has been nothing but amazing with him."

"Do you like Eve, Drew?" the judge asked.

"Absolutely," Drew answered without hesitation. "Eve's the best."

The judge smiled. "She was unable to accompany you this morning?" he asked.

"Yes, she owns a restaurant—"

"I'm here!" Eve stood swiftly and stepped into the aisle, facing the judge.

Kevin turned, obviously shocked to see her. "You came?"

She moved forward until she was beside the table next to Mrs. Rosner. "Of course."

"You must be Eve," Judge Henricks said.

"That's right." Eve took a deep breath. "Can I say something?"

"Oh, that's not—"

"It'll be fast."

The judge sighed. "Sure, why not?"

Kevin stayed on his feet, still staring at her.

She met his gaze. "I know I'm not perfect. I've made mistakes. But I've learned from them and I think Drew can learn a lot from someone like me."

"I agree," Kevin said quickly. He looked at the judge. "Eve and I are great role models for how to fall down and get back up again."

"Mr. Campbell, it's important—"

"And all of these people are amazing," Eve said, inwardly

cringing and hoping the judge didn't have a gavel he could bang —or throw at someone. "But I've seen Kevin with Drew. Even when things were rocky and Drew was pushing him away, Kevin was there. He hung in there. He was determined to show Drew that he had someone he could depend on. I know, because he's done the same for me."

"Eve too," Kevin said as the judge opened his mouth. "She stepped in to help both Drew and I, but she stayed and was there for him even when she was fed up with me. Drew will never have to worry about being alone."

The judge started to speak but then hesitated as if expecting to be interrupted.

Kevin and Eve stood grinning at each other instead.

It occurred to her that maybe she should feel amazed by the things Kevin had said, but instead it felt right. She wasn't surprised, because deep down she knew he felt that way about her.

"Anyone else have anything they'd like to say?" the judge asked the rest of the room.

There was a second of silence—maybe a millisecond—then everyone stood and started talking at once.

The judge held up his hand and everyone got quiet.

"I was being sarcastic," he said. "Mr. Campbell, as I was about to say, I see no reason why you and *Mrs.* Campbell, shouldn't be Drew's temporary guardians."

Eve gasped and Kevin looked startled.

"Mrs. Rosner's report brought up concerns but it addressed each concern and now meeting you—and your entourage—today, I believe Drew will be in good hands."

Everyone stared at him.

"Mr. Atwall, the GAL, agrees."

The man next to Drew nodded.

"And Ms. Shelby has no concerns," the judge said.

The woman next to Mr. Atwall also nodded.

"Your request for guardianship of Drew Hansen is hereby granted."

No one made a sound. No one even blinked.

Judge Henricks looked up from the paper he'd signed, then handed it to a young woman who delivered it to Mrs. Rosner. Then he looked around the room. Eyebrows up he said, "That's it."

Kevin's friends moved in, surrounding them, hugging both Kevin and Eve. Drew climbed onto his chair and grinned at Eve over everyone's heads.

She gave him a wink and then turned to the judge. "Sir, do you ever perform wedding ceremonies?" she called.

"One of my favorite parts of the job," he said as he rose from his chair.

"Are you busy right now?"

That got everyone's attention. They all fell silent.

"Actually," the judge said, looking around. "I think I could spare a few more minutes."

Kevin stared at her. "Right now?"

She nodded. "Kevin Campbell, will you marry me—again?"

His grin was quick and bright. "Hell, yes."

She laughed and everyone started talking at once again.

"Really? Right now?" Drew jumped down from the chair. "Today? *Now*?"

"Yep, right now," Kevin said. He crouched down and asked, "Will you be my best man? I need somebody to stand beside me."

"Your best man?" Drew repeated. "Really?"

"Of course. You're my..." Kevin cleared his throat. "You're my brother. My only one."

"I'm only your half-brother."

Kevin blew out a breath, clearly trying to get past the tightness in his throat. "Well, I'd rather have you as a half-brother than anyone else as a full brother."

Eve sniffed and both guys looked up to find her wiping a tear. They looked at one another and grinned.

"Mom and Lacey and Libby cry over dumb stuff too," Drew told him.

"This is *not* a dumb thing," Eve protested. "This is the *best* thing."

Kevin and Drew shared another grin and Drew nodded. "Yeah, I'll be your best man."

Everyone moved and shifted, until Kevin, Eve, and Drew were directly in front of the judge.

Kevin turned to face her, taking her hands. "You ready for this?"

"I've been ready for this for twelve years," she told him confidently.

And fifteen minutes later, Kevin Campbell kissed his bride.

Again.

*Thank you for reading Why You Should Never Kiss Your Ex-Husband! I hope you loved Kevin and Eve's story!*

**Keep reading for the extended epilogue, Just Count On Me!**

**And check out the epilogue novella, Why You Should Definitely Kiss Your Groom!**

*Expect the unexpected…especially when a Bradford is expecting.*

As family and friends gather to see Dooley and Morgan get married, anticipation is high—but no one saw this much excitement coming. A wedding that doubles as a baby shower, a limo that doubles as an ambulance, a hospital room that doubles as a honeymoon suite… Sure, why not? It's a Bradford wedding, after all.

Dani's in labor, Sam's in a daze, Ben's taking charge, Sara's crying, Jessica's got a secret, Dooley's missing his honeymoon—in other words, things are crazy. As usual. But through it all they've got each other. As always.

Go to **ShopErinNicholas.com**
and look for the title or
go directly to this link:
shoperinnicholas.com/b/1ypJH

*Now read on for the extended epilogue, Just Count on Me!*

# EXTENDED EPILOGUE
## JUST COUNT ON ME

"You've got to be fucking kidding me."

Mac Gordon came up short in the break room at St. Anthony's hospital. He and the rest of his EMT crew were just coming on shift. And right in the middle of the sofa in the break room was a gigantic stuffed dog with a big pink bow tied around its neck.

Without reading any kind of tag, he knew exactly who it was for. And who it was from.

"I'm going to kill him."

Sam Bradford chuckled and slapped him on the shoulder. "You say that at least twice a week."

Kevin Campbell crossed to the dog and read the big heart shaped tag. "I'm happy to follow you around like a puppy. Happy Birthday. Love, Conner."

Mac stomped forward, "Oh, he did not sign it love."

Kevin laughed and stepped back out of the way. "No. He didn't sign it at all, actually."

Mac reread the card. "This is over the top."

Dooley Miller was grinning like a dumbass. "You had to be expecting it. There's no way Conner would let Sara's birthday go by without doing something stupid."

Mac stared into the dog's eyes. Dooley was right. He had been expecting Conner Dixon to do something to commemorate Mac's wife's birthday. Conner claimed he was madly in love with Sara and would never find another woman to compare. Mac knew that seventy-five percent of that was simply a convenient way for Conner to fuck with Mac's head. But there was that other twenty-five percent that he knew was true. Conner had met Sara without knowing she was married to Mac and had immediately hit on her. But, even after finding out she belonged to Mac, he kept up his flirtation. "People break up every day" was his favorite saying when Mac was around.

And there were his jabs about how much older Mac was. And how Conner was exactly the right age for her. And his crazy statistic that seventy percent of married women cheat. And his endless supply of compliments and come-ons that had made Sara blush more than once.

Still, Mac hadn't killed Conner yet. Hadn't even hurt him. Because the kid was actually pretty cool.

He was a phenomenal paramedic, for one. On calls, Mac knew that Conner would make the right decision, would make it quickly, and would give a one-hundred-and-ten percent effort every time. That got him a lot of forgiveness.

Then there was his off-duty side. He was funny, he could take as much shit as he gave, and he was a good friend and leader to his crew. He was also the big brother to four dynamic younger sisters. The Dixon Divas were something. They were gorgeous, out-going, bright and flirtatious. Mac had to admit that he felt a little sorry for Conner. At least some of the time. Conner was protective of his sisters and he was always there for them, no matter what trouble they got into. Mac admired his ability to keep his cool and do the right thing even while clearly wanting to lock them all in a convent permanently.

"He shouldn't have delivered the damn thing here," Mac said, still staring at the dog. Sara was going to love it. Sure, she'd end up giving it to Elijah, their three-year-old son. Still, she would think Conner was sweet for getting her something for her birthday.

"He had to deliver it here. That's the only way to be sure we saw it and could give you crap about it," Dooley said, plopping onto the couch next to the dog that was bigger than he was, and looping his arm around its neck.

"Look at it this way," Kevin said to Mac. "He's got great taste in women, and he idolizes you as the man who got Sara Bradford to fall for him."

Mac had heard that argument before. It was a good point. It still didn't mean that the guy should be giving gifts to another man's wife.

"Maybe I'll give Conner some ideas about where he should shove this dog," Mac grumbled.

"Hey, I wonder where those guys are," Sam commented, twisting the cap off a bottle of water. "It's really quiet in here and I'd expect to see Conner's smug face by now."

"I'll go check on him," Mac said. "I can't wait to see him."

Mac headed for the front of the ER to get the news about Conner's crew from the front desk staff. When the rigs went out on calls, the girls up front kept track, knowing that the ambulances would often be returning with patients for the ER staff.

"Hey, Lisa," Mac greeted as he came to the reception desk. "Where's Dixon's crew?"

"Hi, Mac." Lisa gave him a smile. "Just heading back. Code blue at one of the nursing homes."

"If you see him before I do, tell him I want to talk to him."

She grinned. "He told me that you might leave that message."

Mac shook his head. This kid was something.

"So you saw the dog?"

"Yeah. He carried it through the main doors so everyone would see it."

"Okay, be honest—is it sweet? Sara will like it?" He already knew the answer. Sara would be flattered by Conner's attention but would take it as nothing more than a compliment. Mac wasn't worried. But he had a theory going and he wanted to test it with Lisa.

"Of course, it's sweet," Lisa said. "Any woman would love to have a guy try so hard to win her over."

"Even if she's already with another guy?"

"Even better," Lisa assured him. "Having two great guys crazy about you is a fantastic fantasy."

Uh, huh. So far his theory was working out.

"So tell me, what's wrong with him?" Mac asked. "Why can't he get a girl of his own? A single girl?"

Lisa laughed. "There's nothing wrong with him. Conner's got it all. He's hot, sexy, heroic, funny—and obviously romantic."

Yep. That was part of the theory. Conner was showing his charming, romantic side to all the women by being supposedly ga-ga over Sara. Sara—a woman who wouldn't expect any kind of actual commitment or a promise or a diamond ring. He was winning all the women over and not making one single can't-get-out-of-it-later promise. He was essentially seducing them all without any expectations of next day phone calls.

It was kind of brilliant.

"Do all the women hate Sara?" he asked. The women in his life—his friends' wives and sisters—weren't the jealous types but he worked around enough women in the hospital to know all about female envy.

"No," Lisa assured him. "Everyone loves Sara. Because she's never going to actually have Conner."

"Damn right."

"But I will say, he's set the bar high. Sara's also got it all. The next girl he actually asks out should feel pretty good about herself."

Mac groaned inwardly. And Conner was setting it up so all the women he did finally pay attention to would be totally flattered.

"Plus, watching a guy flirt with another girl calls attention to him—and how cute and sexy he is. It makes you automatically judge whether or not you would say yes to him."

"How does Dixon do most of the time?"

Lisa gave him an I-know-you-already-know-the-answer-to-this look. "He could have any single woman in this hospital."

Exactly as Mac suspected. Conner was setting himself up to be able to just snap his fingers and have woman all over him.

Definitely brilliant.

"I want to see him the minute he gets back."

Lisa gave Mac a wink. "I'll tell him"

"Mac!" Kevin shouted from the doorway. "Let's go. Got a call."

"See ya'," he called to Lisa as he broke into a jog. "Where we goin'?" he asked as he hit the break room.

No one said anything. They were all looking at Sam. Sam looked like he was about to be sick.

Mac was instantly concerned. "What the fuck, Bradford?"

Sam swallowed, with obvious effort. "It's a fire."

"Where?" Dooley demanded.

Mac felt his gut clench before Sam said the words.

"Fifteen seventeen Washington."

Everyone stopped breathing for just a moment. They knew that address. Very well. It was the address for the Bradford Youth Center.

The crew all reacted at once. Without another word, they ran for the rig, going through their checklists by habit and tearing out into the night, siren wailing within minutes.

The Bradford Youth Center was the non-profit center that kept kids off the streets and gave them a place to go when things got shitty at home.

Sam and Sara's dad, David Bradford, had founded the center

and it was still run under the supervision of the Bradford siblings and supported by David's trust, private donations, and lots of volunteer hours. Many of those hours were put in by the Bradfords and their friends and spouses.

Sara was the acting Administrator.

"Who's there right now?" Dooley asked as they all sent their wives texts.

"Sara's there," Mac said, feeling cold seep through his body as he let the reality in.

"Jess was supposed to go over tonight too," Sam said, his voice tight. "Dani's at home with the twins."

Their crew worked the seven p.m. to seven a.m. shift so it was about bath and bedtime at Sam's house.

"Morgan and Eve?" Mac asked about Dooley and Kevin's wives. The girls were all friends. It wasn't uncommon for one or more of them to show up at the Center to help with something or just to hang out.

"Morgan's at the Bed & Breakfast," Dooley said. "She had a couple checking in tonight around eight."

It was seven thirty-six.

"Eve's at home," Kevin said. "She's been going to bed really early the last couple of months. The morning sickness is hitting her hard."

Mac pulled in a relieved breath. At least they weren't all at the Center.

The pain in his stomach wasn't any better, but he was glad the others were safe. Sara was at the center. That was a fact. And until he saw her and held her again, he wouldn't be pain free.

"Sorry, Ma—"

Mac slapped a big hand against Dooley's chest before the man could get the rest of the words out. "Don't you fucking be sorry. More than half the girls are safe and Sara and Jess are going to be, so just shut the fuck up."

Dooley nodded.

"They've got procedures," Kevin said in the calm voice they

all depended on at times like this. "They have smoke detectors and emergency exit plans. The girls are smart. It's going to be fine."

Mac appreciated the words. They were true. But they didn't do a thing to make him feel better.

Sam took the next corner sharply and they all hung on.

"Someone should call Ben," Kevin said, pulling out his phone again. Ben was Sam's other brother-in-law, married to Jessica. He was also a trauma surgeon at St. Anthony's. "He working tonight?"

Sam shook his head, gripping the steering wheel to the point his knuckles turned white. "He might be there too."

Ben was fond of the Center and spent a lot of time there, as they all did.

But if Ben was there tonight, it meant that their young daughter, Ava would be too.

Fuck. Mac gritted his teeth and gripped the bar on the door by his seat. They had a siren. That was the only way to speed up the trip and Sam was doing everything he could to dodge the cars that were slow to get out of the way.

"I can't get him," Kevin said a moment later after dialing Ben's number.

"Dammit," Dooley muttered.

Sam and Mac weren't even able to say that much.

Finally, they came to a screeching halt in front of the Center.

There were already three fire trucks on scene and an ambulance.

"Dixon and his crew are here," Dooley said, bailing out.

Mac took in the details of the scene on autopilot. There was smoke and flames coming from the window on the east end of the building. The end with the kitchen.

A wave of nausea swept over him, and he had to stop and force himself to breathe. He closed his eyes and dropped his chin to his chest, pulling air in through his nose and then letting it out through his mouth.

*The right personnel are already on scene, they're taking care of things.*

He lifted his head and looked around, fighting the urge to run into the middle of the chaos. But that would only add to the commotion. He knew better. He had to give the guys room to work and he had to get a hold of himself.

He scanned the scene. There was a small group of kids huddled together near a tree on the west end of the building. Two others were sitting in the back of the ambulance, breathing through oxygen masks. Dooley was there getting a report from one of the female paramedics on Dixon's crew.

Kevin put a hand on his shoulder. "Do I need to worry about you going in there and making things worse?" he asked.

Mac looked over to find that he had a fistful of Sam's shirt. Clearly Sam needed to be held back. Mac understood that. They were trained emergency professionals… but this was personal.

Firefighters were running around and yelling, but Mac knew from experience that their actions were carefully orchestrated. They knew what they were doing.

Him barging ahead, shoving people out of the way, and knocking down the front door wasn't going to do any good.

Still, he itched with the desire to do exactly that.

"No. I'm good," he told Kevin.

Kevin met his gaze, studying him. Finally, he said, "Don't make me regret believing you." Kevin Campbell was the nice guy of the bunch and the most laid-back, but he was a big guy with a rock-solid sense of right and wrong, and if you fucked with him, he'd knock you on your ass.

Mac took a deep breath and then gave him a nod. "Promise."

Kevin strode toward where Cody Madsen, the fire chief, was standing talking into his headset, directing his crew. Kevin kept a hold of Sam's shirt, like Sam was a four-year-old who couldn't keep his hands out of the candy bins. But Sam wasn't fighting Kevin's hold. He probably knew, deep down, that he needed his friend to keep him in check.

"Mac."

Mac turned at the sound of his name. It was Conner.

"Where is she?" Mac asked without preamble.

Conner looked exhausted. He had soot smudges on his clothes and face, his eyes were blood shot and he pretty much looked like hell. He and his crew had already put in twelve hours and fires with multiple possible victims were always hard.

He shook his head. "They haven't brought her out yet. We've treated about twenty kids. You have any idea how many might be here tonight?"

Mac felt the chill that had permeated his body on the ride over, seep deeper and begin to freeze. No. Sara had to be okay. She had to. Too many people needed her. Elijah needed her, their baby needed her, and Mac would, quite simply, die without her.

He cleared his throat, determined not to be a reason for anyone to pull their attention from the fire and the people inside. If he freaked out, passed out or punched someone, the cops and paramedics would have to attend to him rather than the people who really needed them.

"There could be up to fifty, but there's not really an attendance sheet, you know? It's whoever shows up," he told Conner. "Can't the kids tell if someone got out or not?"

"They're trying to take a roll call but they're pretty shaken."

"What happened?"

"Not sure yet. Kids say they were using the microwave, but no other appliances."

"Jessica's probably in there too," Mac said, feeling that he was on the verge of beginning to shake. He was ice cold. He recognized the signs of shock, but he also knew he had to keep his shit together. If he couldn't help, then he shouldn't have come.

Making himself look back to the Center, he knew that there was no way in hell he could have stayed away. So, he needed to hold it together.

"I'm calling in the rig from Methodist," Conner informed

him. "We haven't had a lot of work to do yet. All those kids got out on their own and we've treated only two for smoke inhalation. No burns. But if there might be twenty more kids inside, I'm gonna need some help and you guys aren't going to be any good to us."

Mac started to protest. They were all here. "We're the best crew in this city."

"Yeah, yeah. I'll give you that, when it's not this personal," Conner said. "But not tonight. Tonight you're civilians."

He started to turn away to talk to the man who'd just approached them, but Mac grabbed his arm. "Dixon."

"Yeah?"

Mac swallowed hard. "When they pull Sara out, I want *you* to make it personal. Got it?"

Conner didn't say anything for several seconds. Then he gave a short nod. "I got it."

Mac gave him a nod back.

Then Conner gestured to the man next to him. "Mac, this is Shane Kelley. He's a buddy of mine, an offensive lineman for the Hawks, and a cop. That last part is the important part right now. If you try to go into that building, he's going to knock you down or shoot you."

Mac felt his eyes widen. He knew Shane's name from some of his own cop buddies. He was one of the best. He'd also watched the guy play football. The he's-going-to-knock-you-down thing would hurt. "You got me a watch dog?"

"Something like that." Conner slapped Shane on the shoulder and headed for his rig.

Shane gave him a grin. "You're not the only reason I'm here, if that makes you feel any better."

Mac shrugged. "Nothing's really going to make me feel better right now."

Shane nodded and started in Cody Madsen's direction.

"You're not going to stick by my side to make sure I don't do anything stupid?" Mac asked.

Shane glanced back at him. "I'm a pretty good shot even from a distance."

Ah. Fantastic.

Mac looked over to where Conner was already calling in another ambulance to be there for the victims they expected out of the building. He was right to make the call. He was right to keep their crew out of there. No way could even Dooley or Kevin stay detached enough to do their job effectively. One third degree burn on one of the kids they cared about, and they'd be a mess. If it was anything worse…

Mac shut that down. That definitely wouldn't help.

He watched Cody stride toward Conner and say something before they both broke into a run toward the building.

It was the damnedest thing, but if Sara needed attention he wanted it to come from Conner. Conner would make sure everything was above and beyond for Sara.

Just like that fucking stuffed dog.

Conner jogged toward the fireman carrying the girl from the front of the building. She was small and blond and for a moment his heart beat sped up.

But it wasn't Sara. Still, he was glad to see every single survivor they carried from the building.

The building was huge. It had been an elementary school at one time. He knew from the briefing at the scene that the west end of the building was mostly offices and storage space. The east end, where the fire had broken out, was the more "lived in" part of the building where they had a huge common room, a gymnasium with showers and locker rooms, and, of course, the kitchen.

One of the firemen was speculating that they had put something in the microwave that had caused sparks. One of the kids had said something about an explosion, but they hadn't been able to get a good explanation. Just that they heard a loud boom and that flames and smoke had come pouring out of the kitchen right after that. Most of the kids in the common room had immediately run for the doors. Though Mac had told him there could be up to fifty kids there on any night, the kids were telling them that there had only been a handful in the TV room on the other side of the kitchen.

But from the description they gave and the layout of the building that one of the firemen had, it was clear they would have been trapped if the fire had come out of the kitchen.

In any case, it was taking a hell of a long time to get the blaze under control.

"Okay, sweetheart, I've got you," Conner told the girl as they shifted her from the fireman's arms to Conner's.

She immediately burrowed close and wrapped her arms tightly around his neck and burst into tears. He continued crooning comforting words until they got the rig. Dooley Miller was there with Sierra.

"She's conscious, I see," Dooley said.

Conner smiled. "Yep. Though she hadn't said anything, so I don't know if she's making sense." And she didn't seem inclined to loosen her grip on him even the tiniest bit.

Dooley studied her for a minute, then he said, "I heard the new running back recruit for the Huskers backed out and is going to Kansas State."

The girl's head came up fast and she looked at him. "Travis Humphry?"

"Hey, Tasha," Dooley greeted with a grin. "You okay?"

Her eyes filled up with tears again, but Conner felt her hold relax slightly. "I don't know."

"Well, come here and let me make sure," Dooley said.

The girl obviously knew and trusted him. She immediately let go of Conner and he swung her feet to the ground. Dooley put an arm around her waist and helped her to the ambulance.

"You sure you're good?" Conner asked the other man. "I told Gordon I was calling in another rig."

"Good idea," Dooley agreed. "Sam and Mac shouldn't go near anyone. But Kevin and I are fine. We'll just help out. Get the Methodist guys over here."

Conner appreciated a cool head in a crisis. "They're already on their way."

"Dixon!"

He turned and nearly got plowed over by Mac Gordon himself. Conner was the quarterback for the best team in the amateur league. He was, unfortunately, periodically plowed over by big guys who didn't mind hurting him. Still, he was very glad Mac didn't play. "What's up?"

He was as anxious as anyone else. He hated the waiting, knowing there were people inside that might need their help, knowing that minutes counted, yet having to hang back while the firemen did their thing. It was hard. But he kept cool. It was his gift. Perfected over the years of growing up with four younger sisters. It was hard to rile Conner up.

Only four things could really do it and they were named Amanda, Emma, Isabelle and Olivia Dixon.

"Sara texted me."

Conner perked up. "What? Seriously? She's not here?" That would be awesome. Not awesome that there were still people inside, but if Sara wasn't one of them…

"She's in there," Mac confirmed. "But they headed in the opposite direction from the kitchen. They went for the showers in the girl's locker room. She figured the tile wouldn't burn."

"There's no back exit?" Conner asked, as he started for Cody to tell him the news. "This is an old school for Chrissake."

"There is, but the door is stuck. Or locked. Or something is against it from the outside. She's not sure, it just won't move."

Conner pulled up short. "She's on the line now?"

"Yeah."

Conner grabbed the phone from Mac. "Sara?"

"Conner, is that you? Oh, my god, are you out there?" She sounded panicky, but not hysterical, which Conner appreciated about her. She had to keep her cool for those kids.

"Yeah, it's me. We're gonna get you out of there."

"You better."

He wove in and out of firemen, searching for his friend, the Chief.

"Well, listen lady," Conner said, trying for light and flirtatious like he always was, hoping to reassure her that everything would be fine. "When you get out of there, I'm first in line for mouth to mouth."

She laughed, sounding tired. Though it wasn't like he really knew her well enough to know if she sounded tired or not. "When I get out of here, I'm pretty sure I'm going to feel like kissing everybody."

*Goddammit where was Cody?*

"That's why us paramedics do what we do, babe."

She laughed again, but this time it ended on what was definitely a sob. Conner would know that sound anywhere. His gut tightened and his fist tightened on Mac's phone.

He stopped suddenly. Mac ran directly into him, sending him two steps forward before he swung around with a scowl. Did the guy have to be right on his ass?

He still didn't see Cody so he took the phone away from his ear, covered the mouthpiece and bellowed, "Somebody tell me where the fuck Madsen is!"

"Over here!" someone shouted.

He headed in that direction. Back on the phone with Sara he said, "Honey, tell me where you are in the building exactly."

"The girl's locker room."

"Right, but walk me to it. Like from the front doors." He arrived next to Cody and covered the mouthpiece again for a moment. "Sara's in the building... and on the phone. She's going to walk you to where they are."

Cody lifted the microphone on his headset. "Dennings, listen up," he barked.

"Okay, Sara, go. I'm right here," Conner said. "I'm going to repeat everything to Cody."

Sara started walking him mentally through the building, giving him lefts and rights, things that would be in the rooms, how many doorways to count off, and other information that would lead the firemen inside to where they were at.

"It's the last doorway in the hallway," she finally said. "We're all in here."

"How many of you?" Conner asked.

"Eight," she said. "Me and my sister and then six kids."

Conner repeated the information to Cody, then felt a heavy hand on his shoulder. "Jessica is in there?"

It was Sam Bradford. He'd come over to join Mac.

Conner nodded. "Yeah. And six kids."

"Ben's not in there?" Sam asked with a frown.

"Sara, honey, is Ben there?" Conner asked.

"No." There was a pause. Then she said, "Was he supposed to be?"

Conner repeated the question to the guys.

"We can't get him on the phone," Sam said. "We thought maybe he came down here."

Conner knew Ben Torres from the hospital. He was one of the trauma surgeons so, unfortunately, their paths mostly crossed when Conner and the crew were bringing people in who needed Ben's skills. But occasionally he'd pass Ben in the hallway or stand in line behind him in the cafeteria. Torres was a nice guy and a hell of a surgeon.

"Does Jessica know where Ben is?" Conner asked Sara.

Jessica Bradford Torres was a nurse and was the head of the ER. Conner knew her well too.

"He's supposed to be at home with Ava," Sara reported. "Jessica can't get her phone to work in here. None of the others will, actually. We figure it's all the cement and stuff. Don't know why mine's working."

Conner made himself smile as he replied. "'Cuz we were meant to connect, Sara. You should just accept this as one more sign."

"Conner." She said it in that sweet, chiding tone that she always used when he flirted with her. He loved it.

She was always going to turn him down. He knew that. And if she was married to anyone but Mac Gordon, he probably would have laid off a long time ago. She was taken. He got it. But wow, it was such a great way to antagonize Mac. And Gordon had plenty of fun antagonizing Conner when he'd been a rookie and filling in on their crew, trying to build up his hours of experience. It was only fair.

Plus, Sara Gordon was it. She was the perfect woman. Gorgeous, funny, smart, sweet, baked like nobody's business, and blushed so adorably whenever he flirted. If he didn't have a crush on her it would have been a sad commentary on his intelligence.

"Fuck."

Conner's attention was pulled to Cody—and the deep scowl his friend wore.

"They can't get through. They're blocked getting into that hallway."

Conner's stomach twisted. They'd have to find another way. And quick. If the fire was blocking that hallway, it was getting too close for comfort. Sara was right about the concrete of the locker rooms not burning, but that wasn't the only risk in a fire. Smoke inhalation and toxic fumes were a real risk as was the chance for an explosion that would propel debris that could seriously injure someone. Debris like concrete pieces, for instance.

"There's a door in back."

They all turned. Ben Torres had arrived.

"Where?" Cody took off at a run, Ben right behind him.

"The door opens into the backyard. It's not right by the locker rooms, but you can come from the back instead of the front where the flames are."

Conner, Mac and Sam were right behind them.

"The door's locked," Sara said in Conner's ear. "We couldn't budge it."

"We're gonna need tools," Conner called to Cody.

"Thomas, Buckely, Peterson, come with me!" Cody shouted. "Bring the tool box"

The door was, indeed, locked. Tight. It took three fireman leaning on the crowbar to finally pop the lock and wrench the door open. No smoke billowed out—a wonderful sign that the fire wasn't anywhere near this area.

Conner turned immediately to Mac as the heavy metal door swung open, bracing a hand on the bigger man's shoulder. "No way, big guy. You don't have equipment on and this isn't your show."

Mac strained forward for just a moment, then he took a deep breath and leaned back on his heels. "Okay."

Conner knew that Mac knew he was right, but adrenaline was pumping hard and the guy's wife—his pregnant wife—was just inside, in danger.

"Here, talk to Sara," Conner said, thrusting the phone at Mac.

Mac put the phone to his ear. "Hey, princess."

Conner almost got choked up at the emotion in Mac's voice.

"I love you too." Then Mac cleared his throat. "Here." He handed the phone back. "She wants to say something else to you."

"Hey, Sara."

"Conner, you better be close by. Because you are getting that kiss," Sara said.

He grinned. He'd take it too. There would likely never be another opportunity and he was all for taking advantage of good fortune.

"I'll be the good-looking guy dressed as a paramedic," he told her.

She laughed and there was no tension now. "Noted."

He handed the phone back to Mac. "Lucky bastard," he said.

"I know," Mac said sincerely. Then he put the phone back to his ear.

"Let's go, Mac." Kevin Campbell appeared out of the darkness, Dooley at his side.

"Yep, come on Sam," Dooley said, gesturing in the direction they'd come. "Let's get out of these guys' way."

The firemen were suited up. They pulled their helmets and masks into place and then turned on their high beam flashlights and plunged into the darkness inside the Center.

"Put the oxygen mask on or I'm going to tell Conner that Sara said his uniform pants make his ass look great."

Mac frowned at Gabrielle Evans, the other paramedic on Conner's crew. "She never said that."

"No, but Conner will want to believe it, so it will be like gasoline on that fire. No pun intended."

That pun was totally intended. Mac grudgingly took the oxygen mask and put it over his nose and mouth. He didn't need it, dammit. But as he breathed for a few seconds, he had to admit that some of the fogginess in his head faded and the tightness in his chest let go a little.

Fine. He'd had a tiny panic attack waiting for the firemen to get Sara out of the locker room. He watched as they escorted all six of the kids out first. He knew that Sara had insisted on that, even though she was pregnant.

He reached over and bumped the oxygen flow up just a bit on the machine, breathing in deeply. Gabby, bless her, pretended not to notice.

Finally, he saw Jessica walking toward the trucks with one of the firemen. Ben met her halfway across the yard, folding her into his arms, his shoulder shaking with the waves of adrenaline he could finally let loose. If the guy wasn't crying, Mac would be shocked.

He kind of planned to do a little of that himself.

And then there was Sara.

One of the guys was carrying her and Mac immediately dropped the oxygen mask and started forward.

"I twisted my ankle a little when we got to the locker room," she said, holding up a hand and explaining before he even asked. "Otherwise, I'm fine."

"Gee, three-inch-high heels and slippery tile floors don't mix, huh?" he asked dryly, watching as the fireman set her on the bumper to the fire truck.

Mac immediately knelt in front of her, inspecting her ankles.

"These are only two inches high," she said.

"They're almost practical then."

"Exactly."

He focused on her ankle, prodding and rubbing, rotating the joint, checking the pulse… and not registering any of the information. That was all he could handle at the moment though. Taking care of that one little thing, that one small part of her, was far less overwhelming that looking up into her eyes, seeing her smile, taking in the slight swell of her belly and realizing that he could have lost her.

"Mac," she said softly, her hand going to his head.

He leaned forward, resting his forehead against her knee, one hand cupping the calf of her leg while the other took her hand and linked their fingers.

He just sat like that, letting it all wash over him… and out of him. It was over. She was here, she was fine.

Sara stroked her fingers over the top of his head, comforting him. When he should be comforting her.

He drew in a long, shaky breath and finally made himself look up at her.

"I might prefer this to yelling," she told him, her hand still resting on his head. "Though seeing you torn up kind of kills me."

He nodded. "I'm torn up. Too torn up to know that I'm even

supposed to be yelling."

Sara's eyebrows rose, but then she just nodded. "Right. Exactly. There's nothing to yell about."

"I thought I told you to replace that fucking thing!"

Looked like Sam knew what to yell about though.

Mac pivoted on the balls of his feet, still crouching in front of Sara. "Back off, Bradford. This can wait. Whatever it is."

"Yeah, apparently Sara thought so too. That microwave is ancient," Sam said, his attention back on his sister.

"I will definitely be replacing it now, don't worry," Sara said, her voice calm.

"That's not funny," Sam admonished.

It wasn't. Mac turned back to her. "That's the old microwave?"

"The torn-up thing's over, huh?" she asked.

"The torn-up thing is why I'm yelling," Mac said, stretching to his feet. "That microwave is the reason I lost six years off my life tonight. God, I've never been so sick and worried in my life."

And just like that Sara was crying.

"Dammit," Sam muttered. He didn't do well with women's tears, especially his sisters and his wife.

"Well, crap." Mac did even worse than Sam did with Sara's tears. He hauled her to her feet and up against his chest.

Holding her was his undoing. He felt the sting of tears in his own eyes and buried his face in her hair, breathing in her scent, absorbing the feel of her, the warmth, the curves, the silkiness of her skin.

They just stood holding each other like that for several long minutes.

Finally, he let her go and turned her into her brother's arms, swiping his hands over his eyes.

Sam held her tight too.

"I'm sorry," she blubbered. "I'm sorry. I know it's all my fault. I should have just done it right away. I didn't know they were going to try to use it tonight—"

"It's okay," Sam told her, his face tight with emotion. "It's okay. You didn't mean for anything to happen."

"But I should have—"

"Yes," Sam interrupted. "You should have. But it's over now. Everyone's okay and that's what we should all be concentrating on."

Sara was next passed to Ben, then Jessica. Then Conner.

He'd been standing at the end of the hugging line and gave her a huge grin as she came face to face with him.

"I'm right here, where you told me to be." He essentially directed the comment at Mac.

Mac gripped both hands into fists. Okay, Conner could hug her. He'd been great tonight. He'd been focused and commanding, yet lighthearted on the phone with Sara to keep her calm. He'd directed his crew, he'd worked with the firefighters, he'd taken care of the kids that needed him.

Fine. He could have one hug.

Sara stepped into his embrace, and it was a nice, platonic hug.

For exactly three seconds.

Then Conner dipped her back and put his lips to hers.

In a very non-platonic kiss.

Mac's fists clenched harder, and he could almost feel the satisfying thud of his fist meeting Conner's jaw. He stepped forward. "Dixon, you're going to hurt for days."

As if that was his cue, Conner brought Sara back upright and grinned at her. "And that, sweetheart, is just a little of what you're missing." Then he spun her toward Mac and sauntered off.

Mac had to admit that Sara looked a little stunned… and not at all pissed off.

Mac took her shoulders in both hands. "You okay?"

Sara's eyes widened. "Well… yeah."

She said it as if it was the dumbest question he'd ever asked. Gabby snorted behind him and Sam was clearly fighting a smile.

"Uh, huh. I think you might need treatment after all. Clearly there's something wrong with your head," Mac told her.

Sara exchanged a glance—and a grin—with Gabby. Which Mac completely noticed.

"Sure," Sara said. "That must be where these tingles are coming from."

Mac gave a little growl, then swung her up into his arms and headed for the ambulance that would take them back to St. Anthony's. "I think I need to remind you what real tingles are like."

She laughed and wrapped her arms around his neck. "That's what I was hoping you'd say."

"The locker room is off limits for the next thirty minutes."

Sara buried her face in Mac's neck and giggled as he strode through the break room the paramedics used at St. Anthony's. There was no question what he was talking about—exactly why he'd carried her through the break room like this.

He was still technically on the clock, but he needed to shower, and he was taking her with him.

Not that she couldn't use a shower. But this was much more than a convenient way to get clean—this was a way of staking his claim

Conner Dixon was in the break room.

As was her big brother.

"Seriously?" Sam asked from where he was standing next to the coffee pot. "You couldn't just walk through quietly?"

"She's pregnant," Dooley said, throwing a Styrofoam cup at Sam. "Probably time to get over the Mac and Sara having sex thing."

"Yuck," Sam muttered.

But Sara knew it was a strange day when Mac not only failed to respond to Sam with the usual very suggestive comment about his and Sara's sex life, but he didn't even slow down.

He'd swept her into his arms as soon as the ER doctor had said "she's fine", clearly on a mission.

As if Mac had to stake his claim. Everyone knew she belonged to him. Even Conner. Especially Conner. If Mac wasn't madly in love with her and she wasn't head over heels for him, Conner would never joke and tease as he did.

Not that it wasn't fun being the object of Conner's supposed obsession.

He was a good-looking, charming guy who seemed to know a bit about romance. His four sisters had likely taught him a thing or two about how to get on a girl's good side.

And he could kiss.

She giggled and Mac squeezed her. "What's funny?"

"Nothing," she quickly assured him, running her hand up the side of his neck. "I'm just feeling good."

"You do feel good."

She smiled. He was trying to keep his tone and words light, but she knew he was on edge. Not because of Conner. Not really. Conner pushed his buttons, no doubt about it, but the tension vibrating through Mac's body as he held her wasn't Conner related. It was about her and their baby and the fire. And when she thought about it, she got choked up. Knowing that he was hurting, that he was letting himself think about all of the horrible things that could have happened, made her hurt.

She'd been in love with Mac for years before she'd done anything about it. But even in her best daydreams she hadn't imagined being loved back as fiercely and deeply as she was by him. It had taken him some time to come around, but when he had—her heart sometimes felt like it couldn't hold all the emotions he made her feel.

He'd helped her make a home, he'd helped her find her place, he'd helped her become a mother, he'd helped her become less selfish while making her feel treasured. She was a better woman since he'd been in her life. And even when she'd been in love with him as a kid, had him on a pedestal, thought he was perfect, she'd felt nothing compared to how she felt about the real man.

So, him hurting, made her hurt.

He shoved the door to the locker room open, stepped inside and swung her feet to the floor before turning and locking the door.

"What if the guys need something in here for a call?" she asked.

He started unbuttoning his shirt. "Don't care."

"You don't care about the victims they'll be going out to help?" she asked, knowing it wasn't true.

"They've got everything they need for the call out there. In here they've got extra socks, gum, and hair gel. They'll be fine."

She laughed. "Besides, you said it would only be thirty minutes."

He tossed his shirt to the side and toed off his shoes. "You feeling especially dirty?"

She breathed in relief. He was teasing. That was a good sign.

She pulled her shirt up and off, letting it drop on top of his. "I always feel dirty when you're around."

He stepped in close, possessive heat in his eyes. Then his gaze shifted to her cheek and his brows pulled down. He lifted a hand and ran his thumb over her cheekbone.

"Mac?" She could feel the change in his emotions.

"Soot," he said simply. When his gaze returned to her eyes there was pain again.

She put her hand against his face. "Stop it. I'm fine. We're fine."

His head dropped forward, and he took a deep shuddering breath. "I know. Deep down I know that. But…" He lifted his head. "Let's get the smoke smell out of your hair. That'll help."

He went to the shower stall and turned on the water, letting it warm up. "Come here, princess."

The nickname never failed to make her tummy flip. She crossed the cold tile floor to him, limping only slightly on her sore ankle and trying to hide even that. It was a twist, not even a sprain. She was fine. But if Mac saw it…

"Dammit." He met her, hoisted her up against him with one arm and turned toward the shower, setting her down just outside.

"It barely hurts."

"Just let me… take care of you."

He always took care of her. Always.

He reached behind her and unhooked her bra. She let it slide from her shoulders and drop to the floor. His eyes heated slightly as he looked at her breasts. They were definitely bigger with the pregnancy and while he'd never complained before, she knew he loved holding the heavier weights.

He cupped one, brushing his thumb over her nipple. Increased sensitivity was another plus to the new hormones. She gasped and pressed closer.

His other hand got busy on the button at the front of her jeans. With surprising dexterity he got the button undone and the zipper down.

She hooked her thumbs in the waistband of the jeans and her panties, pushing both to the floor and stepping out of them.

She reached for him next, but he stepped back. "In the shower."

She had no hesitation about sex in the shower, but he was overdressed. "Mac—"

Again he picked her up and put her inside the shower stall, right under the spray. She was drenched before she could protest.

"You're coming in, right?" she asked, swiping her wet hair back from her face.

"I'll…" He cleared his throat. "Let me wash your hair."

Sara took a deep breath. He was holding back. She could feel it. She hated when he did this. It hadn't happened in a long time, but Mac had a misplaced idea about how vulnerable and fragile she was sometimes. It had faded before the pregnancy, but since he'd found out that she was expecting their first baby it had amped up again.

"Come in here with me," she said, running her fingers through her hair.

The motion thrust her breasts forward and she knew her husband wouldn't be able to resist getting closer.

She was right.

He shucked out of his pants, leaving his underwear on, and stepped into the shower with her.

He grabbed the generic shampoo from the shelf and poured some into his palms. Sara turned to present her back to him and sighed with pleasure as his hands began massaging the shampoo into her hair, his fingers pressing deliciously against her scalp before spreading the suds along the long tresses. But it wasn't long until his slippery hands slid over her shoulders and down to cup her breasts.

His thumbs rubbed the stiff points and she reached back, her hands on his butt as she pressed against his erection.

"How's my hair smell now?" she asked huskily.

She felt his deep breath.

"Lemony," he answered.

She smiled and turned, tipping her head back to rinse the shampoo.

His hands drifted over her waist to her hips, but he simply held her, watching.

When the soap was gone, she looked up at him, trying to read his expression. He looked thoughtful. Not exactly hot or turned on, which frankly was a little tough on her ego.

Whenever she was naked, he looked hot and turned on.

"Mac?"

"I could have lost you today." He drew in a deep breath. "Jesus, Sara."

He almost never called her Sara. He called her princess and

honey.

"You didn't lose me. I'm here. I'm right here." She put her hands at the back of his head and pulled him in for a kiss. He was a lot taller than her, even when she wore heels, which she definitely wasn't at the moment. But he bent to meet her lips.

The kiss wasn't intended to be sweet. She needed to show him that she was fine, not fragile, not hurt. She was more than fine.

She opened her mouth under his, stroking his lower lip with her tongue. He groaned and she felt his fingers curl into her hips as he brought her closer.

Sara tipped her head, pressing her body against his.

His hands moved to her butt and lifted her slightly, bringing her up against him more fully.

"Make love to me, Mac," she whispered against his lips. "I need you."

"You were just—"

"I'm fine. I'm great." And she'd prove it. She moved her mouth to his ear and bit his lobe gently. Then she moved her lips to his neck, then his collar bone and down to one nipple, where she licked, then sucked.

One of his hands went to the back of her head. "Sara," he said, roughly. "We shouldn't—"

"Everyone in the break room thought I was about to get some… including me," she reminded him. "You better not back out now."

He chuckled lightly. "It doesn't matter what they think."

She knew deep down that was true. What did matter was what Mac thought and right now he was consumed by thoughts about what could have happened, about a loss that he could have sustained. He needed to think about what he had, what was here and now, what was alive and well.

She licked over his ribs and the well-defined muscles of his abs. She wanted him to lift her up against the shower wall and thrust deep. And she knew exactly how to make that happen.

"Sara." His hand tangled in her hair and he stopped her southward progression.

But she was on her knees, with her mouth at his belly button and she'd just slid his wet briefs out of the way. She wrapped her hand around his cock, stroking then squeezing the hot shaft.

"Yeah, babe?" she asked, lifting her eyes to his face as she clasped his throbbing erection.

His hot gaze met hers. "I don't remember."

"Was it something about me not feeling well or not being up for this or something else ridiculous?"

"Maybe. But it might have been 'put your sweet mouth on my cock'."

She grinned and licked her lips. "That's better."

"Sara." His voice was thick.

"Yeah?"

"Put your sweet mouth on my cock."

There was her Mac. The hot, sexy, demanding but sweet man who made her love him more every day and who could get her hot and wet—in or out of the shower—in three point two seconds.

She leaned in and did as he'd said. She sucked the tip into her mouth, sliding slowly down as far as she could, then applying her tongue as she dragged back up the length. She swirled her tongue around the tip before lifting her head, then doing it all again. Her hand grasped the root of his shaft, pumping slowly as she sucked.

His finger tightened in her hair, but he didn't move her head, or his hips. And she knew he was holding back. Mac always tried to let her take the lead, tried to lie back and give her some control, but it never lasted long. It was his nature to be in charge and she didn't mind a bit.

And she loved making him lose the little bit of control he did try to have.

She picked up the rhythm, sucking and stronger harder and faster.

His fingers tightened and she felt him move slightly, the smallest thrust, but she grinned to herself.

She looked up into his eyes—knowing he loved that—and took him deeper, then released him to lick down the length of his cock. His eyes were riveted on her, and she took the opportunity to lift a hand to her breast, circling then tugging on the nipple.

His nostrils flared and he thrust again, seemingly unable to control the urge.

"Put me up against the wall," she said. "Please. I need you."

"You're messing with me," he accused, but his words were a bit breathless.

She stroked up. "What do you mean?"

"I was worried about you. I needed to take care of you, make sure you're okay, but you're getting your way. You know just how to play me."

She nodded. "I know what you really needed. You need to feel me being okay, Mac. You need to know that I am so good that I can go down on you in the shower."

"You're so good, huh?"

"So good."

"Up for anything? Ready for it all?"

She shivered in anticipation. She occasionally got cocky with him to push him to the point where all he wanted was to make her beg, then scream with pleasure. When Mac got that tone in his voice it meant he was going to test her bravado. And that was always fun. "Anything you've got," she told him.

"Get up and turn around."

She did, slowly.

"Let's go, Princess Sara. Our thirty minutes is almost up."

Ah, Princess Sara. That was different than the times he just called her princess. It was a role-playing thing that had started one night spontaneously. But it was rooted in some reality.

She'd always been considered a princess by her family and friends. Everyone looked out for her, everyone considered her softer and sweeter than her sister Jessica, but she was also spoiled and had been able to get away with almost anything. And Mac had been the worst. He'd constantly been there to watch over and indulge her.

In their role playing, she was the princess, used to everyone waiting on her, jumping at the snap of her fingers, and he was the servant who had nothing to offer but the best sex of her life—and it was so good that she was willing to give up her riches, her power, everything, just to have him touching her.

Mac gave her so much more than that, but there was something that really got him going when they pretended that he could so overwhelm her sexually that nothing else mattered.

"Hands on the wall and bend over, your Highness."

She grinned and complied, wiggling her ass as she did it. "Like this?"

"Now say please. Really nice and sincere." His hand slipped around to her belly. He rubbed over the curve before sliding down to cup her where the familiar, delicious ache was already starting.

"What do you want to hear me beg for?" she asked, putting some haughtiness into her tone. "An orgasm? Or a good hard—"

His finger slid into her as his thumb pressed her clit and she gasped, widening her stance and letting her head fall forward.

"Whatever you want, princess. I'm here to serve you. As long as you're sweet about it."

She heard the humor in his voice. He loved making her wild and if she was going wild, he'd only be thinking about that—not all the fear and worry of earlier.

"Sweet girls don't say things like 'I want you inside me now'."

He stroked his finger deep, then added a second, his thumb circling her clit.

"Oh, I don't know. That sounds pretty sweet to me."

"I want you inside me now." She thought she'd made that clear.

The pleasure his hand was creating shimmered through her

body, setting fires along her nerve endings. She pressed closer to his touch. Her hands slipped on the wet tile wall, but Mac had a hold of her, supporting her with his big hands.

"You didn't say please."

"Please, Mac. Please." She added the second one just to be sure.

"See, I like that. A lot."

Like that, his hand was gone and she felt him press closer.

"Hang on, princess."

She laughed softly. "I don't have anything to hang on to, big guy. The tile's slippery."

He spun her around, put his hands on her ass and lifted her against the wall, her legs going around his waist automatically.

"Then hang on to me."

He thrust, sliding deep and sure in a way that was familiar to her as her own face and yet felt amazingly new every time.

Her breath caught in her throat at the possessive way he was looking at her. She wrapped her arms around him. "Always."

A man simply shouldn't have to pick his sisters up from a sex club.

That seemed like a reasonable rule.

No matter what his faults and flaws were, getting a call to pick up younger sisters from an x-rated club seemed like an over-the-top punishment.

Conner worked to unclench his teeth as the light at the intersection a block from Frigid—the anything-goes adult club— turned green.

Of course, this was Emma and Isabelle.

His two middle sisters were trouble. Plain and simple. He was beyond being surprised or shocked.

Frustrated though, that was something else. Something he was a lot.

He supposed he should be happy he wasn't picking them up from the police station. Like he'd had to do three months ago.

Apparently, tonight punches had been thrown *about* them versus being thrown *by* one of them.

Conner pulled up at the curb.

He could at least be grateful that only fifty percent of his sisters would ever show up at a place like Frigid. At least he could trust that Amanda and Olivia to stay out of trouble.

Then he spotted his sisters, flirting with the bouncers, and Conner wondered, not for the first time, what exactly he'd done in his previous lives to deserve this.

And there had to be previous lives. Plural. No way could he have racked up enough sins to deserve four beautiful younger sisters in only one lifetime.

Conner slammed the car door with enough force to shake the whole vehicle.

"What the hell, Emma?"

"Conner?" She frowned at him. "What are you doing here?"

"What am I doing here? Shane called me." Conner glanced at Isabelle.

She and Shane were seeing each other. Not that Iz would admit it to Conner. Shane and Conner were friends, more or less. They were teammates if nothing else and they ended up working scenes together often. Shane had fallen for Isabelle the first time they'd met and he'd made no secret of it. But Isabelle knew Conner's rule—no dating between his sisters and friends.

"Shane called you?" Emma repeated. "Well, great."

Shane had responded to the call about the fight in the club. Isabelle was probably lucky he was on duty and had to take the three drunks who'd been duking it out over her and Emma down to the station.

The girls hadn't technically done anything wrong, so weren't being charged, but they'd been asked by the club management to leave.

"Well, maybe this will make Shane rethink his undying devotion to you at least," Conner said to Isabelle.

"Don't count on it," Isabelle said sweetly. "Shane likes my naughty side. He'd love Frigid."

Conner groaned and held up his hand to stall any further commentary on Shane's preferences. "Alright. Get in the car." He should have never brought it up.

"What happened to your hand?" Isabelle asked, stepping forward with a frown.

"Oh, thank you very much for noticing," he said dryly.

He'd wrapped gauze around his hand before heading over here to pick up his sisters from a sex club.

"I cut it at the big fire I worked today."

"Are you okay?" Iz sounded worried.

For just a moment, he was tempted to milk it. Getting a little concern and attention from his sisters wouldn't hurt any of them.

But the cut was really no big deal. And he'd rather have pretty nurses fussing over him at the hospital. Which could be happening at that very moment if he wasn't picking his sisters up from a sex club.

"I'm fine. It's nothing." That was true regarding the cut anyway. Not necessarily the sisters-at-a-sex-club-thing.

"I heard some pretty ladies might need checked over for bruises and lacerations."

Conner groaned again. No. This was already irritating enough. He didn't need to run into anyone he knew. Especially anyone from work.

"Hey, Dooley." Emma greeted the other paramedic with a huge smile.

Of course, Emma greeted most men with a huge smile.

"As soon as I heard the Dixon Divas might need something kissed and made better, I hightailed it over here," Dooley said, looping his arms around both Emma and Isabelle. He gave Conner a big grin. "I didn't bring Mac. You're welcome."

"What are you doing here? You're supposed to be working,"

Conner said.

Sam Bradford strode up, also wearing a huge fucking grin. "Shane stopped by with the three drunks who started this whole thing. Two of them needed stitches before he took them downtown. He filled us in and said you'd be showing up here."

"We were heading out for some sandwiches anyway," Dooley said. "So I generously volunteered to run over and make sure the girls are okay." He looked Emma up and down, then treated Isabelle to the same visual exam. "They look mighty fine from here though, I will say."

"We probably need a more detailed check though," Sam said. "With better lighting."

Emma gave him an air kiss and Isabelle grinned.

"And what will your wives say about this good deed of yours?" Conner asked.

Sam laughed. "Ah, hell, they'll know that the real reason we came over here was to see you. I think we should check your blood pressure."

"And there is a nasty vein bulging on his forehead," Dooley said.

Conner was sure there was. Right in front of the pounding headache he suddenly had.

He looked from one sister to the next to the next. Then over at Dooley and Sam. Then he looked up at the front of Frigid.

"You know what? I think I have just the cure for what ails me at the moment," he said, a brilliant thought occurring to him.

Beautiful women and liquor were right inside that building.

Emma raised an eyebrow, following his gaze to the club's front door. "Oh, yeah?"

"Guys, you make sure the girls have whatever they need and make sure they get home, okay?"

"You're going in?" Isabelle asked.

"Well, let me ask you this," Conner said, pressing the button on his key fob that would lock his car doors, then sliding his keys into his pocket. "Is that club full of gorgeous women?"

EXTENDED EPILOGUE 309

Emma nodded. "Definitely."

"And will any of those women need me to know their favorite holiday or their shoe size or anything else about them? At all?" he asked.

Emma's smile grew as she shook her head. "Absolutely not."

"And will any of them need to me to worry about anything like how they're getting home or what time they need to be to work in the morning?"

"I sincerely doubt it," Emma said. "I'd be shocked if any of them even ask your name."

Frigid wasn't exactly the type of place a person went to find true, lasting love or meaningful relationships. The typical clientele made decisions based on much simpler criteria—how good did the other person look in their clothes and how willing were they to get out of those clothes, for instance.

Conner took a deep breath. "And, most of all, will anyone inside that club call me to borrow anything, fix anything, or pick them up or drop them off anywhere for any reason?"

Emma's grin was big, but she rolled her eyes. "No. I feel quite confident that none of that will happen."

"Then this is absolutely where I want to be right now," Conner said.

In fact, a place where he didn't need to remember birthdays and shoe sizes, where he didn't need to worry about safety and schedules, and where he wouldn't be called upon for favors of any kind sounded like nirvana.

He might never leave.

Dooley chuckled. "Have a good time. Be good. Call us if you need anything."

Conner nodded. "I will. No way. And thanks."

Sam slapped him on the shoulder. "And we won't tell Mac."

"Oh, tell Mac," Conner said. "Definitely tell Mac. Tell every guy you run into, but especially the married ones."

Frigid was a relatively new club, but its reputation had spread quickly.

No matter how in love they were, any normal, straight male was going to be a little jealous of the things Conner planned to do inside Frigid.

💋

"It clearly means *I'll never forget that kiss*",' Conner said, sticking the entire cookie he held into his mouth.

"It clearly means, *this is the only kind of kiss you'll be getting from me from now on,*" Mac countered, plucking a second and third cookie from Conner's fingers.

"I love when Sara brings food down," Dooley said, dropping into the arm chair perpendicular to where Ryan was sitting. "While they're busy fighting over it, I can steal more than my share." He grabbed three cookies from the plate and tossed them to Ryan, then snagged three more for himself.

Ryan grinned as he bit into the first one. "I was just thinking that very thing." Sara Bradford was a cookie master and she'd brought down a huge plate of treats as a thank you to the guys for their action on the scene two nights before.

The cookies tonight were peanut butter with chocolate kisses stuck in the middle.

They were Conner's favorite.

"Well, I'm going to have to be sure to thank Miss Sara appropriately the next time I see her," Conner said, moving past Mac and toward the cookies.

"It's Mrs. Sara, you jackass," Mac muttered. Then he raised his voice. "Okay, fine Dixon. Enjoy the cookies, enjoy reliving those few very short seconds with Sara, and enjoy the memory of bossing me around because none of that is ever going to happen again."

"Your thank you could use a little work, but you're welcome," Conner said, lifting a cookie in salute. "You can count on me, Mac."

Mac gave a little growl and headed out the door just as

Gabrielle and Sierra came into the room carrying two plates—one filled with brownies and one filled with sandwiches.

"See, even our own crew mates know how awesome we are," Conner said, taking the plate of sandwiches from Gabby. "Thanks, girls."

"Oh, these aren't from us," Sierra said, setting the brownies near Dooley and earning a huge grin for the gesture. "These are from a few of the nurses."

Conner smiled. "You don't say. I guess maybe the tales of our heroics have spread."

"They spread pretty fast when you're the one telling the tales," Gabby said.

"I don't know what you're talking about," Conner said, biting into a sandwich.

Gabby snorted. "You had that teeny tiny cut on your hand from the other night but you whined and moaned to the nurses about it enough that they had to look at it, and treat it, and ask you all about how you got it."

"It's hardly teeny tiny," Conner said, clearly offended. He held up his hand with the white bandage around it.

"For God's sake," Gabby said. "I saw the cut before you got it all dolled up. It hardly needs that much bandaging."

"It might be a little overkill," Conner admitted. "But it makes the girls feel good about helping me."

Sierra laughed. "I'm not even completely convinced you got that cut at the fire. I mean, what the hell were you doing?"

"Oh, I heard the whole story," Ryan piped up. "Straight from the horse's ass."

"I think the term is horse's mouth," Conner said with a frown.

"Whatever." Ryan gave his friend and partner a grin. "I believe you cut it with the knife you were using to free one of the victims. Wasn't that it?"

"That was it," Conner said with a nod.

"A young girl, right? She was really scared and told you over and over how strong and brave you were?" Ryan went on.

Conner narrowed his eyes slightly, but he nodded again. "Yeah, that's about right. She was about seventeen and really freaked out."

"And you freed her from what exactly?" Gabby asked. "The group with Sara was blocked in, but no one was really trapped, right?"

"The tie on her hoodie was caught in the hinge on a door," Ryan said.

"The tie on her hoodie?" Gabby asked. "You mean the draw-strings up at her neck?"

"Yeah." Ryan managed not to smile.

"But—" Gabby started.

"Hey, I'm a dedicated professional," Conner said quickly over the top of her. "Nothing is too small a need. I'm there for people no matter what."

Ryan grinned. Conner could certainly bullshit with the best of them. "That's really big of you. No wonder you're everyone's hero."

Sierra chuckled. "Well, that and you telling everyone that you're their hero."

Conner moved in closer to Sierra and gave her a little smile. "Oh, come on, Sierra. If you know that if you were tied up—no matter what the reason—you'd want me there."

Ryan grabbed a brownie and settled back to watch the exchange. If anyone could take Conner Dixon down a peg or two it was Sierra and Gabby. They worked right beside Conner and Ryan, just as hard, just as heroically. They were not easily impressed by muscles and bravery.

She crossed her arms. "And what might these reasons be?"

"Well, one reason would be something dangerous that would require me to barge in to save your pretty butt."

"Okay." Predictably, Sierra looked less than awestruck. "And the other would be?"

"Well, depending on what you were tied up with and what you were tied up to…"

She stared at him for a second. Then burst out laughing. "You've got absolutely no ego problem do you?"

Conner grinned. "I want to be sure you know that I'll be there for you, no matter what your needs are."

Sierra patted his cheek. "Conner, I've seen you covered in blood and vomit and… well, you remember the call for Mr. Harrison."

Conner grimaced. As did Gabby and Ryan. They all remembered Mr. Harrison's trip from his apartment to St. Anthony's. And the clean-up required afterward.

"I just can't look at you as a sexy, hot, demigod anymore," Sierra told him.

Conner looked at her for a heartbeat, then said, "Anymore. That implies that you did at one time."

Sierra sighed. "I know it's important to you to think that, so I'm willing to go with it."

"He'd think it whether you "let" him or not," Gabby muttered.

Ryan laughed out loud at that. The girls headed into the kitchen area and Ryan popped another cookie in his mouth.

Conner sighed and slumped into the seat across from Dooley.

Ryan just chewed and waited.

Conner reached for a brownie, then leaned back in his chair. He also chewed for a few seconds.

Ryan crossed one ankle over his other knee.

Finally Conner looked up at him. "Thanks for not telling them."

"Telling them what?" Dooley asked, looking between the two men.

Ryan grinned. "You bet, buddy. I've got your back."

"Telling them what?" Dooley asked.

"And I appreciate it."

"How's the deep battle wound feeling?" Ryan asked.

Conner held up his hand with a grin. "Better every time one of the girls says, "I heard about the call the other night"."

"Telling them what?" Dooley asked again.

Ryan looked at Conner. Conner looked at Ryan. Then he sighed. "The girl's hoodie was caught but... she wasn't wearing it. She was just carrying it. She could have easily left it behind. But she was panicking and I figured the easiest way to get her out of the building was to slash the drawstring and bring the sweatshirt with us."

Dooley shook his head. "Nice."

"Tell him the best part," Ryan urged, not containing his smile any longer.

Conner couldn't help but give a half grin too. "She showed up yesterday. I was assuming she was here to thank me."

"Yeah?" Dooley said.

"She was here to ask me for money to replace the hoodie I ruined."

There was a beat of silence, then Dooley hooted with laughter. "And you gave it to her?"

Conner shrugged. "Yeah. I wasn't going to argue with her."

If nothing else, Conner Dixon knew when to debate with a woman and when not to. He had plenty of antagonized females in his life at any one time.

"But that means one more woman who doesn't think you're a big hero," Dooley pointed out.

Conner smiled. "I gave her the money. That doesn't mean she didn't leave here thinking I'm the greatest guy in the world."

"You charmed a girl after ruining her favorite sweatshirt?" Dooley asked. "How?"

"I told her I hoped that the next one she bought was green because it would make her eyes look beautiful."

"Oh my god." Dooley slumped back in his chair, laughing. "That's great."

"I thought so and her big smile and soft, sweet "'bye Conner" said she did too," Conner agreed cheerfully.

"If you're not careful, you're going to be the next Sam Bradford," Dooley said, pushing himself up from his chair.

"Or Mac Gordon," Conner quipped.

Dooley gave him a raised eyebrow. "You want to be like Mac? You might have some work to do."

"Work like what?"

"You know about edible body powder?" Dooley asked.

"Heard of it."

"Get some. Try it out. In fact, acquaint yourself with the entire catalog at Scandalous Somethings dot com."

"Then Sara might be interested?" Conner asked.

Ryan groaned.

Dooley laughed. "No. But it'll help you back up some of this flirting when the right woman finally decides to make you prove that you're as hot as you think you are."

Conner shuddered. "Women make things complicated if you let them stick around too long. The last thing I need is another permanent woman in my life."

"Don't think I'm not going to remind you that you said that one of these days," Dooley said, heading for the door. "And I'm going to enjoy the hell out of it."

Ryan regarded his friend as Dooley shut the door behind him. Come to think of it, Ryan was going to enjoy the hell out of that too. He hoped that woman came along soon.

Conner Dixon in love was going to be something to see.

*I hope you enjoyed Why You Should Never Kiss Your Ex-Husband and the extended epilogue Just Count on Me! I hope you loved Kevin and Eve!*

The hot, sexy fun continues with **Why You Should Never Kiss Your Brother's Best Friend** and hot, role-playing, whipped-cream-loving EMT Ryan Kaye and Conner's sister Amanda!

When a stranger walks up and punches him at a bar, Ryan Kaye assumes there's a good reason. But he's stunned to learn it's over a one-night stand that never happened —with his friend's straight-laced sister, Amanda. When he confronts her about the lie, she apologizes, but he realizes he doesn't want her to be sorry…he wants the night they supposedly spent together.

The last thing she needs is to add to her long list of commitments. But when tempted with the chance to go crazy and fulfill a few fantasies with her brother's best friend that she's had a little–or maybe not such a little–crush on, she can't resist.

Thank goodness one night isn't enough time to fall in love…

*Grab it now!* **Or read on for an excerpt!**

ლ

**Find all of my books (including a printable book list) at ErinNicholas.com**

ლ

**And join in on all the FAN FUN!**

Join my **email list!**
**bit.ly/Keep-In-Touch-Erin**
(be sure you get those dashes and capital letters in there!)

And be the first to hear about my news, sales, freebies, behind-the-scenes, and more!

Or for even more fun, join my **Super Fan page** on Facebook and chat with me and other super fans every day! Just search Facebook for Erin Nicholas Super Fans!

3

## Enjoy this excerpt from Why You Should Never Kiss Your Brother's Best Friend

Ryan tugged Amanda through the crowd to the corner near the back door. It wasn't exactly private, but it would work for a few minutes. That was all he would have, he was sure, before Conner realized one of his friends had one of his sisters off in a dark corner alone.

"Yes, I talked to Tim Winters," Ryan said when they were as alone as they were going to get. "Right after he clocked me and knocked me on my ass."

Amanda gasped. "He hit you?"

"Yeah, because I slept with you."

"I… Oh… Um…"

Ryan fought a smile. "But it's weird. That really seems like something I'd remember."

She rolled her eyes. "We all probably blend together after a while." She said it quietly, more of a mutter really, but he heard it.

"What's that mean?" he demanded. He put a finger under her chin and tipped her head so she had to look at him. "Amanda, what does that mean?"

She shrugged and pulled her chin away from his touch. "It means that it's got to be difficult keeping track of everyone in and out of your bed without making them all wear name tags."

He grinned. He couldn't help it. She was sassy too. He liked that. And liked even more that it didn't show all the time. He liked knowing that there might be layers to Amanda Dixon to discover.

"Where would they pin the name tags?" he couldn't resist asking.

For a moment, Amanda seemed surprised. Then she smiled. "You'll have to get the adhesive ones, I guess."

"Might cover up something I need to see."

"You could try only dating women named Jennifer or something."

He smiled. "But then Tim Winters wouldn't believe whatever you told him about you and me."

Amanda pressed her lips together. Then said, "I'm really sorry he hit you."

"I'll live. What I want to know is why he did it."

"I thought he...told you."

She actually blushed and Ryan wondered if he could remember the last time he'd seen a woman blush. Not off the top of his head.

"I want to hear it from you."

She looked at the collar of his shirt instead of his eyes. "I told him I had a one-night stand with someone and had feelings for him."

"Me."

"Yes."

"How'd I get to be the lucky one?"

She snorted.

He hated that she thought he was messing around. "Amanda."

She finally looked up into his eyes.

"Why me?"

She swallowed. "You're...the type, I guess."

He frowned at that. That was what she thought of him? That he was the type of guy to screw around with another man's girl?

"I don't touch what isn't free to be touched."

She sighed. "Tim and I are not dating. We haven't done more than chat and dance. I was trying to let him down easy without the whole 'you're a great guy, but—' routine. I thought another guy was the easiest way."

"Especially if the other guy ruined you for all other men. Who can argue with that?"

Her eyes widened and she blushed again, but then she

laughed. "That's what I thought. Ruined is ruined, after all."

He'd love to be the one to ruin her.

The thought snuck up on him, and Ryan had to take a quick breath before saying casually, "Clearly he's a little more into you than you thought."

Amanda wet her bottom lip and looked up at him and said softly, "Sorry."

He didn't want an apology. He didn't want her to be sorry for having the idea of the two of them burning up the sheets one night. He wanted her to keep that idea firmly in mind, in fact.

"Did you tell him it was a one-night stand?"

He liked the idea that she would think he was so amazing that one night would cause her to be head over heels. Even if it was only in her imagination.

Amanda took a deep breath. "Yes, just one night."

Ryan moved in closer, wanting her full attention on him. "Okay. Make it up to me."

"How?"

"Give me that night."

"What night?" she asked carefully.

"The one we allegedly had. And whatever it was that ruined you for all other men."

Amanda stared at him as if he were crazy. Which he probably was. She'd made up a fling. It was simple and innocent—mostly —and nothing he really needed to worry about. Winters had slugged him and gotten it out of his system. It was probably over. And if it wasn't, Amanda had plenty of people—including him—who would step in to dissuade Tim. It wouldn't require any of them pretending to be her lover.

But Ryan didn't want it to be that simple. Obviously.

"What are you suggesting, exactly?" she asked.

Ryan grinned. "You, me, some whipped cream and twenty-four uninterrupted hours."

*Grab it now!*

# WHY YOU SHOULD NEVER... THE SERIES

**Why You Should Never...**

# MORE FROM ERIN

*

# ABOUT ERIN NICHOLAS

Erin Nicholas is the New York Times and USA Today bestselling author of over thirty sexy contemporary romances. Her stories have been described as toe-curling, enchanting, steamy and fun. She loves to write about reluctant heroes, imperfect heroines and happily ever afters. She lives in the Midwest with her husband who only wants to read the sex scenes in her books, her kids who will never read the sex scenes in her books, and family and friends who say they're shocked by the sex scenes in her books (yeah, right!).
Find her here:

facebook.com / ErinNicholasBooks
bookbub.com / authors / erin-nicholas
goodreads.com / author / show / 3155383.Erin_Nicholas
tiktok.com / @erinnicholasbooks

www.ingramcontent.com/pod-product-compliance
Lightning Source LLC
Chambersburg PA
CBHW031156160725
29698CB00007B/247